GROWING UP

A Novel by

Angela Thirkell

LARGE PRINT

Oxford

First published in Great Britain 1943
by Hamish Hamilton

Published in Large Print 2003 by ISIS Publishing Ltd,
7 Centremead, Osney Mead, Oxford OX2 0ES
by arrangement with Penguin UK

British Library Cataloguing in Publication Data
Thirkell, Angela, 1890–1961
    Growing up. – Large print ed.
    1. Barsetshire (England: Imaginary place) – Fiction
    2. World War, 1939–1945 – Fiction
    3. Large type books
    I. Title
    823.9'12 [F]

ISBN 0–7531–6889–8 (hb)
ISBN 0–7531–6890–1 (pb)

Printed and bound by Antony Rowe, Chippenham

CHAPTER
ONE

To the youth of England, except to that small and misguided section who prefer model aeroplanes to model railways, the station at Winter Overcotes, as all students of Barsetshire know, represents History and Romance in their highest form, for here is one of the few remaining survivals of the main or high level line crossing the low level or local line. Every right-minded little boy who has travelled by this route has wished to spend the rest of his life at the station, with the firm though unexpressed hope of becoming station-master when he is grown up. Under the spell of Winter Overcotes the noble names of Hornby and Bassett-Lowke become as dust. In vain did those benefactors, in the days of peace, vie with each other in producing engines, coaches and trucks, finished to a thousandth of an inch, exquisitely painted, running by clockwork, methylated spirits or electricity. Something was wanting. Their young patrons, having spent all their Christmas tips and drawn heavily on their Post Office Savings Bank accounts to boot, found that all was vanity. In vain did they exercise their ingenuity in constructing viaducts propped on volumes of the *Encyclopædia Britannica* or the *New English Dictionary*;

in vain did they compose flights of stairs from cardboard, or the nursery box of bricks. Again and again would the engine fall from the viaduct and lie on its back kicking and whirring. No rails were subtly enough curved to represent the great sweep by which the low level rejoined the main line some four miles nearer London, and by which one through train a day used to run to Worsted and Skeynes. Such words of blasphemy and despair as "Mother! Hornby's an idiot!" or "Mother! why doesn't Bassett-Lowke have some *sense*?" would burst from the mouths of young gentlemen between six and sixteen. Even undergraduate brothers had to confess themselves at a loss, while fathers would devote an entire week-end to the railway, rising at last to their feet shakily, dusting the knees of their trousers, and uttering such obviously untruthful words as "Of course it would be quite easy if you had a few more left-hand curves, and now you had better put it all away before you go to bed," thus reducing the owner of the railway to soft, sullen rebellion. For every owner knows that if only he had one more box of nuts and bolts he could attain the unattainable, or so Tony Morland said, and Tony was, by his own account, the world's highest authority. And though his railway system had long ago been given by him, rolling-stock and all, in a rather ostentatious way to a much younger boy, it is not impossible that Tony, on leave from his guns and out of uniform, might have spent a whole week-end on hands and knees, wrestling with the enchanting problem.

Though Mr. Beedle the station-master no longer appeared to Tony and his contemporaries as a demigod, ten feet high, endowed with miraculous powers and if not wearing a halo, at least surrounded by a golden effulgence, it was the fault of the times. Gone were the happy days when Mr. Beedle, born of a line of railway men in a tradition of faithful service to the Best Line in England (and hence in the world), was proud to touch his gold-laced cap to the local nobility and gentry, who had an equal respect for him, taking at Christmas the form of game, cigars, bottles of wine and treasury notes. Gone were the days when he could usher old Lord Pomfret who hated motors, returning from a visit to General Waring at Beliers Priory, into the first-class smoker which he had kept locked for his lordship. Old Lord Pomfret was dead, Sir Harry and Lady Waring now used their local station of Lambton, changing at Winter Overcotes for the main line. Both these changes grieved Mr. Beedle, a staunch upholder of the old order, but even more was he grieved that first-class carriages, except on a few long-distance trains, had been abolished. England was at war; English locomotives, unable to voice their dislike of the sea and foreigners, had been sent abroad; porters had been called up; no longer was the station after dark or on foggy days a great beacon of light on the high level platform; all this Mr. Beedle hated, but understood. In moments of stress he had helped to sort luggage and unload goods vans with his own sacred hands; he had even swept the up platform in a moment of emergency when five of his six porters had gone; for to him

3

nothing connected with what he proudly called Our Line was below his dignity. But the abolition of first-class carriages struck to his heart, and Mrs. Beedle was able to state with truth that he hadn't never seemed to fancy his supper since. Mr. Beedle was loyal to the core. What Our Directors did was right, but his personal sense of shame at having nothing better than third-class to offer to his own local magnates did not lessen with time. In fact, so unhappy did this change make him that he was, as it were, made immune to any further bludgeonings of fate, and when two women porters were appointed for the duration of the war, he made no sign of disapproval, though Mrs. Beedle knew that his uniform hung more loosely about him and he did not sleep well.

Here fate was kind. Doris Phipps and Lily-Annie Pollett, though they looked incredibly plain and depraved in oyster satin blouses, tight-seated, bell-bottomed trousers, red nails on dirty hands, greasy curls hanging on their shoulders, a cigarette for ever glued to their lips, were really very nice, kind girls. Their families lived at Worsted, a few stations down the line, and the two girls bicycled in summer and came by the local train in winter. The summer route had the advantage of taking them past a large aerodrome, but on the winter route they could shout at friends out of the carriage window at every stop, besides having more time to make up their faces.

When Doris and Lily-Annie had been at the station for some months, and doing very well, a new porter was sent to join them.

"It doesn't seem natural," said Mrs. Beedle to Mr. Beedle while he was having his tea. "In my young days the girls liked to have a boy about, but Lily-Annie ran in for a talk in her lunch hour and she and Dawris don't seem at all keen on your new young man. What's his name?"

"Bill Morple, from Melicent Halt," said Mr. Beedle. "His mother was old Patten's niece, Mr. Patten that's station-master at Worsted, but his father — well, Ed'ard Morple was a foreigner."

"Ah," said Mrs. Beedle. "Loamshire?"

"Not so bad as that, Mother," said Mr. Beedle. "But somewhere the other side of Barchester. A talking kind of man he was and a one-er for an argument. Young Bill's like that. Talk the connecting-rod off an engine he would."

"I do feel sorry for those girls," said Mrs. Beedle with unfeigned sympathy. "Argument's no use to girls. What they want is a nice talk like, and if Bill Morple did happen to kiss them it wouldn't break any bones."

"More likely they'd slap his face," said Mr. Beedle, as he girded on his official coat preparatory to returning to the station. "That Lily-Annie's as strong as a man any day and Dawris is getting quite a hand with the milk cans. When I see her putting them in the van, it makes me think of our Henry."

There was a moment's silence.

"Cheer up, Dad," said Mrs. Beedle, clattering the tea-things together in a noisy way unusual in her, for she was a very neat, quick, quiet woman. "You'll see the war'll be over by next Christmas and we'll have Henry back in the station."

"It doesn't seem right him being a prisoner," said Mr. Beedle, looking out of the window. "Him being so fond of the country and christened after Sir Harry and all."

"Don't you worry, Dad," said Mrs. Beedle, carefully not looking at her husband. "He said in his last letter that he was liking the land-work fine. It's not as if he was an officer, having to sit about and read a book all day, poor gentlemen."

Mr. Beedle picked up his gold-laced cap and left the house, concentrating his mind fiercely on the new regulations about bombs that were high-explosive as well as incendiary, and rather relieved that the latest ruling was to the effect that the less civilians did about anything the better. And in any case the air-raid warden for the station was his own booking-clerk in whom he had great confidence.

His first duty, after unlocking his office and reading a couple of letters, was to walk about on the platform when the 6.25, the down train from London, came in. As it was mid-November it was by now almost dark. A faint light came from the booking office, and the red and green of the signals glowed in the north-east. Two points of fire revealed themselves as Doris Phipps and Lily-Annie Pollett smoking cigarettes while waiting for the train. Mr. Beedle thought of the days when his station was what a station ought to be. He saw in his mind's eye the bright electric lights, the gaily coloured bookstall, the brilliant scarlet cigarette and chocolate machines, the round-faced weighing machine, the well swept platforms watered in elegant patterns, the shining brass handles on waiting-room doors, the refreshment room with its stacks of crockery, its piles of sandwiches, pies and cakes under neat glass domes, the neatly painted seats. It was his great grief that a garden was not possible on the high level platform, but he had at his own expense put green window-boxes outside his office and the booking office. His porters were the liveliest and most willing on the line. No wonder they had won the silver cup for the best-kept station on that stretch three years running, with the right to keep it.

Now the lights were removed or dimmed to darkness made visible, the bookstall was only open for an hour in the morning with little or nothing to sell, the penny-in-the-slot machines were battered and empty, the platform dusty and strewn with bits of paper and cigarette cartons which their owners had flung there sooner than use the wire baskets provided, the brass dull and tarnished. In the refreshment room he knew there would be a few heavy little pasties with nothing particular inside them and some dyspeptic buns made from the vitamin-stuffed and indigestion-producing Government flour. Cups there were few and saucers none, for travellers stole them to that extent that the Catering Department had stopped replacing. Only sugar remained for some mysterious reason abundant, so that travellers who said "No sugar, thank you" from motives of taste or patriotism found themselves provided with a nauseously sweet draught by the scornful middle-aged woman in charge who saw no reason to pay any attention to national economy or anyone's likes and dislikes. The window-boxes had so often been rifled that Mr. Beedle had with his own hands removed them and Mrs. Beedle now grew mustard and cress in them outside her kitchen window. Where his porters had stood, alert for the down train, were two girls in trousers, smoking; good girls, but no pride in themselves nor in the station.

As for the silver cup — but of it Mr. Beedle could hardly bear to think. Placed upon a fretwork bracket, in a glass case which was fixed to the wall, it was the pride of Mr. Beedle and his staff, the admiration of all travellers. Every week Mr. Beedle would unlock the case and his senior porter would lovingly polish it. In the first days of the war Winter Overcotes was invaded by a crowd of unruly London evacuees. Big loutish boys and equally loutish girls made the station arches, the station approach and finally the station itself their playing-ground. In vain did Mr. Beedle use his authority, in vain did he appeal to their schoolteachers. The boys and girls defied him with malicious words and deeds, the teachers were powerless or unwilling to interfere. More damage was done to the station in a few weeks than had been done since the line was opened. After a very unpleasant incident when spoons were stolen from the refreshment room and the benches in the waiting room hacked with knives, Mr. Beedle decided to remove the cup. But when he approached the case on the following morning the glass was smashed, the cup gone and in its place a dirty piece of paper on which were scrawled the words, "Old beetles a fool." Mr. Beedle had said nothing in public. His friend, the chief inspector at the police station, caused inquiries to be made, but though he knew within twenty-four hours where the cup was, there was not enough evidence, as he regretfully said, to hang a louse. Mr. Beedle ordered his son Henry to take down the shattered case. Then Henry went into the Army and was made prisoner before Dunkirk.

Though Mr. Beedle was a gentle man, no one dared to speak to him of his losses except General Waring, under whom Mr. Beedle had fought in the last war and who had consented to stand godfather to Henry Beedle.

"I take it kindly of the General," Mr. Beedle had said to his wife, "to speak to me about the cup and ask about Henry, him having lost his own son. And it's worse for him, for young Mr. George won't ever come home and our Henry will, when the war's over."

To which in a general way Mrs. Beedle agreed, though she privately wished sometimes that her Henry had been killed, sooner than have to live with foreigners for years on their nasty foreign food and not enough of it and no one to look after his socks, besides his poor dad worrying his heart out all the time. Then she would blame herself for ingratitude, cry quietly, and get on with preparing Mr. Beedle's next meal.

The tide of evacuees had surged back to London, with the exception of a certain number of the younger children whose parents were not disposed to tempt a Providence which had made it unnecessary for them to take any further financial or moral responsibility for their offspring, and a small gang who found it wise to keep away from the London police. Foreign regiments from counties beyond Barsetshire had been billeted in the town or put in camp in the neighbourhood. The volume of traffic through Winter Overcotes increased as the staff diminished; Mr. Beedle's gentle face became more lined; but the war showed no signs of ending.

His brooding thoughts were broken by the whistle of the 6.25 from the beginning of the viaduct.

"Here it is," yelled Doris Phipps to Lily-Annie.

Mr. Beedle shuddered. That anyone should be unconscious of the pervading femininity of a fast passenger train was to him almost criminal and certainly showed a feeble intellect.

"I hope Sid's in the van," yelled Lily-Annie to Doris. "He's a lovely man."

Mr. Beedle shuddered again. No porter he had known would ever have dared to speak of Sidney Crackman, with thirty years' service behind him, honoured guard of the Line's best passenger trains, as anything but Mr. Crackman. And here were a couple of silly girls, wearing trousers too, calling him Sid. If it had been light he would have Given them a Look. But it was dark and he was honest enough to own that if it had been light they probably wouldn't have noticed the Look, and would only have thought he had indigestion if they had. And after all they were good girls, calling the name of the darkened station loudly and as clearly as it was in their nature to do, answering questions with uncouth goodwill, helping mothers to drag children and suitcases out of the train, and now rallying at the guard's van where Crackman seemed to be giving them as good as he got. It was a funny world. He moved towards the booking-hall to keep an eye on Bill Morple who was acting-ticket-collector, very much under protest, for at Melicent Halt he had been in the booking-office, and though he had doubled this duty with porter, he felt that he had lost status and that things would have been better ordered in Russia.

This evening all was going smoothly, though Mr. Beedle could not help contrasting the passengers with his pre-war friends. When cars and petrol abounded Winter Overcotes had been the distributing centre for some fifteen miles round. Lord and Lady Bond at Staple Park, Mr. and Mrs. Palmer at Worsted, Sir Harry and Lady Waring at Beliers Priory, Mr. and Mrs. Middleton at Skeynes, all the best people in fact, were as apt as not to use Winter Overcotes, for there was even before the war only one through train a day down the local line which runs to the small junction at Shearings. Now all Mr. Beadle's friends got out on the high level, stumbled downstairs in the blackout to the low level, waited for half an hour, and steamed slowly and jerkily in cold dark carriages to their various stations. The people who passed through Mr. Beedle's booking-hall would always be treated courteously, for he knew what was due to himself and to the Line, but they were an alien race without the law, and very often on the shady side of it, trying to use a day return after the legal hours, or get away with a last month's season ticket, thus driving the new ticket-collector to pale-faced frenzy.

On the other side of the barrier a tall, good-looking, grey-haired woman was waiting for the crowd to go through. Mr. Beedle recognized Lady Waring and touched his cap.

"Good evening, Beedle," said Lady Waring. "I'm meeting Sir Harry for once, because I've been on Red Cross business all day and have a car. Do you think he has forgotten and gone down to the low level?"

"I will go at once myself and see, my lady," said Mr. Beedle. "Will you wait in my office? I have the stove going."

"Thanks, Beedle, I'd love to," said Lady Waring, "but your platform ticket machine is empty."

"That will be quite all right, my lady," said Mr. Beedle, shocked that Lady Waring should assume herself to be as other mortals. "Come through. Morple, don't let that happen again."

Ever since the staff had been called up, the question of whose duty it was to look after the platform tickets had raged, dividing the remaining staff vertically, horizontally, sideways, causing friction at least twice a week. Willingly would Mr. Beedle have attended to it himself, but none knew better than he the exact point at which prestige is impaired. He could help with parcels, he had even as we know once swept the platform; but the line had to be drawn somewhere and the platform ticket machine was the limit. Unfortunately, Bill Morple also felt that it was the limit. A man who had (to help the war effort) taken a position far below his proper rank and what was more had to put up with sauce from people who thought themselves someone just because they had an out-of-date season to London; such a man, if he had any proper pride, would not fill the platform ticket machine. But unfortunately Mr. Beedle was his superior officer and could be quite nasty (by which Bill Morple meant that Mr. Beedle never lost his temper) if crossed. So as the last passenger had gone, Bill Morple, whistling the "International" rather badly to himself, went and did as he was told, while Mr. Beedle conducted Lady Waring to the station-master's office, handed her to a chair, and went to look for her husband.

By this time the 6.25 had gone and the station appeared empty. Fearing that Lady Waring might be right, Mr. Beedle walked down the platform towards the steps which led to the low level, when a group detached itself from the darkness and came rather noisily towards him. To his horror it consisted of Sir Harry pulling a large porter's truck, Doris Phipps and Lily-Annie Pollett, with cigarettes in their mouths, pushing behind.

"Evening, Beedle," said Sir Henry, "I found these young women in difficulties, so I'm giving a hand. All these heavy cases are too much for girls. What's in them, eh?"

Mr. Beedle turned a small torch on them.

"Stationery, Sir Harry, for the Barchester Life and General Assurance," he said. "Their office in Barchester was taken over by the Ministry of Textile Shortage, so they took the Old Court House here where the Town Council had its offices, and the Town Council took over

Woolstaplers' Hall that had been got ready for an army convalescent home, and —"

"Oh, that's why they took my house for a convalescent home," said Sir Harry. "I always wondered. Still, I don't see why an insurance company needs all this stationery when there's a paper shortage. Well, well. Is her ladyship anywhere about?"

"In my office, General," said Mr. Beedle.

Sir Harry gave the trolley a strong pull to get it going again. Doris and Lily-Annie, who had been sitting on the back of it, were violently jolted and screamed with delight.

"There you are, girls," said Sir Harry, stopping suddenly outside the station-master's office, so that both girls screamed again. "Run along and don't smoke too much. Bad for you."

"Thanks ever so," said Lily-Annie.

"Isn't he a lovely man," said Doris Phipps, loudly and admiringly.

"Now then, you girls," said Mr. Beedle. "That's enough. It's Sir Harry Waring that's been kind enough to help you. Time you went off duty now."

Both girls said "Ow," and Lily-Annie remarked that she'd laugh fit to die if she called anyone Sir Harry, to which Doris Phipps answered that it was reelly Sir Henry, but people called him Sir Harry because he was a Bart.

"What's that?" said Lily-Annie.

"Ow; just what they are," said Doris. "Come on, or we'll miss the train. Sid Pollett's in the van to-night.

Hullo, Bill. Lazy boy you are. Why didn't you give me and Lily-Annie a hand with the truck?"

"Old Beedle made me fill the platform ticket machine," said Bill Morple. "If we was in Russia things 'ud be different. In Russia they're all alike and no one gives orders. If we was in Russia old Beedle'd get the Order of the Boot, coming it over me the way he does."

"There's plenty of help for them as asks," said Lily-Annie. "Dawris and me got a ride on the truck. Sir Henry Waring gave us a ride with the parcels."

"And he's a Bart and a reel gentleman," said Doris Phipps.

"He's a lovely man," said Lily-Annie. "Quite my ideel."

"In Russia," said Bill Morple, "both you girls would be in the Red Army and a good job too."

"If we was in Russia we shouldn't be here," said Lily-Annie, "and then we shouldn't see you, and that 'ud be a blessing. Come on, Dawris."

With loud laughter both girls clattered down the steps, leaving Bill Morple to hang angrily about till the 7.5 up had come and gone and he could go off duty. Mr. Beedle put the Warings into their car and retired to his office and his papers, somehow cheered by the meeting.

Beliers Priory, towards which the Warings were driving through the dark, was built near the site of a pre-Reformation abbey of which little now remained but the ground-plan, exquisitely inlaid in green turf by H.M. Office of Works just before the war, and a string of pools known as the Dipping Ponds, probably stew ponds for the abbot's table. The Priory, so called for no reason, unless the proximity of the abbey ruins was one, was built some seventy years ago by Sir Harry Waring's grandfather. His wife, a City heiress of considerable beauty, had persuaded him to employ an architect much in favour in her circles. The result was a pile which combined inconvenience and discomfort in the highest form. It was built round a central hall into which a skylight gently dripped whenever it rained, so that Sir Harry's earliest remembrances were of bowls and basins on the floor tripping up the unwary. The bedrooms on the first floor were approached by a dark corridor, only lighted by leaded casements opening upon the hall. The kitchens were down several hundred yards of stone passage, the housekeeper's room looked north into a fine laurel hedge, the kitchen, like the hall, was lighted only from the roof and badly at that. Guests, ladies' maids and valets were often lost for a quarter of an hour at a time. The one bathroom in the original plan was about twenty feet by thirty and fifteen feet high and the bath a massive affair in a wide mahogany surround on a kind of dais, with an apse over the round end. Sir Harry's father had divided the original bathroom into cubicles for his hunting friends and sacrificed one or two of the smaller dressing-rooms to make bathrooms for the ladies, but the original water system which burnt about twenty tons of coal a week was still in full fling, copper pipes and all.

When the war fell on England the Warings were at their wits' end and saw themselves reduced to living in the staff quarters and letting the rest of the house decay, so they were on the whole grateful when, as we have heard, the army convalescent home that was to have been in Woolstaplers' Hall was transferred to the Priory. The owners found themselves indeed living in the servants' quarters, but though a more lavish age had thought them poky, they were far more comfortable than the great cold suites of rooms in the house, and the War Office, while putting in central heating and several dozen fixed basins, saw no objection to running the heating across to the servants' wing and installing five surplus basins, two baths and an up-to-date gas cooker. An elderly kitchen-maid and an elderly housemaid were saved from the wreckage of the staff. Lady Waring's ex-nannie who had been retired on a pension (there would never be any grandchildren for her to spoil since George Waring was killed just before the Armistice) ordered her widowed daughter to leave London and those nasty raids and come to her ladyship as useful maid. Selina Crockett came on approval. A pretty, plump creature, nearer fifty than forty, with uncontrollable tendrils of dark hair streaked with silver, and liquid eyes which filled with tears on the slightest provocation, she was as mild as her notable old mother was fierce and snappish, and being immediately approved, slipped into the life of the Priory as if she had always been in service.

Lady Waring sometimes wondered whether she ought to be so comfortable, but as Sir Harry worked in town four days a week on matters connected with regimental charities, spent two days' hard work on county jobs and was rarely free on Sundays, besides doing a good deal of the gardening, she hoped her comfort would be forgiven, wherever these things are judged, because it made a restful home for her husband. Sir Harry in much the same way felt that his lines had fallen in far too pleasant places for an old soldier, but was thankful that his wife, who between Red Cross, Girl Guides, Working Parties, Women's Voluntary Service and a dozen other activities was as busy as he, besides less often having her evenings free, had a safe refuge for her brief leisure and Selina to look after her.

Lady Waring drove the little car straight into the garage. Her husband locked it and they walked over to their own quarters. It was a cold raw evening and as Sir Harry opened the front door the blast of superheating which the War Office bestowed on them was extremely welcome. Selina Crockett came hurrying into the sitting-room to take her mistress's coat and parcels.

"What's the matter, Selina? You've been crying," said Lady Waring.

"Oh no, my lady," said Selina, crystal drops welling in her large eyes, "it's only I was upset about Matron."

"What has Matron been up to?" asked Sir Harry, amused. "By Jove, it's nice to see a fire. I get sick of all these offices with nothing but central heating. Been pinching the nurses' rations?"

"Oh *no*, sir," said Selina wiping her eyes. "It's her cat she was so fond of. It's dead. She *is* so upset, my lady."

"Dear, dear," said Lady Waring, not much interested in a cat with whom she was not personally acquainted.

"It was dreadful, my lady," Selina continued, again shedding a few lustrous tears. "Private Jenks borrowed a gun from Mr. Margett after tea to shoot a rabbit and he saw pussy climbing a tree and thought she was a squirrel, so he shot her, and it was the first time he'd got a squirrel and he *was* so pleased, and then he went to pick it up and it was Matron's cat. He knew pussy at once because she was quite a favourite and only the day before some of the boys put her in a gas-mask and took a snap of her with her little face peeping out. Private Jenks *was* so upset, my lady. He wrapped her up in his handkerchief and brought her to Matron and said, 'You'll never guess what I've got here, miss,' and Sister said Matron *was* so upset. And she's coming in after dinner, please, Sir Harry."

"Who? Sister?" asked Sir Harry.

"Oh *no*, Sir Harry. Matron," said Selina. "She wants you to speak to Mr. Margett about letting the boys have guns. She says they'll be shooting each other next, though that's not so bad, she said, as a poor innocent little cat. Poor pussy looked so lovely when she was dead, Sir Harry. I know I oughtn't to cry about a cat, my lady, but I *am* so upset."

She wiped her eyes apologetically, picked up coats and parcels and left the room.

"Wonderful the way that woman can cry without sniffing," said Sir Harry.

"Dear Sophy!" said his wife.

Sir Harry looked up from his evening paper.

"Only literature, Harry," said Lady Waring.

19

"That's all right, my dear," said Sir Harry admiringly, and Lady Waring felt for the many thousandth time since her marriage what a prig she was and how little was the value of all the books she had been brought up on and lived by, whose people and phrases coloured her daily thoughts and modes of speech, compared with the honesty and common sense of her husband and his unfailing sense of duty. She wished, as so often before, that she could put this into words for her husband, to express her almost humble admiration of his goodness and kindness; but, as usual, too many tools to her hand, she hesitated among the exquisite choice of words that the English language offers, was helplessly dumb, and found no better solution than to kiss the thinning hair on the top of Sir Harry's head.

"I'm going to have my bath now," she said, in a voice meant to explain to any unseen power that was hovering about how very unsentimental she really was. "I always feel so dirty after a day in Winter Overcotes. And Lucasta Bond was more trying than usual."

Sir Harry made an affectionate, absent-minded and approving noise.

"Please, my lady," said Selina, appearing at the door, "it's Mr. Hamp. He says he is sorry but he couldn't get here sooner and could you see him now."

"Oh, dear," said Lady Waring. "I suppose so, Selina. Harry, do you mind?"

"Mind what, dear?" said Sir Harry, looking up over the newspaper.

20

"Mr. Hamp," said his wife. "He has had my black skirt for four months and if I don't let him try it on now I'll probably not get it for another four months. I would take him into my bedroom but Selina stupidly turned the heating off when she was cleaning it and has only just turned it on, and he feels the cold in his head ever since nineteen-fifteen. We won't disturb you."

"Carry on," said Sir Harry.

Selina opened the door again and let in Mr. Hamp, carrying over his arm the black skirt, swathed in a kind of cerecloth of shiny holland. Reft from the bespoke tailoring business at Worsted during the last war he had been sent to India where he got sunstroke and was kicked on the head by a mule. The result of these combined operations had been the loss of most of his hair, which had never grown again, and on the top of his head a peculiar bump or shelf which had a morbid attraction for his customers. By a providential arrangement he was a better hand with skirts than with coats, so while he circled about his ladies on his knees, his mouth full of pins, or measuring stick in hand, they were able to have a good look at the bump or shelf and wonder where on earth he kept his brains. Ever since his double accident he had been morbidly sensitive to cold, and his head was apt to assume a violet hue very terrifying to those who were not used to it. Though really a man's tailor, he was willing to do his best for the local ladies and was not a bad hand at alterations.

Lady Waring greeted him and said she would slip the skirt on in her room and come back. Accompanied by Selina, she disappeared.

"Evening," said Sir Harry. "Sit down."

Mr. Hamp, who had risen to the rank of corporal on the very day the mule kicked him, knew better than to sit down in the presence of a general and stiffened.

"Things going all right?" said Sir Harry, who had already forgotten exactly who Mr. Hamp was and why he was in the room, but wanted to show good feeling.

"Well, sir, if you like to call them all right I suppose they *are* all right in a manner of speaking," said Mr. Hamp cautiously, "but not what you'd really *call* all right."

"Bad show, eh?" said Sir Harry, still feeling his way.

"Well, I don't know about *that*, sir," said Mr. Hamp broad-mindedly, "but what I say is, only a man as has *cut* trousers knows what trousers is."

"Rather," said Sir Harry.

"You see, sir," said Mr. Hamp, encouraged by Sir Harry's interest, "take a nice pair of gent's trousers, say in a light summer suiting. If you leave a cuff, or turn-up as you may say, you make your turn-up and there it is."

He paused to let this sink in.

"Eh?" said Sir Harry. "Oh, yes, there it is."

"Well, sir," continued Mr. Hamp, "here comes the Government and says the cuff, or turn-up if I make myself clear, uses too much stuff, so it says, No more cuffs. Well, sir, a gentleman like you can easy see the mistake *there*."

"To tell you the truth, I can't," said Sir Harry. "It seems to me that a trouser with a cuff must use more stuff than a trouser without a cuff."

"Ah! that's what they say," said Mr. Hamp. "But if you'll permit me to demonstrate, sir, I'll prove to you the exact contrary. Now, look at your cuff, sir, a nice well-tailored cuff. To make that cuff, sir, you cut the leg so many inches longer than you need it, you turn it up so, stitch it so, and there you are."

As he spoke he kneeled in his enthusiasm and gave a practical demonstration by seizing the cuff of Sir Harry's right trouser leg in his practised hands and turning it down. A halfpenny rolled out.

"Good God! there's the halfpenny I couldn't find last night," said Sir Harry, who always balanced his petty cash before he went to bed. "And what a filthy lot of fluff."

"You'll always find that, sir," said Mr. Hamp, still on his knees. "In the days when gentlemen had gentlemen to look after their clothes proper, sir, you wouldn't find that. Everything's altered now."

"That's a nasty bump," said Sir Harry, who had been staring at the top of Mr. Hamp's head. "Fall, eh?"

"No, sir," said Mr. Hamp. "Mountain battery mule's off hind-leg, sir."

"Lord! I didn't know we had any of them about here," said Sir Harry.

"Mutta Kundra, sir, nineteen-fifteen," said Mr. Hamp.

By a delightful coincidence Sir Harry had also been at Mutta Kundra in 'fifteen, so when Lady Waring came back in the black skirt she was surprised to find her husband and her local tailor in animated converse, while Mr. Hamp delicately picked the fluff out of the turn-ups of the General's trousers.

"Funny thing, my dear," said Sir Harry. "Hamp was at Mutta Kundra in 'fifteen. Mustn't keep you, Hamp, her ladyship is ready."

Mr. Hamp, swivelling round on his knees, quickly made the small adjustments necessary and Lady Waring went back to her room to extricate herself from the pin-larded skirt with Selina's help.

"Now, Hamp, about this business of the trouser-ends," said Sir Harry, who hated to leave a job unfinished.

"Well, it's this way, sir," said Mr. Hamp. "A gentleman's instep is higher than the back of his foot, leastways than the place on the back of his foot that the trouser comes to, if you follow me, so the bottom of the leg has to be graduated like. And that way, with sloping and all, you'll find you'll cut into the material something cruel; cut to waste as we say. Besides which it takes a tailor as *is* a tailor to cut that line. Talk about those ready-made tailors, sir. They haven't the art. If I've cut one pair of trousers, sir, I've cut a thousand, and it's the personality as counts in each. Now, sir, if the Government was to put the Master Tailors in charge of this cloth rationing business, men as *do* know their job, well, it'ud make a lot of difference, sir, and go a long way towards winning the war. At least that's *my* humble opinion."

Selina now came in with the skirt which she delivered to Mr. Hamp.

"Her ladyship's just going to have her bath, Sir Harry," she said, "and dinner's at a quarter past eight I was to say."

Sir Harry glanced at the clock, saw he had half an hour to wait, and resigned himself. Mr. Hamp, with the skirt in its winding-sheet looking like a soft mummy, was now preparing to go.

"Good night, Hamp," said Sir Harry. "Interesting about those trouser legs. I must get you to give some of mine a press one of these days."

"Very pleased to be of any service to you, sir," said Mr. Hamp, the top of his head going bright purple as he reflected on the glory this connection would shed on him at the Wool-pack, many of whose *habitués* were ex-soldiers. "And if you are speaking to any of those Parliamentary gentlemen, sir, perhaps you'd bear in mind that the master tailors haven't had a fair deal this war. If a young gentleman as has just got his commission goes to one of these ready-made houses, sir, for establishments I reelly cannot call them, well, he may get rigged out, for tailored is a word I reelly could not use not in this connection, but what will he look like, sir?"

Sir Harry, rather wishing the fellow would stop talking and go, said he thought a lot of the young officers got their things off the peg.

"Begging your pardon, sir, the young gentlemen may do so, but that is not the point I wished to make," said Mr. Hamp. "The point is, have their uniforms that natty look that a gentleman's uniform had ought to have? I know to my cost, sir," said Mr. Hamp almost

25

tearfully, "the difficulty there is with the shocking, shoddy suitings we have to use nowadays, but there is always the Cut, sir, and I've got a few rolls of prewar material that it's a pleasure to get the shears into."

There seemed to be no reason why Mr. Hamp should ever stop talking, especially as Sir Harry could not use his orderly-room manner for fear of offending the tailor who spared his wife various tiring journeys to London. He was wondering if he could offer him something to go and buy a drink, or if this would be against the Master Tailors' code, when Selina came back and by plumping up cushions, emptying ashtrays, and picking up the pins that had fallen from Mr. Hamp's mouth, managed to create a small whirlwind that enveloped him and drove him out of the room.

"Talks a lot, that tailor," said Sir Harry.

"Oh yes, he does, Sir Harry," said Selina. "But I'm so sorry for poor Mr. Hamp, Sir Harry. His son was such a pride to him and he can't get over it."

"Killed? Or missing?" said Sir Harry. "Poor fellow."

"Oh no, Sir Harry, he's got a lame leg and he's in the Home Guard, but he's taken a very good job in The People's Tailoring Limited, and poor Mr. Hamp *is* so upset. He'd set his heart on his son taking over his business," said Selina, her eyes liquid with sympathy, "and now he says when he dies it's the end of the firm. It does seem hard, Sir Harry. Excuse me, Sir Harry, it's the bell."

She went out, but Sir Harry had not had time to settle to his newspaper again before she was back.

"It's Mr. Margett, Sir Harry, about Private Jenks and poor pussy," said Selina.

"Oh, all right, show him in," said Sir Harry, wishing not for the first time that the war were over and he comfortably installed in his own house with an office to see the outdoor men in; or better still that there had never been a war at all. But such repining was useless, so he got up and braced himself to meet his old keeper.

Mr. Margett was one of the three families, Margetts, Polletts and Pattens, who were the real life and fibre of that part of the county and had probably been so long before Barsetshire was carved from forests and downs and river valleys. Of old Anglo-Saxon stock they had intermarried as far back as church registers existed, rarely taking wives from among the foreigners, but from time to time allowing a gipsy man who wanted one of their girls to come into the clan. Jasper Margett belonged to this mixed race, his grandmother, half-gipsy by blood, being a witch who lived in Golden Valley towards Skeynes Agnes, and in her younger days had frequently been met as a large black hare. In his youth Jasper had hesitated between poaching and running away to sea. His mother, the witch's only child, longed passionately for her son to be respectable, perhaps the more because her husband, one of the most accomplished poachers in the district, and the village ne'er-do-weel in his spare time, wished his son to follow his own profession. Young Jasper very naturally wished to disobey the wishes of both parents, and at twelve was well on the way to inheriting the position of ne'er-do-weel which his father had forfeited by falling down the front steps of the Woolpack after closing time and breaking his neck, when Providence intervened in the shape of the head keeper at Beliers Priory who wanted help with the pheasant chicks. As soon as Jasper Margett saw the young birds he knew that no life would be worth living that did not include the handling and rearing of such pleasing objects. He was taken on approval. His hereditary instincts made him as clever and gentle with birds as he was quick with a gun. The head keeper reported favourably to Sir George Waring, father of the present baronet, Jasper was formally engaged, and in time became head-keeper at the Priory, and a silent or acrimonious devotee of the whole family. Harry Waring, then at Oxford, became the chief object of his devotion. Little George Waring had had his first lessons in shooting and fishing from Jasper. Now the under keeper and the other men had gone, but Jasper still kept watch over the woods, a taciturn man, smitten to the heart by the decay of landed estates and game preserving, seeing no possible successor in his craft. The village, which felt kindly towards him, for he had often been lenient to their boys, did a little poaching from time to time to cheer him up, but were grieved to find that he did not respond. When young Alf Margett, brother of Bert Margett the porter at Worsted, home on leave from the tanks, snared six fat rabbits and sold them to the convalescent home at the back door, Jasper merely fought him in the backyard, knocked him down and took him out to shoot young rooks next day.

"You'll never make a poacher nor a fighter, young Alf, nor a shot neither," were his parting words. "Better stick to them tanks," a remark which caused Alf to feel small for the first time in his very cocksure life.

"Well, Jasper, it's about Matron's cat, I suppose," said Sir Harry. "Sit down. Selina, have we any beer? Then bring a bottle, please. You'll have a glass, Jasper, won't you? It's all we can get now. Her ladyship is getting quite a taste for it."

Selina brought a tray with bottles and glasses. Jasper lifted his glass, uttered an unprintable toast to the German Chancellor, and drank it at one draught.

"I'm all with you there," said Sir Harry. "Have another, and tell me the trouble."

By long experience Sir Harry knew that Jasper found it difficult to express himself on most subjects, and particularly difficult when he was in the Priory. The four walls of a room were always a cage to him. His dark eyes glanced restlessly from door to window as if calculating the chances of escape, and he would have found it easier to submit to Red Indian tortures than to say what he had come to say. After drinking the best part of two bottles of beer he so far relaxed his caution as to admit monosyllabically that he had come about the subject he had come about.

"Selina says Private Jenks thought the cat was a squirrel, and that was why he shot it," said Sir Harry. "He must be quite a good shot then, if it was dusk. Selina said after tea."

Jasper nodded.

"Why on earth did you let him have a gun?" said Sir Harry. "It isn't safe to let any of those fellows have guns. You remember those evacuees we had here, and the father that came down to see them and told you a tall story about being a good shot and all he did was to pepper his own children."

Jasper was understood to say that it served them right, with a rider to the effect that they were thieving varmints and were well known to eat pheasants' eggs. "Besides, they weren't his," he added after a pause. "They were his wife's. And the lodger's."

Slightly taken aback by these revelations Sir Harry repeated that it was not safe to let any stray soldier have a gun.

"Might have been mine in a manner of speaking," said Jasper, thawing a little, "if I'd a listened to that woman, but I've never listened to a woman yet."

Sir Harry, ignoring these interesting confessions, repeated that guns must on no account be lent to convalescent soldiers who had probably only shot at fun fairs.

"Not Tom Jenks," said Jasper. "Lord Pomfret's head keeper, that's his father."

"Lord! old Jenks with the broken nose," said Sir Harry. "I remember old Lord Pomfret telling me his boy was a remarkable shot. Well, well, I must see what I can do. But don't let young Jenks have a gun anywhere near the house again. I shall have the dickens of a time about it. Selina says Matron is coming over after dinner. By the way, young Jenks seems to have told Selina he'd never shot a squirrel before."

"Bit of swank," said Jasper. "If I'd a listened to women *I'd* be telling lies. Silleena. It's a good name for a woman. Silly by name and silly by nature."

At this point Lady Waring came in. For her Jasper had an admiration as wife of Sir Harry and as mother of George whom he had taught to shoot and fish, and even as herself, all of which made him tongue-tied in her presence, or ostentatiously gruff, which deceived nobody. Overcome with confusion at his last remark, which Lady Waring must certainly have heard, he sidled his way out of the room against the wall and went away. In the little hall he met Selina.

"Isn't it dreadful about Matron's pussy, Mr. Margett?" said Selina piteously. "And poor Private Jenks too. He *is* so upset. He was at the back door just now and he *was* so upset about poor pussy that I gave him a cup of tea, poor boy."

Jasper looked darkly at her.

"If I went about making up to silly women, *I'd* get cups of tea," he announced witheringly.

Selina went back to the kitchen and told the cook that poor Mr. Margett was quite upset and no wonder, a poor little cat that never did anyone any harm and Matron *was* so upset and poor Private Jenks *so* upset. Then she dried her eyes and went to tidy Lady Waring's bedroom.

Meanwhile the Warings ate their dinner, which was quite a good one but would have been nicer if the telephone had not interrupted so often. Mr. Palmer at Worsted, who refused to dine till half-past eight war or no war, rang up to consult Sir Harry about a case of fowl-stealing that was coming before the magistrates next week. Lady Bond, who to her husband's great annoyance made him dine at seven on patriotic but unappetizing food, rang up to say she did not think Lady Waring had quite understood the point at issue in that afternoon's meeting. Mrs. Tebben, who enjoyed her own discomfort and did not notice other people's, rang up from Lamb's Piece to tell Lady Waring a delightful dish she had discovered of some left-over fish and some cold potato mashed together with a teaspoon of made mustard and any bits of cold cabbage one had and you could eat it just as it was, cold, for Sunday supper. As an afterthought she said her daughter Margaret Dean had just had another baby, a girl this time, and was doing nicely, and her son Richard was enjoying the Middle East so much and said Cairo was just like Piccadilly, but had not yet had time to go to the Museum. Roddy Wicklow, Lord Pomfret's agent, rang up to say his leg was still keeping him away from active service and would Sir Harry like the loan of the tractor next week and his wife and both the children were well. Mrs. Brandon, who to everyone's surprise and most of all to her own, was in charge of the local Land Girls, and doing the job very well in her own peculiar way, rang up from Pomfret Madrigal to ask if Norma Hopkins was giving satisfaction on the farm, and to say that her daughter Delia Grant's little boy had chicken-pox, but Nannie thank goodness had gone to take charge and was going to bring Delia and little Freddie back to Stories next week, and Delia would work at the W.V.S. while her husband was in Washington.

And so the county news came filtering in, from one marooned homestead to another. Such was the press of news after seven o'clock that Palmyra (called after Mrs. Palmer) Phipps at the telephone exchange was often able to give a subscriber who couldn't get through to a friend the exact information she needed.

The Warings were always glad to hear of their friends and to give help or advice when possible, but they did wish they could eat their dinner in peace. Lady Waring had once suggested that Selina should answer all telephone-calls during dinner and take messages. Sir Harry agreed, though secretly convinced that it would never work. To his wife's triumph Selina had proved invaluable at the telephone, intelligent, quick and accurate, but when she had received and written down the message, her kind heart nearly always led her to summon her master or mistress because the telephoner sounded so upset, so that in the end it was simpler for one of them to go to the telephone in person.

"Shall we wait and have our coffee when Matron comes?" said Lady Waring, when they were back in the sitting-room. "It might soften her a little. I mean she can't kill us if she has eaten our salt."

Sir Harry, who wanted his coffee very hot, and directly after his dinner, looked disappointed and said nothing.

"No, we'll have it now," said his wife, ringing.

"You women never know your own mind for two minutes together," said Sir Harry kindly.

His wife smiled at him and said nothing.

Selina brought the coffee.

"Anything wrong, Selina?" said Sir Harry, noticing her tearful eyes.

"Oh yes, Sir Harry, it's dreadful," said Selina. "The gentleman said on the radio that there was a big ship sunk and it does seem dreadful."

"Why you girls listen to that filthy noise I can't think," said Sir Harry, roused upon one of his favourite topics of hate. "Gentleman!"

"The lady then, Sir Harry," said Selina, wiping her eyes.

"It's not a lady. It's an announcer," said Sir Harry. "And whose ship was sunk, ours or the enemy's?"

"I never heard, Sir Harry. The gentleman said it was sunk by an American destroyer, Sir Harry. I *was* so upset and so was Cook."

"Listen, Selina," said Sir Harry. "The Americans are our allies. Have you got that?"

"Oh yes, Sir Harry, like the poor French."

"Good God!" said Sir Harry. "Oh well, we'll leave it at that. So if the Americans sink a ship, it's an enemy ship, and you ought to be glad."

"Oh yes, Sir Harry," said Selina, her tears ceasing by magic, her cheeks dimpling and her hair curling in wilder tendrils than ever. "Cook *will* be pleased. Oh dear, the coffee will be cold. I'll bring some fresh in a minute, Sir Harry."

Her employers looked at each other in amused resignation.

"Please, my lady," said Selina reappearing with the coffee, "it's Mrs. Phipps. She says could she see you a moment, my lady."

34

"Mrs. Phipps?" said Lady Waring.

"Yes, my lady. Miss Phipps is on the railway. It's about her Mrs. Phipps wanted to see you."

"I can't think who it is," said Lady Waring, "but she had better come in. Do you mind, Harry? No, Matron may be here at any moment. I'll see Mrs. Phipps in the hall, Selina. Matron will come by the passage door from the house and you can show her straight in. And bring some more coffee when she comes."

She went into the hall. Sir Harry, left alone, drank his coffee and wished his wife would spare herself, though this was a thing she had never done since the day he married her more than forty years ago. She had made as happy a home for George as a boy could possibly have. When George was killed she had met the blow with a strength and courage that sustained them both. Between the wars she had seconded him devotedly, ably, in his military life, been liked by all his junior officers and made the best of impressions on his superiors. When he retired to take up the management of his estate she had thrown herself with equal vigour into country life and was liked and trusted by all ranks. And the extraordinary thing, thought Sir Harry admiringly, was that she always looked so handsome and was hardly ever in a hurry. It was pure selfishness, he told himself, to want her to do less and rest more; a wish to have a few peaceful evenings at his own fireside. Then he sighed inwardly and had to admit that he was as busy as she, that he was often out at night and away for days at a time, and that his wife never complained. Well, some day the war would be over and perhaps they would settle down; or perhaps everything would be taken from them and they would be glad to go on living in the servants' quarters as they were now; and after all, what was it all for? There was no child to inherit; the place would go to a cousin in the Navy, who had spent much of his life out of England. What a weary business it all was, giving one's best to a place where one's widow wouldn't even have the right to live. Still, one could keep the place going, and there was Jasper, and there were old men about the place who had known his father, and young men who looked to Sir Harry to get them out of trouble, and old women who wanted advice about old-age pensions and were afraid to ask at the post office. One must keep going for them.

From the hall came an interminable monologue, from which his wife would, he knew, come back exhausted, but probably having done some kind deed. Damn Mrs. Phipps, whoever she was. And damn Miss Phipps, who was on the railway. People didn't come to *their* houses badgering their wives to death at all hours of the night. He remembered the two young women at Winter Overcotes station. Dreadful-looking girls they were, but good-humoured as could be, grateful for his help, and probably helping to win the war just as much as he was, in their own way. No place for old men in the world now, he thought; though no one would have called him an old man. Angrily he took up the evening paper and read what Mrs. Betty Higgins, aged ninety-seven, had to say about the war. Oh, Lord!

He was almost glad when Selina appeared at the far door and announced, "Matron, Sir Harry."

"Tell her ladyship, Selina," he said. "Good evening, Matron. Come and sit by the fire and we'll have some coffee."

He managed to keep the conversation on neutral ground till the coffee came, and then said:

"Well, Matron, I'm sorry to hear about your cat. Whose fault was it?"

Matron, who had arrived full of pent-up emotion of various kinds: anger, grief, the holy feeling that a good cry leaves behind it, and several more, was rather taken aback.

"Whose fault?" she repeated.

Sir Harry looked at her. She was a handsome, middle-aged woman with grey waving hair and a firm mouth. Her dress was as precise as it could be; a long line of ribbons on the bodice spoke of honourable service in many places and campaigns. He was willing to wager that she was one of those rare nurses who look even better out of uniform than in it.

"Yes, Matron. Jenks had no business with a gun, but why was he out after tea? I thought they had to be in unless they had special permission."

"He had no business to be out at all," said Matron severely.

"Then why was he out?" said Sir Harry.

"I really thought Nurse Poulter understood that no one could go out unless he had a proper leave pass."

"Who is Nurse Poulter?" asked Sir Harry. "I don't think I've met her."

"She only came in on Tuesday. She is an excellent nurse and will be a help to us. But really, Sir Harry, I do not quite see what this has to do with my pussy. He was as faithful as a dog and far more intelligent. It's a shocking thing if men are to be allowed to shoot dumb animals and nothing is to be said."

Her voice rose a little and she clasped her hands, signs which did not escape her host.

"How old was he?" he asked kindly.

"Five — I had him from a kitten and he was one of those cats that prefer people to places. Never did I have to butter his paws. Wherever I went was home to him. And that's what makes it so hard. Your keeper is, I am afraid, answerable for the death of that poor dumb beast."

"Margett had no business to let any of your patients have a gun," said Sir Harry, "and I have already spoken very seriously to him about it. It will not occur again unless you and I both give permission. I am extremely sorry."

"Well, I'm sure nothing could be more handsome," said Matron, visibly softened, "but what to do about Jenks I cannot decide. I should like to send him straight back to his regiment, but I don't think doctor would pass him as fit. He is only just recovering from appendicitis which," said Matron, fearing she might be relenting too much, "makes it all the worse, of course. Pussy would never have hurt a fly."

"They make them mangy, don't they?" said Sir Harry sympathetically. "My wife had a Persian who used to eat beetles, and its fur came out in handfuls. But now, Matron, about Private Jenks being out of bounds after tea. If you did not give precise instructions to this Nurse Poulter, it seems to me the responsibility is yours. You couldn't possibly have foreseen what would happen. It is all very sad and you are being very brave about it."

For a moment Sir Harry feared that Matron was going to cry, but she fought down her weakness and said "Thank you" in a small voice.

Sir Harry breathed an inward sigh of relief. And even greater was his relief when the door from the hall was opened and his wife came in, for he felt he could not handle the situation much longer.

"Good evening, Matron," said Lady Waring, shaking hands. "I can't tell you how sorry I am about your poor cat. It's dreadful that it happened here and Sir Harry has told Margett he must never let any of your patients have a gun without his and your permission. Will you excuse me one moment. Harry, Mrs. Phipps lives at Worsted and she has bicycled over to thank you for being so kind to her girl who is one of the porters at Winter Overcotes. Do you mind if she comes in?"

Without waiting for the answer which she knew Sir Harry would have to give, she ushered Mrs. Phipps into the sittingroom. That lady wore a disgraceful blue felt hat crammed down on her grey clipped hair and a brown coat with a little old fur on it, and was carrying a basket.

"This is Mrs. Phipps," said Lady Waring. "This is my husband, Mrs. Phipps, and this is the matron of our convalescent home."

"Pleased to meet you and Matron," said Mrs. Phipps. "My Dawris told me how nice you'd acted to her and Lily-Annie this evening and having to visit my sister in the village I come over on my bike to thank you. She's a real good girl Dawris is, and she said you gave them a hand with the truck. I said, 'That's no work for a gentleman, my girl,' but Dawris said, 'All right, Mother, you ask the gentleman.' Lily-Annie and her said you were a lovely gentleman."

"That's all right, Mrs. Phipps," said Sir Harry. "They are good girls. I hope your daughter likes her work."

"The Wrens would have her any day," said Mrs. Phipps, "so would the Waafs. But the railways is in the family as you might say, Bert Margett at Worsted station being my second cousin. Him and Dawris have been going together six years, so I s'pose they'll be getting married one of these days. But Dawris always had her heart in the railway, and she said to me, 'All right, Mother, it's no good you and Dad talking, because Lily-Annie and me's going on the railway.' 'Why not go in telephones like your cousin Palmyra?' I said, but Dawris talked her Dad and me round, so there it is."

"Thank you very much for coming, Mrs. Phipps. You will have a cup of tea before you go," said Lady Waring, ringing.

"I don't mind if I do," said Mrs. Phipps. "It's a nasty hill up to Worsted on a bike. I had words yesterday with one of my ladies, I thought you'd like to know, the one I work for on Tuesdays and Fridays, so if you want anyone I dare say I could manage it."

Lady Waring was about to say that she would inquire, when Selina came in, so she asked her to give Mrs.

Phipps some tea before she went, and put out her hand to say good-bye. But Mrs. Phipps was struggling with something in her basket and paid no attention.

"The mother's our old Flossie," said Mrs. Phipps, at last extricating a small bundle wrapped in a piece of blanket, "but the father's a full Persian. I chased him away twenty times if I chased him away once, but my fine gentleman got the better of me. We call this one Winston. Me and Dad thought you'd like him, being as you was so kind to Dawris."

She unwrapped the bundle carefully. In it was a silky, smoke-coloured kitten half asleep. It opened its mouth, showed some little sharp white teeth and a rose-petal tongue, and mewed.

"How *very* kind of you, Mrs. Phipps," said Lady Waring, madly racking her brain for a plausible excuse for not taking a kitten that she didn't in the least want.

The kitten mewed again piercingly.

"He wants some milk," said Matron suddenly. "Will you excuse me, Lady Waring. Come to auntie, then."

She poured some of the still warm milk into a coffee saucer and offered it to the kitten which lapped twice, sneezed, and mewed again.

"You'd better take him on your lap, miss," said Mrs. Phipps. "He loves a bit of warmth."

Matron sat down. Mrs. Phipps deposited the bundle on her lap. The kitten stretched itself and settled down to the milk with delicate voluptuousness.

"It's extremely kind of you, Mrs. Phipps," said Sir Harry, suddenly inspired, "and we would love to have

Winston, but it's a bit awkward when we are out so much and the milk so short. Would you mind if I asked Matron to take care of him? She gets all the milk she wants and plenty of fish, and we can see him every day."

"That's all right," said Mrs. Phipps. "But don't feed him too much. His mother's a rare mouser and I always keep her short, or she gets lazy. Well, good-night all, and I'll be sure to tell Dawris what you said, Sir Harry. You can keep the kitten's blanket, miss."

"What *did* I say about Doris?" said Sir Harry to his wife when Mrs. Phipps had left, accompanied by Selina, who was already crying because the kitten was such a dear wee little thing.

"I haven't the faintest idea," said his wife.

"You ought to go to bed, Lady Waring," said Matron, looking at her with a professional eye. "And take a day in bed to-morrow if you will excuse my saying so. I apologize for staying so long, and thank you very much for all your kindness, Sir Harry. I shall take the greatest care of Winston. Come along to beddy-byes with auntie, then."

"Diplomatist!" said Lady Waring to her husband when they were alone.

"I thought you didn't want the kitten, my dear," said Sir Harry. "And Matron was quite right; you must go to bed. There's the telephone again."

Selina came in.

"Please, Sir Harry," she said, "it's a gentleman at the camp. I said could I take a message, but he said he wanted to speak to you particularly."

"What gentleman?" said Sir Harry.

"Captain Harper, or some such name, Sir Harry. I didn't like to ask again because he seemed so —"

"No, he was *not* upset, Selina, and he's not a gentleman, and his name is Hooper. All right, I'll come. What the dickens does he want at this time of night? You go to bed, my dear."

But Lady Waring did not go to bed. Her husband's voice, speaking with the patient courtesy that he used for anyone he did not like, told her that Captain Hooper from the camp who was not a gentleman was interrupting him at every other word.

"Now is the moment when I wish brandy wasn't such a price and rotgut at that," said Sir Harry coming back.

"Shall I get you some?" said his wife. "I have that bottle that Lord Bond gave us put away."

"No, my dear, it's all right. But rather a nuisance. The fellow Hooper wants to know if we can put up an Intelligence officer."

"Yes, of course we can," said Lady Waring. "After all, we have got the empty room and it's better than evacuees."

"Bless you, my dear. But I'm afraid there's a wife too. I told Hooper I'd ask you."

"You didn't, Harry. You said you would take them. Don't try to deceive me. It will be a bit of a squash but we'll manage. They can have the big room and Leslie can have the little room next to Selina's. That's the best we can do."

"Is Leslie coming?" asked Sir Harry, who seldom thought about his young cousin, sister of his heir, though he liked her when he saw her.

"You know she is, darling," said Lady Waring, suddenly looking very tired.

"Go to bed at once," said her husband with kindly ferocity. "Oh *Lord*! there's the front-door bell again!"

Once more Selina appeared, to say it was the under-housemaid from Mr. Palmer's who had lost her ration cards and her clothing coupons and wanted Sir Harry to witness her declaration of loss as he was a J.P., and it was her evening out, so she thought she might as well look in on her way back.

"Oh damn Palmer's under-housemaid," Sir Harry exploded. "Oh, all right, I'll see her. And you go to bed at once, my dear; and you too, Selina. I'll let the girl out."

"She's not a girl, Sir Harry," said Selina, "or she'd be called up, Sir Harry. She's Mr. Margett's aunt."

"If she is the devil himself, I'll show her out," said Sir Harry. "Go along to bed, both of you."

CHAPTER
TWO

Sir Harry breakfasted at a quarter to eight four days a week, walked to Lambton station, and got the one up train by which there was no change at Winter Overcotes. Before he left on the morning after Matron's visit he went to say good-bye to his wife as usual. She was in bed, a breakfast tray on a table at one side, a large dispatch-box on a table at the other side, dealing with the morning's post before she got up. Sir Harry bent cautiously over the breakfast tray and kissed her, expressing a hope that she hadn't been kept awake by all the visitors last night, and that the Intelligence officer and his wife would not be too much for her.

"If you think you can't manage it, my dear," he said, "I'll let Hooper know he must try somewhere else. I can't have you working yourself to death."

"I shall manage quite well," said Lady Waring. "And it came to me in the small hours of the night that Mrs. Phipps is the solution. If she can come here on Tuesdays and Fridays and Mrs. Officer isn't too exigent, we shall do quite well. Leslie can help Selina a bit and after all it isn't for ever."

Sir Harry looked at his wife with admiration, took her letters to post in London and went off. His cold, dark walk to the station was solaced by the thought that few other wives would have given such loyal support as his (though here he was quite wrong) and that in all their married life she had never failed him (in which he was quite right). So absorbed was he in these pleasant reflections that he showed his season ticket in a dream, acknowledged the station-master's salute from habit, and strode up and down the platform oblivious of his surroundings. Gradually the fact penetrated his consciousness that every time he passed the ticket office there was a noise as of unrefined giggling. Next time he stopped, and in the dismal light which was now filtering through heavy clouds saw two young women from whom the giggling appeared to come. Loud whisperings were exchanged, more giggles and a good deal of pushing followed. Then Doris Phipps, detaching herself from her friend, came forward.

"Thank you ever so for taking Winston," she said. "Mum said she'd drown him and I cried ever so. Mum's coming to oblige at the Priory, she said to tell you."

Sir Harry said he didn't think anything had been arranged.

"Oh yes," said Doris Phipps. "Mum says she's going up on Friday to commence working. She says the young lady that gave her the tea was ever so nice."

Sir Harry, feeling a little unequal to these plans so early in the morning, asked if they were going on duty by the train.

Lily-Annie, who had not yet spoken, said, "Ow now, Sir Harry," and overcome by her own courage in saying the gentleman's name, though not quite sure if it was etiquette to say Harry, which she knew was short for Henry, got behind Doris Phipps.

"It's our day off," said Doris, "so Mum said to bike over to Lambton and tell you she'd be over on Friday, Sir Harry."

"But how did she know I would be here?" said Sir Harry.

"The young lady told her you got the 8.25, Sir Harry," said Doris, "and Mr. Pollett, he's the station-master at Worsted, said you always went up on Wednesdays, because he takes duty at Lambton if Ernie Pollett, that's my uncle, is on leave."

Doris Phipps might have gone on for ever, making Sir Harry more and more confused as he realized for the hundredth time how fierce was the light of public interest that was directed at him from all quarters, had not Lily-Annie given her friend a hearty shove, with the words, "You and your Bert!" upon which both girls shrieked and ran giggling out of the station.

The 8.25 came in and Sir Harry was carried away to London, rather battered by this unexpected rencontre, but very glad to hear that his wife was to have help. For from what he had seen of Mrs. Phipps, he was quite sure she would come if she meant to.

When Sir Harry had gone Lady Waring finished her letters and read her *Times*, which did not come till after her husband had gone to town. In spite of her cheerful assurances to him, she had not slept very well and thought longingly of Matron's advice to stay in bed. There was a good deal to be done. She must find out if that Mrs. Phipps was really free; she must visit Selina's mother, Nannie Allen, who lived down in Ladysmith Cottages and took offence rather easily. Captain Hooper must be rung up on the private number her husband had left with her. How very nice it would be, she felt, if the unknown Intelligence officer and wife could suddenly find a billet somewhere else. And then there was Leslie coming to-day.

By rights, Lady Waring thought, or at least by all the rules of novels, she and her husband ought to hate the heir who would possess George's inheritance. If Harry were a proper uncle, like Ralph Nickleby, he would do his best to ruin Lieutenant-Commander Cecil Waring, R.N., and if possible persecute his sister Leslie: though even that wouldn't do much good, for Cecil would meet Admiral Cheeryble, K.C.B., and Leslie would marry Captain Frank Cheeryble, R.N., his nephew, and Harry would hang himself from the hook in the drawing-room where the gas chandelier used to hang in his grandfather's time; for there were not any hooks in the servants' wing as far as she could remember. This delightful plan did not seem to leave any place for her, so she laughed at herself, and thought how much nicer it really was that Harry was on good terms with Cecil. As for Leslie, her visits had always been a pleasure, from her early nursery days to her late long-legged schoolgirl days. Lady Waring never pretended to herself that she loved Leslie like a daughter. "I couldn't, you know," she said aloud to herself, "because I've never had a daughter so I don't know how one loves them." But she was fond of the girl and found her a useful person to have at the Priory in the days when they had house-parties, for she was willing to listen, played tennis well, danced well, and took a really intelligent interest in the estate. Lady Waring had once said to her husband that it was a pity brothers and sisters couldn't marry, like the Ptolemies, as Cecil and Leslie seemed so admirably suited to one another and Leslie was so fond of the place and could help her brother with it. To which Sir Harry said the Ptolemies were a dashed queer lot and what Leslie ought to do was to marry some nice man and have a family and he hoped his wife wouldn't say things like that in public. So she kissed him and said she wouldn't.

Since Munich Leslie Waring had been secretary of a large organization connected with naval charities. In the workings of this Sir Harry had taken a great interest and had been able to help her more than once at difficult corners. Of late this work had grown greatly and Leslie was so indispensable that she had been left in her job, though she would willingly have become a Wren and in many ways preferred it. After more than three years' work, including being bombed in London and Portsmouth and two journeys to America, she had had a kind of breakdown and been ordered three months' complete rest.

"And that," said Lady Waring, on whom the general strain and tension of the war had the effect of making her talk aloud to herself as much as Alice, "is quite a good thing, because if she hadn't been ill I couldn't have had her here."

This led her to a consideration of how very difficult it must be for people to write novels, because all the young heroines were in the Forces or civilian jobs and all the young heroes the same, so that there was very little time for novelists to make them fall in love with each other, unless they made the hero be a flying officer and the heroine a Waaf, and then one would have to know all the details of the R.A.F. or one would make the most dreadful howlers. Unable to find any real solution to this problem, she determined to wait till she saw Mrs. Morland, who wrote a novel every year to earn her living and would be able to tell her exactly how these things were done.

By now the sky was as light as it proposed to be and as Nannie Allen used so truly to say to George, "Laying in bed doesn't get you up," so she rang for Selina and said she would wear her blue tweeds.

"Selina," she said, "do you know if anyone is going over to Worsted today? I want to send a message to Mrs. Phipps to say that I would be glad to have her on Tuesdays and Fridays. If the officer and his wife that Sir Harry was speaking about do come, we shall need extra help. Do you think we shall be able to manage? I don't want Cook and Baker to feel put upon."

"Oh yes, my lady," said Selina. "Cook said it would be quite like old times and really she said she can't do herself justice with your ladyship and Sir Harry out to so many meals. And I'm sure Baker won't mind. She quite took to Mrs. Phipps."

"But we don't know if Mrs. Phipps can come yet," said Lady Waring.

"Oh yes, my lady," said Selina with kindly pity. "It was all arranged when we was having a cup of tea with Mrs. Phipps last night and she's coming on Friday to begin. Private Jenks is her sister's nephew, my lady."

Marvelling at all the things she didn't know, but delighted to hear of one difficulty smoothed out, Lady Waring finished dressing and rang up Captain Hooper's private number. After some delay a voice said, "Captain Hooper speaking."

"This is Lady Waring," said she. "My husband tells me that you rang up last night about billeting an officer on us. He has gone to town, but if you will tell me what you want I will see what I can do."

"Great minds meet, Lady Waring," said the voice. "I was just going to ring you up. I hear you are going to be a friend in need."

"Oh, not at all," said Lady Waring, who did not in the least mean what she said, but already made a little nervous by her husband's words about Captain Hooper, was not reassured by that officer's voice. "What is it exactly?"

"Well, in these stirring times it's difficult to get a house anywhere," Captain Hooper continued, "and happening to pass the remark to the General that we were to have an Intelligence officer billeted on us who wants to have his wife with him, he said would we inquire. This Major Merton is due to arrive to-day. I suppose you couldn't do anything about it. I mean having a big place and all that I thought you might be the Lady Bountiful in the case."

Lady Waring's mind during the foregoing had rushed like an express train through suspicion, repulsion, fear of the unknown major, a general wish to disoblige Captain Hooper in every possible way, remorse for nourishing evil thoughts of a soldier who was doing his best for a brother officer and couldn't help being himself, the determination which was her fixed guide never to refuse help to the army, a second wave of repulsion, and finally the decision to settle everything at once and not give herself time to think how horrid it would be. So she said she would do all in her power to help and could Major Merton come and see her as soon as convenient.

"I assure you, Lady Waring, that your taking my request in the spirit you do is very much appreciated," said Captain Hooper, obviously relieved. "I'll tell the Major to report at your place as soon as he comes. Of course we can put him up for a day or two, but it's the question of the wife. I might drop in with him myself. I feel we quite know each other after this little chat and in times like these we must all pull together."

"Yes, thank you *so* much," said Lady Waring, hearing herself sounding quite idiotic. "Good-bye."

When describing this conversation later, Lady Waring averred that as she put the receiver up she distinctly heard the words "Chin-chin," but this was generally considered a flight of poetic fancy.

"What can't be cured must be endured," she said aloud to herself and prepared to go down to the village and call on old Nannie. It was a dull day, raw and dark. As she walked round the house to get from the servants' wing into the drive she saw disconsolate soldiers looking out of the windows and remembered how much gayer they had looked in the last war in their bright-blue flannel suits and red ties. Some of her convalescents were old friends as friendship goes in war-time, having been there for a fortnight or more, so she waved to them. A soldier tapped on the window and held Winston up for her to look at. He had put a tie round the kitten's neck and was trying to make it hold a cigarette behind its ear. Winston opened his mouth and gave a silent mew behind the great plate-glass window. Lady Waring wondered if he was happy. Then she saw him arch his small head to be tickled behind the ears and felt he could well look after himself. In the drive Matron was having ten minutes' walk up and down before going back to her duties, so Lady Waring stopped and greeted her.

"I really can't thank you enough, Lady Waring," said Matron, with the gleam of devotion in her eyes, "for your sympathy and forbearance last night. But I mustn't talk of myself. I see you have not taken my advice about staying in bed for a day. You really need someone to look after you."

Lady Waring asked after the kitten.

"He is quite devoted to me already," said Matron proudly. "He follows me everywhere. He wanted to come out with me, but I said, 'No, Winston' — you know it feels quite funny to call a cat Winston, but I dare say Mr. Churchill has quite a number of cats called after him — 'No, Winston,' I said, 'Auntie is going walkies and it's too wet for little pussy-paws,' and he understood every word I said. So Sergeant Hopkins happened to be passing and pussy — Winston, I should say, but I always called the old pussy pussy — rubbed against his legs as much as to say, 'Auntie's going for a walk, so you take care of me, Mr. Soldier.' Sergeant Hopkins is one of our really nice men, so helpful to the nurses and always willing to go down to the village for any little thing."

Lady Waring murmured her interest.

"And I am sure you will be pleased to hear," said Matron, "that Private Jenks has given Winston a ping-pong ball to play with. Where he got it I cannot think, but Winston was so pleased, and played with it as if he was human. I think Jenks has had his lesson against cruelty to animals, and after all there's a war on."

Whether Matron meant that cruelty to animals was a venial offence when so much cruelty to humans was going on everywhere, or that humanitarians ought not to be hard on our gallant men who were giving their lives, and in Private Jenks's case their appendix, for their country, or, as seemed most probable, that she uttered the phrase without attaching any meaning to it, Lady Waring could not say. She took leave of Matron and went on down the drive, wondering not for the first time whether it was very horrid of her not to have any particular love for animals, and why the relationship of auntie was so peculiarly repellent as between middle-aged spinsters and kittens. Still, if the breach between Matron and Private Jenks was healed, that was all to the good.

54

Ladysmith Cottages where Nannie lived were at the Worsted end of the village, opposite the Sheep's Head, Geo. F. Pollett, licensed to sell wines and spirits, Pampler's Entire. They had been built by Sir Harry's father and though hideous were warm and comfortable. The walls, of ugly grey brick with a diamond pattern of ugly red brick, were draught-proof; the dark grey slate roofs never let in a drop of rain; the pitch-pine doors fitted closely; the depressing art-brown wall-papers defied dirt and use; and the scullery and wash-house taps rarely needed attention. They were mostly let at nominal rents to old servants and pensioners and carried with them a prescriptive right to coal, which the Warings always used to lay in by truck-loads in the summer. Nannie Allen lived at No. 1, which, with No. 6 at the other end, was the most genteel, having a bow window in front on both floors and a little builtout hall, so that the front sitting-room could be the whole width of the house instead of having the passage sliced off it. But in one respect No. 1 was superior to No. 6, for over the hall was a little room which in No. 6 was used as a bedroom, but in No. 1 had a real bath. This had been put in by Sir Harry to please Nannie when she retired from nannying, for after a life of nurseries she felt a bath was a necessity, and though she seldom or never used it herself, she kept it exquisitely clean and saw to it personally that any old charges who came to stay with her used it to the fullest extent.

Nannie Allen, the good-looking daughter of a small Barsetshire farmer, had married very young and against her parents' wish Albert Allen, a dashing commercial traveller who had drunk himself and his business into the grave in a couple of years, leaving his widow with one child, a girl called Selina. Her parents offered to take them both, but the widow would not be what she called beholden. She left little Selina at the farm and went into service as nurserymaid, rising very soon to be nurse with one or more under her. Selina grew up with her dashing father's curly hair, her mother's good looks and a happy disposition. Her marriage to Mr. Crockett, a middle-aged greengrocer in Blackheath, had been a happy one, but though she cried bitterly after his death she could not help cheering up, and as we know was ordered by her mother to come and look after Lady Waring.

It was when Selina was about seven that Nannie had gone to the Priory, and the little girl was sometimes asked to spend a week of her school holidays there, under her mother's care. When little George Waring went to his first school, Nannie had stayed on as maid to his mother, but a few years later Sir Harry had been ordered abroad. His wife was to accompany him and Nannie felt the call of the nursery too strong, so with many tears she went to take charge of Cecil and Leslie Waring, the latter from the month. From them she had moved to other families, always giving complete satisfaction, but never obtaining it herself for two reasons: the first that babies will have parents who are apt to imagine that they can bring up their own children, the second that babies are so blind to their own advantage as to grow up. About ten years previously she had got her old-age pension and on this and her savings decided to retire for good. The Warings, who had never lost touch with her, suggested that she should come and live at No. 1. Her parents were dead, so she furnished the house with their things and the photographs of all her charges, whose parents were delighted to be able to send a child or children to stay with their old Nannie to recover from mumps, or be away from an outbreak of measles, or because a father was abroad and a mother doing war work. Nannie cooked and slaved for them with grim affection, bullied them about their hair and nails, and refused to let them help in the house on the grounds that young ladies and gentlemen didn't do such things; but somehow Miss Mary and Master John were usually to be found in the kitchen, helping with the beds, or getting in her way on washing-day. By virtue of her nurse's mysterious power she was always able to get girls from twelve to fifteen from the village to help her, and not one of them dared to use her cheap lipstick while Mrs. Allen could see her.

Perhaps because she had stayed longer at the Priory than in other places, George Waring had been her favourite. Other little boys had been killed between 1914 and 1918, but it was George's death that she had most mourned. Photographs of him at every stage, from a long-clothes baby to a second lieutenant, hung on her walls and stood framed in every room in the house. Lady Waring knew, though she was too honest to feel any shame about it, that George was thought of more often at Ladysmith Cottages than he was at the Priory. Lady Waring could welcome Cecil Waring without restraint as heir to the estate, but she knew that

Nannie, although she had taken Leslie Waring from the month, would always look upon Cecil as an interloper. She could not help admiring Nannie's uncompromising loyalty and at the same time she hoped it was not hypocritical in her to be glad that she could like her husband's nephew and feel that the place would be in good hands in years to come. She might have added, "if Cecil survives the war," but she did not, for in spite of talking aloud to herself she remained very sane and could look the most unreasonable facts in the face and give them their proper value.

She knocked at the door and was admitted by Nannie, who had already heard through the village grapevine that her ladyship was on her way down. In the sitting-room a fire was burning. The room was a little too full, owing to the amount of furniture for which Nannie had sentimental feelings, but everything was exquisitely clean. The mantelpiece was thick with photographs of her soldier-charges from a stout general whom she had often bathed as nurserymaid in her first place to the youngest round-faced boy in battledress fresh from his public school. The gem of the collection however was undoubtedly her great-nephew Sid, brother to Mrs. Barclay's nurse over at Marling Hall, with a pair of Kitchener moustaches and a chest which could best be described as a strikingly handsome military bust.

"You know Sid is a sergeant-major now, my lady," said Nannie.

"How splendid," said Lady Waring. "Do sit down, Nannie."

"Of course if you wish it, my lady," said Nannie, pulling up to the fire a chair with carpet back and seat. This ceremony was invariable and Nannie would have felt much hurt had this form of protocol been omitted.

After all proper inquiries had been made after Nannie's nieces and nephews and such of her ex-charges as Lady Waring knew personally, Nannie offered a cup of tea.

"Thank you so much, Nannie, but I really must be going on," said Lady Waring.

"It's no trouble, my lady, and I'm going to have one myself in any case and the kettle's just coming to the boil," said Nannie; which again was part of the invariable ritual. While Lady Waring waited for the kettle to make up its mind an idea came into her head.

"Nannie," she said, when the tea was poured out, "I've been asked to take an officer and his wife. I could do it, but Miss Leslie is coming and we shall be rather a squash. Your rooms are free, aren't they? Would you like to take them? I would see them first and inquire about proper references for the rent and so on."

Nannie's face assumed a guarded expression from which Lady Waring augured the worst.

"I'm sure, my lady, I would like to take anyone to please you, but officers' wives — well, you never know. Besides, Lady Graham wrote yesterday to say they had measles at Master John's school and could she send him here when school breaks up till he is out of quarantine, so of course I said I would keep the rooms till I heard from her, and really I couldn't manage Master John with people in the house, he's such a tow-row boy. Just like his Uncle David used to be. So I hope you'll be able to manage, my lady, not but what I'd always like to oblige you."

Lady Waring felt it was not worth pressing the matter at the moment. If John Graham was as tow-row as his Uncle David Leslie used to be, Nannie's little house would hardly hold him and an officer and wife.

"How is Mr. David, Nannie?" she asked, looking at a very rakish snapshot of him at St. Moritz on the mantelpiece.

"Somewhere abroad, my lady," said Nannie. "I've no patience with the Government not letting us know where anyone is. As if it could do anyone any harm me writing to David and sending him some of my socks. But he sent me a lovely card, my lady. It was a view of York Cathedral, with 'Posted at Sea' on it, so we must suppose he was in a ship. Dear, dear, never will I forget the time Lady Emily took the two younger ones to Dieppe for the day. Miss Agnes was as good as gold, but poor Master David was as green as a cucumber. I've never seen a child so sick in my life. And the moment we landed, running about as bold as brass."

As there was no stopping Nannie when once launched the perfections of the Leslie family, Lady Waring got up.

"I really must go, Nannie," she said. "Selina sent you her love and is coming down to see you to-morrow afternoon."

"Tell her to bring an apron then," said Nannie. "I'm turning out the big bedroom and she can give me a hand. All those curtains will have to be washed. I hope she is giving satisfaction, my lady."

Lady Waring said, with truth, that Selina was a great help and she didn't know what she would do without her, and so departed.

Apart from a meeting of the W.V.S. at the village hall at two o'clock, a meeting of the Red Cross at the vicarage at half-past three and a lecture at the convalescent home at five o'clock, Lady Waring had nothing to do. The lecture was provided once a week to amuse the men by the Army Education Officer at Winter Overcotes. The idea, namely that any local people who had anything interesting to tell should tell it, was a good one, but had the drawback that it necessarily included a number of people whom the soldiers would sooner have died than hear. Their likes and dislikes were incalculable. A lecture on the reconstruction of the Middle East after the war by Lord Bond had caused his audience to whistle "I've got spurs that jingle, jangle, jingle" very softly to themselves. On the other hand, a talk by Mr. Tebben on "Some Aspects of the Elder Edda" had mysteriously kept them enchained for an hour and a quarter, while Mr. Middleton's monologue on the "Antiquities of Skeynes" had caused such convalescents as were not directly under Sergeant Hopkins's eye to melt like clouds in the silent summer heaven.

To-day the speaker was Dr. Ford from High Rising, who with his hands in his pockets told his audience exactly what would happen to them and what they would look like if in defiance of the War Office they neglected elementary precautions against various sub-tropical diseases. These unpleasant details were avidly supped up by his hearers, though the elder men permitted themselves some scepticism.

"Keep on at the whisky and you'll be all right," said Sergeant Hopkins to a small knot of friends when the lecture was over. "Whisky'll tan you proper inside and then the bugs can't get you. I was in the Cameroons last war, and I know."

"Tan your inside if you like, but *I* know what it will look like," said Dr. Ford as he passed, which so frightened Sergeant Hopkins that he rated Private Jenks severely for not getting himself and his chair out of the lady's way.

"It isn't a bit in my way," said Lady Waring. "Come and have a cigarette, Dr. Ford. I would like to say a drink, but we literally have nothing but beer at the moment."

Dr. Ford said there was nothing wrong with beer, so he and Lady Waring went by the passage into the servants' wing. In the sitting-room they found Sir Harry reading the evening paper and delighted to see Dr. Ford, who was the friend of half the county. Local news was exchanged and Lady Waring asked after Mrs. Morland at High Rising.

"Very well," said Dr. Ford. "The way that woman sits down and writes a book every year beats me. I can't think where she gets all the ideas from. You ought to get her to come and talk to your men about writing novels. Might encourage a few budding writers."

"Lord forbid!" said Sir Harry, frightened. "Don't want that in the Army."

"By the way, Dr. Ford," said Lady Waring. "My niece is coming here for a rest. She had a kind of breakdown in London. If you are anywhere about, will you come and see her some time? Dr. Davies in the village is very nice, but I cannot quite fancy a woman doctor. I have to have her myself of course for politeness, and because she is taking our man's practice while he is in the Middle East, and luckily as I'm quite well I don't need her, but I think Leslie needs someone that really understands. She ought to be here at any moment now. Harry, did you tell the village taxi to meet her?"

Even as she spoke, the front door bell rang.

"Nice girl, your Leslie," said Dr. Ford. "I'll do anything I can for her. Who's her doctor in town?"

Lady Waring mentioned a name.

"Oh, he's all right," said Dr. Ford. "Knew him at Guy's when I was lecturing there. I'll write to him. I look forward to seeing that young lady again."

Selina opened the door and announced, "Captain Hooper and the other gentleman."

"Jolly nice of you to ask me to come along, Lady Waring," said the first officer, who from his three stars was evidently Captain Hooper. "This is quite an antique old place of yours, Sir Harry," he added, shaking hands warmly with Dr. Ford.

"Eighteen seventy-two. Ford's my name," said Dr. Ford unsympathetically.

Captain Hooper shook hands with Sir Harry, evidently thinking but poorly of him for not being someone else. One must not, he said, let etiquette go by the board even in these times of change, and he must introduce Lady Waring to Major Merton. Everyone behaved extremely well.

"Etiquette is not the word," said Dr. Ford, at which Captain Hooper laughed in a gratified way.

Sir Harry, who knew Dr. Ford's intolerance for people to whom he took a dislike, hastily invited Captain Hooper to have some beer. Though far from being a drinker himself, said Captain Hooper, he would not say No to the offer. And by the way, he said, he thought a man of his, Sergeant Hopkins, was at the hospital and would much like a few words with him if possible. Sir Harry consulted his wife with a look, understood that the sooner Captain Hooper got what he wanted and went away the better, and took him away to the big house, accompanied by Dr. Ford who wanted to see Matron.

"Is Captain Hooper a friend of yours?" said Lady Waring to Major Merton.

"I only met him for the first time yesterday," said Major Merton.

"And I only met him for the first time to-day," said Lady Waring deliberately.

"In that case," said Major Merton, offering Lady Waring a cigarette, which she gently refused, "I gather that we see eye to eye. Do you mind if I smoke?"

"Oh, please," said Lady Waring. "And now we have a few moments to ourselves while our common friend is in the other part of the house, would you like to talk business? I gather from Captain Hooper that you are looking for some kind of lodgings for yourself and Mrs. Merton."

"How few women would have said 'common' rather than 'mutual'!" said Major Merton admiringly. "Yes, that is what I want. If you can give me any help in finding rooms, or a small house, or really anything, though in a caravan live I will not, my wife and I shall be more than grateful. We were married during the war and I have been moved about all the time, and we have no home except my old chambers in London."

"You are a lawyer, then?" said Lady Waring.

"A barrister. I like to mention this because we pique ourselves on being the Senior Service. But I expect I've forgotten all the law I ever learnt. My wife's people lived at Northbridge, but their house has been taken over."

"I used to know a Mrs. Keith at Northbridge," said Lady Waring. "She had a house near the river."

"My wife's mother," said Major Merton.

"But then you ought to be called Carter," said Lady Waring, perplexed.

"No, I do assure you I oughtn't," said Major Merton. "If I were Everard Carter I'd have married my sister-in-law, Kate Carter, and though I am very fond of Kate, that is what I *will* not have done. I married Kate's younger sister, Lydia."

"Oh, but *Lydia*!" said Lady Waring. "Now I know all about you. You are Noel Merton. Lavinia Brandon has often talked of you and your wife."

"Bless that woman," said Major Merton. "I have never known anyone so silly and so perfectly satisfactory. She has such an effect on me that I practically dance a minuet and flick a grain of snuff from my lace jabot whenever I see her."

"I do so agree," said Lady Waring. "Mrs. Brandon is really what would be called a Universal Favourite."

"I could talk with you for ever," said Major Merton warmly, "but time is flying and my gallant and odious friend Captain Hooper may be back at any moment. Have you any hope for Lydia and myself? She is staying with the Carters till we can find somewhere near the camp."

"Well, not at the moment," said Lady Waring. "There isn't a house for miles and my old Nannie who lets rooms in the village can't promise anything just now because of Christmas holidays. But Captain Hooper did suggest that we might put you up here —"

"Insolent puppy," said Major Merton.

"— and though I would sooner die than do anything to please Captain Hooper," said Lady Waring earnestly, "it would really give me great pleasure to ask you and your wife to come and stay here, at any rate for a few weeks while you look about. Or Nannie's rooms might be free. Or anything might happen. And I know Harry will be delighted."

Major Merton accepted this offer with real gratitude. He was intelligent enough to realize that Lady Waring would not have made it unless she meant it, and hoped that he and his wife would give satisfaction. He also felt, with even more intelligence, supplemented by heart, that to accept a kindness without any self-deprecating argle-bargle (his phrase, not ours) was what would most please his hostess, who indeed looked as if she were pleased.

Just as they were approaching, sideways and with occasional withdrawals, the really interesting questions of whether Lady Waring would get her way and have the Mertons as her private guests while they looked for rooms, or Major Merton would have his way and come as a paying guest with his wife; thus leading on to the even more absorbing question of what was the most Lady Waring could bear to accept from her guests, or the least that the Mertons would allow themselves to be browbeaten into giving; and to the further consideration of whether the rent should include such few drinks as still existed (in which case Lady Waring was determined that Sir Harry should strain every sinew to get some sherry at least), or the Mertons should buy their own beer, wine and spirits in a phrase which now had little meaning (in which case Major Merton was determined that the Warings should drink knee to knee with him or he would throw it all out of the window); just, we say, as this fascinating topic presented itself, the further door was opened and a young woman in a tweed coat came in, with a small suitcase.

"Leslie!" said Lady Waring. "You are all wet. What on earth has happened? Didn't the taxi meet you?"

"No one seemed to know anything about a taxi," said Leslie Waring, with a flat, tired voice, but without resentment. "I tried to ring you up from the station, but your line was out of order. The station-master said he'd send my luggage up by the railway van in the morning, so I walked up and came in the back way. Rather nice to walk in the rain after that stuffy train."

"My poor child," said Lady Waring, and rang the bell.

Major Merton took Leslie Waring's bag from her, helped her off with her coat and politely pushed her into a chair by the fire. Selina appeared.

"Please, my lady," she began, "Mr. Coxon from the garridge is just rung up and says the line was out of order this afternoon or he'd have let us know sooner, my lady, that he couldn't fetch Miss Leslie from the station because his taxi's broken down and he tried two other places but there was nothing to be had and he seemed *so* upset about it. Cook said she knew the line was out of order because she tried to ring up the fish at lunch-time and they wouldn't answer but she didn't want to upset you, so she didn't tell anyone, but Private Jenks said he'd ring up the exchange from the big house, and he's just come in to say it's all right now, so I thought you'd like to know, my lady."

As it was obviously impossible to stem the flood of Selina's speech, Lady Waring waited till she had finished, and looking towards the fireside where Leslie was almost hidden, lying back in a large arm-chair, said that Miss Leslie had walked up and would Selina take her things, and Miss Leslie would go to bed at once and have her dinner there.

"Really not, thank you so much, Aunt Harriet," said Leslie, in the high voice of intense fatigue. "I'm not a bit tired, simply walking half a mile from the station. Besides, I'd loathe to go to bed. You'll have to excuse my being a bit untidy, as I've only got my little case with things for the night. I'm really fearfully fit now. I wish you wouldn't worry, Aunt Harriet."

She got up as she spoke.

Her aunt stood undecided. It was obvious that Leslie must go to bed. People who had had breakdowns and walked uphill from the station, even if it was only a mile (and Leslie knew she wasn't speaking the truth when she said half a mile), and had very wet feet (Leslie's shoes had left dull patches on the pale gold carpet) were in no fit state to stay up to dinner. On the other hand Lady Waring had schooled herself to interfere as little as possible with the young, having with her usual sanity taken into account the fact that they would do whatever they wished, regardless of her wishes. She felt helpless, and inclined to slap her niece by marriage. But even as she hesitated Selina picked up Leslie's suitcase, coat, gloves and scarf and hurried out of the room to run Miss Waring's bath and put a hot bottle in her bed, pausing at the kitchen door to tell Cook how upset she had felt at seeing poor Miss Leslie looking so dreadful. And in the same moment Major Merton remarked how curious it was that great fatigue made women talk more and men talk less. But he said it so kindly and yet with such authority that Leslie, conscious that she had been almost hysterical a moment ago, felt no resentment, being now quite aware that she had spoken foolishly and at unnecessary length. Bed was an extremely attractive idea, and one would certainly look horrid at dinner with nothing to put on one's feet but bedroom slippers, because it was years since she had grown out of Aunt Harriet's.

"How wise you are," said Major Merton.

She looked at him, common sense piercing her tiredness for a moment, and smiled.

"All right, Aunt Harriet, I'll go," she said. "Oh, an officer at the station carried my suitcase up. I did ask him to come in, but he was late already as the camp had forgotten to send a car for him and he'd have to walk. If he rings up, will Selina take a message for me."

As she finished speaking Sir Harry came back with Captain Hooper and Dr. Ford. Sir Harry kissed his niece heartily.

"Here is an old friend, Leslie," said Lady Waring, "Dr. Ford. And this is Captain Hooper — my niece, Miss Waring."

"A pleasure, I'm sure," said Captain Hooper.

At the door Leslie turned.

"Oh, his name was Colonel Winter," she said.

Major Merton looked interested.

"I'll remember, dear," said Lady Waring. "Go straight to bed now. Every one will excuse you. Leslie hasn't been well and she had to walk up from the station because of a stupid mistake about the taxi," she added to the company in general, and Leslie went away.

"And what is this about our Colonel Winter?" said Captain Hooper waggishly.

"Is he at the camp?" asked Lady Waring, wishing Captain Hooper would go.

"Not yet," said Captain Hooper, "if the young lady says he was walking. We might pick him up and give him a lift. He's only attached to us for a course. Not quite your sort, Lady Waring. Schoolmaster in private life, you know. They're all a bit morbid. He hasn't got the right idear about Russiar either. Oh, definitely not quite, our Philip."

"Philip Winter is an old friend of mine," said Major Merton, addressing himself pointedly to Lady Waring. "I didn't know he was here. He is a very brilliant Latin scholar when he isn't a soldier."

"Not the Winter who wrote that little book about Horace?" said Sir Harry, who had always kept up an interest in the classics. "The kind of book an old amateur like myself can thoroughly enjoy. We must have him here, my dear."

Captain Hooper said no one would be learning Latin in a few years and mensar and all that useless rot. Biology and aerodynamics and sensible stuff, he said.

"And we must be off, sir," he added to Major Merton. "Time and tide, you know. Is it all fixed?"

"Lady Waring has been kind enough to ask my wife and myself here for a few days," said Major Merton, trying hard to remember that Captain Hooper was a conscientious soldier who had got promotion by hard work (for of this and many other things Major Merton had been informed before coming to the camp).

"Well, you'll be better off than I was in my last billets," said Captain Hooper. "That was in '40. Place called Northbridge. I was at the rectory. Well, well. Meals with the Rector and Mrs. Rector — Villars, that was the name. Not at all your style, sir."

"Verena Villars? Cousin of mine. A most delightful woman," said Sir Harry. "Good-looker too. Her second boy has bombed Italy six times."

Major Merton so far forgot himself as to cast a despairing look at Lady Waring and met a gleam of amusement. He said good-bye, promised to ring Lady Waring up next morning, and went away with Captain Hooper.

"New Army!" said Sir Harry, very unfairly. "He managed to get across Merton in two minutes. We shan't need to have him here again, my dear, shall we?"

"I don't think we shall have much say in the matter if he decides to come," said Lady Waring with a sigh. "But it was you who told him he could come, you know."

"I admit it," said Sir Harry thoughtfully. "I must say I didn't much care for the fellow when I met him at the camp and I must say I like him even less in the house. But the Colonel says he's a good officer. Perhaps after the war we'll be able to have our house to ourselves."

"Or no house at all," said Lady Waring sadly.

"Or a house and no one in it, like me," said Dr. Ford.

Sir Harry and Lady Waring made sympathetic noises, for Dr. Ford was well known to have broken his heart twice: once when Mrs. Morland's secretary Anne Todd married the well-known biographer George Knox, and again when the vicar's elder daughter broke off her engagement to him, in which she was probably wise, as though a very nice girl she was at least twenty years younger than he was and quite unsuitable. Since these calamities he had remained a peaceful bachelor, getting, as his old friend Mrs. Morland often told him, far too much sympathy on false pretences.

"Your bath is ready, my lady," said Selina at the door, "and Miss Leslie's in bed."

"I'll go up and have a look at her in a friendly way," said Dr. Ford, "and then I must be off."

"Did you find a dressing-gown for Miss Leslie, and everything she wanted?" Lady Waring asked Selina. "I suppose the station will send her things up to-morrow."

"That's all right, my lady," said Selina. "Jasper was talking to Cook at the door and happened to pass the remark that Sergeant Hopkins and some of the boys were down at the Sheep's Head, so I phoned up Mr. Pollett, and one of the boys brought Miss Leslie's cases up on the back of Mr. Pollett's bike. I *was* so upset, poor Miss Leslie not having her things, but she's quite comfortable now, my lady, and she gave me a pair of silk stockings that Mr. Cecil sent her from abroad where he is. It does seem dreadful to think of him at sea, my lady, with the war going on," said Selina, brimming over suddenly into dewy tears.

"Don't talk nonsense, Selina," said Sir Harry, looking up from the paper. "Where do you suppose a sailor ought to be?"

"But Mr. Cecil's an *officer*, Sir Harry," said Selina.

Sir Harry gave it up and went behind his paper.

CHAPTER
THREE

Mr. and Mrs. Everard Carter were seated at breakfast, with Master Bobbie Carter, aged four, who could feed himself very nicely when it wasn't a boiled egg. Everard Carter had the largest house in Southbridge School and was right-hand man to the headmaster, Mr. Birkett. In the early days of the war, the Hosiers' Boys' Foundation School had been housed at Southbridge and the two schools had a working amalgamation, but as the war went on most of the London school had gone back to its old quarters, leaving behind it some forty boys and two masters who had by now almost become part of Southbridge. Kind Kate Carter had seen in the refugee boys a good excuse for the managing and fussing for which men, in her opinion, were created, and "Ma Carter" was as popular a figure as the headmaster's wife, "Ma Birky," had been in the days when her husband was head of the Preparatory School.

"What a blessing that the hens are laying again," said Everard. "An egg makes all the difference in my life. If it weren't for your hens I would chuck being a schoolmaster. If Birkett and I have to run this place much longer with elderly clergymen and middle-aged come-backs and cheerful women with exemption we shall burst. We haven't had legless officers discharged from the Army yet, but I dare say we shall — poor devils."

"What would you do if you did chuck it, Everard?" said Kate anxiously.

"That's just the trouble," said Everard. "Probably there's nothing else I could do now. Go into the M.O.I., I suppose."

"You are *far* too clever for that sort of work, darling," said Kate.

Everard looked affectionately at her.

"There is nothing," he said, "like a Good Woman's love. And have you heard if Peppercorn is measles or chickenpox?"

Kate said she hadn't seen Matron yet and at this moment the door was opened with controlled violence and her sister Lydia came in.

Lydia Merton, whom we have not seen since the black days of Dunkirk, when her husband was one of the last to get back, was still the Lydia who had helped Geraldine Birkett to tear the frock she didn't like and spent a hot Sunday with Tony Morland and his friends clearing out the pond. But during the last two years, married to her own blissful content, willing to please Noel Merton in all outward things in her deep security of pleasing his heart, she had so schooled her old wildness and conformed to his excellent taste in matters of dress and appearance, that we might be forgiven if we did not recognize her for a moment. The well-groomed hair, the well-cut tweeds, the well-made shoes, even the well-kept hands, were what Lydia Keith would have characterized as a lot of rot, but to Lydia Merton they were as comfortable and normal as an old pair of gloves. In her carriage the old Lydia appeared, with brusque though not ungraceful movements, and Noel Merton said he would know her under any disguise if he only saw her as she vanished at the corner of a street, or got off a bus; and her speech was still apt to startle new friends by its downright quality.

"Sorry I'm late for breakfast," she said, sitting down. "Good morning, Bobbie. How are you?"

Master Carter said he was quite well, and paused with a spoonful of porridge half-way to his mouth, tilting it up so that the milk gradually ran over the handle and his fat hand.

"Small pig," said his Aunt Lydia, wiping him up in a rough-and-ready way with his feeder. "I say, Kate, the reason I was late was that Noel rang me up. He couldn't get on last night. It's frightfully good news. Lady Waring at Beliers Priory will let us stay with her while we look for a cottage or something. Noel says it's quite near the camp, at least it's about four miles but they may let him use his car a bit."

"I *am* glad, darling," said Kate. "When do you go?"

"Saturday," said Lydia. "Do you think my washing will be back by then, Kate? I sent a lot of Noel's and my things last week."

"Oh dear," said Kate, her kind face troubled by care. "The laundry is quite dreadful now. It says it will come twice in three weeks, but of course that means absolutely *nothing*. Sometimes it is twice in one week and then one has nothing to give it the second time, and sometimes Matron takes all the boys' sheets and pillow-cases off, ready for it, and it doesn't come for a fortnight. And it often brings the things back at the next time but one, which is so confusing. Most luckily I bought a lot of sheets soon after the war began, or I don't know how we'd manage. I will telephone and ask about your things and if they don't come to-day, which is the day the laundry-man told Matron he *might* come, only he said he thought it might be the last time before the end of term because of the petrol, which will mean leaving the beds unchanged for a fortnight and a half, then I'll post them on to you, registered of course, because you never know with the post. Not that one thinks anyone is dishonest, but it is silly to let clothes go about the country tempting people to steal them."

"I do hope they have done Noel's shirts properly," said Lydia earnestly.

"I looked through them before they went," said Kate, "and I wrote in the laundry book, 'Please note that these shirts have all their buttons,' so perhaps they won't break them or pull them off."

"It's a bit vague, like all commercial language," said Everard. "Still, I don't know that one could put it better. Could you say, 'These buttons are all on. Please don't pull them off'?"

"One might offend them," said Kate, growing pale.

"Yes, I suppose you might," said Everard. "It's all part of war blackmail. They know you couldn't get another laundry round here, and that's that."

"Still, they are very nice," said Kate, who could not bear to think ill of anyone. "Last time they did come they were a hamper short and the man said he thought it might have fallen off near the gates because he heard a funny noise, so Edward went down with the wheelbarrow and there it was and he brought it back. And if the laundryman hadn't told us, someone might have stolen it."

"I suppose it didn't occur to him to go and get it himself, as he heard it fall off," said Everard. "No, of course it didn't. I'm sorry you're going, Lydia."

"Thank you very much, Everard," said Lydia with earnest gratitude. "I hate going too, but I've not seen Noel for three days, and till Saturday will make nearly a week, quite five and a half days anyway."

Kate so sympathized with her sister's feelings that she cast about for a way of cheering her up, and as they had now all finished breakfast she suggested a visit to the nursery before Everard went into school. Accordingly, Kate took Bobbie's feeder off and he got down from his chair and taking his Aunt Lydia's hand stumped upstairs, two feet on each step, followed by his parents.

In the nursery Miss Angela Carter, aged two, was sitting in a tall chair made of cane and mahogany. Her stout form was confined to the chair by a wooden rod passed through holes in the arms, with a wooden knob at each end that screwed on and off, and she was banging the table with a spoon. By the fire Nurse had just finished bathing and dressing Master Philip Carter, aged very little indeed, and was about to give him his second breakfast, for he had already had a slight repast at seven o'clock that morning.

"Would you like to give Baby his bottle, Miss Lydia?" said Nurse, who had known Lydia before her marriage and did not mean to stand any nonsense.

"Rather," said Lydia.

So nurse gave the comfortable warm bundle to Lydia who sat down, less ungracefully than Lydia Keith would have done, by the fire and held the baby in a strong, competent arm. Everard took a chair to the nursery table to talk to his daughter for whom he had a distinct partiality. Kate, an exquisite needlewoman, found some mending in the nursery workbasket, Bobbie played on the floor with his bricks, a relic of Kate's nursery days, the fire burned brightly, the world outside looked perfectly revolting, and inside all was great comfort and peace. Nurse brought the bottle wrapped in a piece of white flannel to Lydia. At the sight of it the baby, which had been lying on Lydia's arms, its blue eyes apparently seeing heavenly visions, its small features composed in seraphic peace, suddenly went bright red in the face. Its whole body stiffened, its mouth opened wide and became quite square, dry shrieks of rage proceeded from its little throat, and its whole being became rigid with baffled gluttony and milk-lust.

Its unsympathetic aunt laughed so much that she nearly dropped the bottle.

"Give him the bottle *quickly*, Lydia," said Kate, a mother's anguish at the sight of her starving child showing clearly in her mild eyes.

"Greedy little beast," said Aunt Lydia and shoved the teat of the bottle into the baby's mouth.

At first the baby was so transported with wrath that it shrieked more loudly than before, but after a while nature asserted herself against imbecility and with one great final heave and spasm of fury it suddenly became like a jelly soother than the creamy curd, its vengeful limbs relaxed, and with long shuddering breaths it began to suck its bottle, both hands clutching the beloved object and an angry suspicious eye roving the nursery against the possible approach of milk-thieves.

Nurse, who was going and coming, emptying the bath and generally tidying things, stopped to look.

"Take it out of his mouth now and then, Miss Lydia," she recommended, "or he'll give himself the wind."

"I can't think," said Lydia, forcibly withdrawing the bottle from her nephew's toothless gums, "how any babies ever lived before people knew how to take care of them properly. I mean anyone might let Philip drink it all up and then he'd feel frightful."

Kate began to explain how Mother Love had a wonderful instinct for cherishing its young, but the baby, realizing with a kind of delayed action that its second breakfast had left it, rent the welkin again.

"Oh bother," said Lydia, shoving the bottle back into its mouth. "Come on, baby. I say, Kate, I must go and see Mrs. Birkett this morning. Will you come with me? I want to ask about Rose and Geraldine. Where are they?"

Kate was just beginning to give Lydia what news she had of the Birketts' married daughters when the baby emitted a wail of misery.

"He can't get at the milk, Miss Lydia," said Nurse looking over her shoulder. "Tilt it up a little more, miss."

"Oh, I say, I *am* sorry, baby," said Lydia, tilting the bottle well up.

The baby applied itself to its work again with such concentration that a light perspiration broke out on the top of its bald, crimsoning head. It then seized its bottle in both hands and pushed it violently away, at the same time gnashing its jaws together. The teat came off the bottle and all the rest of the milk fell out on to the baby.

"Hi! Nurse!" said Lydia. "Help!"

"He nearly always does that just before the end of his bottle," said Kate proudly. "It means he has had enough. Nurse, do you think we gave him another ounce of milk a little too soon?"

But Nurse's face expressed such long-suffering resentment that Kate quickly said of course it would really be safer to keep him as he was, as changes weren't a good thing. Nurse relented, picked up the baby and took him away to sleep off his meal.

Lydia got up and gave herself a violent shake, reminding her brother-in-law of the summer he had first met her when she was about sixteen and spent most of her time on or in the river. She was twenty-four now and as handsome a young woman as one could see, but Everard had been very fond of the old Lydia and sometimes felt a little shy of this new, distinguished-looking sister-in-law.

"Gosh! I can't think how Nurse ever does it!" said Lydia.

"Does what, darling?" asked Kate.

"Oh, all this," said Lydia, including nursery and babies in a sweep of her arm.

"It's quite easy when they are One's Own," said Kate, whose loving placid nature appeared to thrive on Nurse's afternoon off and was never happier than when she could get all three children under her wing.

Lydia made no answer and was obviously referring the question to herself for further consideration. Everard said he must be going now, and Kate said she must ring up Mrs. Birkett, so they all left the nursery whose waters at once closed over their heads.

At about half-past eleven Kate and Lydia were preparing to go across to the Headmaster's House when Matron came in to report that doctor had been, and Peppercorn was only a rash.

"Not that rashes are to be wondered at, Mrs. Merton," said Matron, "with all these vitamins. My eldest nephew, the one who is a wireless operator and has been torpedoed twice, was in a boat for five days before he was picked up and he had quite a Nasty Eruption when he came home on leave."

Both Kate and Lydia were doubtful as to the relations of cause and effect in this interesting story, but felt it would be simpler to accept it.

"Oh, I say, Matron," said Lydia. "Do you think the washing will ever come back? I'm going on Saturday and nearly all my husband's shirts are at the laundry."

"Well now," said Matron, "that was exactly what I wanted to speak to you about, Mrs. Merton. I said to Jessie only this morning — you remember Jessie, the head housemaid, such a nice girl and I used to get quite annoyed with her because she would not wear her glasses and was ruining her eyes, but all things have turned out for the best because her sight is so bad she won't get called up — Well now, Jessie, I said, the Major will be wanting his laundry, I said to her, because gentlemen cannot understand these little war difficulties and a gentleman like the Major must have his shirts, and you never know when the laundry will call. So Jessie, who is really a thoughtful girl, gave her cousin, who is the manager, a ring and your things will come out with the fish to-morrow, Mrs. Merton."

Lydia thanked her warmly.

"Well, what is the good of a war, as I said to Jessie," said Matron, "if officers can't get their laundry back. We might as well be in peace-time for all the good it does *us*, Jessie, I said."

There were renewed thanks and Matron went away to tell Jessie how pleased Mrs. Merton was and what a pity it was there were no children and she had always thought Mrs. Merton would have started early.

"For children, Jessie, are a great comfort," said Matron, "and what my married sister would have done without my nephew when her husband died I cannot think. He was at sea then, but he wrote her a lovely letter and always takes her to see his dad's grave when he's on leave. She doesn't hear from him for months at a time now of course and then it's only a wire as often as not, but your son's your son till he gets him a wife, as the saying is. Poor Mrs. Merton. Still, it's early days, and now, Jessie, you can do Peppercorn's bed as the doctor says it's nothing but a rash and he can get up."

By this time Kate and Lydia had arrived at the Headmaster's House and were sitting with Mrs. Birkett. The drawing-room had been shut up and Mrs. Birkett had turned the dressing-room into her own sitting-room, which made her, she said, feel like Mrs. Edmonstone in *The Heir of Redclyffe* and also made the room warm for her husband to undress in at night.

"I do all my writing and see my committee people here," she said to Lydia, "and in the evening we sit in the study, where the fire burns our own wood very nicely and the furnace for the boiler is in the cellar underneath, so I can keep Henry warm. And now tell me all about yourself, my dear. How is Noel?"

"Oh, he's awfully well," said Lydia, "at least," she added, suddenly going pale inside with apprehension of unknown and improbable dangers, "he was quite well when he rang me up this morning. He's at the hush-hush camp near Lambton now, and some people called General and Lady Waring have very kindly asked us to stay with them till we can find a cottage or something."

"Waring?" said Mrs. Birkett. "I think we know them. I'll ask Henry when he comes in. He is taking the

84

Upper Sixth for Latin just now, but he wants to come up and see you. How is your mother, Kate?"

Kate said that Mrs. Keith was still quite happy with her sister at Bournemouth which suited her heart, and she and Everard hoped to have her to stay with them in the Easter holidays when the weather might be nicer, though probably it wouldn't. And in her turn she asked about Mrs. Birkett's daughters, Rose and Geraldine, who had married two brothers called Fairweather. Rose's husband was a sailor and Geraldine's a soldier.

Mrs. Birkett said Rose was very well. "You know she is in America," she added for Lydia's benefit. "John was at sea for eighteen months when they came back from South America and now he is on a two-year job at Washington and got permission for her to join him with the children. She writes very happily and sends us the most enchanting snapshots of Henry and Amy — called after Henry and me, bless her — and she is going to have another baby in June."

"I say, that's a bit quick, isn't it?" said Lydia.

"She was married before the war, and the war will have been going on nearly four years by next June," said Mrs. Birkett with a sigh, "and she adores the children."

"And how's Geraldine?" said Lydia, who had never known Rose, her senior by several years, very well.

Mrs. Birkett looked worried.

"She is quite well, and Geoff has been all through Libya without a scratch so far," said Mrs. Birkett, "but she finds her little John so tiring. Not that she doesn't adore him, but she is longing to go back to the Red Cross with Geoff away all the time and she cannot get a nurse in that out-of-the-way place where she would take a cottage, and it worries me very much. Last time she came to stay with us Kate most kindly had little John in her nursery and Geraldine looked a different girl. But she cried as I have never seen her cry since she was a little girl the night before she went away."

There was a pause. Mrs. Birkett thought sadly of poor Geraldine, pining to nurse, chained hand and foot by a baby whom she loved but could not take in her stride. Kate pondered on the peculiarity of people who found babies any trouble. Lydia was a prey to various bewildered emotions. If Kate said it being One's Own children made everything easy, she must be right, for anything happier than Kate could not be. Yet there was Geraldine, with only one little boy, miserable and crying. Lydia Keith would have felt, and probably expressed, great contempt for people who cried because they had a baby to look after, their own baby too; but Lydia Merton became thoughtful and was silent, while Mrs. Birkett and Kate discussed rationing and points, till Mr. Birkett came in. As he and Everard met every day, and Mrs. Birkett and Kate met at least six times a week, not to speak of after chapel on Sundays, and they all supped at each others' houses on alternate Sunday evenings, there was naturally a great deal to discuss and Lydia felt a little out of it, so she sat thinking her own thoughts; an occupation which Lydia Keith would have condemned as tending to melancholy and on the whole rot. Her attention was at length caught by the mention of her dearly loved second brother Colin, now a staff captain and very much enjoying his life. He had not much time to write and his letters were mostly to Lydia, so she had to pull herself back to reality and give her latest news which was but scanty.

"Henry," said Mrs. Birkett, "do you know people called Waring at Lambton? Lydia and her husband are going to stay with them. He is Sir Harry."

"Waring, Waring," said Mr. Birkett. "There was a George Waring here during the last war. I never knew him, of course, but Lorimer used to speak about him," he said, thinking of the old classical master who had died some years previously. "He said he had never met a nicer boy but totally resistant to Latin. His name is on the Roll of Honour in the Chapel. He went straight into the Army from school and was killed almost at once — now they put it off a bit longer, otherwise it's all the same."

"Have you any news of Philip Winter?" asked Kate, sorry for the headmaster.

Mr. Birkett said not very lately. When last Philip had written he said he expected to be moved again and would write. She knew, he supposed, that he was now a lieutenant-colonel. Then he went back to his work and the visitors took their leave.

The next two days passed at their usual rate, though to Lydia, in spite of her great affection for her sister and her sister's family, they appeared to drag. The washing came back by kindness of the fish, packing was done and Saturday morning dawned. When we say this, nothing would ever have happened if the world had waited for the dawning, for the blackout did not end till

8.33 and even then, owing to wind and rain, it was pitch dark for another hour or so and as Matron said to Jessie, one might just as well not try to dust at all as to dust by electric light, for as soon as it was really daylight, lo! and behold everything looked as if you hadn't touched it.

The journey from Southbridge to Lambton, which in the forgotten days of peace would have taken about thirty-five minutes by car, was now one of great inconvenience and slowness. Everard, who was very good at trains, had made a previous survey of the terrain and prepared the plans. After lunch the taxi owned by Mr. Brown of the Red Lion, who was allowed petrol for station work, was to fetch Lydia and two small suitcases and take them to Southbridge station. A large suitcase had been sent off by rail two days earlier, as the dearth of porters made it advisable to take no more than she could carry at a pinch, though even so she had overflowed into a large shopping-bag and a coat and a rug strapped together. From Southbridge she would go to Barchester where her train arrived at the precise moment when the Winter Overcotes train steamed out. After a decent interval she would take the next train for Winter Overcotes, arriving at the high level station three minutes after the departure of the low level train to Lambton. This left her with a wait of seventy-three minutes before the next train, and with luck, and if Mr. Coxon remembered to send the taxi to the station, she would get to Beliers Priory very late for tea.

Lunch was rather silent. Everard had some school affairs on his mind; Kate was thinking how dreadful it was for Lydia to be leaving Bobbie and Angela and the baby; Lydia's thoughts were with Noel, as indeed they mostly were, whether she knew it or not. The taxi was announced. Lydia, half-ashamed of her own impatience, hugged Kate and Bobbie, flung herself at Everard and rubbed her face against him, and shouldered her baggage. And when we say shouldered, it is no figure of speech, for having calculated that with only two hands she could not carry two suitcases, a large bag, a rug and coat bundle and her own handbag, she had ingeniously fastened two or three of them together with the other strap from her rug bundle and hung them over one shoulder after the manner of a Continental porter. With Mr. Brown's help she got into the taxi. Edward, the invaluable odd man and an old friend, appeared round a corner and saluted, Everard and Kate waved, Bobbie's hand was waved for him by his mother, Angela and the baby were held up at the nursery window by Nurse and Jessie, Lydia waved from the taxi with love and remorse for not wanting to stay longer, the taxi leapt and jarred itself down the drive and her visit was over.

Everard and Kate went back into the house with Bobbie, for it was cold. Everard went into his study.

"Go up to Nurse now, Bobbie," said Kate, "and tell her Mummie is coming quite soon."

She watched Bobbie begin his stumping journey upstairs and followed Everard into his room.

"I remember," said Everard, "the summer I first came and met you and Lydia, how she suddenly discovered the Brownings. She said, with that delightful way she had of making discoveries as if no one else had ever made them before, that there was something about happy married life even more beautiful than being in love with people. Bless her, she is a living image of it."

"I am so glad it is Nurse's afternoon out, Everard," said Kate, "it will cheer me up to be with the children. I do wish you could be with us instead of in school."

"Well, I can't," said Everard, "and well you know it, my love. But I expect I'll find school will cheer me up considerably. We shall miss our Lydia, shan't we?"

"Oh, Everard," said Kate, almost in tears.

"Never mind," said Everard, putting an arm round her.

"I don't really," said Kate, "because I know she wants to be with Noel. Do you know what I wish, Everard?"

"Of course I do," said her husband. "You want to know why Lydia hasn't got any children. Your prophetic gloatings over young married women are patent to the meanest observer."

"I do *not*," said Kate indignantly. "It is nothing to do with me at all. But, Everard, it does seem so sad."

"Why, darling?" said Everard. "She is nicer than ever and looks very well and very happy. Nothing sad about it. Give the girl time to look round."

"I was thinking," said Kate earnestly, "of the day Lydia gave Baby his bottle and how beautiful they looked, and I thought how heavenly it would be if it was a baby of her own. She looked as if she wished Baby were hers."

"My precious idiot," said Everard, kissing the top of her head and releasing her, "if ever I saw a young woman thoroughly bored by a job she was trying her competent best to do, it was Lydia. She was either laughing at Baby or wanting to shake him. And I must say," added the fond father reflectively, "that he was making a perfectly hellish noise."

"You don't understand at all," said Kate with much dignity. But she relented and stroked Everard's coat sleeve before going up to the nursery. Here her offspring were happily and virtuously employed, Bobbie and Angela on the floor with toys, the baby lying on his back holding his own toes and quite unable to account for their presence in his cot. Nurse, who had left everything tidy and the tea-things ready, now came out of the night nursery dressed to go out.

"We shall feel quite lonely without Miss Lydia, madam," she said. "What a picture she and Baby were when she gave him his bottle. As I was saying to Mrs. Birkett's maid, it's much to be hoped that Miss Lydia will be having a nice family of her own before long. After all, with a war on, there's not much else to do, madam," said Nurse, by whom every world event was judged by the probability or improbability of its producing nurse-fodder.

"They looked very nice, Nurse, but Miss Lydia wasn't very good at giving Baby his bottle," said Kate, basely going over to Everard's camp.

"That is quite to be expected with the first, madam," said Nurse, with the condescension of one to whom all babies were an open book. "Good-bye, Bobbie and Angela, and mind you're good. Baby's bottle is all ready for you to hot up, madam."

Lydia's feeling of remorse soon vanished as she clanked towards the station, passing several old friends on her way through the village. Admiral Phelps and the Vicar were arguing about the care of the church bells outside the lychgate; Mrs. and Miss Phelps were to be seen over the hedge of Jutland Cottage chasing a large billy-goat in the field. Miss Hampton and Miss Bent from Adelina Cottage came down the street with their elephant-faced little dog, at present called Eisenhower. Eileen, the exquisite blonde from the Red Lion, was patting her coiffure in front of a shop window. It all felt very friendly and Lydia suddenly had a small pang for a real home. Life with Everard and Kate, after two years of hotels and rooms, had seemed so pleasant, so natural, so unwarlike. She had an impulse to ask Mr. Brown if he could drive her to her old home, Northbridge Manor. True, it was let for the duration, but she would dearly love to see it. Perhaps the present occupiers would let her look at the drawing-room, where Noel had come to her in her loneliness after her father died, or walk on the terrace where she had once walked with him on a cold winter's day, and neither of them had known what their hearts were saying. Then she reminded herself that one could not take a taxi for more than ten miles, that she would miss her train, and that by so doing she would delay her meeting with Noel. She did not laugh at herself, for she did not readily laugh, but she shook herself impatiently.

The short journey was soon over and Lydia found herself on the platform of Southbridge station with plenty of time. Here there were no familiar faces and her nostalgia began to fade. Presently the train came in, so she lugged her suitcases into a carriage and in fifteen minutes was in Barchester. Not a porter was to be seen, so glad of her foresight she slung her suitcases about her and went to the exit to ask the ticket-collector, the only official in sight, the platform for Winter Overcotes. Her way lay by the whole length of the longest platform, down a flight of steps, through a subway narrow at the best and impeded with anti-blast sandbagged barriers, up a flight of steps at the further side, and along the platform to a bay where a train was waiting with WINTER OVERCOTES on a board above it. Strong though she was, her hands, arms, back and shoulders ached from the unwonted strain and she was glad to rest in an empty carriage. After half an hour or so a train came in at the other side of the platform, gorged with people. As Lydia idly contemplated it, a porter went down the platform shouting, "Winter Overcotes and London only." A horrible doubt leapt to Lydia's heart.

"Hi!" she shrieked out of the carriage window. "Am I right for Winter Overcotes?"

The porter looked round and stopped.

"Over the other side, miss," he said, with the kindly manner of Barsetshire porters.

"Oh Lord!" shouted Lydia. "But this train says Winter Overcotes."

"That's the local, miss," said the porter. "She doesn't go till half-past seven. You'll have to run, miss."

In a panic Lydia got out of the carriage, picked up her luggage somehow and dragged it across the platform. The guard had his whistle to his mouth and his flag raised. Lydia dashed at the nearest door, pushed her luggage in, and almost fell in after it. The whistle sounded and the train started.

Lydia, who had not been able to get to Barchester during her stay at Southbridge, had vaguely hoped that she might see a friend or two in the train; perhaps the Dean, or Mrs. Crawley, from whom she could get news of her friend, Octavia Crawley; perhaps Sir Edmund Pridham, who was often in the town on county business; even her old headmistress, the much disliked Miss Pettinger. But the carriage was full of people who had no business to be in or near Barchester at all. Alien faces, alien languages, were on every side. Cheap tobacco, cheap lipstick, cheap nail-polish, cheap furs, cheap scent characterized the women; a ring on the right hand, pointed unpolished shoes, black-shaven faces distinguished the men. Nearly every one sniffed continuously. As both sides of the carriage were full and no one showed any symptom of making a place for her to perch on, Lydia, recognizing their perfect legal right to remaining four a side, dragged her luggage through the compartment under eight pairs of unfriendly, contemptuous, or indifferent eyes, and got into the corridor which was indeed full of soldiers, but Lydia felt she could stand more happily with them than with the insolent strangers in the carriage, and her spirits rose again at the thought of Noel, so that when the train passed through Northbridge Halt she could look across to the trees to where her old home stood without any sad thoughts.

At Winter Overcotes a soldier obligingly helped her down with her luggage and the train went away. Seeing the station-master, she asked him when the next train for Lambton went.

"Five-ten, miss, from the low level," said Mr. Beedle. "Only twenty minutes to wait, miss. The London train was very late."

"I don't suppose there is a porter," said Lydia, looking at her luggage. "I'm going to Lady Waring's."

"Oh, are you Mrs. Merton, madam?" said Mr. Beedle. "Excuse me, but I had a message about you. There's an officer, Major Merton, your husband I believe, madam, was here this morning. He was going to London and he said I was to be sure to look out for you because he mightn't be back in time to meet you. He said he would be down for the 6.25 from here at latest, madam."

"Oh, thanks *awfully*," said Lydia. "Do I go from this platform?"

"No, madam, from the low level," said Mr. Beedle. "You have plenty of time and I will send one of the young lady porters to help you with your things. Five-ten, madam."

Lydia was cheered by this proof of Noel's thought for her — not that she wanted any proof — but rather dashed by the thought that he would not be at Beliers to help her to meet her unknown host and hostess. As she stood wondering what the Warings would be like, Doris Phipps and Lily-Annie came up, impelled thereto by Mr. Beedle's authority and their own curiosity.

"Well you *have* got some luggage and no mistake," said Lily-Annie. "Why don't you put it in the van?"

Lydia said she would with pleasure, but there usually weren't any porters.

"We'll put it in for you all right," said Doris Phipps. "It's a pity Sid Crackman isn't the guard on your train — he's a lovely man. He let Lily-Annie and I go to Barchester in the van with him one day."

"You *are* lucky," said Lydia with undisguised envy. "I've only once been in a guard's van in my life, when I was quite small."

Conversing amicably in a way that would have shocked Mr. Beedle to the core, Lydia and her attendant nymphs walked along the platform to the steps.

"Remember the day Bill Morple chucked the sack of potatoes down the steps?" said Doris Phipps to Lily-Annie. "I've never laughed so much, seeing him pick them all off the line. I thought they'd have rolled to Worsted. There you are," she added kindly to Lydia. "Lily-Annie or me'll come along and give you a hand when the train comes in, see?"

Left alone in the gathering gloom of a dark day on a platform overshadowed by the great viaduct of the high level, Lydia felt depressed again. She thought of waiting for the 6.25 and Noel's company, but he might be detained, it would be dark, and if she had to meet the Warings it had better be done. Besides, a taxi was to meet her at the station and it would be uncivil to delay. Passengers for the Shearings Junction line began to arrive, mostly village women with shopping-baskets. Some soldiers on leave found friends among them and there was a good deal of laughter. Lydia's mood of depression returned. Doris Phipps carefully pushing a truck with a number of cardboard boxes on it stopped to light a fresh cigarette.

"Five-ten's late again," said Doris to Lydia.

While she spoke Lydia was conscious of a tiny insistent sound, rather like a kettle on the boil, or the noise made by a little jet of gas burning in a lump of coal. She looked at the truck.

"Noisy little beggars, aren't they?" said Doris.

"Go on," said Lily-Annie, who was making up her lips. "I bet you made more noise than that when you were a day old."

Both girls laughed loudly.

"Day-old chicks," said Lily-Annie, seeing Lydia's perplexed look. "Come from Southbridge they did and going on to Lambton."

"All alone?" said Lydia.

"Well, the old hen was coming, but she got called up," said Lily-Annie, but seeing Lydia's look of real concern she added, "They're all right, miss. The head porter at Barchester takes them off the Southbridge train and puts them in the porters' room till the London train comes. And if we didn't treat them nice when they got here, Mr. Beedle would fair skin us, wouldn't he, Dawris? Remember the day Bill Morple dropped one of the boxes? Mr. Beedle didn't half tell him off."

Lydia anxiously inquired what had happened to the chicks, and was assured that they had escaped injury.

"A dozen in a box seems rather a lot," said Lydia.

"Keeps them warm," said Doris Phipps. "Look through the holes, miss, you'll see they're all right."

Lydia bent over the boxes, and through round holes in the sides saw tiny fluffy restless bodies moving about, cheeping softly all the time.

"Going to General Waring's place, they are," said Lily-Annie. "He's a lovely man."

"I'm going there too," said Lydia, suddenly seized with ridiculous compassion for these frail, undaunted objects, going about the world alone and changing trains for an unknown destination, though a moment's reflection would have told her that they were having a much easier journey than she was, having no luggage, no tickets, no anxiety about their present and a complete want of interest or curiosity about their future.

"Ow," said both girls, much impressed. "Well, we'll be along, don't you worry," and the truck rolled on to the far end of the platform.

As the chicks, like herself exiles from Southbridge, were wheeled away, Lydia felt the darkness thicken round her. No light came from a heavy clouded sky, the station lamps were few and very dim. Again she began to wonder what the Warings would be like and contemplated hiding till the 5.10 had gone and waiting for the next train and Noel, when a tall man in uniform surged out of the thick gloom.

"Noel!" she said, with great relief.

The figure stopped.

"I am so sorry, but my name isn't Noel. Are you looking for someone?" it said.

Lydia stared madly through the darkness.

"Philip!" she cried.

"I am honoured," said the voice, "but who is it? Not Lydia? Oh, my Lydia!"

"Oh gosh! how pleased I am," said Mrs. Merton, grasping Philip Winter's arm with both her hands and shaking it violently.

"Not pleaseder than I am," said Colonel Winter, putting his other arm round Mrs. Merton and giving her as close a hug as the thickness of a British warm will allow. "My precious Lydia, what the dickens are you doing here?"

"Or you, either? Oh, *Philip*!" said Lydia.

The 5.10, though so late that it was only so by courtesy, steamed in. No one could hear a word, milk-cans clanked, Doris Phipps and Lily-Annie yelled unintelligibly, Bill Morple came bumping down the steps from the high level with a perambulator, two dogs on leads had a friendly quarrel, the engine let off steam at high pressure.

"WHERE ARE YOU GOING?" shrieked Lydia.

"LAMBTON," Philip shouted.

"Hurrah!" said Lydia. "Come on," and she got into a carriage followed by Philip. Doris and Lily-Annie pushed the luggage in, overjoyed at the sight of what they very rightly took to be Ro-mance. Lydia was feeling in her bag, but Philip, with a man's contempt for the whole question of small change, gave the girls the coin that felt largest in the dark. With the exquisite, imperceptibly gliding motion of the Best Line in the World, the train moved out of the station, and Philip and Lydia found themselves alone in a carriage which was so lighted that anyone could read or knit if they held book or work well away from themselves into the middle of the compartment, and smelt of cold dirt and tobacco.

"How much did you give them, Philip?" Lydia asked, still fumbling in her purse.

"By the feeling, a half-crown," said Philip, "but it may have been a florin. It's no joke trying to feel a milled edge with gloves on."

"Here you are then," said the honest Lydia, pushing some money at him.

"Good God, my girl," said Philip, shocked. "Hasn't Noel taught you never to give money to men?"

"Oh, all right," said Lydia. "Besides, you're a colonel now, so I suppose you can afford it."

"I'm only a colonel because I had an unfair start at the beginning of the war, having territorialled so long," said Philip. "And any way, it's lieutenant-colonel, though I keep this in the background. But I do like getting more pay. And what's more, that aunt of mine died and left me some money, so I am quite well off. I used to think I'd start a school with it if she did, but this doesn't seem a good moment. Besides I don't think the Army would let me go. What are you doing now?"

100

Lydia said that she and Noel had been moved about a good deal and now expected to be in this part of the world for some time, as he had an important job at the hush-hush camp. Philip said he hoped to be there for some time too and was living at the camp for the time being. Lydia asked if it was in a tent or a hut.

"Neither, thank God," said Philip. "Tents are out of date and as for Nissen huts, the worms they crawl in the worms they crawl out, I mean water streams up, down, by, with and from those infernal creations and all one's food and bedding taste and feel damp. No, we've got a nice old house called the Dower House between Lambton and Worsted for our headquarters, and there the important people, which includes me, live in a chastened kind of luxury. Is Noel coming there?"

Lydia explained that they were looking for lodgings and had been invited to Beliers Priory for the present.

"Beliers Priory?" said Philip. "I carried a suitcase for a girl who lived there. Waring her name was."

Lydia said the people she was going to stay with were called Waring, and then the conversation passed to really interesting subjects, for Philip Winter had been senior classical master at Southbridge School before the war and was a great friend of Everard and Kate Carter, and he wanted all the news of the school.

"And Mrs. Birkett says Rose is going to have another baby, that's three," said Lydia, when she had given him all the gossip she could remember. "I say, Philip, do you remember the day we cleaned out the pond at home and Rose broke off your engagement and you threw your ring into the pool."

"What a day!" said Philip. "I was never so glad in all my life."

"Do you know, they were clearing the channel of the stream the summer after the war began," said Lydia, "and Twitcher found it. You remember Twitcher the gardener that married our old nannie. I meant to tell you, but I got married to Noel and forgot. I'll give it you. And then when you get engaged again you can use it," said the practical Lydia.

"God forbid!" said Philip.

"It's a very pretty one," said Lydia.

"It is," said Philip, thinking of all the trouble that a young assistant master who could then ill afford it had taken to have a ring made with little diamond petals round a ruby core, to look as like his love's name as possible. "Look here, Lydia, you give me the ring, to warn me against getting engaged to anyone as silly as Rose again. And when I do get engaged to a very nice, sensible girl, I'll send it back to you."

"Like a secret code," said Lydia, taken by the idea.

By now the train had got to Lambton. Between them they carried Lydia's luggage to the exit.

"There's to be a taxi to meet me," said Lydia.

"For me too," said Philip. "I'll ring you up soon. Give Noel my love."

"Beg pardon," said Mr. Coxon from the garage, "but are you for the Priory, miss?"

Lydia said she was.

"And you for the Dower House, sir?" said Mr. Coxon. For although the Dower House's name for the duration was Camp XZ 135, and people who wanted to ring it up had to ask the exchange for that number, and people who lived there were supposed, when rung up, to pretend they did not know where they were, the original inhabitants saw no reason for such silly goings-on.

Philip said yes.

Mr. Coxon embarked upon a long, rambling statement, the gist of which was that her ladyship had ordered the taxi and a gentleman from the Dower House had ordered the taxi, and there wasn't but the one taxi, and no one could expect a taxi to go to two places at once, but as the Priory was, in a manner of speaking, on the way to the Dower House, the gentleman had better get in along of the young lady and he'd take him on to the Dower House when he'd taken the young lady to the Priory, but first he must get them chickens on board. So Philip and Lydia got into the taxi, by no means sorry to have a little more of one another's company.

Coxon collected the boxes of chickens and in ten minutes they were at the door of the Warings' wing. Philip got out to help Lydia with her bags, which in the darkness, with three unknown steps to the door to be negotiated, caused a little delay. Just as he was going to say good-bye the door was opened and Sir Harry appeared in the subdued light of the little hall.

"Come in, come in," he said hospitably. "We mustn't show too much light. Coxon, wait a minute, will you. I want you to take a note down to the village for me. Come in, Mrs. Merton. Your husband I have already met."

"I am sorry, sir," said Philip, "but there is a mistake. My name is Winter. I am an old friend of Mrs. Merton's. We were in the same train, and when we got to the station the taxi driver said he would drop her first and take me on to the camp."

Sir Harry apologized, saying that he had only met Major Merton once and they were about the same height and looked much the same in the black-out.

"But you must come in and meet my wife," he said to Philip, "and have a cup of tea, before you go to the camp."

Taking no denial, he hustled Lydia and Philip into the sitting-room. Here Lady Waring was writing letters and Leslie Waring knitting. Lady Waring welcomed Lydia kindly and introduced the two young women. Leslie was now more rested, but she looked so pale and languid that Lydia felt very sorry for her and tempered her usual handshake.

"And this is — what did you say your name was?" said Sir Harry to Philip.

"Philip Winter, sir," said that gentleman.

"— who is going on in Coxon's taxi to the camp," said Sir Harry. "Colonel Winter, my dear. And my niece, Leslie Waring. I can't think how I came to take you for Merton. He is dark and you are quite fair."

"Ginger was my name at my prep. school, sir," said Philip. "Also Carrots and Fireworks and a few other names."

"It's awfully difficult to tell in the dark," said Lydia. "I met Philip at the station where I changed and I thought he was Noel for a moment."

"Winter," said Sir Harry, ransacking his memory. "Wait a minute. Why, you are the man who wrote that book about Horace. I liked it. I have to read my Horace with a crib now, just as if I were at school, but I liked your book very much."

Philip, reddening to the roots of his red hair, thanked his host. His little book on Horace, published while he was still at Southbridge School, was his only literary child, and though he wished he could have rewritten it again and again, pruning, correcting, improving, it was very dear to him.

"Perhaps," said Lady Waring, glad to find someone who could share her husband's interest in the classics, "Colonel Winter will come over to dinner one evening, Harry."

"I must thank you again, Colonel Winter, for carrying my bag for me last night," said Leslie Waring with, so Lydia felt, a slight but unnecessary tone of proprietorship, though she at once blamed herself for the feeling.

Philip declined tea, as he was already due at the camp, and went away, with Sir Harry's letter to be delivered in the village by Coxon. Lydia said good-bye to him with her usual warmth, which had the effect of making Leslie Waring think that Mrs. Merton and Colonel Winter seemed to be on very good terms, a feeling which she condemned as uncharitable.

Lydia, drinking her tea and talking amicably, took stock of her new friends. For the Warings she felt an immediate liking. Lady Waring looked the kind of person Noel would approve, well-dressed, good-looking, with pleasant manners. The General was just right for a retired soldier who was a country gentleman, with a fierce appearance, due perhaps to his grizzled moustache, high forehead and piercing blue eyes, and obviously very kind. About Miss Waring she had not decided. Her face and figure she admired; and if she was a bit floppy, perhaps that was because she was not well.

As for the Warings, they had both taken to their guest at sight. Lady Waring, amusedly observing a certain gallantry in Sir Harry's manner to Mrs. Merton which suited him very well, hoped that this young woman would be a pleasant companion for her husband, who throve on, and indeed pined without, a little old-fashioned flirtation. Anything that made Sir Harry feel a little young and dashing was approved by his wife, who feared for him, above all things, the stagnation of a war-restricted life at home, with no fresh faces or conversation. And she was delighted to see that Mrs. Merton and Leslie were getting on so well, for she was anxious about her niece, who obviously needed to be taken out of herself, poor child. So that, as usual, Lydia was cast for the role of general utility.

"See you again, Mrs. Merton," said Sir Harry when he had drunk two large cups of tea. "I've got to go to the British Legion meeting at six."

"Don't be late if you can help it, Harry," said Lady Waring. "It looked as if there might be a fog coming up. And will you ring for Selina."

"Can I have your keys, please, madam?" said Selina, when she had cleared away the tea-things.

"I suppose my big suitcase hasn't come?" said Lydia. "I sent it off two days ago by passenger train, but that means nothing."

"Oh, yes, madam; they rang up from the station this morning to say it was there," said Selina.

"Why didn't you tell me?" said Lady Waring. "Coxon would have brought it up when he fetched Mrs. Merton. I am so sorry, Mrs. Merton," she added to Lydia.

"Well, my lady," said Selina, "I thought the lady would like to find things nice when she got here, and Private Jenks happened to let drop that Sergeant Hopkins was going down to the station with the lorry, so I thought he'd better bring it up, so I'll unpack it and see if anything wants pressing, if you'll let me have the keys, madam."

"Oh, thanks most awfully," said Lydia, giving Selina the keys. "Oh, and please don't undo the little blue case, because it has all the bottles and things in it. I can't tell you," she continued to her hostess, "how exhausting it has been to live in one's boxes all the time as we have since I was married and never knowing if you'll give offence by using your electric iron. But you would know even better than I do, because you must have lived in your boxes with Sir Harry for years and years."

Lady Waring was touched. How many of the girls she knew would, she wondered, have realized that although she was over sixty and doubtless decrepit and mentally doddering by their standards, she had travelled a great deal and lived in all sorts of mild discomfort for her husband's sake. And Lydia's slight air of deference pleased her. Not that she wanted it for herself, but living as she did by older and by no means despicable standards of conduct, she approved courtesy to one's elders. It might come from the heart, it might be only an outward form, but it helped to keep civilization going, and it was her opinion that if more people practised even the form of civility they would have a good chance of becoming Happy Hypocrites and be polite and kind off guard as well as on.

"I expect you would like to see your room," she said. "Leslie dear, will you take Mrs. Merton up? We dine at a quarter past eight, Mrs. Merton, so if you are tired, do rest before dinner. If not, we shall be delighted to see you down here."

The two young women got up. As Lydia looked back from the door she saw Lady Waring settling at her writing table where papers were ranged in pigeonholes, boxes, clips, and even on a spike, though it came from Magnum's and had a painted base and cost fifteen shillings and sixpence. Sir Harry had gone out in the cold, misty, dark evening to do his duty. An uncomfortable little thought assailed Lydia, but she pinched it, and it disappeared for the moment.

"This is where you and Major Merton are," said Leslie, opening a door.

Lydia drew a deep breath of delight. After more than two years of hotels, lodgings, furnished cottages, her own old home occupied by an insurance company, Noel with only his now cheerless chambers as a background, her heart leapt at the sight of what she mentally called a proper bedroom. Good furniture, not so young as it was but well cared for, good rather shabby chintzes, good brocade curtains though faded and patched, the right engravings of ancestors after Reynolds and Lawrence on the walls, a large writing-table, a reading-lamp to each bed. It was like a plunge back into a past life.

"Aunt Harriet is a marvellous arranger," said Leslie, gratified by the guest's obvious admiration. "Of course all this part was the servants' wing, but she has made it look quite ancestral. Still, I'm glad she's got electric light and central heating — that's thanks to the War Office. And —" she added, proudly opening what Lydia thought was a cupboard in the wall, but turned out to be a little recess with a fixed basin and an electric light of its own.

Lydia nodded gravely. Leslie's "and" needed no amplifying with this enchanting vision before her.

"You open the door and the light goes on," said Leslie proudly, "and when you shut it, the light goes off."

"How can one be sure?" asked Lydia, the practical. "There isn't room to shut oneself up and see."

"I know," said Leslie seriously. "I did think of that. But I put out the lights in the room and shut the cupboard door, and then I lay down on the floor and looked under the door which doesn't fit very well, and there wasn't a sign of light."

"I say," said Lydia, warming to anyone who did such sensible things, "do sit down and watch me unpack. I hate anyone to unpack this case for me, because it's always full of things I'm ashamed of, like dirty handkerchiefs, or face tissues that one thinks one can use just once more."

As she spoke she wheeled an arm-chair vigorously towards the fire that leapt and crackled in the old-fashioned grate.

"Thank you, I'd love to," said Leslie, sitting down with obvious relief. But as if unwilling to let anyone notice her fatigue, she quickly continued: "It's lovely to have proper fires here, and as there is unlimited timber we can be warm to the last, at least as long as Jasper is alive."

Lydia asked who Jasper was.

"He's the old keeper," said Leslie. "He is nearly as old as Uncle Harry. And anyway there's enough dead wood to burn for years. If you like we'll take the pony-cart and collect some to-morrow. It saves Jasper and he has a lot to do."

She stopped suddenly and lay back in her chair.

"I'd love to," said Lydia, who was arranging bottles, brushes, combs and such small fry neatly on the dressing-table, "what sort of pony is it?" and she pushed the less reputable toilet accessories into a drawer. There was no answer. She looked round and saw Leslie, rather like a deserted marionette, limp in the chair.

110

"I say, you look *rotten*," said Lydia. "I *am* so sorry. I thought you didn't look very fit downstairs. Shall I tell Lady Waring?"

"Please not," said Leslie. "It's all right, but I get these stupid fits since I was ill. If you could just take no notice —"

But Lydia, who believed in taking on any job that came in her way, was not to be put off by such evasion. True, she did not, as Lydia Keith would have done, sit down with her knees wide apart and her toes turned in and lay down the law, but she did plant herself before the fire in a rather gentlemanly way and looking down with kind firmness at Leslie, asked her exactly what the matter was.

"I've done all my Red Cross exams," she said, "and I'm frightfully strong, so if I can do anything for you, do let me know."

Leslie was so struck by Mrs. Merton's air of competence and benevolence that she thawed a little more, and haltingly at first, but gaining confidence by the delightful method of talking about herself, told Lydia how she had been secretary of a large naval organization for several years, which had meant a great deal of hard work and two visits to America, after the second of which she had been ill and just couldn't get better.

"But don't say anything to Aunt Harriet, please," she said. "She would worry and then I'd get cross. I am really doing my best, but the weather is a bit against me, and then there's Cecil."

Lydia, divining that Miss Waring was relieving some strain by talking to her, looked down with kindly interest and asked who Cecil was.

"My brother," said Leslie. "He's in the Navy and this place will go to him when Uncle Harry dies, which I hope he never will, because Cecil adores the Navy and doesn't a bit want to do death duties and things and take an interest in the crops and the shooting. If only there were the sea here and he could have a sailing boat he wouldn't mind so much, but there's no water at all, only the Dipping Ponds. I haven't heard from him for six weeks, which is really quite short, but one does imagine things at night and I expect I'll get a letter or a cable any day. It's awfully good of you to listen to this."

"I think it's extremely reasonable of you to be ill when you haven't heard from your brother," said Lydia, in measured but vehement tones. "My brother Colin, who is really the nicest person in the world except Noel — that's my husband — is in the Army, and I go quite mad sometimes when I don't hear. But what one has got to get into one's head," said Lydia earnestly, "is that if they were killed or anything the War Office — I mean the Admiralty for your brother — would let one know. So the longer you don't get any news the safer they are, in a way."

Leslie was so grateful for Lydia's bracing sympathy that she accepted this rather specious reasoning, and declaring that she now felt quite well got up and put her hair straight.

"Thank you very much, Mrs. Merton," she said. "I must go and rest before dinner, which is a hideous thing I have to do, but I'm afraid it does me good. And I wish you'd say Leslie."

"Of course, and I'm Lydia," said Mrs. Merton. "And what's more," she added proudly, "no one, not even Noel or Colin, has ever called me anything else, not Lyddy or anything."

"I should think not," said Leslie, with meaningless but flattering indignation. "Oh, by the way," she added, "who is Colonel Winter?"

"Colonel — oh, *Philip*," said Lydia. "He was a master at Southbridge School where my brother-in-law is a housemaster and he was engaged to the headmaster's daughter but she broke it off and then he went into the Army, at least he was a Territorial, so he was there anyway, and he was at Dunkirk and I'm frightfully pleased he is near here."

Leslie went down the corridor, thinking how horrid the headmaster's daughter must be. As she turned to go up the stair that led to the little room next to Selina where she was sleeping, she saw Major Merton, escorted by Sir Harry who was showing him Lydia's room. Major Merton knocked and went in. Leslie, pausing at the foot of the stairs, heard a confused noise which she guessed rightly to be Lydia, pouring out her day's adventures to Noel, giving him a rapid account of the Carters, rejoicing with him that Philip would be their neighbour.

"I'd hate to marry anyone," said Leslie to herself as she went upstairs, "but if I had someone to talk to about Cecil, I wouldn't even mind his being my husband."

CHAPTER
FOUR

Next day, being Sunday, Lady Waring asked the Mertons at breakfast if they would like to go to church. As Noel's work very kindly didn't want him on Sundays, the Warings and their guests walked across the chill, misty park to the church, which was at the Priory end of the village. An angry elderly clergyman hustled them through the service with such vigour that they emerged breathless but glowing with virtue at five minutes past twelve. Sir Harry, who was a church-warden, stopped to talk to the verger, while the others walked on.

"We haven't got a proper Vicar at present," said Lady Waring. "Our dear old Vicar died in October, and Canon Tempest, who has really given up active work, kindly takes the service on Sundays. He has been staying near here with a niece, but he is very anxious to get away to Devonshire, as the winter is too much for him. The living is in my husband's gift, but it is so difficult to find the right man," said Lady Waring with a sigh. "And we can't even offer a Vicarage at the moment, as our dear old Vicar's sister lived with him and we don't feel we can turn her out the minute her brother is dead. It is such a nice little house. Harry's father built it because the old Vicarage was so large and expensive. This is it."

The Vicarage was indeed a delightful little abode, more like a particularly nice cottage, built of Barsetshire stone which mellows quickly.

"It is like something in a novel," said Noel admiringly. "Home paddock and well-stocked kitchen garden if my eyes do not deceive me."

"And there was a shrubbery to walk in on wet days," said Lady Waring, "but we cut it down, because it simply ate up the garden and no one ever walked in it."

"I wish I were a Vicar," said Noel with undisguised envy, "and then I would ask to be inducted, if that is the right expression, at once. But I don't think the Army would quite like it."

"I wish you were, too," said Lady Waring. "It would be a very nice temporary home for you and Mrs. Merton. When we shall find a suitable incumbent I don't know. You see, the people here have their likes and dislikes, and they don't want a good preacher, because they say they can get that at the chapel. And they so much prefer one of the gentry. There was a most zealous young man called Moxon, who was curate at Worsted under Dr. Thomas, who wanted this living, but he used to be Christian, in the social sense, in the Woolpack at Worsted and play darts, and the village didn't like it at all. But I am thankful to say he has gone abroad. He writes a cheery letter for the parish magazine every month."

"If I see a nice clergyman I will let you know at once," said Noel earnestly. "The Dean of Barchester is rather a friend of mine. Unless of course your parish prefers someone from the Palace."

"What's that about the Palace, Merton?" said Sir Harry, joining them.

On hearing that Major Merton had been inquiring whether Lambton would consider an incumbent approved by the Bishop of Barchester, Sir Harry asked his wife in an audible aside whether he was a Bishop's man.

"No, Harry, Major Merton stays at the Deanery," said Lady Waring, so Sir Harry was able to pour his dislike of the Bishop into the sympathetic ears of his guests.

"Octavia Crawley is engaged to a very nice clergyman called Tommy Needham," said Lydia. "He's in Africa, or you might have had him."

"Harry, we really ought to go and see Nannie," said Lady Waring. "We haven't been for two Sundays. Nannie Allen," she explained to her guests, "was our boy George's nurse — he was killed in 1918."

"I expect," said Sir Harry, "Major and Mrs. Merton would find it rather dull. There is a very pretty way home, Merton, if you take that stile beyond the Vicarage and keep left, leaving the old kennels on your right. Only don't go through the second gate, because it leads nowhere. Take a little path that goes a bit up and a bit down, only not past the pond; turn left again just before it and keep slanting across the field to a bridle path on the far side, and just beyond it you will see a shed and a track going downhill. It is rather muddy at the bottom and you must be careful of the plank bridge over the stream, because it has broken twice lately and we haven't a man to put on it at present. And at the other side of the marshy ground you will see Jasper's cottage and then it is only a quarter of an hour to the Priory."

Lady Waring saw interest, bewilderment and stupefaction succeed each other rapidly on her guests' faces, and came to the rescue, suggesting that the men should walk home by the woods and she and Lydia should visit Nannie. Sir Harry looked relieved and took Noel off towards the stile.

"I do hope," said Lady Waring as she and Lydia walked down the village street, "that it won't bore you. Nannie is a most faithful old friend, and she does miss it when we don't pay her a call on Sundays."

To which Lydia replied that she liked Nannies very much and her family had an ex-Nannie themselves, who married the gardener and took lodgers.

"Nannie Allen has lodgers too," said Lady Waring. "In fact I was thinking of her for you, but she is keeping her rooms for one of Lady Graham's boys who is in quarantine. And may I say that I am glad of this, as it gives us the opportunity of getting to know you and your husband."

"Oh, thank you most awfully," said Lydia. "If it really isn't a bother, Noel and I will be so grateful to you for having us. I'd nearly forgotten what a real house is like. And if you don't mind, could we settle soon how much we may pay you, because it is so much more comfortable. We are really quite well off, if it isn't boastful," she added.

She had thought of asking Lady Waring not to say Mrs. Merton, but an instinct told her that Lady Waring, though she did not look elderly or behave as if she were, belonged to a generation which did not expect its juniors to take the lead. So she wisely left this question for the moment. Lady Waring, still thinking of Lydia, though in a most friendly way, as Mrs. Merton, the wife of Major Merton, was amused by Lydia's eager honesty about payment and rather liked her for it.

At No. 1 Ladysmith Cottages Nannie Allen was to be seen seated at her window with an uncompromising countenance, which did not relax as she grimly watched her visitors come up the little gravel path.

"Nannie is offended," said Lady Waring, "because we didn't come last Sunday."

With what Lydia considered superhuman courage she opened the door and went in. The little oilclothed passage smelt of cleanness and Sunday dinner. The sitting-room door was shut. Lady Waring behaved with the courage of a General's wife. Opening the door boldly, she walked in, followed by Lydia, and advanced to the window. Lydia carefully shut the door.

"Well, Nannie," said Lady Waring, "how are you? I've brought a lady to see you."

"How do you do," said Lydia, shaking Nannie's unresponsive hand.

"You'll excuse my getting up, miss," said Nannie, sketching a pantomime of arthritic knees, trembling ankles and twisted feet. "This weather is very hard on me and no one takes any notice of me, not even my own daughter."

"She was down here only the day before yesterday, Nannie," said Lady Waring, "helping you to turn out the bedroom."

"That's how I got my rheumatism so bad," said Nannie. "I didn't expect you to-day, my lady. When you and Sir Harry didn't come last week, I said to myself, It's the weather that keeps them. They won't want to come and see me now."

"Now, Nannie, that's nonsense," said Lady Waring. "Sir Harry sent you his love and I've brought this lady to see your house. She is staying with me."

"It's a pity you never had a daughter, my lady," said Nannie. "Someone like this young lady. But they're all alike. Selina never comes near me now."

"Is that your daughter that unpacked my things?" said Lydia. "She *is* nice, and so pretty."

"They used to say she took after her father," said Nannie, a shade less grimly.

"Well, I think she is awfully like you," said Lydia.

Nannie said beggars couldn't be choosers, but it was so evident that she said this merely because she couldn't think of anything else depressing to say, that her guests were much cheered.

"And she's awfully kind," said Lydia. "The lock of one of my suitcases has been broken for weeks because one simply can't get anything mended now, especially if you're moving about, but she said Sergeant Hopkins would do it for me."

"*That's* why she doesn't come and see her old mother," said Nannie. "Sergeants and privates, that's all she thinks about."

"But you aren't a bit old," said Lydia.

"I've got my old-age pension, miss," said Nannie relapsing.

"Well, that's sixty now," said Lydia cheerfully.

"It's Mrs. Merton, Nannie," said Lady Waring.

"I thought the young lady was married, my lady, as soon as she came in," said Nannie untruthfully, "but you didn't say. How long have you been married, madam?"

This question from a complete stranger might have appeared to betoken a wish to pry, but such was Nannie's authority that Lydia, without hesitation, said, "Two years and a bit. It was after Dunkirk," and almost looked at her hands to see if they were clean.

"Major and Mrs. Merton have been moved about a good deal and haven't a home at present," said Lady Waring, rather wanting to get this stage of the conversation over. "Major Merton is at the Camp, and I am glad to say they will stay at the Priory till they can find a house. You remember, Nannie, that I spoke to you about your rooms," said Lady Waring, not betraying her impatience.

"Yes, my lady," said Nannie, looking abstractedly at and through Lydia. "It was at the end of 1900 that I came to the Priory when Master George was still on bottles, and you were married in the June of '99, my lady, because the silver wedding was in 1924. I was with young Lady Lufton then, taking the new baby from the month. She married his lordship in '21 and little Lucy was just two when the baby came. Just a nice interval between them, we used to say, and little Lucy was so pleased with the little baby sister."

Lady Waring raised her eyes to heaven in despair. Nannie was an old dear, but one never knew what mood one would find her in. Quite obviously to-day she was in the mood when the thought of nannie-fodder bulked very large in her mind. Some sixth sense had told her that the Mertons had as yet no family and it was more than likely that she would ask Mrs. Merton why before the visit was out. But most luckily Lydia, whose attention had been wandering to the photographs on the mantelpiece, gave an exclamation and got up.

"I say, there's Octavia," she said, pointing to a photograph of Mrs. Crawley with her eighth child on her knee in a condition of sulks. "Do you know her?"

Nannie said she was at the Deanery as temporary when Miss Octavia was nine months old and the trouble she had to make that child eat her greens no one would ever know, and milk-pudding the same.

"That's funny," said Lydia. "Octavia simply loathes cabbage, and rice-pudding too. Was she really like that, Nannie? She's a great friend of mine."

When addressed by her nursery name, Nannie had been known to blight people by saying, "Mrs. Allen is my name, madam, if convenient." But whether it was professional interest in Lydia, or the fact that she was a friend of one of her ex-babies, Nannie replied that Miss Octavia was a nice baby though with quite a will of her own, and getting up with no visible pain or distress, extracted from the sideboard or chiffonier an album bound in red plush with a brass filigree lock that didn't work, and treated Lydia to a Private View of some of her old babies, from the period when they were photographed by a time exposure face downwards on a fur rug with nothing on, to the large blurred faces of mother and child pressed together of the illustrated weekly. Lydia was enchanted and showed such intelligent admiration of the gallery that Nannie offered to take her upstairs to see some more. But Lady Waring said they must go home for lunch, and Nannie must come up to tea some day soon.

"Miss Leslie shall come and fetch you in the pony-cart, Nannie," she said.

"I'll write and tell Octavia all about you," said Lydia. "She's engaged to an awfully nice clergyman called Tommy Needham, but they don't mean to get married till the war is over."

Nannie said she had no patience with that sort of nonsense, but when informed by Lydia that Mr. Needham was in Africa, relented and said she supposed what couldn't be cured must be endured, and to give Miss Octavia her love and to remember her respectfully to Mrs. Crawley.

"How good you were with Nannie," said Lady Waring as they walked quickly homewards by the short way.

Lydia said she liked her awfully and it was great fun.

"It's lucky that we did not get onto the subject of Leslie," said Lady Waring. "I think she was Nannie's pet baby — next to George, of course — and she would do anything for her."

"If it's not interfering, could you tell me about Leslie," said Lydia. "I mean she isn't well, is she? and if I could do anything, or if there is anything I oughtn't to do, I would be so glad if you would tell me. She looked so ill in my room last night that I thought she would faint. I'm pretty good at nursing and I know what to do, but she asked me to leave her alone. It was a kind of breakdown, she said."

"Poor Leslie," said Lady Waring. "Yes, she overworked for two years with hardly any break and then she was asked to go to America to speak about her work and the second time she was torpedoed coming back and in a boat for two days."

"No wonder she doesn't look well," said Lydia.

"And I think, though I wouldn't say this to my husband and I know you will keep it to yourself, that she worries more about her brother because of what she went through. When George was killed," said Lady Waring, "it was far worse for his father than for me. For me George went when his leave was up and didn't come back. That was hard. But my husband had been in France and knew exactly what it was like and what George might have felt."

Lydia was silent.

"I don't want to make you think that it is serious," said Lady Waring, taking her silence for a wish to avoid too painful a subject. "She will get over it when she is better."

"It wasn't that," said Lydia. "I was thinking about Colin — that's my special brother. I was thinking when he goes abroad and gets killed I can never know what it felt like."

Lady Waring looked at her guest and saw that she was suddenly and deeply moved.

"If you can amuse Leslie, it will be the best thing in the world for her," she said. "Dr. Ford says it is simply a question of time."

Lydia looked gratefully at her.

"I am so sorry about your brother, my dear," Lady Waring said. "And now we must really hurry, or we shall be late for lunch. I oughtn't to have let Nannie keep us so long, but she does love talking about her babies."

Leslie Waring made her appearance at the lunch table, looking better for a long morning in bed and ten minutes' walk. During the meal she asked Sir Harry if she and Lydia might take the pony-cart for a little drive. Her aunt looked anxious, but contented herself by saying that they must go out soon after lunch and be back by four at the very latest, as it was such a nasty day. Sir Harry, who had enjoyed his walk back with Noel, offered to take him round the woods and introduce him to Jasper, so that he could walk where he liked without question. Noel, who had had from Lydia a rapid sketch of Leslie's adventures and illness, thought Miss Waring could have no better medicine than his wife's company and accepted Sir Harry's invitation with pleasure, which left Lady Waring free to write her letters and do the thousand and one things that made up her busy life.

124

By the end of lunch a pale sun had struggled through the mist, so Lady Waring felt less misgiving when Leslie and Lydia went off together, carrying rugs. Leslie led the way to the stables where a stout pony with a small head was standing in a loose box thinking of nothing at all. The whole stable spoke eloquently of changed times. Where hunters and driving horses had champed and stamped, old mowing machines, mysterious wooden boxes, iron bedsteads and deal chests-of-drawers removed from the servants' wing, a couple of baths left by the contractors till needed, a rusty kitchen range, chicken meal, a bath-chair, a giant weighing machine and twenty other pieces of now useless furniture were stored, dating from different epochs in the history of the Priory. The bath-chair, or rather invalid's chair, which the occupier could propel by laboriously turning two wooden rims outside the wheels (a description which will be absolutely unintelligible except to those who have such a chair in their memory), had been bought for an aunt of Sir Harry's. She, being the unmarried daughter left at home to look after her old parents, had found it advisable to lose the use of both her legs at about forty. Sir Harry's childhood had been terrorized by the chair and his aunt. Cecil and Leslie Waring had pushed, pulled and propelled themselves and each other, sometimes into the lily pond, sometimes down the terrace steps, sometimes down the long passage from the house to the kitchen, driving footmen with trays nearly demented. On the weighing machine which used to stand in the hall, a monstrous structure with a padded mahogany chair at one end of a brass beam and a bowl for giant weights at the other, they had weighed themselves, their nurse, the dogs, any maidservants they could catch and, once, the butler. A stuffed pike in a glass case, degraded from billiard room to steward's room, thence to boot and knife room, was in a manger, and a dressmaker's dummy, known to Cecil and Leslie as Mrs. Grabham, from the name of her maker, stood with firm, well-developed bust and hips, and a kind of cage for a skirt, in a corner.

The only living inhabitants were the pony and a cat who liked to live there and pretend she was an outcast, though the gardener's children to whom she belonged spent all their spare time bringing her and her frequent families back to their cottage.

"Hullo, Crumpet," said Leslie, addressing the pony, who turned his small head and looked at her. "Come out."

She opened the door and Crumpet walked neatly out. Leslie, with Lydia's help, took his harness from the wall, dressed him, and led him to the coach-house, which was packed with furniture from the big house under dust-sheets. At one end was a governess cart, which must have been a smart turn-out in its time. Leslie backed Crumpet into it, fastened the harness, and led the equipage into the stable yard.

"Would you like to drive?" said Leslie.

Lydia said would Leslie drive first as she knew where they were going, so Leslie took the reins, Lydia got in opposite her, and Crumpet trotted in a leisurely yet nimble fashion down the back drive. The once neat surface was green with moss and weeds, littered with damp twigs and rotting leaves, and when Leslie turned down a drive into the woods the sound of the pony's feet and the wheels was no more deadened than it had been on the metalled road. At the top of a little rise Leslie stopped the pony. Before them the drive dipped and rose again with a misty perspective of trees. At the far end a tapering column gilded by the low sun closed the view.

"Obelisk," said Leslie, pointing with her whip, "erected by my great-grandfather, Uncle Harry's grandfather, Lord knows why. It used to have a gilded ball on top, but the gilding faded and last year the ball fell down and Uncle Harry can't get it put up again, so there is only a rusty spike. All very sad."

"I know," said Lydia, looking wistfully down the long vista to the obelisk. "We had a stone figure at the end of the terrace at my old home and last time I went there the pedestal had split and the little statue had fallen down, and the business people the house is let to didn't care."

"It must be rotten for you to have your old home let," said Leslie. "We'd better get our wood or Aunt Harriet will begin to think I am dead. She is rather given that way."

She got out and showed Lydia a heap of dead branches, roughly chopped into lengths.

"Jasper's wood-pile," she said. "He brings them up in the cart when he has time, so I always help him when I'm here."

She produced some cord and began to collect branches.

"That's awfully bad for you," said Lydia. "I'll stack them and you can tie them up and I'll put them in the trap."

Leslie looked up, but apparently did not resent this interference. Lydia made neat piles of wood, reft the cord from Leslie's hands in a kind, business-like way, carried the bundles to the cart and came back for more.

"We can't manage all this," she said, "but if I leave it by the road we can fetch it another time."

She beat the dirt and bits of bark from her hands and clothes vigorously and shook herself. Leslie, looking at her handsome face flushed with the exercise and her violent, free movements, suddenly felt very envious, which so affected her that she sat down on a log, looking very tired.

"Here, you'll get green marks all over your skirt if you sit there," said Lydia. "Are you feeling queer? I oughtn't to have let you tie up that last bundle."

"Well, they are my bundles — at least, Uncle Harry's," said Leslie with the unreasonable perversity of fatigue.

A retort sprang to Lydia's lips, but remembering that she was a guest and Leslie an invalid, she said nothing, looking at her with anxious compassion.

"I apologize," said Leslie after a brief silence. "I suddenly got rather cross because you can do so much and I can't do anything now. Can't keep my job; can't even keep my temper."

"Rot!" exclaimed Mrs. Merton, becoming again for a moment Miss Lydia Keith. "Look here, you get into the cart and I'll drive for a bit. You look cold."

Leslie obediently got up, walked silently to the pony-cart and got in. Lydia tucked one rug in a business-like way round her companion's legs, put the other rug round her shoulders, loaded the faggots onto the cart, exchanged a word with Crumpet, climbed in over the wood and turned the pony towards home.

"Along that drive to the left," said Leslie. "We'll go by Golden Valley."

Lydia turned as she was told.

"I am normal now," said Leslie. "Thank you."

"But you always were normal," said Lydia, letting Crumpet drop, not unwillingly, to a walk. "If you knew how low and wormish you make me feel."

"*I?*" said Leslie, in extreme surprise.

"Well, you've held down a very difficult, important job, though I don't know what it was, for *years*," said Lydia, "and you've been to America twice to help the government, and you've been torpedoed, and your brother is at sea, which is enough to make anyone worry, and I think you are simply splendid. I've done absolutely nothing at all except bits of V.A.D. and land work and working parties and all that sort of easy stuff. Every time I thought I'd found a job Noel was moved on again and by the time we had moved everyone had lost interest in me. I know everyone says, why aren't I called up, but if I said I hadn't had any luck yet no one would believe me. Anyway, I shall try again."

"Do you mean get a job and leave your husband?" said Leslie.

"I suppose that's what it boils down to," said Lydia, looking straight in front of her. "It would be quite ghastly as long as Noel is in England. Of course when he is sent abroad again nothing will matter. But somehow if one is happy one feels one isn't really helping the war, and I am so very happy, except when I think how wormish I am and really almost a Traitor," said Lydia knitting her brows.

Leslie could not think what to say. Of one thing she felt quite certain, that Lydia was being unfair to herself. What Lydia had done in the way of war work she did not know, nor did Lydia's contemptuous reference to easy stuff give her any real information. But in her job she had learnt to wait before judging people and to get sidelights when possible.

"Now to the right," she said, "and we'll see if Jasper is in."

Lydia turned Crumpet's head to the right, into a lane that crossed the drive. Inspirited by the sound of his own hoofs on the road the pony tossed his head and broke into a smart trot. A couple of hundred yards further on they came to a cottage over-towered by a large pear-tree. In front of it was a vegetable garden where Jasper was digging. He looked up as they approached. Crumpet recognizing him stopped abruptly and jerking his head forward began to tear at a few scanty blades of grass under the hedge in a manner expressive of starvation and ill-treatment.

"Hullo, old Crumpet," said Jasper, straightening up and sticking his fork into the ground, "you're a nice little old pony, aren't you."

Crumpet tearing away at the grass and two withered nettles paid no attention.

"Good afternoon, Jasper," said Leslie. "I've brought a friend with me who is staying at the Priory. Can I bring her in to see your cottage?"

Jasper leant his arms on the top of his gate and surveyed the cart and its occupants with an unwinking stare.

"If Crumpet'll stand," he remarked after a pause.

Taking this as an invitation, Leslie opened the little back door of the pony-cart and prepared to descend.

"That's a fine lot of wood you young ladies has got," said Jasper admiringly, "but you don't want mucking up old Crumpet's trap with all that. I'll bring it up to-morrow in the cart."

He came out of the gate, took the faggots out of the trap and piled them by the hedge. The young women got out. Jasper pulled a piece of cord from his pocket and hobbled the pony.

"No good a-hitching the reins on my old thorns," he said. "Only scratches the leather. You'll be safe enough now, old Crumpet. You won't go straying away."

He strode up the path, followed by his guests.

The cottage, which was so Early English Water Colour as to be almost incredible, stood below a hanger, a small stream purling beside it. The walls were of a kind of wattle and daub, of a creamy colour, the roof was thatched, the windows latticed and very small.

A deserted pigsty leaned drunkenly at its side, a well was near the pigsty with a bucket standing on its stone rim. There was, quite unbelievably, a bench before the little porch. A thin plume of blue smoke rose lazily from the chimney. A gun and a fishing-rod stood against the white-washed wall of the porch. Jasper, with his autumn leaf coloured coat, breeches and leggings, almost melted into his surroundings.

Owing to its position the cottage suffered from every conceivable drawback of picturesque rural life. The hanger prevented any sun from reaching it except in the late evenings of midsummer when it is almost in the north. The purling brook overflowed every spring and autumn, leaving mud and old leaves all over the garden and sometimes in the cottage. The well was apt to run dry or at other times produced water with a peculiar and unpleasant taste, attributed by Jasper and the older men to they old monks at Beliers Abbey in a general way. The windows let in draughts and kept out what light there was and the pigsty, although untenanted since pig-control came in, still smelt of Domesday swine kept by the Margetts of that time, who thought but poorly of foreigners.

Again and again Sir Harry had tried to put Jasper into a better cottage. Jasper, more than half-gipsy in nature if not by blood, cherished his solitude and his independence of newfangled contraptions. Electric light, water laid on, the neighbourhood of shops, the companionship of his kind except at the Sheep's Head, were suspect in his mind. His well gave water which he had drunk all his life and when it ran dry the stream, analysed as ninety per cent fatal to humans, was there. A tin of paraffin supplied his lamp. Bread and a few groceries he bought once a week in the village, milk he got from Sir Harry's farm, potatoes and herbs he grew, game could be got in some shape all the year round by a man who knew how, for newspapers he had no need and probably could not have read them. He knew no one that he wanted to write to and in any case had forgotten so much of the art as he learned while forced to attend the village school. As for the wireless, he felt great contempt for people who could listen to what he called, though in less refined terms, an old box of tricks, when, as he said, it stood to reason you couldn't hear no further than what your own ears heard, and his were sharp enough; and indeed they were, as the local poachers knew. When Cecil and Leslie Waring were little, they were convinced that Jasper's cottage was really old Jacob Armitage's cottage in *The Children of the New Forest*, and longed for the Priory to be burned down by the Roundheads, so that they could go and stay there.

His one room, which was kitchen, living-room and everything except bedroom, for a little wooden stair in the wall led to an attic above where he slept, was now almost dark. Jasper courteously brought forward two rush-seated chairs, made by his Romany kin years before, and sat down at the other side of the table. Lydia looked round, a little daunted, but much interested. As her eyes got used to the gloom she saw that the walls were almost covered with skins of vermin, and the dry corpses of others hung in bunches as onions or bits of bacon might hang in a more normal kitchen. A black pot was cooking on the fire, giving out a smell that reminded her of the gipsy's stew that Mr. Toad partook of.

"Seed my old grandmother last night, Miss Leslie," said Jasper, who was occupying his fingers by making a snare.

"How was she?" said Leslie. "Jasper's grandmother," she explained to Lydia, "was a witch."

"All right, old granny was," said Jasper. "I was down at the big Dipping Pond, laying for some of those lads as come over from the camp. Poor lot they are. Make enough noise to scare every old rabbit on the place. And there was a big black hare, as plain as you are."

"Did she see you?" said Leslie.

"See me?" said Jasper with a sardonic laugh. "Old granny seed me all right. Sat up as bold as brass, looking at me. I was just going to have a shot at her, when two of those lads came out of the coppice and scared her away. I gave them both a proper old hiding and they won't come again in a hurry."

Lydia listened with serious attention, fascinated and hardly believing her ears.

"Jasper's grandmother died sixty years ago, so it is quite troublesome of her to come back like this," said Leslie with an air of courteous explanation.

"But would you really shoot her?" Lydia asked, a little afraid of offending her host.

"Yes, miss. I'd shoot old granny if I could get her," said Jasper. "I'd learn her not to rest quiet in her grave. But I've never got her yet."

134

"Some people," said Lydia, "say you can't shoot witches except with a silver button."

She waited nervously for Jasper to take offence, but he appeared to consider her remark worth attention.

"Yes, I have heard tell as an old silver button is the thing," said Jasper. "Thank you, miss. If I find a silver button I'll mind what you said. But they aren't as common as all that."

So carried away was Lydia by the events of the afternoon, the twilit room, the general feeling of mystery and even sorcery, that she said, almost without meaning to:

"I'm sure I've got a silver button somewhere, if you'd like one."

It was now so dark in the room that she could not see Jasper's face, and before he could answer Sir Harry's voice was heard outside. They all went into the garden and found Sir Harry and Noel, who had been for a long walk and were taking Jasper on their way home. Noel was formally presented to Jasper, who appeared to feel well disposed towards him and offered him the freedom of Sir Harry's woods and fields. His taciturnity then descended upon him again like a cloud. Crumpet was released, Leslie got into the cart and the others said they would walk beside her.

"Well, good-bye," said Lydia, not wishing to leave her host without a farewell, and not knowing whether she ought to call him Jasper or Mr. Margett, "and I won't forget."

Jasper gave her one of his quick sidelong looks, but must have thought she was in earnest, for he said in a low voice, "Have you seen that Sillina?"

Lydia said she had, and how very nice she was.

"Silly by name and silly by nature," said Jasper, who had been storing this witticism in his mind for future use. "But you're right, miss. She's nice, that old Sillina."

Lydia felt a certain Barkis-like flavour creeping into their conversation and wondered if he was going to ask her to tell Selina that he was willing, but Crumpet began to dance and the cavalcade moved off. As they went up the lane they came into the last light of sunset of which Lydia was glad, for the hollow behind them, though Leslie had called it Golden Valley, was a little sinister in the fading light.

"Jasper saw his grandmother last night, Uncle Harry," said Leslie. "She was in the wood down by the big Dipping Pond."

"A cold place for an old lady," said Noel.

Sir Harry laughed.

"His grandmother was supposed to be a witch," he said. "I can just remember her when I was a boy. She was a white witch and lived down in Pear Tree Cottage, where you were this afternoon. She was supposed to turn into a black hare on moonlight nights. I sometimes wonder if it wasn't true. All the old people round here believe that she walks. Jasper believes that if he can shoot her she will be laid, but somehow he has never got that hare."

Lydia was undergoing a violent inward conflict. Ought she or ought she not to tell her host about the silver button? Down in Jasper's cottage it had seemed reasonable enough. Looked at now, in daylight or what was left of it, it seemed foolish. And what the etiquette was about witches she did not quite know. If the witch was on Sir Harry's property and had been his tenant in her lifetime, it would perhaps be discourteous, or against the Game Laws, for outsiders to interfere.

"Some people say you can't shoot them unless you have a silver button," said Sir Harry, with a tone of scientific detachment.

Lydia's innate honesty got the better of her.

"Oh, Sir Harry, I do hope you won't mind," she said, "but I told your keeper I would give him a silver button if I can find one."

Sir Harry was for a moment taken aback. To have been personally acquainted with a witch is one thing; to find other people sharing your belief is another. They might be laughing at you, they might be taking you too seriously and bringing up the question of folk dancing. In either case you would courteously retire into yourself. But either Lydia's face, or her voice, or both, combined with the good impression he already had of her, gave him a sense of security.

"It's very queer about these things," he said judicially. "Mind, I won't commit myself one way or another, but there always might be something in it. Look at the Witch of Endor, eh?"

This appeal to Holy Writ appeared to have settled the question. Crumpet stepped out, the three walkers had to quicken their pace, and before the frozen sea of pale gold and green in the west had faded, they were safely back at the Priory. Sir Harry sent his niece indoors to get warm and took the pony-cart round to the stables, accompanied by Lydia, who had become a fast friend of Crumpet. Noel, who confessed without shame that harness was as much a mystery to him as the internal combustion engine, went in with Leslie and found Lady Waring in the sitting-room and Selina bringing in tea.

Lady Waring asked what they had done that afternoon, looked searchingly at Leslie, and decided that her niece was none the worse for her chilly drive; in fact, rather the better, which she attributed partly to Mrs. Merton's company and felt grateful to her guest.

"We won't wait for the others," she said to Noel. "My husband will be so delighted to have someone to talk to about the stables that he will probably keep your wife out till dark. I hope she won't be bored."

Noel said, with truth, that he had never known Lydia bored in his life. Then he and Lady Waring discovered common friends in London and were able to give each other news of births, deaths and marriages, while Leslie listened, a little too tired to talk, but with a pleasant relaxed tiredness such as she had not known for a long time, a state of things which her aunt discerned with the corner of her eye but made no comment on it.

"How is it that we have never met before?" said Lady Waring. "You must have been in these parts a good deal."

"I really belong to them," said Noel. "My father was a solicitor in Barchester, but I was at school and Oxford and reading law and then practising and had lots of friends and wasn't much at home. I only began to know this country again when I first visited the Keiths, from which moment I never looked back."

Lady Waring asked about Northbridge Manor, the Keiths' old home.

"When Mr. Keith died his son Robert had it," said Noel, "a very good fellow, another Barchester solicitor, but he couldn't live there and he has let it to a business firm. They are quite good tenants, but the estate is the trouble. Lydia ran it when the bailiff rejoined the Navy, and she has run it ever since, though I'm afraid marrying me and moving about England and Scotland rather cramped her style, not to speak of her land work and her nursing. But we hear that the bailiff may be invalided out of the Navy and if so we hope he will come back. Then Lydia will probably get a whole-time job. I know she wants to."

"What are your own feelings?" said Lady Waring.

"To be quite truthful, I should like my wife simply to be my wife and be there to welcome me every evening with a well-cooked repast and darn my socks," said Noel, "without prejudice, of course, to a very well paid war job that called for no exertion. Of course when I am sent abroad —" He did not finish the sentence.

"My brother Cecil is like that," said Leslie from her chair by the fire. "He says if he were the government he would conscript the women to live at home and look nice for when he came back. He hates me doing my job."

"I like Cecil," said Noel. "But the awful thing is that people like you and Lydia do your jobs so well. Lydia was practically offered a hundred pounds a minute to stay at the hospital where she worked when we were in Yorkshire, and I know the farm where she was all last year when we were in Scotland would have given her free food and lodging and every rationed luxury for the rest of her life."

"I think it is frightening," said Leslie. "Most of the women I had under me were incredibly efficient and I don't think they were any more trying than the men. But it's all upside down. It is quite horrid not to be able to feel that men are superior beings. I'd much rather I did."

Lady Waring looked as if she did not quite like the turn the conversation was taking and said this was one of the ways in which war upset everything and when it was over she hoped we would settle down.

"But that's just the awful part, Aunt Harriet," said Leslie, sitting up and speaking with an energy she had not shown since she came. "Most of the women in my department don't *want* to settle down. They want to go on living with lots of other women like the Fifth Form at St. Ethelburga's and having all their fun in crowds. That's why such a lot of girls don't want commissions. They really like cocoa suppers in the dormitory."

"It is a very sad prospect for the men when the Army is demobilized," said Lady Waring, who as an old soldier's wife was apt to forget that we have other defenders.

"There won't be so very many, Aunt Harriet," said Leslie sadly. "There were too many of us before the war and there will be millions more too many afterwards. No; it frightens me."

In spite of her affection for her niece and her genuine wish to sympathize with younger people's point of view, Lady Waring was liking the argument less and less. Noel, sensitive to this, asked Lady Waring whether the convalescent home was keeping the Priory in good repair.

"They could not have behaved better," said Lady Waring. "If we can ever afford to live in our house again, it will be very much more comfortable. And Matron encourages the men to keep the drive tidy and work in the kitchen garden. We are very lucky — what is it, Selina?"

"Matron rang up, my lady," said Selina, "and she's *so* upset she couldn't get over before, but they had a visiting specialist down. She is coming over now, my lady, and says not to keep tea for her."

"I had quite forgotten she was coming," said Lady Waring, conscience-stricken by the appalling gulf between her precept and her practice, her heartfelt praise of Matron and her entire want of interest in that estimable woman. "Bring some fresh tea as soon as you can, Selina."

Selina collected the teapot and hot water-jug. In a few minutes she came back with fresh tea, announced Matron and retired.

"Now, you have had fresh tea made for me, Lady Waring, and you shouldn't," said Matron. "What would our good Lord Woolton say? But I shall throw patriotism to the winds and have a refreshing cup if you will let me. Sir Abel Fillgrave talked till I thought he would never go, all most interesting about his experiences with shell-shock in the last war, but as I said to Nurse Poulter, what we really want to know is if Private Jenks will have to be operated on again. No; no sugar, Lady Waring, thank you; I have my saccharine. I always say one of a nurse's temptations is to forget how all you kind folk are rationed and nibble at your little store."

Lady Waring, who had long ago made a principle of not protesting against other people's economies, did not explain that fresh tea would have been needed for Sir Harry and Mrs. Merton in any case, and introduced Noel.

"My niece you have met before, when she was down here," she said. "She has not been well and is on leave, which is very nice for us."

A gleam came into Matron's eye and she was obviously about to ask the most pressing questions as to Leslie's illness and the ordering of her convalescence, when Sir Harry and Lydia came in.

"Well, well, Matron, men all right and all that?" said Sir Harry. "This young lady, my dear," he continued, sitting down near his wife, "knows nearly as much about the place as I do. Put Crumpet in his stall like a groom, gave me some good tips about the compost heap and helped me to saw some logs like a Trojan. And she is hand in glove with Jasper already."

"Harry! you haven't been making Mrs. Merton saw wood!" said Lady Waring.

"I loved it," said Lydia. "One doesn't often get a chance to work with a two-handed saw."

She then applied herself to her tea with the same energy that she brought to everything she undertook.

"By the way, Matron," said Sir Harry, "one of your men was in the backyard as I came in. I told him he could go and have a shot at some rabbits whenever the keeper is with him. Can't remember his name. The man that shot your cat. How is the new kitten?"

"Well, fancy your remembering kitty," said Matron, much gratified. "Winston we call him. He is quite a little favourite with the men. But really now, it is quite a coincidence your mentioning Private Jenks, because Sir Abel Fillgrave was here to-day and it seems he will have to be operated again."

Sir Harry said he didn't know people could have their appendix out twice.

Matron said Sir Harry would have his joke, but it wasn't appendix that Private Jenks was to be operated for this time. It was, she said, something More Serious, which made Sir Harry wish he had not spoken. "It does seem a shame," Matron continued, "just when we were so pleased with him, and I consider that the Barchester General ought never to have sent him to a convalescent home. What is the use of the War Office taking over the hospital if they send men out when they aren't fit? As I was saying to Nurse Poulter, it is in and out, in and out, all the time."

"He seems to be in and out of the backyard pretty often," said Sir Harry, who was apt to use the back entrance if his boots were muddy, or as a short cut to the home farm.

"I think he was a typewriter mechanic," said Leslie, who knew about people on the place almost as well as her uncle and often sooner than he did, "at least he mended my typewriter the day before yesterday when the carriage stuck. And Selina says he is mending her sewing-machine."

"He's too young for Selina," said Sir Harry. "Quite unsuitable. But it's not my business."

"Really, Harry!" said his wife. "You might as well suspect Jasper."

Lydia remembered Jasper's lover-like words about that old Sillina and decided to keep them to herself.

As was inevitable when Matron was there, the conversation now centred on the hospital. No one had yet discovered any other subject, apart from pussies and the Royal Family, in which she took any interest. Yet she must have seen much of the world and of life, the service ribbons on her uniform were enough proof of that. But whether she did not like to speak of her work in the last war, or whether such parts of Europe as she had nursed in had merely meant so many cases to her, no one knew. Sir Harry and Lydia discussed the care of green-houses when they could not be heated, while Lady Waring, supported by Noel, showed the appropriate emotions and made the appropriate exclamations to Matron's chronicle of her nurses and convalescents.

"And one thing I specially wanted to ask you about, Lady Waring," said Matron. "You know those nice lectures we have on Thursday afternoons for the boys."

Lady Waring said she did.

"I have enjoyed them all thoroughly," said Matron, "and so do the boys. We are going to have one by Lord Stoke on Viking remains in a field near Rising Castle, and I believe the remains were found in a field called Bloody Meadow. Now I *know* the boys will give his lordship a good laugh if he mentions the name, but that isn't quite the spirit for a lecture on human remains, so I wondered if you or Sir Harry could just say a word to him before the lecture. It is often a little point like that, that just makes the success or otherwise of a lecture."

Lady Waring said she quite saw Matron's point and would try to explain to Lord Stoke, but he was now almost stone-deaf besides being very obstinate.

"You know I really felt quite ashamed of the boys when Lord Bond was kind enough to lecture on the Reconstruction of Europe," said Matron, "and they commenced to whistle, so I thought I'd just mention it. Well, I must be getting back. We are short-handed at present and really where to turn for nurses or V.A.D.'s one hardly knows in these days. I wonder if your guests would like to see over the hospital some time, Lady Waring? Mrs. Tebben came over from Worsted last week to see a man in her son's regiment, and brought us an art repoussé copper jar for the sitting-room and

145

Sergeant Hopkins has kept it filled with foliage and it really gives quite an effect."

Noel said he was unfortunately at the camp all day, but his wife would be much interested, he knew, as she had done a good deal of nursing herself. Lydia, hearing her name mentioned, turned towards Matron, who graciously inquired which hospital she had trained at.

"Oh, I'm not a proper nurse," said Lydia, "only V.A.D. But I'd most awfully like to see your hospital if I may."

Matron said she had known some very good V.A.D.'s. Miss Crawley, the daughter of the Dean of Barchester, had been a most enthusiastic and helpful nurse when she, Matron, was at the Barsetshire General in the early months of the war.

"Octavia, you mean," said Lydia. "She's a friend of mine. She's frightfully keen on nursing. She wants to train properly and go in for facial surgery or else frightfully difficult baby cases. Did you know Nurse Chiffinch?"

It appeared that Matron not only knew Nurse Chiffinch but, with reservations as to her own perfect superiority, considered her an excellent nurse. She and Lydia plunged into hospital talk, but though Lydia was genuinely interested, her enthusiasm was kept within bounds and her voice did not dominate the conversation as it did in former days.

Matron then said again that she must be going and bade a gracious farewell. "Oh, and one more thing, Lady Waring," she said at the door. "We need a lecturer for one of our Thursdays. The Army Education People are finding it difficult to send lecturers every week and have asked us to collaborate. I believe you know Mrs. Morland that writes those lovely books. Could you ask her if she would come and give a talk to the boys about her books? They are all great readers and would thoroughly enjoy it. We had Mr. George Knox for a literary talk once. I couldn't be there, unfortunately, but the boys seem to have thoroughly enjoyed it. About the Inquisition it was, and Sergeant Hopkins said it gave them some good ideas to try out on the Germans. So if you will be so very kind as to ask Mrs. Morland —"

"I will do my best," said Lady Waring, almost interrupting Matron, though as she afterwards explained it was because she knew Matron was going to say the boys would thoroughly enjoy it, and she could not bear it again.

When she had crackled away everyone said what a nice woman she was, after which effort they all relapsed into Sunday coma, even Lady Waring, so rarely idle, looking at the fire and apparently thinking of nothing, though as a matter of fact she was arranging in her own mind a short speech which would effectively crush Lady Bond at the next Red Cross meeting at Winter Overcotes. Sir Harry read the lower and more interesting of the Sunday papers which the kitchen kindly allowed him to have after tea on Sundays, and called Lydia's attention to various points of interest. While they were looking for the days on which they would be lucky in love or business, Noel talked to Leslie. Partly by nature, partly because it belonged to his profession in peace-time, he had the art of making people talk about their own subjects, and of taking an interest which was quite unforced, for in his experience most people could tell you something which was of use one way or another, at some time or another. Leslie did not as a rule like talking about herself or her work. Her thoughts about herself she poured out to her brother when he was on leave and in long letters when he was at sea, and did not wish to share them with any other person. As for her work, she preferred to keep it away from her private life and during the last three years there had been many things it was advisable not to mention at all. Even with her uncle and aunt, of whom she was very fond, she found it better to keep her own counsel. She trusted their discretion, but she felt that a good many people of their age still looked on the war work of the younger generation as a kind of amiable hobby.

But when Noel, with real kindness and real intelligence, began to speak to her about a department of her office with which he had had something to do, asking her opinion and listening attentively, she began to thaw. Her aunt was surprised but pleased to see Leslie's animation and felt grateful to the Mertons, who in their different ways had roused her niece from the state of apathy in which she had been since her arrival, an apathy that Lady Waring found slightly irritating, though she at once blamed herself for want of charity.

"What I want more than anything at the moment," said Noel, "is an intelligent person, male or female, to do a good deal of reading for me and make notes. It isn't hush-hush, but I need it. Do you happen to know anyone in London who would read hundreds of books and pamphlets and make a sort of digest, though the word has unfortunately become rather debased?"

Leslie said it seemed to stand for a mixed literary diet guaranteed to give any educated person literary indigestion in ten minutes. She then opened her mouth to go on speaking, but apparently thought better of it and shut it again.

'If you could hear of anyone, I would pay union rates whatever they are," said Noel, "and he or she, though more probably the latter I fear, unless I got a superannuated professor, could use my chambers if they like. My Mrs. Cripps is there every day and stirs the dust about."

"What you would need —" said Leslie, sitting up, reaching over to her aunt's writing-table for a pencil, and flattening open an old envelope which she took out of the waste-paper basket.

"No," said Noel, taking the envelope away from her and presenting her with a blank leaf which he tore out of one of those note-books that are held together by rings, "that is the kind of economy in which women are infamous, petty, and not in the least helping to win the war. Now, what would I need?"

"What you would need," said Leslie, half-annoyed, half-amused, and in any case determined to say what she wanted to say in her own words, "is someone under military age, which is practically too young to be any use now, or someone quite doddering with decay: there

149

doesn't seem to be much choice. Or someone with fallen arches or T.B."

"This is what Rose Birkett, now Mrs. Fairweather, the girl Philip Winter was engaged to, used to call foully dispiriting," said Noel, "but I expect you are right."

"What an odious girl that Miss Birkett must have been," said Leslie.

"She was one of the prettiest creatures I have ever seen," said Noel, wondering vaguely why Miss Waring suddenly looked so animated and really handsome. It had not occurred to him before that her pale face, with its wide forehead, pale greeny eyes and pointed chin could be so attractive. "But a nitwit *hors concours*. Philip was well out of it."

Miss Waring said carelessly that she supposed he had got engaged to someone else. Men always did.

"Not so far as I know," said Noel. "He worked very hard at the school and at his own classical stuff and being a Territorial, and then he got into the war."

"Why don't you ask him up here some time?" said Leslie.

Noel said he would love to, but being a P.G., not that they had managed to get down to brass tacks about the money side yet, made it a little difficult.

"I know Uncle Harry wants to talk to him about Horace," said Leslie. "I'll speak to Aunt Harriet about it."

"That is very kind of you," said Noel. "Lydia and he are very old friends and I know she will love to see him."

No, Miss Waring was not really so good-looking, he decided. It must have been a trick of the firelight suddenly dancing on her face. And she looked tired. Probably the afternoon had been too much for her.

"I will write to some people in London," said Leslie after making a few notes on the piece of paper, including the correct mode of addressing Noel by letter, which included an M.C. "By the way —"

She stopped.

"By which way?" asked Noel.

"Oh, any way," said Leslie, "but what I *did* mean to say was, do you think I could be any help? I can't go to town and work in your rooms, but I can work here. I've got a typewriter, and I am gently going to go mad out of London, without any work to do, and worrying about if the office is getting on without me — which of course it is. I'm afraid I've not got fallen arches or T.B., but I'm under orders not to do my own work at present. Would you like to give me a trial?"

Noel said he would like it very much, but it must be union rates. In Leslie he found one of the rare women who do not squabble and protest about money, and a rate of payment was settled.

"We don't change for dinner on Sundays now," said Lady Waring, which made them all look at the time, exclaim how late it was, and disperse to wash their hands.

CHAPTER
FIVE

The bargain between Noel and Leslie was duly ratified. Leslie worked for a couple of hours in the morning and very often again between tea and dinner. Her aunt fed her on milk and eggs from the home farm, her own restless mind was eased by a feeling that she was not entirely useless, and between the two she got a little fatter, slept better and was more content in mind. Lydia looked on benevolently, and apart from her general inclination to want to do any piece of work that she met, was delighted that Noel should have such a good secretary, for she herself had been splendidly resistant to education as practised at the Barchester High School under Miss Pettinger and had not the art of reading through a book with her eyes only and letting her subconscious mind pounce on the facts it needed. But she put in some valuable work on the farm, groomed Crumpet, sawed wood with Sir Harry, began to clip the hedges in the garden and wrote to Kate to ask her to look in the big trunk she had left at Southbridge and see if there was a little box with some horrid peasant silver buttons in it and send it to her.

Matron had not forgotten her promise to show Lydia the hospital, but she was a nurse short and the home suddenly filled up, so the treat was still to come. Private Jenks was frequently to be found in or about the kitchen, where he was a general favourite and mended everything from the cook's alarm clock to the hinge of the scullery door. His frequent and cheerful allusions to his next operation made Selina's large brown eyes overflow more than once, but though Private Jenks was a great one, in his mother's phrase, for comforting the girls, more particular those as didn't need it, a certain vague respect kept him from encircling Selina's buxom waist with a solacing arm. Perhaps her mother's long association with the gentry was reflected in Selina, perhaps her present position as what was almost confidential maid to her ladyship set her a little apart. But whatever the reason, Private Jenks felt for her a slightly reverent passion to which his easy-going soul had hitherto been a stranger.

At times Jasper, coming up to the house on estate affairs, would find the kitchen enthralled by Private Jenks's extremely untruthful stories of his own prowess, or his brilliant execution of popular melodies on the mouth-organ, while cups of strong tea went round. Jasper would accept from Cook a very large cup, kept specially for him, and sit stirring it in sardonic silence, watching that old Selina's Desdemona-like reactions to Private Jenks's lies; for such, we regret to say, they undoubtedly were. And as the liquid pearls gathered in Selina's eyes and her cheeks became flushed and her breath came in pants like a frightened bird — a simile which had dimly occurred to Jasper in connection with his profession, but remained unformulated owing to his opinion of the greediness, viciousness and general unprincipledness of the feathered race — he would choose a moment to let fall a word about taking a gun into Forkman's Spinney, or unbagging a ferret near that old rabbit-hole on Copshot Bank. Then would Private Jenks show himself in his true colours as a head keeper's son. At once he would be on his feet, ready to start immediately; kitchen, tea, brown eyes, all forgotten. Jasper would finish his cup and go out, Private Jenks in tow, casting a triumphant look at the femininity. Had Othello been a head keeper's son, much discomfort would have been saved. Cook would then bang the cups and saucers together, and the party would disperse, Selina already upset by the thought of the poor little rabbit and also, for her charity was universal, for the poor little ferrets going down that nasty hole.

Leslie Waring had not forgotten her promise to Noel that she would speak to her aunt about Colonel Winter; and if she chose to persuade herself that she was doing so entirely out of kindness, who are we to blame her? Lady Waring, who had for her part not forgotten that her husband had expressed a wish to see Colonel Winter again, quite agreed, and Lady Waring telephoned.

"Number, please," said the exchange.

"Oh, will you give me the camp, please," said Lady Waring.

"What number's that?" said the exchange, whose voice to-day was unfamiliar to Lady Waring.

"I never can remember," said Lady Waring. "You know, the office at the Dower House."

"I'm afraid I'll have to put you through to inquiries," said the voice icily. "We can't give numbers here."

"Oh, dear," said her ladyship, turning to Leslie, "what a trouble they are. One cannot possibly remember all these new numbers and everyone knows that the Dower House is the camp headquarters."

On her official or London side, Leslie felt it only right that regulations, however trying, should be carried out. On her private side, as a countrywoman and kin with the Warings, she fully shared her aunt's indignation and was just preparing to do battle with the exchange for her when Lady Waring held up her hand.

"Hush!" she said, listening earnestly to the receiver, and then putting her hand over the mouthpiece, "there's an extra-ordinary noise going on. A kind of quarrelling noise with a lot of booming, but the exchange always does boom. It must be the acoustics."

She reapplied herself to the receiver.

"Is that Lady Waring?" said a voice.

"Yes. Is that you, Palmyra?" said Lady Waring.

"Oh, good morning, my lady," said Palmyra Phipps, head of the exchange and niece of Mrs. Phipps, "was it the Dower House you wanted?"

Lady Waring said yes, and was there any difficulty?

"It's only a new young lady we've got here, my lady," said Palmyra. "She's from Barchester and doesn't quite understand the work. She boards with Margett and goes home for her day off. I'll put you through to the

Dower House at once, my lady. Who was it you wanted?"

Lady Waring said Colonel Winter.

"My sister, the one that's got triplets, used to be second housemaid at Mr. Carter's house at Southbridge School," said Palmyra, "and she says Mr. Winter as he was then was ever so nice, but a very quick temper. He was engaged to Miss Rose, but they broke it off. Just one moment, my lady."

Lady Waring thanked Palmyra, and blessing the fact that feudalism was by no means dead, listened for a reply. In an incredibly short time a voice said, "Colonel Winter speaking."

Lady Waring gave her invitation, Philip Winter accepted it, Thursday week being a date convenient to both. Leslie thought it would have been a good plan to invite Colonel Winter a little earlier, say the very next day, or even that very evening, but reflection told her that she was unreasonable, and that Colonel Winter was probably not very interesting and in any case would want to talk to Lydia who was his old friend. It then became obvious to her that Thursday week was one of those days that would never come. Wednesday week might arrive, nay, certainly would; Friday week was infallibly bound to arrive; but of the arriving powers of Thursday week she entertained the gravest doubts. So she applied herself vigorously to her précis writing and had several intelligent questions to ask Noel when he came back from the camp. Lydia, seeing them deep in talk, was delighted that Noel was getting such help in his work. For a moment she felt wistfully that it would

156

be great fun if she could help too, but she had a humble nature and fully recognized that she was not, in her inelegant phrase, brainy, and went off to attend to the stable dog who had an abscess in his paw.

The day of Philip Winter's visit happened to be also the day that Matron was at last free to show Lydia the hospital. This treat was arranged to take place before the men's tea, and at five o'clock Lord Stoke was to give his lecture on the Viking remains.

The whole plan for the lecture was nearly upset by Lord Stoke's patriotism. Having grasped the fact that petrol came in ships, that ships and men and petrol were needed for the demands of war and not for his comfort, he had put down his car, exhumed a very old brougham, last used by his step-mother, Lady Bond's mother, in 1911, and caused himself to be driven within a ten-mile radius in wet weather, in fine weather contenting himself with a stout old cob who was still equal to his thirty miles a day. When he had consented earlier in the year to lecture at Beliers Priory, he had not counted on December weather. The Priory was about fifteen miles from his residence of Rising Castle. The brougham could not go so far. By daylight he could and would have gone over quietly with the cob, making a long day of it, but with the early darkness and a five o'clock lecture this was impossible. There was a taxi at High Rising, but the Priory was outside the ten-mile limit for which taxis might be used, and the whole plan was about to crumble when it was discovered that Dr. Ford had to visit the hospital professionally on Thursday afternoon.

"I'll run you over, Stoke," said Dr. Ford, who often looked in at the Castle, for his lordship, though his deafness was past cure, liked to talk, 2nd Dr. Ford was one of the few people who could make him hear. "I'll run you over, but you will have to go rather early as I have business at the Priory. I'll wait and bring you back."

Lord Stoke expressed his thanks.

"Mustn't get you into trouble with the police, though," he said. "The Castle's out of your way. I shall walk down to the village and wait for you at Reid's Stores. There's always something to hear there," said his lordship, who was as inveterate an old gossip as could be. "Then no one can blame you for taking me to the Priory."

On the Thursday afternoon Lydia went through from the Waring's quarters by the long corridor into the big house where the hospital was. She was received by Matron in her sitting-room, formerly known as the Old Bookroom because some bound volumes of *Punch* and the *Graphic* lived there beside an unused rack for billiard cues.

"Such a quaint old room," said Matron, who in common with a great many other people thought any house was old if it was large enough. "You see I have given it quite a homey touch with my photos."

She indicated with a wave of her hand some three or four dozen photographs and snapshots of relations and friends, most of the female ones in the nursing profession. Among them Lydia was delighted to discover Octavia Crawley, winding a skein of wool with the assistance of an armless patient who was obligingly holding it on his feet.

"A real turn Miss Crawley had with our mutilated cases," said Matron. "She was always the first volunteer for any specially distressing case. Quite devoted. Here she is again, Mrs. Merton, in a group."

Lydia looked at a professional photograph done in Barchester of the Bishop, the Mayor and a number of other celebrities, flanked by nurses and convalescent soldiers, outside a house.

"Hullo, that's Barchester High School," she said. "I was there with Miss Pettinger."

"The photo was taken when the school hall was given up as a recreation room for the boys," said Matron. "Of course, I should have been in it, as Senior Sister at the time, but Miss Pettinger pushed in front of me just at the critical moment, really so unnecessary. But I beg pardon, she is a friend of yours."

"If you call a headmistress a friend," said Lydia vengefully. "She was a beast — we always called her B.P. behind her back for Beast Pettinger — and was always talking about the honour of the school and giving one bad marks for not hanging one's shoe-bag on the right peg. The boarders said it was ghastly, because she would come and kiss them in bed just when they wanted to talk."

"Well, I must say," said Matron, her opinion of Mrs. Merton rising by leaps and bounds, "if I hadn't been in uniform I would have spoken Right Out to Miss

Pettinger. But of course I was on duty and one can't think of oneself then. Nurse Poulter, who was there — that's her, just not in the picture on the right, you can see her elbow — said she wondered some people had the face to go on as they did."

With such a basis a firm friendship was very soon established between Lydia and Matron, who led her guest from room to room expressing her own admiration so ungrudgingly that Lydia found it quite unnecessary to say anything. When the Priory was taken over the basement was dismantled and used for furnaces that supplied the central heating and baths, or made into store-rooms. The top story had also been closed and the best bedroom furniture stored there, so that the hospital proper was housed on the ground and first floors. On the first floor, in the bedrooms on two sides of the central hall, the nurses slept and had their sitting-room, the other two sides being given to patients who required special care. On the ground floor a new kitchen and offices had been made in a suite of built-out rooms known for no reason as the pavilion; the big drawing-rooms and the dining-room were turned into wards, and the hall and billiard-room were used as reading and recreation rooms. Matron's office, in an angle of the hall near the pavilion, commanded a strategic position from which she could see what she wanted, ignore what she wished to ignore, and pounce when convenient.

The nurses' bedrooms and sitting-room with a wireless full on, though the room was empty, were duly admired. One or two nervous convalescents were woken from an afternoon sleep by Matron's quiet withdrawal. The wards downstairs were of course little used except at night, but Lydia was introduced to some bad cases and was an instantaneous success. Matron beamed at her new friend; Nurse Poulter came up on the pretext of asking Matron about Simmons's dressing but really to take notes of what in subsequent conversation in the staff sitting-room she called Mrs. Merton's costume; the other day nurses hovered.

The billiard-room, from which the billiard-table had been removed to the basement when the hospital took over, was already prepared for Lord Stoke's lecture. Ping-pong and card tables were pushed to the wall, chairs had been requisitioned, and a table and chair for the speaker placed under the portrait of Sir Harry's grandfather, which was so large and hideous that its owner would have been glad if the military had used it as a target for darts. The hall had been left much as it was, with its own furniture, and here men were writing, reading, smoking, and in various ways getting through a dull December afternoon.

From the door that led to the Warings' quarters came Dr. Ford and Lord Stoke.

"Good afternoon, Matron," said Dr. Ford. "This is your lecturer. Lord Stoke. Matron. I had to bring him early or else he couldn't have come, because of petrol. I'll leave him with you now. Mind you don't let him talk too long, as I've got to get back."

Matron shook hands with Lord Stoke.

"Oh, hullo, Dr. Ford," said Lydia. "I'm Lydia Keith, at least I was."

One of the soldiers who was writing looked up, looked at Lydia, and resumed his employment.

"Lord!" said Dr. Ford. "I've not seen you since you were a hoyden with a passion for riding on a cock on roundabouts at flower shows."

"I do adore cocks," said Lydia, "but I'm married now. I married Noel Merton, you know, Lavinia Brandon's friend."

"Bless that woman," said Dr. Ford. "Look here, you know how deaf Stoke is. Don't let Matron shout too loud. It only annoys him if he sees people bellowing and doesn't like to confess he can't hear. See you after the lecture. I've got some men to see."

He strode away, leaving Matron with her guests.

"You'll have some tea with me, Lord Stoke, I hope," she said. "It's only a quarter past four and the lecture doesn't commence till five."

Bearing in mind that Lady Waring had said his lordship was deaf, she was not surprised to get no reply, and led the way towards the sitting-room. The writing soldier looked up again as they passed.

"Tea will be here in a moment, Lord Stoke," said Matron at the top of her voice.

Lord Stoke nodded in a friendly way, but it was so obvious that he had not heard, that Matron made the motions of drinking a cup of tea, and pointed to the table to indicate that this refreshing liquid would shortly be served.

"What the dooce does the woman mean?" said Lord Stoke aloud to himself, without heat.

"Tea, Lord Stoke," said Lydia right into his ear.

"Yes, yes, of course," said Lord Stoke. "Now, who are you, young lady? I ought to know your face."

"I used to be Lydia Keith and now I'm Lydia Merton," said Lydia at the full diapason of her powerful lungs.

"That's right," said Lord Stoke, much pleased to talk to someone sensible who didn't mumble. "Your father had some cows at Northbridge. Nice animals, but he never did much good with them. How is he?"

"Dead," said Lydia in a bellow. "About two and a half years ago."

"Dear me, dear me," said Lord Stoke, patting Lydia's hand. "How time does fly. Well, well, I suppose it's what we'll all come to. Pomfret's dead, his wife's dead, Bond's cowman died the other day. Bond doesn't look what he was," said Lord Stoke, who in common with other elderly gentlemen took an enthusiastic interest in the decay or demise of his contemporaries. "Last time I saw him I said to Lucasta, 'Bond's breaking up fast, Lucasta,' she's my half-sister, you know. 'I'll be surprised if he lasts through the winter,' I said. He's younger than I am too, a good deal younger, but no stamina, no stamina."

The arrival of tea now eased the situation. Lord Stoke was loud in his approval of the hospital catering and ate a great deal of cake, ably seconded by Lydia. Matron poured out, gave an excellent pantomime about milk and sugar, and quite won Lord Stoke's heart by providing for him a very large teacup, for ordinary china was his abomination and he often asked for the slop-basin when among friends; especially among those who had cups that turned out and over at the rim, thus causing the tea to run down both sides of a thirsty man's mouth. Only one thing marred Matron's perfect pleasure, the question of Bloody Meadow. Lady Waring had promised to do her best to influence Lord Stoke, but how could she find out whether her ladyship had done so? The efforts she made to reassure herself on this point were vain, as Lord Stoke was telling Lydia about the infamous conduct of the Government in regard to pigs and finding in her an intelligent and sympathetic listener. Still, as Dr. Ford and Lord Stoke had come by the door from the servants' quarters, it probably meant that they had called on Lady Waring first, and she was more at ease. Had she been better acquainted with either of these gentlemen, she would have known that Dr. Ford preferred to visit his more distinguished patients by the back door as he said it made him feel eighteenth-century and in his proper place, while Lord Stoke found an approach via the stables and kitchen quarters of his friends far more productive of local gossip than the more usual approach by the front door.

At five minutes to five Matron said they ought to be moving. Lord Stoke caught her meaning, looked wistfully at Lydia and pulled out of the pocket of his old shooting-jacket, with some difficulty, a large and very untidy mass of papers.

"Hope they'll like it," he said. "Doesn't seem to me quite the subject with all this war going on. I should have thought a really constructive talk on dairy-farming after the war — but I dare say there'll be no cows after the war. If the Government have their way, there certainly won't."

Matron led Lord Stoke towards the billiard-room, Lydia in their wake. As she passed, the soldier who was writing got up and came towards her.

"Excuse me, miss," he said, "but I thought you mentioned the name of Keith."

"That was my name," said Lydia. "I'm Mrs. Merton now."

"Beg pardon, miss," said the soldier, whom Lydia now recognized to be a sergeant, "I mean madam. I just happened to hear you mention the name and I thought it might be a relation of Captain Keith."

"Colin?" said Lydia.

"Captain Colin Keith, that's right, miss," said the sergeant. "You haven't any news of him, have you, miss?"

"I wish I had," said Lydia. "He had a sort of embarkation leave and I haven't heard anything since, not for weeks. He might be in Africa, or he might be on a course in England."

"I *am* sorry, miss," said the sergeant. "My name's Hopkins, miss. I don't know if the Captain ever happened to mention it."

"I don't think so," said Lydia, "though I'm sure he would have if he had known we were going to meet," she added, with an insane wish to give pleasure.

"No, I expect not, miss," said Sergeant Hopkins, rather dashed. "I've a lot to thank the Captain for."

"Do tell me all about it," said Lydia sitting down, the lecture banished from her mind by the chance of talking about her dear Colin.

Sergeant Hopkins required little encouragement, and as long as he was allowed to express himself in his own slow, circumlocutory Barsetshire way, would probably have talked all night. His first words were interrupted by the sound of perfunctory clapping from the billiard-room, indicating that Matron had said a few introductory words and Lord Stoke was about to begin his lecture.

"Don't you want to go to the lecture?" said Lydia.

"Not if I'm not keeping you, miss," said the sergeant. "The boys are all right. They meant to be up to some funny business with Winnie, but they won't."

As he spoke he unbuttoned his tunic and pulled down the front of his khaki pullover. Inside it the kitten was curled up in a somnolent condition. It opened one eye, yawned a dislocating yawn and went to sleep again. With no further comment he began to tell Lydia how his wife had died a year ago while he was in camp and how kind Colin had been, pushing through his special leave, giving him the benefit of his legal knowledge about his wife's affairs and allowing him to talk. Lydia's eyes shone at this praise of her favourite brother and she felt an unmanly choke in her throat. Suddenly from the billiard-room came a roar of laughter of an extremely joyful and unrefined nature. Sergeant Hopkins clapped his hand to his chest, but Winston was safely there. Reassured, he continued his simple tale.

166

"Had you any children?" asked Lydia.

"Well, no, miss; no, we hadn't," said Sergeant Hopkins, having apparently thought out this question with some difficulty. "Perhaps it's as well. And then I was for light duties only, so I got sent here to be in charge."

By probing, which she did with her usual ferocious benevolence, Lydia discovered that the sergeant had been in a lorry collision in a fog, and had had injuries which had affected his eyes. If, he said, the Captain had still been there, he'd have seen he went with the battalion, but the Captain had been sent off somewhere while he was in hospital and he had lost his address. While distrusting even Colin's powers of getting an invalid soldier out of hospital, Lydia sympathized heartily with Sergeant Hopkins. Her deep interest in all Colin's affairs and the long letters he had always found time to write to her had made her familiar with the names of many of his brother officers and men, so that she was able to discuss regimental matters in a way that confirmed the sergeant's good opinion of Captain Keith's sister.

During the whole of this conversation further roars of laughter had been coming from the billiard-room at intervals. Lydia was pleased that Lord Stoke, whose celebrity in the cow world had impressed her, was being such a success and wondered what he was saying. Sergeant Hopkins, satisfied that the kitten was not implicated, thought the boys were enjoying themselves and told Lydia more about himself and his nice little greengrocery business in Northbridge which his mother was carrying on while he was in the Army. His mother, he said, was a rare one at business and up at half-past five every morning, summer and winter.

"She's always at me to marry again, miss," he said, "but it seems to take the heart out of a fellow when his wife dies. A bit like Mrs. Crockett, she was, miss, but not so cheerful-like. I'd like you to see mother, miss, if it's not asking too much, when she comes over to visit me."

Lydia said she would be delighted. A tremendous outburst of laughing, cheering, clapping, stamping and cat-calls now showed that the lecture was over. Lydia promised to let Sergeant Hopkins know when she heard from Colin. Lord Stoke emerged, flushed with success; Matron followed him, her eagle eye looking for her sergeant in charge.

"I'm for it," said Sergeant Hopkins resignedly. "But it's worth it to have a talk about the Captain, miss."

Lydia, grasping the situation, begged Matron to forgive her for not attending the lecture, giving the true and reasonable excuse that she had met a man who knew her brother, and apologized for having kept Sergeant Hopkins talking so long. Matron graciously accepted her excuses, Sergeant Hopkins saluted, touched his tunic, winked, and vanished into the billiard-room. Lord Stoke complimented Matron on the nice body of men she had under her, said he had never had an audience with a keener sense of humour, and issued a general invitation to any convalescent who felt like walking fifteen miles each way to come and see his dairy herd, which, he said, he had managed to keep as a pretty good going concern in spite of those meddling fools in Whitehall. A nurse then brought a message that Dr. Ford was over at Lady Waring's and would Lord Stoke join him there, so he and Lydia said good-bye to Matron.

"I suppose," said Lydia, "you don't want an odd V.A.D. You said you were short-handed and I'd be awfully glad if I could help. I've got my uniform and everything at South-bridge, at my sister's."

Matron said she would certainly consider the suggestion, and then Lydia and Lord Stoke went back to the servants' wing, where they found Dr. Ford gossiping with Lady Waring and Leslie.

"How are you, Lord Stoke," said Lady Waring loudly. "I hope the lecture went well."

Lord Stoke, beaming, said it had gone very well indeed. In fact, it had been one of the best audiences he had ever spoken to. The interest the men took in the excavations in Bloody Meadow was, he said, most marked, and several supplementary questions had been asked about it, though he was sorry that, doubtless owing to the acoustics of the place, he had not quite caught them all. Lady Waring, who had a pretty shrewd guess as to the nature of the questions, felt rather guilty, but as she had not seen Lord Stoke before the lecture it couldn't be helped.

"Well, Stoke, we must be off," said Dr. Ford. "You are doing me credit, Miss Waring," he added to Leslie. "Keep going, and we'll have you fit by the time your leave is up; before that, I hope."

Cutting short Lord Stoke's account of how Lord Bond was breaking up, he seized that worthy peer and hustled him away.

"What really happened?" Lady Waring asked, when they had gone.

Lydia said she didn't know, but the men had laughed and cheered a great deal, on which Lady Waring made no comment.

"I didn't really hear it," said Lydia, "only the noise through the door, because I was talking to Sergeant Hopkins who was in Colin's regiment and wanted his address. I promised I'd let him have it as soon as I heard from Colin, but if he is in Africa I shan't hear for ages probably. Or he may be in England and not allowed to write."

"At least I know that Cecil *isn't* in England, which is something," said Leslie generously.

Lady Waring thought of the last war, when letters to and from France were almost as regular as letters to Brighton, and how George's letters had gone on coming after the news of his death. She thought of it now as something which had happened to a young woman whom she hardly recognized; she thought of it very seldom, for which she was grateful.

The telephone bell rang in the hall. Lady Waring was just about to switch it through to the sitting-room when the noise of the front door being shut was heard and Sir Harry's voice answering the call. Then he came in.

"The 6.25 was punctual for once," he said, "and one of the hospital cars brought me up. That was Colonel Winter just now, my dear."

Of course, thought Leslie Waring. He would be kept at the office to-night. Still, we are very comfortable as we are.

"He said someone had just turned up who is going abroad," Sir Harry continued, "and is only down for the night. I asked him who it was but the connection was very bad. It sounded like his brother, so I asked him to bring him here. Is that all right, my dear?"

The General's wife, with one rapid mental glance over her dinner, said of course he was right. Lydia said Philip hadn't got a brother, so it must be someone who wasn't his brother. Sir Harry said it might be someone with a name like Brother. Or even called Brother, he added. Leslie Waring thought, rather bitterly, that friendships between men were very fine things, but such a bore for other people if it meant that one couldn't count on getting a proper talk with people who were coming to dinner. Then she reflected that Cecil would certainly have asked any friend to dinner in such an emergency, nay preferably five or six friends or friends of friends, so it must be right. Also, to be quite truthful with herself, she had always liked his improvised parties, so why should she not like this?

Noel as a rule did not get back till nearly eight, so Lydia usually dressed earlier and left the room free for him to throw his belts and spurs and things about, as she unfairly said, for not only was he very tidy, but he did not wear spurs. On this particular evening she was dressed sooner than usual and found herself alone in the sitting-room. While she was knitting, with only one reading lamp on for economy, she heard the front door bell and Selina hurrying to open the door. There was a noise of people taking off overcoats and Philip came in. Lydia got up to greet him, but suddenly stood quite still and felt almost faint. Then she gave a most unladylike yelp of happiness and hurled herself into the arms of her brother Colin.

"Oh, Colin!" she said, rubbing her face on the front of his tunic with sheer joy, while she held out a hand to Philip. "Why didn't you say it was you?"

"Ask Philip," said Colin. "He rang up."

"I did say it was your brother," said Philip.

"Sir Harry thought it was *your* brother, only I told him you hadn't got one," said Lydia, recovering her wits. "Oh, Colin, how lovely. How long are you here? Why didn't you tell me you were coming?"

Colin explained that he had not been able to let her know that he was coming, in fact he would never have been there at all except that he had been sent to the camp at a few hours' notice without even much hope of being able to get to the Priory, had found Philip and by the greatest luck been able to come this evening.

"Bother the Warings," said Lydia, most ungratefully. "We can't have a proper talk."

"Bother me too, I suppose," said Philip.

Lydia said Rot, he didn't count, which he took as a kind of compliment, for he knew his Lydia.

"Colin," said Lydia, looking up at him with sudden earnestness. "May you tell me if you have come to say good-bye?"

Colin did not answer.

Then Lady Waring came in and was delighted to meet Mrs. Merton's brother, and so was Sir Harry, and so was Leslie Waring when she came down a little late owing to a misunderstanding with her lipstick which had not satisfied her and had to be wiped off and put on again twice. Not that Colonel Winter would notice, for if he had been engaged to a girl like that Miss Birkett he probably preferred a lot of make-up sloshed on anyhow. But when she saw Philip she felt unreasonably glad that she had taken pains. Noel was the last to come in. He had already seen Philip at the camp and was delighted that he could spend the evening at the Priory. Dinner passed pleasantly. Both Leslie and Lydia behaved very well, taking part in the general conversation and deferring prettily to Sir Harry, who was in high good humour with so much military company and had not the faintest idea that any of his guests wished to talk to each other in peace.

After dinner, Lady Waring with great skill managed to fence Colin and Lydia away into a corner behind her writing table and begged them to excuse her if she wrote some business letters. Sir Harry then pounced on Philip to have what he called a good talk about Horace, so Noel went to sit by Leslie and discuss the work she was doing for him. Leslie answered all his questions, but in a rather distracted way.

"I'm so sorry, Major Merton," she said at last. "I'm not attending."

"Are you feeling poorly?" said Noel. "I do love the expression. My grandmother always used it."

"Not so much poorly as low," said Leslie smiling. "It's Captain Keith."

"If you will tell me exactly what he has done, I will have him out to-morrow morning and run him through the gizzard at once," said Noel. "Word of a major."

"It's not anything he has *done*," said Leslie. "It's just his *being*. It makes me think about Cecil, and it is so *dreadfully* long since I heard from him. Sorry. Don't let's talk about it."

"But do let's, if that's any help," said Noel. "Lydia always says she feels better when she has talked about Colin, and better still when she has cried. You wouldn't like to cry, would you? We are quite safe here. Lydia and Colin will gabble for ever if left alone and if my eyes do not deceive me your uncle is going to sleep."

This was indeed so. Although Sir Harry was, in Matron's words, thoroughly enjoying his talk about Horace, which consisted largely in reminiscences of his undergraduate days at Oxford, where he had been better known as a lively member of the Bullingdon than a reading man and had narrowly escaped being sent down, his day in London, his dinner and an unwonted glass of sherry which he had produced in honour of the military, were too much for him. He suddenly, according to his peculiar custom, went to sleep bolt upright in his high-backed chair, looking so handsome with his fine face in repose that Lady Waring nearly got up to kiss the top of his head. Philip, catching Noel's eye, came softly over and joined him and Leslie.

"I do like your uncle, Miss Waring," he said.

Leslie said warmly that Uncle Harry was an angel. So was Aunt Harriet, she added, in a different way.

Noel said Lady Waring was one of the seraphim and the General one of the cherubim; with reservations of course in both cases, he made haste to say.

"I agree," said Leslie seriously. "I can see Aunt Harriet with blue wings being good and wise and Uncle Harry with red wings being quite adorable."

The three then talked in low voices in a conspiratorial way, for though nothing was said it was tacitly recognized that Lydia and Colin must be given as much rope as possible, to which end Sir Harry must stay asleep. But on no account, said Leslie, must they whisper, as that always woke her uncle up at once. So what with the effort of talking in a quiet voice that was not a whisper and the discovery that Cecil Waring and Philip Winter had been at the same prep. school, Leslie enjoyed herself so much that she forgot how anxious she had been to talk to Colonel Winter in peace.

Presently, Lady Waring, having finished her writing, collected some papers and went towards the door. Noel got up to open it. As she passed out she signed to him to follow her into the little dining-room.

"I am so sorry, Major Merton," she said, "that I can't ask your wife's brother to stay the night. Nothing would have given me more pleasure, but we literally have not a bed."

"It is more than kind of you," said Noel, "but Lydia never expected it and of course she would of all things dislike to give you any trouble. And may I say how grateful I am to you for managing to get her this opportunity of talking to Colin. They are quite devoted and I am afraid he is going abroad at once."

"Poor child," said Lady Waring. "Does she know?"

"Colin has not said it in so many words," said Noel, "but I am certain she suspects, and I suspect she is certain."

"I would be glad to do anything I could for her," said Lady Waring. "It is so good for my husband to have young company and someone who loves the country. Leslie usually goes about with him, but with her illness and the dreadful weather we have had, she has not been up to it. Your wife has done her so much good too. In fact," said Lady Waring, with one of her rare smiles, "I am getting almost reconciled to Captain Hooper because he sent you both here."

Noel said God forbid. Lady Waring went away to her room, telling him to make any arrangements that seemed good to him on Lydia and Colin's behalf. Noel was moved by her gratitude and by her praise of Lydia, for Lady Waring, though a charming and considerate hostess, was fastidious in her tastes and conservative in her ways, and it pleased him greatly that his dear Lydia should have penetrated their hostess's defences and been recognized for what he knew she was. The dining-room was comfortably warm, the less Sir Harry was disturbed the less likely he was to wake, so Noel fetched his dispatch-case from his room and sat down to some work.

Meanwhile Sir Harry slept, bolt upright, looking like a handsome stone image of himself, and as he slept the hands of the clock moved on, ignored by Lydia and

Colin in their eager talk of themselves, Kate and Everard, their elder brother Robert and his wife and children, their old home. Colin too had heard that the business firm which had taken Northbridge Manor might be moving back to London and he thought Robert would never really want to live there. The place had been bought by Mr. Keith when Robert was just leaving his preparatory school and had never been to him or to Kate the childhood's home that it had been to Colin and Lydia.

"I wish I could buy it from Robert," said Colin. "Then when the war's over I'd go and live there and keep pigs, and you and Noel could come whenever you liked and we'd have picnics on the river and go to Parsley Island."

"Oh, do you remember the picnic when Rose was so awful to poor Philip?" said Lydia. "And I never told you, Colin, that Twitcher found Philip's ring that Rose threw at him and he dropped it into the pool. I brought it down to give Philip to-night."

She took from her bag the ring with its ruby and diamond flower.

"What a day it was!" said Colin. "And you and Geraldine Birkett and Tony Morland cleaning out the pond. What a sight you were. What's happened to Tony and those other boys?"

Lydia said she thought Tony was a gunner officer now. The others she knew nothing about. There was a moment's silence. If one has not heard of one's friends for some time, one does not always quite wish to know. The news might not be happy, and on Colin's last night one does not want sad things. Lydia wished she had not thought of a last night; very likely, she said to herself, he will have another night, and anyway people often get embarkation leave and then go on turning up till one almost wishes they had gone the first time. If only Colin could have an accident; not a bad one, but just bad enough to make him be fit for light duties only. Then quite suddenly the words, "light duties," roused a memory, and with a pang of remorse she thought of Sergeant Hopkins.

"Oh, *Colin!*" she said, "how dreadful of me! I had quite forgotten!"

Full of contrition she sat staring at her brother.

"I'm sorry you've forgotten," said Colin. "But what?"

"Sergeant Hopkins," said Lydia. "He's in the hospital here and he wants to see you and I promised I'd let him know if I heard from you. I wonder if it's too late. I know Matron quite well. We might try. The quickest would be to ring up the night sister from the hall. Come on, it's only ten o'clock."

Very quietly they left the sitting-room. Just as Lydia was going to take the receiver off, Selina came by.

"I say, Selina," said Lydia. "Have you any idea when the soldiers go to bed? My brother wants to see Sergeant Hopkins."

"Well, madam, I know the sergeant hasn't gone to bed," said Selina, her eyes shining at the thought of being able to help Mrs. Merton's brother, "because he was in the kitchen just now. He's teaching us all to play poker. Cook said not for money, because that's gambling, but Sergeant Hopkins said we'd play for buttons, so we all got our work-boxes out."

"Who won?" said Colin, amused.

"I did, sir," said Selina, "and I *was* so upset, because the sergeant hadn't got any buttons of course, not having a workbox, so he cut off one of his own buttons, sir, off the shoulder-strap on his battledress, and gave it to me. He won't have gone yet, sir, because Cook was just making a cup of tea and the sergeant said he felt quite on top of the wave to-day because of seeing the captain's sister, and if the night sister wanted him she could come and fetch him. I'll run down, sir, and tell him to come up and see you. Would you like to see the button, sir?"

In her plump, pretty, though by no means smooth hand she showed him a bone button.

"It's an awfully decent button," said Lydia admiringly. "What are you going to do with it?"

"Private Jenks says he can make a brooch of it for me, madam," said Selina.

"Oh, was he there too?" said Lydia, struck by the very crowded life that went on in the kitchen.

"Well, you see, madam," said Selina, her eyes beginning to brim over, "he's got to go back to hospital for another operation. I *was* so upset when I heard. He won't say what it is, though Cook and Baker teased him ever so, but he said if he had to go into hospital again he'd enjoy himself while he could. He ought to be in bed by nine, sir, so when he wasn't there the sergeant came over to fetch him. I'll tell the sergeant now, sir."

Lydia and Colin looked at each other and for the first time that evening laughed as if they were at home and the war had never been.

"Do you mind if I stay here?" said Lydia. "I feel if I took my eyes off you, you might vanish."

Colin begged her to stay. Selina returned and delivered Sergeant Hopkins over to Colin. The men were soon well into talk about the regiment and the sergeant's own affairs. Lydia, sitting swinging her legs on a big chest where rugs were kept, idly fingered the railway guide and watched the hall clock telling the moments. Presently a thought came into her head and she consulted the guide; with such concentration that she was startled by the sergeant's good-bye.

While the company were so dispersed, Philip and Leslie sat together in the sitting-room, continuing to talk about nothing very particular very comfortably. Philip had liked the voice of the girl whose suitcase he had carried in the dark. He had thought, as he walked back to the camp, that even if he did not recognize her by daylight, for the night had been too dark and wet for him to get more than an impression of her appearance, he would know her again by her speech. Now he found that he also liked her face and enjoyed her way of looking at things in general. He had heard from Noel about the work she was doing, he saw that her intelligence was considerable, and he vaguely thought that Noel was lucky to have such a delightful assistant, contrasting her in his mind, much to their disadvantage, with two young ladies in uniform in his office who were not remarkable for looks or brains, or indeed for anything except thick ankles and great punctuality in knocking off. Then the talk came round to her brother, and Philip was touched by her truly unselfish pleasure in Colin's visit and said so.

"Well," said Miss Waring very frankly. "I would be jealous of Lydia if I could — no, not jealous, that's a horrid thing, envious, I mean — but I simply can't. In fact, next to having Cecil here, I can think of nothing nicer than having Captain Keith. I wish he hadn't to go so soon."

"So do I," said Philip. "Lydia does care for him so much. More than anything in the world except Noel, I think."

"I care for Cecil more than anything in the world that ever was, or is, or will be," said Leslie, almost savagely.

"I am sure you do," said Philip, thinking of the seas, the nights, the storms that would lie between Leslie and her brother till he came safely home.

"It isn't only that I care for him frightfully," said Leslie, impelled by the hour, the quiet, the peaceful room, to unburden her heart, even while she told herself that she must be boring Colonel Winter, who liked gay creatures like that Miss Birkett, very much indeed, "but he keeps me safe."

Philip looked questioningly at her.

"You know. The place," said Leslie impatiently, but always keeping her voice low for her uncle's sake, possibly too for the sake of a conversation which must not be interrupted.

"But I don't know," said Philip. "You mean he looks after things here when he is on leave?"

"Of course he does that," said Leslie, again with impatience, "but what I mean is that when Uncle Harry dies, which I hope will be never, all this belongs to Cecil. But if Cecil is killed, I am the only one left."

If Dr. Ford had come into the room at that moment he would have been seriously annoyed and probably sent her to bed and told Philip he was a fool to let the girl excite herself. But Philip was no fool. His years of schoolmastering at Southbridge had not included the psychology of war-wrecked young women, but it had included some patience and understanding for troubled youth; a patience and understanding developed against the handicap of his own naturally quick and suspicious temper till, except on very rare occasions, it had become his servant. Looking at Miss Waring, whose face had suddenly become small and peaked, he thought of the early autumn more than three years ago, before term began, when he had come back to the school in his Territorial uniform to visit Everard Carter, and young Holinshed, aged seventeen, had suddenly turned up, half-demented because he could not join the Army and be killed at once. He and Everard had let young Holinshed talk himself out, had convinced him that the best help he could give was to wait for orders, and after a huge tea had sent him away comforted and resolved to be patient. The look in poor Holinshed's face he saw again in Miss Waring's. Unfortunately he could not talk to her for her good, nor, so soon after a very good war-time dinner, would a large meal be of any use. But if patience could help, patience there should be; all that she needed.

"Of course I adore the place," Leslie continued, not looking at Philip, "but I have always adored it with Cecil. How could I live here without him?"

Philip thought of a great many wise and sensible things that he might say, but every one of them sounded priggish. Sir Harry, perhaps reached by Leslie's voice, though she had never forgotten to restrain it, suddenly opened his eyes and was wide awake. At the same moment Lydia and Colin came in, and then Noel, who had heard the noise, returned from the diningroom.

Philip, looking at the time, said regretfully to Colin that they ought to go.

"Will you say good night to your aunt for me, Miss Waring?" he said. "I shall write and make my excuses for not saying good-bye. Will you perhaps let me come again?"

Leslie gave him her hand.

"I would like it very much," she said.

Lydia now approached and took possession of Philip with her old impetuosity.

"How is Colin going to-morrow?" she said.

Philip said one of the camp cars was going to Winter Overcotes to catch the London train and Colin would go in it.

"Then I shall go from here with Sir Harry," said Lydia. "He always goes on the 8.25, which is direct to town. I can see Colin at the junction before he gets into the train. Oh, and here's the ring. Remember your vow. And come again soon."

"Of course I will," said Philip, putting the ring in his pocket. "I can't hug you here, because it wouldn't be seemly and I would hate Noel to kill me, but I will another time. I won't tell Colin. Then if you can't manage it he won't know."

"But I will manage it," said Lydia. "I always saw him off to school and college and I shall see him off to the war."

There was no answer to this. Sir Harry made the leave-taking easier by insisting on seeing Philip and Colin off himself, which was destructive of sentiment. Lydia and Colin made a grab at each other, kissed quickly, and the party was over.

"I think I'll go to bed," said Lydia, a little too off-handedly. "Coming, Noel? Good night, Leslie."

"Good night," said Leslie. "I'm so glad I saw your brother. He is so like you and I liked him so much. I hope he'll be here again very soon."

Lydia smiled her thanks, but did not see fit to speak. Leslie had a moment's illusion that she had held her husband's arm as if to steady herself, but she might have imagined it. Left alone, Leslie wandered vaguely round the room putting things tidy. It was no business of hers if Lydia gave Philip Winter a ring. It might be one that belonged to his mother if he had one, or his aunt if he had any, and Lydia had been getting it mended for him. She bore no malice against Lydia, for anyone who was so fond of her brother must be wholly admirable. But as for Philip Winter, she said to herself, tossing her head at his absent figure, it was a poor sort of man that took a ring from a woman. And though she knew she was being very foolish and unreasonable, she had a sudden wish that Philip was there so that she could tell him exactly what she thought of him and be very cutting and hurt him. At which pleasant thought she nearly cried, falling into a welter of self-pity for which she knew there were no grounds whatever. Then Sir Harry, having seen Philip and Colin off, came back, inquired for the Mertons and hearing that they had gone to bed said it was time Leslie went too.

"What a nice boy Mrs. Merton's brother is," he said, "and I had a splendid chat about Horace with Winter. We must ask him here again, Leslie."

"Yes, do let's, Uncle Harry," said Leslie, much cheered by the thought of seeing the despicable creature again. A man who understood about Cecil so well must have a good side. She kissed her uncle good night.

"You women," said Sir Harry, looking intently at her. "One never knows where to have you. A moment ago you looked done in, now you are looking as pretty as ever. Well, well, *varium et mutabile semper.*"

"Yes, Uncle Harry," said Leslie. "Good night."

CHAPTER
SIX

When Sir Harry came down to his early breakfast next morning he was much surprised to find Mrs. Merton already drinking her coffee. On hearing that she intended to accompany him as far as Winter Overcotes in the hope of catching one more glimpse of her brother he inwardly disapproved. A soldier's life was made of partings and the less womenfolk bothered him the better. He ate his breakfast behind the newspaper, which was what he called a penny-halfpenny rag, for *The Times* in its stately march did not come till later, too polite to tell his guest he didn't want her company, yet unable to be perfectly cordial to her. Lydia, more sensitive to fine shades than of old, felt less and less comfortable. She had told Noel the night before what her plan was.

"I can't stop you," said Noel, his heart wrenched by the sight of her controlled distress, "and I suppose I wouldn't if I could. Is it really worth while, darling, just for a few minutes at the station?"

To which Lydia had replied that she knew it wasn't worth it, but go she must. Noel, who was the only child of his parents, could not understand the peculiar link of brother and sister when the link is there. Often it does not exist, but when it does it is a very strong and enduring sentiment; and an elderly brother and sister who have lived together for many years are often more devoted than husband and wife. But though he could not share the sentiment from his own experience, he recognized its importance to his Lydia and loved her for it; though to be fair he would have loved her just as much without it. So he gave his blessing to her morning pilgrimage, on the one condition that she should do her best not to wake him at an unearthly hour next morning, for it was quite bad enough, he said, to get up in any case in this weather. And, though he did not say this aloud, he did not wish to see his Lydia go off in the cold and dark on a journey which would but turn the knife in the wound. Then he blamed himself for being morbid and wishing selfishly to keep Lydia to himself, and so went to sleep.

"I'd have ordered Coxon's taxi if I'd known you were coming, young lady," said Sir Harry, throwing the mangled body of his newspaper on to the floor. "Are you ready?"

Lydia was ready. They walked together to the station almost in silence. It was a black, blustering morning. No warmth of light shone from the Priory or the village. The station was cheerless and only half awake. Presently the London train came in. Sir Harry and Lydia got into the nearest carriage. As their eyes became accustomed to the faintly illumined gloom they saw a man in some kind of uniform half-asleep in a corner. The train stopped with a jerk, and with a loud shriek began to go backwards. The man woke up.

"Hullo, Waring," he said, leaning forward into the dim light.

Sir Harry looked at him and recognized Mr. Dean, brother-in-law of Mr. Palmer at Worsted. Mr. Dean, a wealthy retired engineer, and his wife had spent a summer at the Dower House before the war and so fallen in love with the country that they had bought a house near Winter Overcotes and settled there. He and Sir Harry met from time to time on committees and county war work, where his practical sense was extremely useful.

"Morning, Dean" said Sir Harry. "I didn't recognize you at first. You're wearing a boiler-suit like the P.M."

"I might take offence, but I won't," said Mr. Dean. "It's Observer Corps."

Sir Harry apologized handsomely, saying his eyes weren't as young as they used to be.

"I thought of saying that myself when you were so offensive about my uniform," said Mr. Dean, who was on very good terms with Sir Harry, "but it might have sounded personal. I've been up at the Observation Post all night. When I say all night I slept a good deal, but it was just as uncomfortable, or even more so. Well, it's about the only thing old fellows like myself are fit for, and now we hear some talk about our being too old and being sacked. Not much sympathy for the elderly who want to help nowadays, Waring."

"I mustn't complain," said Sir Harry, "for I'm probably ten years older than you are, but old generals are about the most useless thing this war has brought up. We'd be more use dead, or just as much use as we are alive."

This led to an interesting discussion of their exact ages, from which it transpired that Sir Harry, who was seventy-six, though he didn't look it, was eight years older than Mr. Dean. Each gentleman then commiserated the other's misfortunes under the discouraging attitude of a world that had no use for age, while secretly thinking, nay knowing, that his lot was much the harder and more persecuted. The train, after banging backwards and forwards in an aimless way so that the teeth of every coach rattled in its head, had now settled down on the stretch between Lambton and Winter Overcotes. Lydia in her dark corner had not taken any part in the conversation. To tell the truth she still felt mildly in disgrace with Sir Harry and was not sorry to remain in obscurity.

The other occupants of the carriage having, owing to excess of courtesy on both sides, left the battle of grievances drawn, were now circling warily for fresh points of attack.

"I've got my niece Leslie down at the Priory," said Sir Harry. "She has had a bad breakdown, poor girl. Worked to death on that committee of hers — very useful work she does — and then torpedoed coming back from America. We are worried about her brother too. He is at sea again, and we have heard nothing for more than two months. It makes me think of the last war. You know we lost our boy in 'eighteen," he added.

Now Mr. Dean was a kind man and respected Sir Harry, and if it gave the old general (for as such he thought of him) any pleasure to boast about a niece with a breakdown and a nephew at sea, he should. But to bring up the son who was killed in France in the last war was a hitting below the belt which could not be tolerated.

"Yes, it is worrying to have anyone at sea," he remarked. "We heard from the twins last week, I am glad to say. You know they are in the same squadron — I mustn't say any more — and seem to be enjoying life and seeing a lot of each other. Laurence is still in Scotland, I am glad to say, doing liaison with the Poles, and Margaret and the babies are with him. Helen is driving for the Wrens as you doubtless know, while her husband is seconded from Oxford for special work at the Censor's Office. We get airgraphs quite often from Gerald in India, and Robin has passed out top from his O.C.T.U. Betty — you know she married an American — has been doing good work for the American Red Cross and may be coming over here with her husband, as he is on a commission to inquire into the reorganization of the peanut industry after the war. They will fly, of course. Susan is working for the prisoners of war at Oxford, and we only have Jessica at home, but she collects salvage in her holidays and is learning ju-jitsu. Yes, Waring, it does make one feel old to see all the young people are doing."

This was an undoubted defeat for Sir Harry, and we may say, well deserved, for if ever a man asked for it, that man was he. But Sir Harry, going on the general principle of never knowing when he was defeated, looked round for his reserves, camp-followers and sutlers, and brought them all into action in the shape of Lydia, whose existence, sitting as she was in a far corner in the dark, he had honestly half-forgotten.

"By the way, Dean," he said carelessly, "I should have introduced you before. Mrs. Merton, this is our neighbour, Mr. Dean. Mrs. Merton, Dean, who is staying with us, she and her husband, Major Merton, who was in France when the Belgians ratted on us and was all through Dunkirk. Her brother is just ordered abroad and she is going to see him off at Winter Overcotes."

By the introduction of Colin, Mr. Dean was temporarily checkmated. The train stopped at Winter Underclose and Mr. Dean got out. After a few words with the stationmaster he came back and opened the door.

"There was an accident higher up the line," he said. "That's why we were delayed. A shunting engine ran into a truck and derailed it. Nobody hurt. I thought you'd like to know."

"Thank you," said Sir Harry. "And remember me to your wife. I hope she is well."

"Rachel? Never been better," said Mr. Dean. "She runs the Land Army for these parts, you know."

He shut the door and went off. Sir Harry was silent, reflecting upon the Deans' large, competent family; upon his own childless old age. And, being an honest man, he had to admit that only very rarely did his childlessness weight upon him. The wound had healed, and he could not truly say that he would have wished it otherwise. He wondered if Dean's anxiety with five sons serving was greater than his own had been with one; whether to lose all with one swoop, or to view the possibility of losing a child at a time was the more cruel. And to this he could give no answer. Then as the unpleasant daylight came into the carriage he saw Lydia's face, and his heart smote him for lack of courtesy to a guest who was not happy.

"I dare say this accident will mean a delay at the junction," he said. "If so, you ought to have more time with your brother, Mrs. Merton. What a nice fellow he is."

This amende at once raised Lydia's spirits and they talked on and off in a friendly way till they got to Winter Overcotes.

Here Doris and Lily-Annie, much excited by the accident, though regretting that there had been no loss of life, were having the pleasure of yelling "All change" up and down the platform. Mr. Beedle was on the platform and opened the carriage door.

"I am so sorry, Sir Harry," he said, "that you will have the trouble of changing. There was a slight accident on the loop to the main line and we cannot run the London train through this morning. It does seem a shame to trouble a gentleman like you, Sir Harry, but you will have go to the high level for your train. In the old days we would have had the breakdown gang out at work and everything clear by the time you came along, but times aren't what they were."

Sir Harry quite agreed, and knowing that without Mr. Beedle's presence the London train would not go, lingered to talk to the stationmaster. But Lydia, on hearing the news, fled like a deer to the steps, mounted them two at a time, took one comprehensive glance up and down the platform and made straight for Colin. He was as surprised to see his sister as anyone could have wished, and much touched by her affectionate devotion, though at the same time fearing that a second parting might be even harder for her than the first.

As they talked, feverishly, not knowing how soon the train would come, Lydia was conscious of someone hovering in their immediate neighbourhood. She also noticed that Colin moved away a step or two from time to time, or turned in a slightly different direction.

"I think," said a not very attractive voice at her elbow, "Mrs. Merton and I ought to be introduced."

"Oh, Hooper," said Colin, trying to look surprised at the appearance of that officer with whom he had driven in from the camp. "Lydia, this is Captain Hooper."

"Pleased to know you," said Captain Hooper. "Nasty sort of day for the last of England and all that. Still, Keith will be having wine, women and song in sunny we-won't-say-where, while you and I, Mrs. Merton, are the girls he left behind him."

Colin wondered for a moment if, in view of the need for good officers and he knew Hooper was one, intentional brother-officercide would be overlooked by the Army Council. Feeling that it would not, he regretfully stifled his wish to push Captain Hooper onto the line and tried to edge away.

"And how is the old general?" said Captain Hooper. "A fine old boy, Mrs. Merton, quite the old English gentleman, isn't he? But quite a relic, we don't want his type now. We want to be progressive, up-in-the-morning-early, like Russiaris."

At this moment Sir Harry and Mr. Beedle came up the platform. Mr. Beedle was telling Sir Harry about the latest letter he had received from his prisoner-of-war son, and Sir Harry was giving a kind, heartfelt, sympathetic attention that was balm to Mr. Beedle's spirit.

"Good morning, sir," said Captain Hooper jauntily. "Are you off to the gay metropolis like me? Take my tip, and it's worth having, if you want a good lunch go to the Poubelle in Hentzau Street. It's run by Les Free Frogs and there's a spot of pre-war Dubonnet if you ask Mademersell Rose at the bar."

Sir Harry had hardly ever been deliberately rude in his life, but undoubtedly he would have snubbed Captain Hooper in a way even that thick-skinned officer would feel, had not Mr. Beedle, with the tact that is given only to the officials of the Best Line in England, spoken to the general.

"I beg your pardon, Sir Harry," he said, "but I've a message for you. Would you mind stepping this way, Sir Harry, and you too, sir," he said to Colin, "and the young lady."

Detaching them with a masterly flank movement from Captain Hooper he shepherded them to his office, led them in and shut the door.

"You'll excuse me, Sir Harry," he said, "but you'll be warmer here and I shall come and fetch you myself when the train is in. Is the lady going to London, Sir Harry?"

194

"Thank you so much, but I'm only seeing my brother off," said Lydia.

Mr. Beedle looked compassionately at her and went away. Sir Harry considerately read a number of recent railway regulations, strictly private, to himself, while Lydia and Colin stood together with little to say.

"You know you were an old goose to come, Lydia," said Colin.

"I had to." said Lydia. "Oh, Colin do you remember the Grand Opening when we used to tidy the boat-house and get the punt and the boat ready and the coracle? All hundreds of years ago. And last time I had the Grand Closing I did it with Noel, before we were married, because you were away in the Army. This is the real Grand Closing, isn't it. Promise not to be killed, or missing, or a prisoner, or *anything*."

"All right, I'll promise," said Colin. "Take care of yourself, old goose. Give Noel my love."

"Sorry, sir, but the train is in," said Mr. Beedle at the door. "I have locked a compartment for you, Sir Harry."

Majestically he preceded them to the train and unlocked a door.

"It goes to my heart, Sir Harry, indeed it does, not to be able to offer you a first-class carriage. I call it a great shame and I hope it is one of the first things the directors will put right after the war. No, madam," he said to a small, wiry woman with a mop of frizzled dark hair and a leopard-skin coat, accompanied by a yellow-faced man with dark sad eyes wearing a béret and huddled in a sheep-skin coat, "this carriage is reserved."

"You can reserve carriages no longer," said the woman, lighting a cigarette. "England is now entirely démocrate. Viens, mon petit Gogo."

"Pardon me, madam," said the unmoved Mr. Beedle. "There is plenty of room higher up. This carriage is reserved."

"Ah-ha, see me this type which says reserved," said the woman to her companion who, obviously terrified of authority, was shrinking further into his sheepskin coat at every fresh outburst. "I will tell you, Mr. Station-chief, that in Mixo-Lydia if you wish a voiture réservée which you say reserved carriage, you address yourself at the Touritza-Büro which you say Tourist Bureau for an affiche qui porte les mots Riservistza ce qui veut dire Réservé avec le nom which it is for Gogo and me Brownscu, et vous la collez à la fenêtre you steek her onto the window and if anyone tries to force an entrance you fight freely. You remember, Gogo, tu te rappelles quand ces deux types ont essayé de nous prendre notre voiture réservée et t'ont battu? Ah, combien je regrette nos chemins de fer Mixo-Lydiens! Et le chef de gare qui t'a giflé, tu te rappelles? Et le juge d'instruction qui t'a condamné à une amende?"

"Czy, pròvka, pròvka, pròvka," said the wretched Gogo, nothing of him now visible but his despairing eyes.

"He says, 'No, never, never, never,'" said Mme Brownscu, stubbing her cigarette out with much

196

determination against her companion's coat. "We will not lose our time to argue. Viens vite, Gogo."

She seized her unhappy companion and choosing a carriage pushed him violently into it, nearly knocking over Captain Hooper as she did so.

"It is Russian you are? Yes?" she demanded, standing on tiptoe and thrusting her face alarmingly near his.

"Oh no, not at all," said that officer. "But I'm all out for the Help for Russiar idear."

"Montez donc, imbécile," said Mme Brownscu, shoving Captain Hooper into the carriage and getting in almost on top of him. "Nous allons lui causer un peu des Russes, Gogo, n'est-ce-pas. Avez-vous jamais vu éventrer une femme par un Russe par exemple?" she added fiercely to her new friend. "On va vous en dire des nouvelles. En Mixo-Lydie —"

But here the engine let off steam and the rest of this interesting conversation was lost.

"It must be some of the Mixo-Lydians from Southbridge," said Lydia, laughing in spite of herself. "No one knows if any of them are married or not. Oh, *Colin*. Good-bye, good-bye."

The guard blew his whistle and waved his green flag. Colin, leaning from the window to Lydia, gave her a hasty hug. The train pulled out round the curve.

"I'm glad Colin didn't wave to me," said Lydia stoutly to herself. "And I'm glad the line goes round so that I can't see him. Well, that's that."

She walked aimlessly down the platform, suddenly realizing that Colin had gone and that she did not know when there would be a train to Lambton. She tried to look at a time-table outside the booking-office, but the figures were slightly blurred and it did not seem to matter very much what they said. Perhaps it would be a good thing to go for a little walk along the platform. Then one could come back and ask a porter when the next train was.

Mr. Beedle, having as it were dismissed the train with his blessing, said a few words to Bill Morple at the barrier and looked round to see that all was well. The waiting passengers had gone by the train, the arrivals had all gone out into the town, only one figure was to be seen at the far end of the platform. A faint drizzle was now blowing across the line from the leaden sky and Mr. Beedle thought that the lady down the platform would be getting wet. Then he recognized the figure as the young lady who was with Sir Harry, the same young lady that had been seeing her brother off; and quite illogically he felt that she would somehow get wetter than other young ladies who weren't staying at the Priory or seeing their brothers off.

Lydia, walking determinedly back from the end of the long platform, her hair and coat frosted with the fine, cold rain, her eyes and mind elsewhere, was suddenly conscious of a figure in front of her and recognized the stationmaster.

"Excuse me, miss," said Mr. Beedle, "but it is coming on to rain quite fast. Won't you come into the waiting-room, miss? We've a nice bit of fire there. It's only the general waiting-room, I'm afraid, but we can't get coal enough for the ladies' waiting-room too. I don't like it at all, miss, having to put ladies into the general, but that's what war does."

"Oh," said Lydia, dragging herself back to the scene before her. "I hadn't noticed the rain. Could you tell me, please, when there's a train to Lambton? I forgot to look up the trains."

"Well, miss, you've just missed the local," said Mr. Beedle. "She pulled out two minutes ago. If I'd known, miss, I'd have held her for you. The next isn't till 12.43."

"Oh, well," said Lydia desolately, "I suppose I could wait. Or is there anything to see in the town? A museum or anything?"

"Well, miss, I'm afraid there isn't much a lady like you would like at present," said Mr. Beedle. "There is the Whatmore Mechanics' Institute, but it doesn't open till twelve and the museum department is closed. It was a fine museum, miss, with a lovely collection of birds' nests and their eggs, but the evacuees broke so many of the cases to take the eggs that the trustees had to close down for the duration. There *is* the exhibition of Mixo-Lydian Atrocities. I dare say you saw the lady who's arranging it getting into the train. But I don't think you'd like it, miss."

"Thank you very much," said Lydia gratefully, "I'm sure I wouldn't. I'll just go and sit in the waiting-room. You see, I was seeing my brother off. He's probably going abroad and I never thought about getting back."

Mr. Beedle hesitated. He well remembered his mother seeing him off to the last war and how Dad had put her arm under his and taken her away as the train got to the curve. He hardly liked to remember how he and Mrs. Beedle had seen young Henry off when he was suddenly recalled from leave, and how they had talked cheerfully to each other of all meeting again soon. The rain was driving more fiercely and the platform and lines glistened in the pale grey light.

"Excuse me, miss," said Mr. Beedle, hesitating no longer, "I'm going off duty now for an hour. I don't hardly like to suggest it, but if you'd care to come back to our place and have a cup of tea, I'm sure Mrs. Beedle would be gratified, with you staying at the Priory. Sir Harry was kind enough to stand god-father to our boy. Prisoner-of-war now, miss," said Mr. Beedle, trying to convey by a cheerful business-like voice that his son was doing very well and that if a like fate awaited the young lady's brother he would find himself quite pleasantly situated.

Lydia grasping at this kindness, accepted at once. Mr. Beedle took her back to his office while he gave some instructions to Doris Phipps and Lily-Annie Pollett, and then requested Lydia to come with him. At the barrier she gave up the outward half of her return ticket to Bill Morple, who eyed with satanic scorn this alliance between bureaucracy and capitalism.

"Look at old Beetle making up to people just because they know Sir Harry," said Bill Morple to Doris and Lily-Annie. "Fair makes me sick. Seeing an officer off she was. Now in Russiar it's all different. Officers don't have no more rights than you or me."

"Well, I hope they've got more moustache than you, Bill Morple," said Lily-Annie, whose tender heart had been much moved by Mr. Beedle's brief description of Lydia's plight. "A lovely little moustache the officer had."

Bill flushed angrily, while both girls indulged in loud, hooting laughter, for his efforts to grow that ornament had never gone further than a few scrubby hairs.

"All right," said Bill, "all right. But you aren't the only clever ones. There's some that knows a bit more than you. Where's old Beetle's silver cup, eh?"

"Well, where is it, then?" said Doris.

But Bill with a sudden access of virtuous industry, began to roll empty milk-churns along the platform, thus drowning all attempts at further questioning.

"Barmy!" said Lily-Annie scornfully to Doris.

Lydia, although friendly and adventurous in casual relationships, had never before been for a walk with a stationmaster, and had an uneasy feeling that everyone would stare. But Winter Overcotes early on a cold, dark winter morning had quite enough to do in getting its rations, hurrying to its office, standing in a queue at the Food Office, rushing into the W.V.S. office for information about a rumour of coupon-free khaki knitting wool, or hopelessly going to Miss Beak at the Morleena Domestic Enquiry Bureau to ask if there was a daily available for half a day a week, was not in the least interested in anything outside its own concerns. Mr. Beedle, walking at a good pace, occasionally touching his cap to some friend or acquaintance, led Lydia down the station slope, round by the Town Hall, up the wide market place, past Woolstaplers' Hall, now the unwilling temporary seat of the Town Council. Here an old wall, relic of Overcotes Palace, a summer residence of the pre-Reformation prelates of Barchester, skirted one side of the quiet road. Mr. Beedle passed through a narrow archway in it, followed by Lydia who, in spite of her heavy heart, stood entranced by what she saw: a double row of mellow red brick houses, each with two stories of small but well proportioned sash windows and a dormer window in the red-tiled roof, and to each house a little front garden with a gate onto the flagged pathway between. Over the roofs could be seen the tall trees that had been part of the Palace garden. Boon's Benefit, as this little backwater was called, was the relic of a foundation for old vergers, sextons and other cathedral servants, built by the executors of Thos. Bohun, D.D., Canon of Barchester, who died in the Great Plague and left moneys to that end. In the middle of the nineteenth century the foundation had fallen into disrepute, at about the same time as the public attack was made on Hiram's Hospital in Barchester. The Charity Commissioners, after considerable delay, had sold it to the railway Company, who had put the houses into good repair and let them at moderate rentals to chosen employees. By an oversight they had chosen a good architect to overhaul Boon's Benefit, and Mr. Barton, father of the present architect of that name, had made the cottages watertight and comfortable without spoiling their appearance. Each house, by a pleasant whim of a director of the time, was called after one of the company's crack engines of the "River" class, and Mr.

Beedle's cottage, the last on the left, was called River Rising, with River Woolram next door and River Rushmere opposite.

Some basely said that Mr. Beedle's fence was so well kept and repainted because he used the company's paint. This was quite untrue. Mr. Beedle, seeing trouble ahead, had hoarded from the beginning of the war seven-pound tins of green and white paint with turps to match and repainted his fence every spring. He also repainted with infinite care the charming window-box, made by his own hands. It had a little white fence with a gate in the middle, carefully modelled on the level crossing gate near Winter Underclose. This gate, envy of all the children in Boon's Benefit, opened on a hinge, and as it opened so did a wooden signal, scale model of the station signals, go up. When the gate was closed the signal went down, the intention being to show that traffic in the shape of lobelias, geraniums and yellow musk could now pass unimpeded from end to end of the window-box. Some younger officials with new-fangled ideas had protested against geraniums as old-fashioned and suggested some nice spring bulbs, but Mr. Beedle was adamant. Hyacinths and crocuses and suchlike were very nice in the front garden, he said, and if some people said the sparrows tore the crocuses to bits, well if those people took the trouble to put a few sticks among the crocuses and wind black thread among them, those thieving sparrows wouldn't come anigh; but geraniums were the proper thing for a window-box. So every summer the red geraniums, tended through the winter in the little glasshouse behind, bloomed fiercely outside River Rising, filling the front room with their pungent smell. Between the geraniums grew lobelias of the most violent blue. But instead of golden-tawny musk Mr. Beedle now grew marguerites, for red, white and blue were our colours, and if old Hitler seed them they'd give him a bit of a shock.

But now in midwinter the window-box was desolate. Lydia, not knowing its summer bower, admired the gate and signal and was enchanted by the little grotto below it composed of broken china, bits of old tile from the ruins of Beliers Abbey, bottle-ends, chips of marble and granite (by favour of G. Smallbones, Monumental Mason, Orders Executed in All Styles), the whole topped by a cherub with a broken nose and one wing, dug up by Mr. Beedle in the back garden. This edifice was the joint work of Mr. Beedle and his son Henry and was immortalized in a picture postcard sold at the stationer's and the toy shop.

"Walk in, miss," said Mr. Beedle, opening the front door and standing aside.

He followed Lydia, shut the door and called out "Mother."

"Coming, Beedle," said a voice, and from the kitchen Mrs. Beedle appeared.

"This young lady is staying with the General," said Mr. Beedle, hanging his cap on a peg. "She was seeing an officer, her brother that is, off this morning and missed the Lambton train. It's a cold day and we can't have a nice fire in the ladies' waiting-room, so I asked

204

the young lady if she would come back and have a cup of tea. This is Mrs. Beedle, miss."

While he was speaking he had taken off his official coat and put on an old jacket.

"There now," said Mrs. Beedle. "There was a stranger in my cup of tea this morning. I've just got the kettle on the boil, miss, and I'll light the fire in the front room in a minute. Or, if you don't mind, the kitchen miss, it *is* more cosier-like."

Lydia thanked her and said she would like tea in the kitchen very much.

"Well then, Beedle, don't stand there blocking up the passage," said Mrs. Beedle, very unfairly, as her husband was behind Lydia. "Come in, miss, and sit down."

Lydia followed her hostess into the kitchen. A good fire was burning in the little range. Through the window she saw a long strip of garden, exquisitely laid out with vegetable beds. Many of these were empty at the moment, but well dug. At the end, through the bare branches of a large pear-tree, the shingled spire of the old parish church could be seen.

Lydia sat down and took her gloves off. Mrs. Beedle cast one all-seeing look at her.

"Well, Beedle, you *are* a great stupid," said his wife, "calling the young lady miss, and her staying at the Priory."

Mr. Beedle said with great truth that he couldn't see the young lady's hands through her gloves and he was sure there was no offence.

"I'm really Mrs. Merton," said Lydia apologetically. "My brother is Captain Keith. He's a gunner and he's in the same armoured division with the Barsetshire Yeomanry."

"Then he'll know our Henry, for sure," said Mrs. Beedle, with the unshakable conviction that anyone in the British Army must know anyone else.

"I expect he does," said Lydia. "Where is your son?"

"Prisoner-of-war, madam," said Mrs. Beedle.

"Oh!" said Lydia. "Oh, I *am* so sorry."

"Thank you, madam," said Mrs. Beedle. "I'll show you his photo. He was able to send us one from Germany."

She took down from the mantelpiece a photograph of a group of men who looked to Lydia exactly like any other group of men she had ever seen; not starved-looking, and some of them apparently in high spirits.

"That's our boy, miss," said Mr. Beedle, putting his finger on a large young man with a grin.

"Don't take no notice of Beedle, madam," said Mrs. Beedle apologetically. "Can't you remember the young lady's married, Beedle?"

"Sorry, mother," said Mr. Beedle. "Yes, that's him, miss. He doesn't look too bad, does he?"

Lydia said he looked splendid. Silence fell. Mrs. Beedle looked at her husband with a look which she meant to express that he wasn't to bother the lady, and which he took to mean a command to get Henry's last card out of the little drawer in the table in the front room. Lydia wondered, as we all do, whether people who tell one about relations killed, or missing, or as in this case prisoner, really want to talk about it. She didn't very much want to talk about Henry Beedle herself, with Colin's departure and the months or perhaps years of anxiety that were to come so fresh in her mind, but it was strongly borne in upon her that Mr. and Mrs. Beedle would not have introduced the subject if it was nothing but pain to them, and that it would be only courteous to take an interest. If they did not want to pursue it further, one could always switch off to something else.

Mr. Beedle was back almost immediately with the prisoner's card in his hand.

"Now, Beedle," said his wife, "you don't want to go bothering the lady with that card."

Lydia saw Mr. Beedle's disappointment, guessed Mrs. Beedle's protest to be mere form, and said she would very much like to see it.

"Well, read it, Dad, can't you," said Mrs. Beedle, basely changing her note, "and don't keep the lady waiting."

Mr. Beedle made a great show of putting on his spectacles, coughed, and read aloud:

" 'Dear Dad and Mum, Thanks for the letter it was fine.' That," said Mr. Beedle, "was the letter Mother and me wrote him in September. It seems a long time to get an answer, but as we have got one we can't complain. 'We had a concert party with community singing it was fine. We have been loading cabbages but the soil isn't near so good as ours. It is fine getting the fags from the Red Cross and the parcels and all the boys say what price the old Red Cross. Well Dad and Mum I'm keeping fine. There is a railway where we load the cabbages but not like Our Line but I kid myself I hear the old 6.25 down whistling at the level crossing. All the best to you and Grannie and all friends from your loving son Henry. P.S. I'm keeping fine.'"

Mrs. Beedle wiped her eyes. Mr. Beedle looked proudly self-conscious.

"That *is* a nice letter," said Lydia, all her doubts gone, speaking with the whole force of her warm nature. "I think it's a splendid letter. Where was he taken prisoner, Mrs. Beedle?"

"After Dunkirk, madam, same as a whole lot of our Barset-shire boys," said Mrs. Beedle.

"My husband was there," said Lydia. "He got back one of the very last. When I got his telegram to say he was in England again I thought it was to say he was dead. Oh, I do hope the war will be over before too long and Henry will come back."

"And I hope your brother, the Captain, will be back safe before very long, miss," said Mr. Beedle.

Everyone now had another cup of tea and there was some cheerful talk about the day Henry would come home and how the engine-driver of the 6.25, an old family friend, would give an extra loud whistle as he passed the level-crossing gates to honour the prisoner's return. Then Lydia was shown photographs of Henry from six weeks onwards, and the wedding group of Mr. and Mrs. Beedle, and Mrs. Beedle's mother, who died at ninety-five and would never wear her false teeth. At last Mrs. Beedle looked at the clock.

208

"Time you was going, Beedle," she said.

"Would you mind," said Lydia, who had been casting about in her mind as to how she could best repay the Beedles' kindness, "if I sent some extra money to the Red Cross and asked them to use it for cigarettes for the soldiers in prison camps?"

This suggestion evidently gave great pleasure; so much pleasure in fact that Lydia felt ashamed that a gesture which to her would be no sacrifice should mean so much to her kind friends.

"Will you be kind enough to give my humble respects to her ladyship, madam," said Mrs. Beedle. "I was nurserymaid there under Nannie Allen just before Mr. George went to school. I hear Nannie's Selina is at the Priory now. A pretty girl she was, and if you'll excuse my saying so, all the men on the place were round her like flies round a honeypot. And then she had to take and marry old Mr. Crockett. I wonder if she's changed much."

"She is very pretty," said Lydia, "and very kind. And certainly there always seem to be some of the convalescent soldiers in the kitchen, or Jasper."

At this Mrs. Beedle laughed heartily. With many thanks Lydia said good-bye. Mr. Beedle went back to the station and Lydia, warmed by tea and her friendly reception, felt less depressed and went for a walk in the little town. She tried to see the church which was locked, tried to get one of Mrs. Morland's novels in a Penguin, and failing that bought a thriller called *Doom at the Deanery* to read at the station. But it was so dull that she asked Doris Phipps, who was talking to Bill Morple, if she would care for it.

"Ow, yes," said Doris. "I don't mind reading a bit sometimes."

"You hadn't ought to read that stuff," said Bill Morple contemptuously. "Now I'll tell you a book you did ought to read —"

"Ow, I know you and your books," said Doris Phipps. "Now I like a nice book like *Film Stars at Home* and *Film Stars and the Men They Love*. They're lovely books. But thanks ever so for the book, Mrs. Merton."

"How did you know my name?" said Lydia.

"You're staying with Sir Harry, aren't you?" said Doris Phipps. "Mum's obliging on Tuesdays and Fridays and she said Mrs. Crockett says you've got some lovely camiknicks. Sir Harry's a lovely gentleman, isn't he?"

Lydia heartily agreed. Then at last the 12.43 came in and took her back to Lambton. Now that the excitement of her morning call had worn off she felt a chill of sadness fall on her again; but she thought of the Beedles, and though she knew she could never be as simply valiant as they were, she determined to do her best. Leslie Waring thought that anyone who could be so cheerful at lunch after seeing her brother off to the wars could not have much imagination. It is probable that Lady Waring gave Lydia credit for unselfishness.

CHAPTER
SEVEN

After a great deal of nervous politeness on both sides the question of terms was approached, shied away from, reapproached, argued, counter-argued, and finally reduced to a provisional agreement.

The Mertons, who were very comfortable at the Priory and very grateful to the Warings for having them, felt that nothing they could pay would represent the kindness they were receiving. This position put before them an alternative of nothing at all, or about a hundred pounds a month. As neither of these sums (if you can call nothing a sum) came anywhere within the region of practical finance, the whole matter had to be reconsidered. Lydia, studying the back page of *The Times*, saw that delightful homes with h. and c., near bus route, cinema, and shopping centre, with use of kitchen and bathroom, vegetables, eggs, golf, fishing, bridge, refined and cultured or bright and cheery society, could be had for anything from three and a half to twelve guineas a week. Against this must be put the facts that she and Noel did not want buses (much preferring the train), cinemas, shopping centres, golf, fishing or bridge; that they did not feel particularly refined or cultured and certainly not bright or cheery, and though they did want to have a bath would have thought twice before meddling in the kitchen. Inquiries among friends of Lydia's who were being or having paying guests were of little more help, as there was always some special factor, such as living in a very large decaying house in a hollow five miles from the lodge gates with no servants, bad and irregular meals, lots of drink and an aerodrome in the grounds, which made the rent outrageously high, or living as one of the family in a very small villa in a dormitory town with excellent but hugger-mugger meals and any amount of talk about the neighbours, which made the rent ridiculously low.

The Warings, who had never taken paying guests before, were equally at a loss. When Sir Harry had said often enough that no guest under his roof should ever pay a penny, not to speak of all the work Mrs. Merton did in the garden and the stables, and what was hospitality coming to, his wife, who had always been paymaster and done the accounts, pointed out that their overdraft was not getting any smaller and it would not be fair to Cecil to miss any chance of improving the financial situation even by a few pounds. This Sir Harry pooh-poohed, but when Lady Waring suggested that Major Merton might feel hurt if asked to accept what would really be charity, and that if Sir Harry did not like to take money from a guest he could always put it into National Savings, her husband was so overcome by this point of view and, we may add, this very fallacious reasoning, that he gave in, on the condition that he should not be bothered about it.

Having got so far, Lady Waring, with affectionate vengefulness, thought it was high time her husband took some responsibility for his own household, so choosing an evening when Lydia was in bed stifling a cold she caught on the wet, bitter morning when she was seeing Colin off, and she and Leslie were going to a Mothers' Union meeting in the village, she told Sir Harry he must discuss the matter with Major Merton after dinner.

Accordingly Noel and Sir Harry dined together very comfortably. Sir Harry, whose conscience was smiting him with a two-edged sword, in one direction for finding it almost impossible to bring himself to the scratch, in the other for neglecting his wife's express wishes, was at first not quite at his ease, but as dinner went on accompanied by a very interesting discussion about a possible successor to the Bishop of Barchester (not that there was, alas, any immediate probability of the present Bishop's resignation) he recovered his spirits, and by the time they had drunk their coffee in the sitting-room he had quite forgotten about the unpleasant subject.

"You remember, sir," said Noel presently, "Northbridge Manor where my wife's people used to live? The insurance people who took it after the air-raids on London are going back. They want to keep part of the house in case of further emergencies, but my brother-in-law to whom it now belongs tells me they did it all up very nicely, so we might be able to live in part of it later on if we came to an agreement with him. Lydia is devoted to the place."

213

"Quite a nice little place," said Sir Harry, not condescendingly or belittlingly, but simply from his mansion and his several thousand acres. "I hope that's not likely to happen just yet, though. We don't want to lose you and your charming wife."

"It's extremely nice of you to say so, sir," said Noel, "and we can't be grateful enough for all your kindness to us. But that brings me to a point that I ought to have spoken about before: what terms you will accept for Lydia and me. I am ashamed to think of the length of time we have been here without arranging our affairs. Had you any sum in your mind, roughly, sir?"

Sir Harry was a soldier. That is, he was ready to fight to the death when necessary, but saw no necessity to seek the bubble reputation in his lodger's mouth.

"Oh, well, Merton," he said. "Time enough to discuss that. Let sleeping dogs lie, you know, and all that. It's a pleasure to us to have you, so let's leave it at that. Any news in the camp this evening?"

"Nothing particular," said Noel. "We've got a new man, a Major Spender, but he has only come for a short time on a special job. But seriously, sir, we can't go on consuming your food and drink indefinitely without paying our share."

"As for drink," said Sir Harry, "except for a bottle of sherry the night Winter came to dinner and your wife's brother, I don't think there's been any, apart from beer of course. No, no, I couldn't dream of it."

"We were thinking of suggesting twelve guineas a week, sir," said Noel.

"Good God, no!" said Sir Harry, and was stricken dumb, thus leaving Noel uncertain as to whether his host thought it too much for one person, or too little for two; or perhaps barely enough for one and ridiculous for two. "Besides, I'm rather busy this evening. Got some letters to write about the Roads Committee of the County Council. We'll talk about it another time, my boy."

So saying he got up nervously and went into the diningroom, where he had a large bureau for his many letters and papers. Noel felt almost snubbed. Two things, however, reassured him — one that he had done what in honour he simply must do; the other that Sir Harry had called him "my boy." This he had not done before and Noel valued it, for he had become very fond of his host.

So after looking at the paper he wrote a few letters and went up to bed, for everyone kept fairly early hours, leading as they did very busy lives.

Here he found his wife Lydia sitting up in bed, her head tied up in a large silk handkerchief, reading Gibbon.

"How's your cold, darling?" he said.

"Rotten," said Lydia. "I say this is an awfully good book. I mean he puts things the way you'd like to yourself if you knew how. It's what I call an educated book."

Noel said it was on the whole very well thought of.

"You're nice and early," said Lydia.

"The fact is," said Noel, "that I tried to make Sir Harry talk about what we should pay him and it frightened him so much that he went away."

"What did you say?" asked Lydia.

"I suggested twelve guineas a week, and all he said was, 'Good God!'" said Noel. "Which was a good sentiment, but not exactly helpful. Then he fled the country and went to write letters, so there we are, exactly where we were. I think, my love, it is your turn now."

"All right," said Lydia agreeably, if indistinctly. "I did try to talk to Lady Waring about it once, but this time I won't let her go till it's settled. I'm beginning to feel like a Mixo-Lydian refugee, living on other people."

"What is this revolting smell?" asked Noel, picking his pyjamas up.

"Eucalyptus," said Lydia. "I thought as I've got a cold I'd better put a lot on your bed and then you wouldn't catch it."

"All I hope is that you will be quite well by to-morrow," said Noel. "Not that I wish you any ill, but I'd like you to get the full blast of this stinking stuff."

Lydia made no answer and stared straight in front of her.

"Anything wrong?" he said, for his Lydia never took offence and he feared she might be feeling really ill.

"No," said Lydia, coming back to consciousness. "It was only Gibbon. It made me think of the summer Tony Morland and his friends came to Northbridge and Hacker had a chameleon he called Gibbon. Do you remember?"

"Someone told me," said Noel, "that Hacker was in the Ministry of Information. I wonder if he has his chameleon with him, and what colour it's turned."

"Flags of all nations, I should think," said Lydia, and relapsed into the *Decline and Fall*.

Next day, whether owing to the eucalyptus, or to Noel's curse, or because it would have been better any way, Lydia's cold was much abated. She came down before lunch and finding Lady Waring at leisure decided to have the matter out.

"I do think, Lady Waring, that it is quite time we settled what the rent is," said Lydia, who saw no reason to beat about the bush in a matter which was useful to both parties. "Noel and I were thinking of twelve guineas a week if that's all right."

"I told Harry he must speak to your husband about it last night," said Lady Waring, "but I gather that he didn't; so you and I had better talk it over now, Mrs. Merton. As a matter of fact, the sum Harry and I thought of on the one occasion when I got him to consider the matter was eight guineas. I mean for the two of you, of course."

"That's very kind of you," said Lydia, "but I honestly don't think it's enough. We are so very happy here."

Lady Waring said she was very glad to hear it, as she and her husband enjoyed having Major and Mrs. Merton with them, not to speak of the young companionship for Leslie, and as they could only offer them simple food and no drink to speak of, twelve guineas would be an unreasonably large figure to ask.

"Let's split the difference then and call it ten," said Lydia.

"Ten guineas a week would suit us excellently," said Lady Waring. "It is really so much easier to settle things oneself. Men talk so much that they get nothing done."

"Or else they are afraid to talk about it at all, like Sir Harry and Noel last night," said Lydia.

Lady Waring smiled and said she was glad it was comfortably settled.

"And now, Mrs. Merton," she said, "as we hope to have you here for some time, I am going to ask if you will let me call you Lydia. It is such a charming name and it suits you."

Lydia blushed with pleasure and as she afterwards said to Noel, was so glad that Lady Waring did not go on by asking her to call her Harriet, for it would have made her very uncomfortable. But no such thought had come into Lady Waring's head, for to her Christian names were not things to be thrown about lightly and she was capable of feeling just as much affection for people without dashing into informal modes of address. It had not slipped Lydia's notice either that Lady Waring, for the first time since they had lived under the same roof, had spoken of her husband as Harry, instead of by a more formal title. All which Lydia, very rightly, took as proof of confidence and was correspondingly pleased.

"We are both grateful to you," said Lady Waring, "for your goodness to Leslie. The work your husband has been kind enough to find for her has really taken her out of herself; so have her drives and walks with you. It is so good for her to have young companionship. I am too old and a very busy woman."

Lydia said, with truth, that they liked Leslie very much.

"Well, that is all very satisfactory," said Lady Waring, kindly, yet with her slightly aloof manner as of one who was for ever the chairman of some committee or another. "And I hope Major Merton will not be moved for a long time to come."

"So do I," said Lydia, "only —"

"Only?" said Lady Waring.

"Well, I've got to do *something*," said Lydia.

"Do something?" said her hostess. "But you are. I really can't think how Harry would get on without you. Don't talk nonsense, my dear."

"Yes, but," said Lydia, frowning as she tried to formulate her ideas, "it's not real work. You see, I'm twenty-four and I haven't got any children and I'll be put into something if I don't do something. I suppose I really ought to be in a factory in the north of England, but while Noel is in England I don't think either of us could bear it, which is very unpatriotic but we can't help it."

Lady Waring's face assumed an expression of faint disgust.

"A factory, my dear?" she said. "Quite unsuitable. Why not the Land Army? You are excellent in the garden and on the farm and then you can go on living here just the same."

"But I mayn't," said Lydia.

Lady Waring looked incredulously at her. Then a light dawned. Of course the child was going to have a baby. Land work would be entirely unsuitable, or indeed any work at all. She must stay here and go to the excellent cottage hospital later, and so quickly did Lady Waring's mind run ahead that she had already turned Selina, whom she didn't really need though it was a delightful luxury to have her, into a nurse and arranged for Nannie Allen to come up to the Priory when Selina was off duty. Her further lightning decision to keep Lydia at the Priory in the event of her husband being sent abroad was rudely broken in upon by her guest.

"You see," said Lydia, "I was on the land for a year when we were in Scotland, and I simply loved it. But that's why I can't be in the Land Army."

Lady Waring was so roused from her usual calm and gentle manner as to say "What?" in an emphatic and almost a fierce voice.

"I know," said Lydia. "That's what everyone says. But it's a law. If you've been on the land more than six months you can't join the Land Army."

"I must look into this," said Lady Waring, all her years of experience in managing other people's lives as a general's wife and a county lady rushing energetically into the fray. "It is quite ridiculous."

"That's what I think," said Lydia, "but there it is. So I think I must do Red Cross. I really am a V.A.D. as well as a land worker, and I was in a hospital in Yorkshire all the time Noel was up there, though why they call it V.A.D. when you have to do it and you get paid for it, I can't think. It's only since we came south again that I have been out of work. It makes one feel a bit of a traitor," said Lydia pensively.

"I am sure Harry could find a good job for you in London," said Lady Waring, "and you could go up with him every day."

Lydia thanked her very much, but said a job in London wouldn't seem like really working, and then Leslie came in to say lunch was ready, so the question dropped for the time being.

Perhaps because of the convalescent hospital there were still two posts a day at the Priory. The second post came directly after lunch and they were still in the dining-room when Selina brought the letters in. Lady Waring and Leslie always had a large second post, as the London letters were often delayed in the morning. Both were fully occupied in opening dull if fairly important letters, Lady Waring about county affairs and Leslie about the office, for Dr. Ford was now letting her do some of her work by post, when an exclamation from Lydia made them look up. She had an air of such distress that they were almost alarmed and begged to know what had happened.

"It's a letter from Octavia Crawley," said Lydia.

"No bad news, I hope," said Lady Waring kindly, and with the unspoken thought that the Dean and Mrs. Crawley, with eight grown-up children, all, whether married or unmarried, serving in some way, could hardly escape some misfortune.

"Not bad for them," said Lydia. "At least it's bad for Octavia. You know she is engaged to Tommy Needham, who was Dr. Crawley's secretary, and he turned into an army chaplain and was in Iceland and then he got sent to Africa, and Octavia hadn't heard from him for ages. And now she has heard from him and he was wounded somewhere with the Free French and his arm had to come off."

"How dreadful!" said Leslie, thinking of her brother.

But Lady Waring, being a practical woman, asked which arm it was.

"Octavia doesn't say," said Lydia, looking at the letter again. "She only says they had to take it off and she wishes she had been there. Oh, *poor* Tommy. I suppose one can go on being a clergyman with only one arm, can't one?"

Leslie said Nelson only had one arm, but of course he was an admiral.

"I think it's worse for an admiral than for a clergyman," said Lydia. "He's got to do more commanding. Only being Tommy somehow makes it different. May I ring Octavia up, Lady Waring? She says she is having a few days off from the Barchester General."

Lydia Keith would have crashed from the table, either banging the door or leaving it open. Mrs. Merton however waited for her hostess to say, "Of course, my dear, and be sure to say how distressed I am by this news, and I know Sir Harry will feel the same."

Lydia went quickly to the telephone, noting even in the middle of her concern for Octavia that Lady Waring had reverted to Sir Harry when speaking of her husband, because, Lydia was certain, her relations with the Deanery though friendly were not intimate enough for her to speak of him as she did to Lydia. In a few moments she came back. Selina was clearing the table and Lady Waring and Leslie talking by the fire.

"Oh, Lady Waring," Lydia said, "what *do* you think? Tommy's letter took so long that he got home almost as soon, and he's at the Deanery. Octavia hasn't seen his arm yet — I mean where his arm was. She says he needs to have quiet and rest, and if he is at the Deanery he is sure to want to help Dr. Crawley, and his parents are dead so he really hasn't a home except his married sister who is doing war work and has no servants, so I was wondering if there was any chance of Nannie Allen taking him. I told Octavia I'd ask."

Lady Waring highly approved the idea. She was going to Winter Overcotes at once for a committee and would not be back till the 5.10, but the girls might drive to the village and sound Nannie about it and bring up the chickens' ration of meal which had sent a postcard to say it was at the station.

On their way down the back passages to the stable yard Leslie and Lydia met Selina, who said she had happened to hear Miss Leslie mention they were driving Crumpet to the village and would they mind taking a pair of curtains her ladyship had given her for her mother. Leslie said certainly and Selina had better put them in the cart.

"And I *was* upset, madam," said the tender Selina, "hearing about Miss Octavia's fiancé. Fancy losing an arm. I had an uncle lost his leg in a boiler explosion and all the skin taken off his face. It was terrible, Miss

Leslie, enough to give you the creeps, but my auntie said it was the Lord's judgment on uncle. Oh dear, what *will* Miss Octavia do?"

"I expect she'll be awfully pleased," said the truthful Lydia.

"Oh, madam!" said Selina.

"To get him back, I mean," said Lydia. "Do you think your mother will take him, Selina?"

"I'm sure she will, madam," said Selina. "Mrs. Graham didn't send her little boy after all and mother and me turned out the best room only yesterday. She *will* be upset when she hears about Miss Octavia's fiancé. If you are going there, Miss Leslie, will you tell her I'll be sure to be down before tea to help her with the curtains."

She ran into the house, got the curtains and was out with them before they had begun harnessing Crumpet. As she crossed the stable yard Jasper came round the corner.

"That old bundle's too heavy for you," he said. "I'll take it. Take you too for that matter, one under one arm, one under t'other. I'll harness old Crumpet, Miss Leslie, and bring him round to the front."

Lydia and Leslie looked at each other and walked back to the front of the house. After an interval, during which either of them single-handed could have put the pony into the cart and taken him out and put everything away again, a patter of hoofs was heard and Crumpet trotted up, Selina driving and Jasper walking beside with his long stride.

"I *am* sorry, I'm sure, Miss Leslie," said Selina getting out. "It's that Jasper, Miss Leslie, he's enough to upset anyone."

"I like to see you driving old Crumpet," said Jasper. "Whoa, old Crumpet, keep still. I'll hold him till you're settled, ladies."

The ladies got in, Selina shut the little back door, and the trap rattled away.

"You're a nice old bundle for a man to put his arm round," said Jasper.

"Don't talk about arms, Jasper," said Selina, her eyes dewy, "poor Miss Octavia's fiancé has had his arm cut off by those Free French. Miss Lydia was telling about it at lunch and to think of him a clergyman too, it doesn't seem right, and I —"

"All right, my girl, you *was* upset," said Jasper grinning. "But I never heard a clergyman needed two arms to marry people with."

At this Selina shrieked and fled into the kitchen passage.

As the ladies went down the drive they overtook Sergeant Hopkins striding in a purposeful way towards the village, accompanied by Private Jenks, who was still waiting for a vacancy at the Barchester General. Outside the post-office Matron was licking some stamps onto her letters: her own phrase.

"Good afternoon, Matron," said Leslie checking Crumpet in his career, "I haven't seen you lately."

Matron said they had been very busy in the hospital.

"But this afternoon," she added, "you find me having a little jaunt, Miss Waring. I am going to tea with old

225

Mrs. Allen. Such a wonderful old character. As I said to Nurse Poulter, quite one of the old type, just one's idea of a duchess."

As Lydia had never met a duchess and Leslie only knew a very dowdy dowager who worked on one of her committees and unbelievably wore a black bonnet, they could not see Nannie Allen in the role, but agreed fervently with Matron.

"We shall be looking in on Nannie when we've got the chicken rations and done the shopping," said Leslie, "so perhaps we can give you a lift back."

"Well, to that I shall not say no," said Matron graciously, "for as I was saying to Nurse Poulter, it may be all downhill to the village, but say what you will it is all uphill coming back. She has a very nice piece she recited at the men's last concert about the road winding uphill; sweetly expressive it was. It is *au revoir* then."

Leslie flicked Crumpet and they were soon at the station where the chicken ration was sitting waiting for them, also a parcel from the Winter Overcotes ironmonger, which appeared to consist entirely of corners. Lydia said it looked as if one of them would have to walk back if Matron was coming, but Leslie said one never knew how much Crumpet's cart would hold till one tried. As Lydia sat screwed sideways, Selina's bundle of curtains looming over her, one of the largest corners of the ironmongery sticking painfully into her legs, and one end of the sack of chicken ration on her lap, she did not really see how Matron was going to fit in, but if Leslie said so she was probably right.

Turning into the High Street again, they saw Philip Winter at the far side of the road.

"Hi! Philip!" said Lydia in a powerful voice.

Philip came across the road and expressed his pleasure at seeing the ladies. Lydia inquired what he was doing. Philip said having his afternoon off, and he had thought of walking up to the Priory and inquiring if anyone was at home.

"Well, we aren't," said Leslie, "and I'm afraid no one else is, because Uncle Harry is in London and Aunt Harriet is in Winter Overcotes. Lydia and I are taking some curtains to my old nurse, who was George Waring's nurse too, and if you cared to come with us we might all go back together."

This seemed to Philip quite a good way of spending his afternoon, so the whole cavalcade, Crumpet reined to a footpace (which we may say was accomplished without any difficulty as it was exactly the pace he would have chosen if consulted), Philip walking beside, proceeded to Ladysmith Cottages. The ladies got out and the curtains were unloaded.

"Can Philip come in?" said Lydia to Leslie. "He'd love to see Nannie."

"Would you care to come in, Colonel Winter?" said Leslie. "It is such a treat for Nannie to see people. She lives quite alone."

Philip said he would love it, but what about the pony.

"Oh, Crumpet. I'll tie him up in the lane," said Leslie. "He knows it quite well."

Crumpet having been stabled in an old cartshed in the little lane, hardly more than a cobbled passage, that ran up beside No. 1 Ladysmith Cottages, the travellers approached the house, from which came a noise of hammering and men's voices.

Leslie, wondering what on earth Nannie was doing, opened the front door and walked in. There was no one in the sitting-room and as the noise appeared to proceed from the first floor front, Leslie led the way upstairs and looked in. Everything in the room was dust-sheeted except one easy-chair, in which Nannie sat enthroned and wrapped in shawls. On a step-ladder near the window Sergeant Hopkins was screwing a block of wood on to the wall, while Private Jenks on the floor was shortening a length of brass curtain rod with a hacksaw. The two warriors looked slightly confused by the appearance of an officer and two ladies, but Nannie entirely unmoved said in a general way, "Have you wiped your feet?"

"I'm very sorry I haven't, if you mean me," said Philip, "because I was carrying a very large bundle of curtains and couldn't see the doormat. But I'll go down again and wipe them at once."

"How often have I told you," said Nannie, apparently taking Philip for one of her ex-charges, "it's no good waiting to wipe your feet till you've dirtied the stair carpet."

"Nannie," said Leslie, agitated by the far from benevolent reception that Philip was getting, "this is Colonel Winter, from the camp. You remember I told you Uncle Harry asked him to dinner. He wanted to meet you."

"Well, here I am," said Nannie, "and I'll thank you to bring the curtains up, sir. These young fellows are putting up a nice new curtain-rod for me and I must get the curtains up before the black-out. It's a nasty dull day too, so there's no time for dawdling," said Nannie sharply, and apparently under the impression, a not uncommon one, that the hour of the black-out varied with the state of the weather. "I've had trouble enough as it is, having to put dust-sheets over my furniture with them messing everything up with their sawdust."

Philip, much struck by the commanding qualities of his hostess, obediently went downstairs, while the two workers exchanged grins.

"And don't dawdle, you boys," said Nannie, exactly as she had said it to Master George and Master Cecil and Master David and many other of England's gently nurtured or gilded youth.

"Selina asked me to say she'd be down before tea to help with the curtains, Nannie," said Leslie. "Aren't you too cold up here?"

Indeed the best bedroom, doing its best to keep within the fuel target, was as piercingly cold as a room which has not lately been used and has no fire is likely to be in the depth of winter.

"It's healthy," said Nannie. "And you know what the Government said, Miss Leslie, about using our fuel to fight the Germans."

The irrepressible Private Jenks said he'd fight Hitler with a nice big bonfire if he had his way and he knew who'd be the guy.

"If you've finished messing about with the curtain-rod, Jenks," said Nannie, "you can go down and put the kettle on. You know where it is. And mind, no carryings on with Marigold. I'll give you all a cup of tea," she added to Leslie.

"Here are your curtains, Mrs. Allen," said Philip, who having met Private Jenks on the stairs had taken the opportunity of inquiring his hostess's name.

"I'm much obliged, sir," said Nannie. "Now, Hopkins, have you finished?"

The sergeant, who had just put the second bracket for the curtain-rod in place, came down the ladder and said, looking at Philip, that he didn't think he'd stay to tea.

"Nonsense," said Nannie. "Who's to help Jenks get the curtains up and put my step-ladder away? Now, you all come down and get your tea."

Her company, now well under her thumb, meekly obeyed and followed her downstairs, just as in their different social spheres they would have obeyed their nurse or their mother. In the sitting-room Selina, who had arrived unheard during the conversation upstairs, was putting out the tea-things and looked slightly puzzled as the large company came into the room.

"Lay for all," said Nannie, sitting down in her special chair at the head of the table. "You'll please to sit next me, sir," she said to Philip, "and Miss Leslie the other side of you. Mrs. Merton, will you please to come on my other side and leave a place for Matron next me. Selina and you boys can sit at the other end. Is the kettle boiling, Jenks?"

Although Nannie's lofty ordering of the guests made it sound as if the table were at least six yards long, it was in reality of a size which made above or below the salt very much the same. Lydia found herself next to Sergeant Hopkins, with Private Jenks beyond him. Selina brought in the teapot and squeezed in between the soldiers.

To add to the glory of the scene, Marigold Smith, the young lady of fifteen who acted as occasional handmaid to Nannie, brought in the kettle, nicely on the boil, and placed it on the hob by the fire to replenish the teapot. At the sight of three men in uniform, one of them being a real officer, she was taken with a fit of that self-consciousness which can only express itself in giggles and writhings of the body.

"That's enough, Marigold," said Nannie. "You can go home now."

With a final wriggle in which she appeared to be doing her best to burst out of all her clothes, Marigold left the sitting-room and could shortly afterwards be seen outside still giggling with her friends in the street.

"Now you needn't look at your watch, Miss Leslie," said Nannie. "It's only a quarter to four and you'll get back before it's dark. And what's Mr. Cecil doing now?"

There was an emphasis on the word *now* so sinister in its implications that Philip said half to himself, "Go and see what Master Alfred is doing and tell him not to." Leslie swiftly turned her head and smiled at him before answering Nannie that she hadn't heard from him for some time.

"If we was away anywhere, like Brighton after the chickenpox, I always made my young gentlemen write home twice a week, Sundays and Thursdays," said Nannie. "But Mr. Cecil was never a one for writing."

Lydia could see that Leslie had flushed angrily at this sideways attack on her brother, whose long letters were part of her life, so over Matron's Banquo seat she obligingly flung herself into the breach.

"Of course he writes, Mrs. Allen," she said, "but when people are at sea they can't post their letters so often and even people on land can't always. Octavia Crawley —"

But before she could finish there was a knock at the front door. Selina went out and came back with Matron, who included the whole company in a gracious smile which had the effect of making Sergeant Hopkins and Private Jenks look rather sheepish.

"You'll please to excuse my not getting up, Matron," said Nannie, "it's my legs."

As everyone present had seen her walk downstairs unassisted and quite briskly, this statement deceived no one except Matron, who sidled, for no other mode of progression in the tightly packed room was now possible, into the seat next her hostess.

"And what a pleasant abode, Mrs. Allen," said Matron. "So snug and cosy. And such a pleasure to have tea before the black-out. I do find the black-out *quite* the most trying part of the war, don't you?"

Having vindicated her dignity by not getting up to receive her guest, Nannie was in a mood of regal condescension and said Matron must have quite a time getting the hospital blacked out. Matron said she had some very good helpers, two of whom were not a thousand miles away from this very spot, which caused Sergeant Hopkins to choke into his tea, upon which Selina slapped his back and her mother frowned at her. Private Jenks was heard to say, in a low but audible aside, that he wouldn't mind choking himself if Mrs. Crockett would slap him.

"What were you saying about Miss Octavia, madam?" said Nannie to Lydia, to cover her daughter's low behaviour.

"Oh, she didn't hear from Mr. Needham that she is engaged to for ages," said Lydia, "and when she did hear it was to say he had to have his arm off."

She was then able to reflect that this was not a comparison calculated to cheer Leslie.

"That comes of going to the front," said Nannie, finally. "I could have told him."

Matron asked where.

"I don't exactly know," said Lydia, "because he isn't allowed to say where he is. Somewhere in North Africa. But anyway he's back now, because letters take so long."

This elliptical mode of expression was understood by all her audience, except Matron who said she meant *where*.

"Oh, I don't know," said Lydia, "because Octavia didn't say. But I expect she's seen it now, so she'll be able to tell me."

"Indeed not, madam," said Nannie. "A young lady to look at a gentleman's arm he's had off! I never heard of such a thing."

Matron, much interested professionally, said it all depended *where*. If of course it were at or below the elbow it would be easy by just pulling up the coat-sleeve. If it were higher, or at the shoulder, at which her eyes gleamed slightly in spite of her very kind disposition, it would of course be less easy. Nannie said she never allowed such goings-on, not in her nursery.

"But Tommy's a clergyman, Mrs. Allen," said Lydia.

Matron said that was indeed shocking. To Sergeant Hopkins the idea of a padre losing an arm appeared to afford a certain cynical satisfaction, while Selina, who was already familiar with the sad story, began to wipe her lustrous eyes.

Nannie said she wondered where it was done.

Leslie, interpreting correctly her old nurse's question, said it was in Africa, fighting with the Free French.

"I knew those French were at the bottom of it," said Nannie. "When I was abroad with Lady Emily Leslie and Miss Agnes and Mr. David I wouldn't let them play with the French children on the beach. They never played fair, beach cricket, or running races, or whatever it was. And now poor Miss Octavia's young gentleman's had his arm cut off fighting them. Still, there's wonderful artificial legs nowadays."

"But I never said Mr. Needham was fighting with the Free French, Nannie," said Leslie. "I said fighting *with* them."

234

Conscious that her explanation, though perfectly clear to everyone present, was wanting in precision, she looked at Philip, next her, for help.

"What you said was that he was fighting with them," said Philip, "because I heard you with my own ears. But I quite see your point."

Private Jenks said his uncle had a hook instead of a hand. "Came in handy in all sorts of ways, it did," he added. "He wasn't born like that of course."

Matron said the work that was being done for our mutilated men was quite wonderful. A Canadian convalescent, she said to Lydia, whom perhaps she felt alone to be worthy of her confidence, had come in with an artificial arm that was as you might say as large as life and twice as natural except when the elbow occasionally bent the wrong way. While they were engaged on this enthralling subject Nannie gave Selina a mother's look which informed her that those boys had better get the curtain up and fold up the dust-sheets and leave the quality to itself. Leslie, seizing her opportunity, asked Nannie if she would be able to take this Mr. Needham, who was engaged to Miss Octavia and had lost his arm, as a lodger. The doctors had ordered rest and quiet, and Nannie knew that these advantages were impossible in an hotel or ordinary lodgings, and poor Mr. Needham had no home to go to.

"I won't have anyone fighting here," said Nannie, "not the French nor anyone. I always said to my young gentlemen, 'Now if you want to fight go in the garden, for in the nursery I will not have it.'"

235

Leslie, with great cunning, said that she was sure Mr. Needham, being engaged to Miss Crawley, wouldn't want to fight anyone, besides being a clergyman.

"Well, I suppose I'll have to say yes," said Nannie. "It's a mercy I got the new rod and those curtains up. Poor gentleman, I expect he feels quite strange without his arm. I wonder how he manages."

"You'll be able to help him a bit, Mrs. Allen," said Philip, who had been listening with amusement.

Nannie said she'd always wondered how them collars did do up and now perhaps she'd know, which was rightly interpreted by Leslie as an enthusiastic reception of the plan. Although it was barely black-out time the darkness was gathering fast under the leaden sky and Leslie, with Crumpet on her mind, said they must be going and kissed her old nurse.

"Good-bye and thank you so much for your tea-party," said Lydia. "I hope you don't mind me calling you Nannie, like Leslie? I've got an old Nannie at home, Mrs. Twitcher is her name."

Nannie, smiling grimly, said she didn't suppose it would be any use saying no, but Lydia could see that she was not displeased by the familiarity.

Matron insisted on having just a wee peep into the kitchen, was loud in praise of everything and profuse in thanks. As they were all putting on coats in the passage Selina and her escort came down, rather squashed together on the narrow staircase.

"If you've finished, you can go along," said Nannie. "I'm tired and want to rest. Marigold's coming in at six to cook my supper. Don't you forget to come in on

Sunday, Selina. I hope you young fellows left everything tidy upstairs. Don't keep me standing in a draught."

Taking this as a general invitation to be gone, the whole party left the house. Sergeant Hopkins and Private Jenks were having a friendly dispute as to which of them should walk back with Selina, who turned her brown eyes on each in turn imploringly, so Philip said he would fetch Crumpet and bring him to the gate as he had a torch. But even as he stepped out of the front garden, a trit-trot of little hoofs was heard and round the corner came Crumpet and cart, produced by an unknown agency, the little lamps discreetly shining in front and a red light behind.

"I knew you'd have tied up old Crumpet in the shed, Miss Leslie," said the voice of Jasper, "and I was down here in the village so I thought I'd bring him along. He's ready to go home, aren't you, old Crumpet?"

He had got out while he was speaking and gone to the pony's head. "Old Crumpet he says 'yes,'" he reported.

"It's that nice keeper," said Matron, which caused Jasper to confide in Crumpet exactly what he felt about some women, "and now if you are really giving me a lift, Miss Waring, shall I mount the barouche? Oh dear!" she said as she began to get in, "it seems to be quite full."

"It's all right," said Leslie. "Just one moment, Matron. I'll get in first and shift the parcels a bit."

"But you are going to walk up with me, aren't you?" said Philip quietly at her elbow.

"Oh," said Leslie, hesitating.

"Lydia, you'll take care of Matron, won't you?" said Philip. "I'm going to walk up with Miss Waring. My legs are bent nearly double with doing office work all the time."

Lydia was perfectly agreeable. She got in, arranged the spiky parcel and the bulky bag as well as she could, and invited Matron to come along.

"There's an old rug there," said Jasper. "I brought it down in case you ladies was cold. Brought it the same as I brought down them old lamps, because I know'd you'd forget."

Matron said again what a nice man and so good to Private Jenks. Having thus thoroughly embarrassed them both she said this was quite like ye olden times. Philip slammed the little back door and Crumpet dashed away at full tilt, suddenly remembering his stable.

"Now, you boys," said the voice of Selina, trembling to a very attractive half-sob, "don't you quarrel. Why not both see me home? We're all going the same way."

"That old Sheep's Head opens at six," said the voice of Jasper. "You young fellows'll be wanting a drink. I'll take Mrs. Crockett home."

Selina's voice was heard protesting that she *would* be upset if there was any unpleasantness.

"There won't be none," said Jasper's voice. "You come along, my girl."

There was a coquettish shriek and the shadowy forms of Jasper and Selina melted into the darkness towards the Priory.

"What's the time?" said the voice of Private Jenks.

"Just after the half-hour when we left the house," said the voice of Sergeant Hopkins.

"Left good and proper, that's what we are," said Private Jenks. "Well, come on, sergeant."

Their shadowy forms melted into the darkness to await the opening of the Sheep's Head.

"Oh, love, love, love," Philip remarked.

"Dear me," said Leslie, "I thought I was the only one that knew Tennyson."

"I got him in a prize at school," said Philip. "It was for physics, a subject I could never understand, but I cheated. Not much, but just enough to make the difference. Shall we walk?"

Without answering Leslie turned towards the church and moved forward. Philip dropped into step with her. As they passed the vicarage, Leslie wondered how the late vicar's old sister was.

"What do you think about old people dying?" she asked Philip. "I mean people like old Miss Horniman, who are deaf and half blind and mostly don't even know where they are, and use up lives and strength and money."

"For the life of me I can't tell," said Philip. "What frightens me is the way most of them talk as if they were going to live for ever, and the more decayed they are the more they grab at life. However, they'll be in a majority soon, so it won't matter what we think. We shall be dead, killed, worn out, and all the paralyseds and paralytics and gagas will be able to dance on our tombstones."

They had now reached the lodge, and the drive began to wind uphill.

"Do you mind if we don't walk so fast?" said Philip. "Partly for my pleasure because it will make the walk longer for me, partly because it is bad for you to walk fast uphill."

"Oh, how did you know?" said Leslie, standing still.

"Eyes in my head," said Philip. "Or as it is dark, let us say that it's part of a schoolmaster's job to see if the young are overdoing themselves. Mind and body are our jobs if we do it properly."

"As a matter of fact," said Leslie, moving on again, "Dr. Ford says my heart is as fit as ever, but he did say to take things easily and not go about like a tank. It's a bit mortifying when you are a good walker."

"I know," said Philip quietly. "And as another matter of fact I will tell you that more people do themselves harm by being snobbish about walking than you can imagine. They dash along at four and a half miles an hour and boast about it. Then they wonder why they look haggard."

"I know I look haggard," said Leslie, enjoying this self-abasement.

"As a third matter of fact you don't," said Philip. "You look much better than when I first saw you. But if you pound up hills, you will. I expect you pound at your work."

"Well, I'm a woman," said Leslie on a half-sigh.

"Yes, fortunately or unfortunately," said Philip. "But being one, do make the best of it. I can't tell you what pleasure it gives me to see you so much better."

240

"It's a good deal Lydia," said Leslie. "It's Noel a bit too, because to do a bit of work for him interests me and keeps me from squirrelling."

"Squirrelling?" said Philip.

"Yes. Thinking round and round about Cecil, about my brother. But it's Lydia more. It's fun to have her to do things with."

"Lydia is a remarkably good girl," said Philip, slackening his pace. "I've seldom known a better and I've known her as long as Noel has. She has stood up to everything good and bad like a Trojan."

"She doesn't look as if she'd had much bad," said Leslie, with a faint twinge of envy.

"Nothing spectacular," said Philip. "Her father died, you know, and she ran her mother and the place. Then she married Noel and he was at Dunkirk. Then her old home was commandeered. She did a year's voluntary work on a farm in Scotland to be near Noel; real five-in-the-morning-to-nine-at-night kind of work. Then Noel was moved to Yorkshire and she wanted to join the Land Army there, but she couldn't because of some regulation about previous employment, so she got into a hospital as a full-time V.A.D. She was very ill up there for a time, but she took it all as part of the job and thank goodness she is as fit as ever, and would be quite happy except that Colin has gone. And now she tells me she is going to do full-time V.A.D. work again — here, I hope."

They had walked more and more slowly as Philip spoke, till now they were at a standstill. Leslie felt rather like a whirlpool in her mind. All she heard about

Lydia made her like and admire her more. All that Philip said about Lydia made her feel how very nice and comforting it would be if he could say things like that about her. But she had to confess that it would be difficult. She knew that she had done her job well, extremely well, she said, looking at it with detachment, but she also knew that it was stereotyping her into the careerist woman. Gradually her interests had narrowed to her work, hardly including her colleagues except as part of her well-running machine. Even when her beloved Cecil had been on leave she knew she had been almost impatient with him once or twice for making demands upon her time, and bored by the girls he wanted her to meet. She had been ill too, but she suddenly wondered whether in Colonel Winter's words she had taken it as part of the job. She knew she had not; that she had been moody for long spells and more than a little irritable with her uncle and aunt, who did their round of unexciting duties so patiently and uncomplainingly with nothing particular to look forward to.

Suddenly she said out of the darkness, "Colonel Winter, I do kick against the pricks."

Philip was again conscious, as he had been on the night she spoke to him about her brother, that he was being asked for help, and was overcome by a sense of guilt in having perhaps appeared to criticize this girl who was asking him to lighten her troubles. He rather wished he could put a British warm arm round her as he would with Lydia and give her a hug, but this obviously would not do.

"Oh, well, I suppose we'd better go on," said her voice, flat and tired.

"You wouldn't care to take my arm, would you?" he asked, almost diffidently. "I oughtn't to have asked you to walk back."

"I liked walking," said her voice. "And I will be rather glad of an arm."

She slipped her arm into his and they covered the rest of the distance in silence. Skirting the hospital they came round to the Warings' wing. At the door she withdrew her arm.

"I will try to be good," she said. "Good lord," she added, "how affected I am."

Her ingenuous surprise at this discovery touched and amused Philip so much that he began to laugh. Leslie, after a second, began to laugh too, though we very much doubt whether either of them really knew what it was that made them laugh.

"Thank you," said Leslie. "I enjoyed my walk."

"But it isn't the first time we have walked up the drive together at night," said Philip. "I hope you don't forget that I was the mysterious unknown who carried your suitcase up from the station. But I didn't know who you were then."

"I didn't know who you were, either," said Leslie.

CHAPTER
EIGHT

Philip Winter, looking back during the next few days upon his black-out walk with Leslie Waring, would dearly have liked to know if he had offended her past bearing. His true desire to help her appeared to him in the unfriendly light of self-tormenting retrospect very near meddling, and the advice he gave her little less than priggish. These thoughts stung him the more that he had lost one love (though relieved beyond measure to lose her) by his same meddling, priggish ways. Lovely Rose Birkett, so suited to amusement and laughter, such a complete nitwit, so quickly dashed by his efforts to improve her a little; never had she flung her arms carelessly round his neck with such affection as after she had thrown her engagement ring into the water. All she had wanted was admiration and a good time; all he had given her, apart from his heart's devotion, was moodiness and a temper which if not bad was far too earnest, and her relief at her freedom was such that he had for a moment feared she might get engaged to him again from pure gratitude.

Not that there was any suggestion of his being engaged to Leslie Waring. They had not even got past Miss Waring and Colonel Winter. Though it was inevitable that Christian names should be used, and almost surprising that they had not been used already, he felt a fastidious pleasure in the slight formality between them. Having always felt a distaste for very competent young women and a certain amount of fear of them, he was troubled at finding this woman with a first-class organizing brain so very unsure of herself; so unexpectedly ready to listen to his advice, yet always a little aloof like a wild creature. Doubtless the illness of which Lydia had told him was largely accountable for her overstrung state of mind; that and the anxiety for her brother. A girl who had been torpedoed and two days in a boat had every right to be shaken nervously, though he felt certain that his Lydia would have as it were defied herself not to recover and won her challenge; as she had so valiantly done when illness stopped her activities for a time. Still, he said to himself, veering from point to point, in spite of his little panegyric on Lydia she had done no more than thousands of other women, married or unmarried. Why had he held her up as an example to Leslie Waring? Just because he was so fond of his Lydia, he supposed, and had watched her career from the violent, untidy schoolgirl to the product of her own self-discipline and Noel's influence, never with the faintest approach to love, but with solid and increasing affection. Still, there was no reason to praise one young woman to another so outspokenly, and he wondered, with a sudden clutch at his heart, if he had made Leslie hate both Lydia and himself.

But these considerations were not going to help him to do his work, so he put the remembrance of his darkling walk with Leslie out of his mind and looked forward very much to their next meeting. Twice when he was free he telephoned, but once Leslie was in town, having been allowed by Dr. Ford to go up on parole and see how the office was getting on, and the second time she was doing a piece of work for Noel against time and had to put him off. Always forgetting that anyone who works is not his or her own master, that he would find it just as difficult to make a sudden appointment or to keep it, he gave himself some quite unnecessary annoyance by thinking that to work for Noel, whom he liked very much, would be much more interesting than to have a colonel whom one hardly knew to tea. Not that he for a moment suspected Leslie and Noel of having more than the most ordinary liking for each other: he knew Noel's feelings for Lydia too well. But Noel was on the spot, he was more a man of the world than Philip, had more amusing friends, was in Intelligence, and being happily married could afford to be charming to women without danger. So he decided not to ring up again.

It had been a disappointment for Leslie that she was really busy each time Philip rang up. Her day in London had been successful and she was not unduly tired; her work for Noel was interesting and she liked him; but behind both her day in London and her work at home had been a slight feeling of irritation that Colonel Winter must choose that particular time to invite himself to the Priory. Of course, she said to

246

herself, he really came to see Lydia, an old friend whom he was obviously very fond of, and if people liked Lydia better than they liked her it was, she had to confess, only natural. So she decided to wait and see if he would ring up again.

This state of things might have gone on for ever, or at any rate till Philip was next asked to dinner, had not a small temporary crisis occurred at the Priory in the shape of a burst pipe in the kitchen which meant a day's joyful saturnalia of the staff, Mrs. Phipps, and any convalescent soldiers who felt inclined, and the absence, if possible, of the family. Luckily the Warings both had to be in town that day, so Leslie and Lydia, refusing offers of a meal on a tray, decided to lunch at the Sheep's Head, which still managed to serve an eatable meal if it was given notice.

Mrs. George Pollett, wife of the Sheep's Head, was renowned far and wide for her fried fish and her steak-and-kidney puddings, which, alas, were now but beautiful memories. Yet even under the peculiar arrangements for fish known as zoning, a word accepted placidly by the population of England and with their genius for misinterpretation at once reduced to a synonym of total disappearance, Mrs. Pollett managed to do wonders with an occasional bit of frozen cod, and her meat ration always went twice as far as anyone else's. Owing to these virtues and to the agreeable atmosphere of the bar, the officers at the Dower House had arranged with the hostess for a kind of informal mess on a small scale, and every day three or four of them might be found there rather than at the canteen, where English-speaking food was supplied by a number of A.T.S. of various sizes and shapes.

In the dining-room, which looked out on a cheerful stable yard now housing army equipment of various kinds, a large round table was kept for the officers, and two small tables, pushed away against a wall, for stray visitors. One of these Leslie had booked by telephone earlier in the day, the other was already occupied by two commercial nondescripts.

Lydia knew that Noel would not be coming, but otherwise had no guess as to who might or might not be there. It was no pleasure to her and Leslie when they came into the dining-room to find Captain Hooper straddling like Apollyon right across the fireplace; however there was nothing for it but to say good morning, which they did. Captain Hooper, continuing to straddle, said seas between them braid had roared since they last met and how were things. Leslie, with her best secretary's manner, said things were doing very well and with Lydia sat down at one of the little tables. The captain had already expressed a gallant wish that the ladies would join their little party, when a couple of officers came in and Captain Hooper had quite enough to do in standing them drinks for which he had no intention of paying if he could help it. These were followed by Philip.

"Hallo, Philip," said Lydia.

Leslie suddenly felt glad that the kitchen pipe had burst.

"Hallo, Lydia," said Philip, not to be outdone. "How are you and Miss Waring?"

This was said not so much in conventional greeting as with a wish to know if London and her work had tired her. Leslie felt this and thanked Colonel Winter.

"I say," said Lydia, "you ought to say Philip and Leslie."

"I always do, to myself," said Philip and then suddenly thought that it sounded rather familiar, so that he was reassured when Leslie added, "So do I. You see, I never hear you called anything else, except by my uncle and aunt, and they don't christian name. Uncle Harry adores Lydia, but he always calls her Mrs. Merton."

"But Lady Waring does call me Lydia," said Mrs. Merton proudly.

"That," said Leslie, "is most unusual."

"Do you think," asked Philip, "that I could have my lunch at your table, Leslie? I address myself to you rather than to Lydia because I want to get used to saying your name at once. I love all those names that haven't any gender, like Leslie and Lindsay and Cecil and Evelyn. Not Esmé, though. One must draw the line somewhere."

"Of course you can lunch with us," said Leslie, avoiding in a cowardly way the use of his name. "As a matter of fact, my brother was to have been a girl called Cecil, and when he turned out to be a boy my people were struck all of a heap and couldn't think of any boys' names, so they kept Cecil, and it was such a success that next time they chose another name like that and didn't mind what the baby was."

"And it was you," said Philip, somehow touched by the thought of Leslie as a baby, a thing he never much liked except to please Kate Carter.

"Yes," said Leslie, which seemed to him a very noble, simple and moving statement, besides being true.

"Another great advantage of having lunch with you," said Philip, addressing himself to the whole company, "is that I am not having lunch with my gallant and insupportable friend behind me. And yet another is that I am going to pay for you both. This is because I am rich to-day. I have just had a cheque from the Oxbridge University Press for one pound three shillings and eightpence, representing a year's royalties on that Horatian bantling of mine. Not a gold mine, but so far a permanent source of income."

"Horace makes me think of that summer you were with the Birketts at the Rectory," said Lydia, "and that beast, Miss Pettinger, set us a whacking great ode of Horace to do. Everard was there for Whitsun and he helped me. I do think it is marvellous to be able to get all the words into the right order."

Philip said it was really only a trick, backed by a slight acquaintance with the Latin grammar, and they fell to talking about the summer at Northbridge Manor and how lovely and odious Rose had been. Leslie felt out of it and was cross with herself for being so self-conscious, when luckily the arrival of Mrs. Pollett with the menu brought a common interest into their lives.

"Good morning, Mrs. Pollett," said Leslie. "This is Mrs. Merton who is staying with us, and Colonel Winter."

"Mrs. Pollett and I are old friends," said Philip. "She gives me gin in the bar when there isn't any, and on Christmas Eve I kissed her under the mistletoe."

"Kiss and don't tell, Colonel Winter, as the saying is," said Mrs. Pollett, with an appreciative giggle. "With a gentleman like you it's just a bit of fun, but there's some that if they tried it would find themselves on the wrong side of the door pretty sharp," she added, with a jerk of one fat bare elbow towards the mess table, a gesture rightly taken by her audience to indicate Captain Hooper. "No fish to-day, Miss Waring. There's a bit of liver, but I'm not letting those gentlemen know."

Liver was gratefully accepted, beer ordered, and they began their lunch. Leslie was still feeling out of things and though she didn't mind listening, a fear of appearing sulky made her smile till she thought her face would be struck so. Philip felt a constraint, could not quite account for it, and wondered if he had said or done the wrong thing.

Before they had finished the liver (which was extremely good, as Mrs. Pollett had a passion for garlic which she grew and used with exquisite art), the door opened and a spare, anxious-looking officer came in; a major by his badges.

"Oh, Hooper," he said, "will it be all right if my wife joins us? She is just down for the day, and Mrs. Pollett told me there wasn't a separate table free."

Before Captain Hooper could answer, the officer was over-borne by what was evidently his wife, not really taller than he was, but by her commanding presence and general air of complete adequacy for any kind of surroundings, giving the impression of being about six feet high. Having swept her husband aside she stood, rather like a heroine of opera making her entrance, surveying the room and its inhabitants and affording to them all the majestic spectacle of a purple checked coat thrown open to display a green checked suit and orange jumper, all rather on the tight side. Her auburn and deeply waved locks, knotted in a bun behind, were crowned by a red felt hat with a green feather. Black shoes, gloves and super-bag completed her toilet.

"Well, wonders will never cease," said the apparition, "and little did I think when I arranged to come down and see Bobbie, who *cannot* understand, poor pet, that a woman is far busier than a man in this war, that I would find an auld acquaintance here, coincidence if you like, but believe you me, my life is one mass, simply one *mass* of coincidences. As I was saying to Bobbums when he met me at the station, I simply cannot move a step without falling over someone I know, and when he told me Sir Harry Waring was the big noise here, of course I said, Well, there you are, Bobbie, talk of a coincidence and it's practically my second name, for who was Bobbie billeted with a couple of years ago, though it seems fantastic to talk of a couple of years still the war has been going on more than three years now though I always say the tide will turn, but the

252

Villarses at Northbridge, cousins of Sir Harry's my dear. Well, I ask you."

During this interesting *aperçu* of life and her relationship to it, Captain Hooper had been eyeing the new arrival with a marked want of favour. But as he was a captain and the lady's husband a major, he had to make the best of it.

"Delighted to meet you again, Mrs. Spender," he said. "The Major has sprung quite a pleasant surprise on us. Come and join our little party. Captain Gumm, our dental bloke, have 'em out as soon as look at you; Mr. Wagstaffe, Signals; Mrs. Major Spender. The Major and I were billeted together with the Reverend Villars and his wife, to whom Mrs. Spender reludes."

Mrs. Spender then took a seat which automatically became the head of the table, so far as a circle can be said to have a head, and from this point of vantage surveyed the neighbourhood. The two nondescript commercials had no interest for her except in so far as anyone not in uniform was probably a spy or fifth-columnist, but the sight of yet another officer lunching with two ladies aroused her curiosity. As there was a lull in the general conversation she did not voice this sentiment, but gave her husband an interrogative glance accompanied by a slight jerk of her head towards Philip's table, meant to express a desire to know all about him.

"I'm afraid there isn't any, my dear," said Major Spender, looking anxiously about on the table.

"Any what?" said Mrs. Spender.

"You were looking for the mustard, weren't you?" said Major Spender anxiously.

"Now, *isn't* Bobbie a dear old silly," exclaimed his lady. "Not mustard, Bobbums, though well you might have thought so, for what you do need with all this American tinned stuff, though it is wonderful of them to lease-lend us all their Spam and what not, is mustard. I must tell you, Captain Hooper," she continued, drawing the whole table into her remorseless orbit, "what our second boy says, a bright lad, though I says it as shouldn't, considering he is only seven, seven last birthday. When all this tinned meat and so forth began to come over, and mind you, at the cost of men's lives, as I always say to anyone who prefers fresh meat, the kiddies thought it was ham. So I said to Billy, he is the eldest, you know, and doing quite too marvellously at his prep, school, said she, coming all over the proud parent, I said to Billy, 'Billy, this isn't ham, it's Spam,' and Jimmy, that is the second of course, thought I said, 'It's Pam,' not 'It's Ssspam,' you see, just the tiniest, weeniest difference in pronunciation but that boy's hearing is so acute that believe it or not he can hear the grass grow as the saying is, so he called it Pam, and the expression has quite caught on, if you take my meaning, in the family, so whenever one of the kiddies says, 'Can I have some more Pam, Mummie?' we all laugh like anything. Well, it's laughter that will get our little friend Adolf down in the end, mark my words. Guns and planes are all very well and of course we owe a deep debt of gratitude to them and of course to the R.N. which ought to come first, for I

254

always say that wherever you see the sea, that is the Front Line, even if it's only Torquay, though in spite of being so far from London it has suffered terribly, though I mustn't mention how, but Mr. Wagstaffe being Signals," said Mrs. Spender, who had a quite royal memory for names and faces of Army people, "will bear me out, hush-hush, Mr. Wagstaffe, is the word, but it is our wonderful gift for laughter and seeing the funny side of things that will get friend Adolf in the end, even if it's only little me as says it. I wish you could see our kiddies. Clarissa, she's the girl, is getting her second teeth all crooked and I wish Captain Gumm could have seen her first teeth, just like a dainty little row of pearls, said she coming over all weepified. No, Bobbums," said Mrs. Spender, who with rare tenacity of purpose always came back to her original thesis, "not mustard, you silly old goose, but WHO ARE THEY?"

These last words she rather mouthed than spoke, in a hoarse whisper calculated to reach the furthest corner of the room. Captain Hooper and Mr. Wagstaffe ate their lunch in gloomy resignation. Captain Gumm, who had always wanted to join the Air Force, but had been forced into becoming a dentist by his father, who had a flourishing dental practice, was merely confirmed in a general grudge against the world. Major Spender, having told his wife as quietly and quickly as possible who Philip was, managed to switch her off on to coupons, and the rest of the meal passed peacefully. By this time Philip was suffering severely from suppressed amusement, for one can hardly use the word giggles when speaking of a colonel. Having done his best to get over this and partially succeeded, he looked at his fellow-lunchers. Though they had exchanged smiles they had evidently not found any difficulty in concealing their feelings.

Considering this, it quite suddenly occurred to him that his Lydia, with all her sterling qualities and delightful defects, had very little sense of humour. How he could have known her so well for the past eight years or so without noticing this he could not imagine, unless it were that he had very little himself. Knowing his Lydia's interest in philosophical discussions, and always enjoying her downright not to say bludgeoning methods of argument, he said to her:

"Lydia, which of us would you say had a sense of humour?"

Lydia, who, owing to her habit of taking most things as they came, was rarely taken aback, looked seriously at him.

"If you mean me," she said, "I don't think I have. At least, not how you mean, or Noel. But I do laugh at things quite a lot, even if it isn't your way. And quite often I laugh at things inside when it doesn't feel polite to laugh at them outside."

On hearing this clear though jumbled statement, Philip felt, as he so often did, what an extraordinarily good fellow Lydia was, and would have hit her in a friendly way on the back, but that the time and place made it a most unsuitable action.

"I expect Leslie's got heaps," said Lydia, looking at Leslie with something of a hen's pride in a duckling. "I mean she is always seeing clever people in London that know about what's going on everywhere and are a bit disillusioned — if that is what I mean," she added anxiously.

Philip, watching Leslie's face, saw a flicker on it which told him that Lydia's muddled explanation had gone very near the mark. He had a pretty good guess at her London world; men and women whose educated and partly trained minds, moving in a small set though many of its names were those of rising or risen stars, had no very great inner resources and through mental laziness preferred to spend their spare moments in idle or sometimes mildly malicious gossip about their circle, always, very gently, discrediting with crackling laughter those who had climbed highest. It all made him a little uncomfortable and he wished he had not spoken, especially when Leslie suddenly looked at him as if she had something to say, but said nothing.

Mrs. Pollett had by now served them with not only the liver but some excellent castle puddings, made with some hoarded white flour, and produced some quite drinkable coffee, saying as she handed it, "Warmed-up's good enough for *them*. I made this fresh for you." Though Philip knew that her obliging preference of his party was dictated by feudalism rather than mercenary motives, he also knew that a tip is never unwelcome and gave her one which almost made her curtsy. They all thanked her for a very nice lunch and were about to go, when to her horror the macaw-like form of Mrs. Spender rose and dragging the unwilling Captain Hooper with her approached their table.

Captain Hooper, remarking Happy Days as a suitable combined greeting, said he wanted to introduce everyone to Mrs. Spender, and not having done so, basely deserted her and went back to his military duties.

Leslie, bravely taking upon her the role of hostess, as representing her uncle and aunt for the time being, begged Mrs. Spender to sit down, named herself, introduced Lydia and Philip, and offered her guest a cigarette.

"Now don't let me be a spoilsport," said Mrs. Spender, "but I never smoke. Why, I cannot tell you, for everyone knows I am the last person in the world to be faddy, but somehow it has just never appealed to me, and when I think of all our brave men risking their lives to bring tobacco I feel I am doing just a tiny bit to save the Empire. But Bobbie is a dreadful old chimney, such an old silly, so you'd love him. Bobbie," she called to her husband, who was comfortably discussing the golf links at Fleece with Mr. Wagstaffe, "come over here. Miss Waring has kindly asked us to join her party. You know, Miss Waring, Bobbie was billeted with the Villarses at North-bridge a couple of years ago, and Mrs. Villars is a cousin of Sir Harry Waring, such a delightful woman, simply hospitality itself and so courageous. There was an air raid the night I stayed there and she was so splendid, and we had such a nice matey time in the dear old rector's study, not that he is old of course, but being a rector, well you know what I mean, little me all in my siren suit and dressing-gown and wouldn't go to bed till the rector absolutely forced her. You must tell Sir Harry, Miss Waring, what a really wonderful time his cousin gave us and then a really too marvellous sherry party another time when I was down there, I mean quite too marvellous."

Leslie said she had only met Mrs. Villars once and liked her very much.

"That's exactly what I mean," said Mrs. Spender, much impressed. "A woman you simply could not help liking. People say I'm psychic, of course there may be something in it or there mayn't, these things are not for little me to judge said she quite solemn all of a sudden, but I say you often know when you meet a person whether you like them or not. I suppose I'm funny that way but something tells me if I like a person or not right from the jump. And of course Mr. Villars, such a saintlike man, though a modern saint if you see what I mean, really not a saint at all, I mean a saint inside, not showing off about it as one sometimes feels the saints did in the olden times, not that I am irreligious, far from it, though I always say these things don't need discussing because one just *knows*, but somehow a man like Mr. Villars who is really such an old pet, there now I've called him old again but you know what I mean, well, what was I saying, oh yes, a man like Mr. Villars really makes you think."

Leslie, as fascinated as a rabbit before a boa constrictor, said she had never met him, but heard he was very nice.

"Nice," said Mrs. Spender emphatically, "is hardly the word, if you see what I mean. I mean a man who does such wonderful good just by his mere influence,

259

though mind you I don't mean like an Indian by simply sitting and thinking of nothing. And all up-to-date too. Now the vicar at home, that is where we live if you see what I mean, for though Bobbie is away the children and I living there makes it seem like home, though we miss Bobbie dreadfully, don't we Bobbums, is really quite bigoted, I mean like the Inquisition. We had quite an argument about this Beveridge plan, though it sounds exactly like beer-rationing if you take my meaning, or even tea and cocoa, and believe me or not he hadn't even read it!"

Lydia, who felt it was her turn, said she hadn't either.

"Nor had I," said Mrs. Spender with great frankness, "but I always say it isn't so much the actual words as the feeling one gets. I suppose I'm a bit different from other people, but you only have to mention a thing to me and I seem to see it, if you know what I mean. I don't need to read, I just sense what things are about. It's funny, but I'm that way. What, Bobbie?"

Major Spender, who had vainly been trying for some time to break into his wife's conversation, said they really must go if she was to catch her train.

"Why didn't you tell me before, Bobbie?" she said, getting up. "You know, Bobbie is such an old dear, but the most unpractical man that ever stepped God's earth, though really when I say that one is hard put to it to know nowadays whose earth it is with all that's going on, said she quite serious like. Well, good-bye all. Where's my coat, Bobbie?"

Her husband collected it from her seat and helped her into it, looking anxiously at the clock as he did so.

"Now this coat," said Mrs. Spender, buttoning it across her determined front, "and the suit, and the jumper, are all utility. Nothing cut to waste, as you see. It's wonderful in the fourth year of a total war, whatever that means, to be able to get such good clothes, and believe it or not, the whole outfit only seven guineas. As the girl in the shop said, it's just as if it had been made for me. Of course the coupons! But there now, we are all in it, and as I say every coupon spent is a nail in little friend Adolf's coffin. And if you want hats, my dears, not little bits of rubbish but real hats, to stand up to anything, I'll tell you though I wouldn't tell just anyone, of a marvellous little woman in Northampton who can do absolutely anything. I got this hat from her, simply for nothing. I call it my victory hat. Now, Bobbie, we mustn't dawdle."

So saying she led her dejected husband from the room.

"Thank God," said Philip, "Mrs. Pollett keeps the dining-room clock seven minutes fast, otherwise we'd have her back on us. I must go back to work now. Would you care to walk a bit of the way with me and go home by Golden Valley? It would cheer the lonely traveller, but not unless you feel like it."

Lydia said she wanted to go and see Mrs. Allen about the arrangements for Mr. Needham's visit, but if Leslie went a little way with Philip they could meet at Copshot Bank, for she was by now well versed in the geography of the Priory estate and knew most of the local names.

So Philip and Leslie walked up the lane towards the Dower House, pleased to be together, yet with a feeling of constraint between them.

"I wish I were like Lydia," said Leslie suddenly.

Philip, suppressing the obvious retort that he liked her as she was, asked why.

"I don't know," said Leslie, trying to think what she really meant. "I suppose it's her largeness. How stupid that sounds."

"I think I know what you mean," said Philip. "Her bigness."

Even as he said the words he felt how inadequate, nay downright silly they were, when suddenly Leslie began to laugh and he began to laugh too.

"We *are* a couple of sillies," said Philip. "We can't even talk English intelligently."

"Never mind," said Leslie. "It *is* such fun to laugh. I haven't laughed properly for ages."

"Yes, you have," said Philip. "You laughed that evening we walked back from Mrs. Allen and I enjoyed it more than I can tell you. Do go on. It suits you."

"You laughed too," said Leslie, not looking at him. "This is where I turn off for Copshot Bank."

"Never mind Copshot Bank for a moment," said Philip. "I was as usual rather priggish about a sense of humour at lunch. I apologize. I haven't an ounce myself, except the schoolmaster kind, but you have a quite enchanting brand of it. I would like to laugh with you a great, great deal."

"What I was thinking," said Leslie, still looking away from him, "was that Lydia was quite right about the clever disillusioned people I know."

"If it made you unhappy, I wish to goodness she hadn't meddled," said Philip, for the first time in his life feeling critical of his Lydia.

"Not unhappy," said Leslie. "Just wishing one could ever get out of being oneself. One does get so sick of it."

Philip nearly said, "None of us can," but checked himself at the fatuity of the words.

"Oh, damn," he exploded suddenly, "what's the good of a sense of humour or anything else if it makes one so self-conscious that one can't think or speak? I like you exactly as you are and that's all. I don't seem able to express myself very well."

Leslie at last looked at him, pleased, yet a little alarmed.

"And now I have put you off again," said Philip, allowing himself to fall into such a fit of rage as he thought he had conquered long ago. "There you sit, like a bird in a bush, looking out at the world, and if one tries to please you, back you go again into your hole," said Philip, with a fine disregard for natural history. "I'm sorry."

Leslie, with a pleasurable sense of suffocation, looked at him in an interested way.

"Well then, I'm not sorry," said Philip. "At least I am."

What fun it would be, thought part of Leslie, to goad Colonel Winter and see what he would do. But the other part, which usually had the upper hand, said that was not the way ladies behaved. So both parts combined to be perfectly tongue-tied and stupid.

"Are you sure you know your way back?" said Philip, with what appeared to him to be courteous though icy detachment.

"Oh yes," said Leslie, in a voice which was mean to express "Ah, do not so reject me," but came out like "Of course I do, you great fool," "and thank you so much for the lunch party," she added, thus causing Philip to feel that he had been given his dismissal.

"Oh, well, good-bye," said Philip.

Someone had to move first, thought Leslie in desperation, so she set her face towards Copshot Bank. Philip strode back to the Dower House and plunged into his work, so well concealing his feelings that Corporal Jackson said to Private Moss that His Nibs was in a fine old paddy.

Leslie walked towards Copshot Bank in a heartfree manner whose outward semblance was a violent pace and absent looks. Suddenly she stopped dead. Colonel Winter had been quite right; to walk very fast was not good for her at the moment. Not that she wished to pay any attention to what Colonel Winter — oh well, Philip then — said, but if a person, even if you didn't like them very much, happened to say something sensible, the fact of not liking them needn't mean that you need disregard their sensible suggestion. So she walked on at a reasonable pace and presently got to Copshot Bank where she found Lydia, and the two ladies went away down Golden Valley.

Lydia was quite satisfied with her visit to Nannie Allen, who was now all eagerness for her new lodger.

"We had a lovely time settling where Tommy's bed was to go," said Lydia. "I thought sticking out from the wall opposite the fireplace where he'd get some light from the window if he stays in bed a bit and wants to read, but Nannie said it ought to be along the inside wall so that he could knock in the night if he wanted anything."

"I'm almost sorry for your Mr. Needham," said Leslie. "If Nannie takes a real liking to him, she is quite capable of killing him with kindness. I wouldn't be in the least surprised if she brought him a bottle at six in the morning. I'm always expecting her to give me a doll on my birthday."

"Our old Nannie's a bit like that," said Lydia. "We had a splendid talk about a text to put up in his room too. Nannie had a lovely Gothic one about the everlasting arms, but we thought it would be a bit discouraging for Tommy, so she is going to look out a safe one. Did you and Philip have a nice walk?"

Leslie said very nice, adding offhandedly that it would be very nice if Lydia rang him up and asked him to dinner again soon.

"You ring up," said Lydia. "He likes you awfully."

They were now approaching Jasper's cottage. Though nothing was in leaf or bud, for that would be unreasonable in January, the open weather had, as usual, deluded the birds into thinking it was spring and a very ignorant, carefree noise of warbling, twittering, shrilling, billing and cooing arose from the neighbouring bushes.

"And a *primrose*," said Leslie in disgust, stooping to a bank.

"And *catkins*," said Lydia with equal scorn. "Well, they'll find what time of year it really is before long. What's Jasper doing?"

"He must have gone mad too. It looks like spring-cleaning," said Leslie. "Let's go and see."

It was not so much a spring-cleaning, so Leslie afterwards said to Noel, as a defenestration. The untidy grass plot before the house was strewn with wooden chairs, rag hearthrugs, two iron kettles and an iron crock, a broom, a jug, and various other household articles. From one of the upper windows hung a patchwork counterpane for which collectors would have given large sums, and Jasper was in the act of arranging a pillow and a bolster on the sill of the other. On seeing visitors he disappeared from the window and came out to meet them.

"Good afternoon, Jasper," said Leslie. "What are you doing?"

Jasper said Having a turn-out.

"It's a bit early, isn't it?" said the practical Lydia. "I mean you'll be having fires for ages and everything will get dirty again."

"That's naught to go by," said Jasper. "You need a fire all the year round in this old cottage."

"Jasper's fire hasn't gone out for years and years," said Leslie. "It's unlucky."

"That's right, Miss Leslie," said Jasper. "Thirty years I've been in this old cottage and thirty years that old fire's been burning. No, miss, I'm having a turn-out. Makes the old cottage clean like."

As Jasper had never been known to turn the cottage out, though always keeping it clean enough, Leslie came to the conclusion that he had gone mad. Not that this mattered, for she was perfectly sure that no amount of madness would affect his competence as a keeper. After a little talk Leslie said they must get back to the Priory.

"Oh, Mr. Margett," said Lydia, fumbling in her coat pocket, "I didn't forget about the button, but my sister took ages to find it. Here it is."

"That'll do nicely for granny, that old button will," said Jasper, looking with satisfaction at it. "Thank you, miss. That'll learn the old lady."

His visitors turned to go, but Jasper, his face more inscrutable than usual, stopped them.

"If it isn't a trouble, Miss Leslie," he said, "will you tell that old Silleena that I'm turning granny's old mattress, and the goose feathers are nice and soft."

He looked at her with his sideways gipsy look and went back into his cottage.

The ladies walked on in silence till they were out of earshot.

"Cold Comfort Farm," said Lydia in awestruck tones.

"I know," said Leslie. "I was waiting for him to talk about the liddle button. What *do* you think his message to Selina means? It sounded like a proposal."

"It did, awfully," said Lydia. "Do you think we ought to give it?"

"I suppose we'd better," said Leslie. "If Jasper found out I hadn't, he wouldn't trust me again. But I do hope Selina isn't going to marry him. It's a dreadful cottage and a frightful situation apart from being so incredibly picturesque. I'll try to catch Selina when we get back."

Accordingly, the ladies went round by the stable yard and in by the kitchen passage. Leslie looked into the kitchen where Cook and Baker and Selina were having tea. Selina looked up, and Leslie saw that she was in floods of tears.

"What *is* the matter, Selina?" said Leslie.

Selina tried to speak, but sorrow choked her.

"It's Private Jenks, miss," said Cook. "Such a nice young fellow, too."

"What's happened?" said Lydia, envisaging Private Jenks dying suddenly in great torment because the Barchester General had not a vacancy for him, and wondering at the same time how she could help.

"He's gone off to Barchester in the ambulance, miss," said Baker. "Cook was just passing the remark he was in here only yesterday. It seems as if it was meant."

"Stop crying, Selina, and tell me what's the matter," said Leslie in her best lady-of-the-manor voice. "Was Private Jenks taken ill?"

Selina obediently stopped crying and wiped her dewy eyes, which beamed with undiminished lustre from her enchanting, unravaged face.

"Oh no, Miss Leslie," she said. "He was ever so well and that's why it seems so dreadful him being taken in the ambulance. They say if a healthy man or woman rides in an ambulance it's a certain sign of death."

This interesting piece of folklore struck Leslie and Lydia with amazement, but Leslie, who had all Sir Harry's parental feelings towards anyone on the estate, whether an old inhabitant or a stranger within the convalescent hospital gates, pressed for particulars, and managed to extract from Selina that Private Jenks was in excellent spirits and was only taken in the ambulance because there was now a vacancy in Barchester General, and the ambulance was going there in any case.

"And there was ever such a nice orderly with the ambulance, Miss Leslie," said Selina, "and him and Private Jenks were going to play poker all the way. I *was* so upset."

"Well, that's all right," said Leslie with professional cheerfulness. "Oh, Selina, Jasper sent you a message. He says he is turning his old grannie's mattress and the goose feathers are nice and soft."

Feeling that this would be a good corrective to any emotion about Private Jenks, Leslie left the kitchen with Lydia, followed by a sound of laughing and expostulation.

"I rather wish Selina would get settled," said Leslie, with the estate-office manner that Lydia found very becoming to her. "It doesn't seem to affect her work, but Matron has nearly complained, because the men are always round the back door. Of course if she can't control them, we can't, and Sergeant Hopkins who is supposed to be in charge is as bad as any of them. But not Jasper. It wouldn't do at all."

Sir Harry got home by the 5.10, so was able to talk to his family at leisure for once. When we say family, he now counted the Mertons, Lydia in especial, as part of his own circle. One of his pleasures was to hear any local gossip that had trickled in or been collected, and the story of Jasper's spring-cleaning and his message to Selina amused him very much.

"But it would never do," he said, becoming serious. "For one thing, he's too old for her. Besides, the cottage suits him very well, but it wouldn't do for married quarters and I can't think of another free, or likely to be free for years."

"Don't worry about it, Harry," said Lady Waring. "I will speak to Nannie. I am quite sure she wouldn't approve of anything of the sort for Selina."

"I'm not worrying, my dear," said Sir Harry, "but I've known Jasper all his life and most of mine and I must look after him."

"I thought it was about Selina you were worrying," said his wife.

"I leave that to you, my dear," said Sir Harry. "Selina is too attractive. A wife that has every man on the place round her all the time is no wife for Jasper. He'd probably kill her, and that wouldn't suit me at all. By the way, I had a talk with Beedle this afternoon. There's trouble at the station, I'm sorry to say. Money has been taken from his office; not much, but bits here and there. It has never happened before and Beedle is very much upset."

Leslie suddenly laughed.

"I am so sorry, Uncle Harry," she said, "but it made me think of Selina."

"You are an impertinent young woman," said Sir Harry, looking at his niece over his spectacles, "but it's good to hear you laugh. Shows you're really on the mend."

"This is very uncomfortable, Harry," said his wife, who was also pleased to see Leslie amused but did not comment on it. "Has Mr. Beedle any idea who it is?"

"I'm sorry to say he has," said Sir Harry. "When I say sorry, it's a local man I'm afraid. A man called Morple who was at Melicent Halt. His mother was a Margett. He got mixed up with some very undesirable people from London, the gang who were concerned in all that damage at the station, and Beedle thinks he has been betting with them. He is very distressed — no, Leslie, not upset — and can't quite make up his mind what to do, and what's more, Morple has had his callingup papers and may have to go any day now. Beedle doesn't want the police in the station, but of course he can't let it go on. And he worries about their boy in Germany. I'm sorry for Beedle."

Lydia also felt sorry for Mr. Beedle and thought of the morning he and his wife had been so kind to her. She was not given to imaginings, but she suddenly saw Winter Overcotes station as an island in the middle of a sea of darkness which was lapping at its walls, and the suspected Morple as a traitor within the gates.

For a time there was a comfortable silence, only gently disturbed by the little noise of Lady Waring's writing and her papers, the rustle of Sir Harry's *Times*, the regular click of Lydia's and Leslie's knitting-needles. Leslie, not too tired by her walk, indeed just pleasantly tired, sank into a reverie in which the conversation between herself and Philip was directed by her into a more soothing form than it had taken that afternoon. But although she recast it more than once, she could never quite bring it to the ending she wished. Indeed what end she did want she did not quite know. All she did know was that she felt it would be very nice to have Colonel Winter to dinner again soon. She knew her uncle and aunt would be delighted to have him, she knew Lydia was very fond of him, she knew that any suggestion coming from her would be well received, but every time she took a breath to mention it, something corked up her throat, the breath all went back to wherever it came from, and the whole thing had to be begun again.

The sound of the telephone made Sir Harry grunt angrily. Selina appeared.

"It's Dr. Ford, Sir Harry," she said. "He says could you speak to him, please."

Sir Harry, who knew that Dr. Ford never rang up unless he had something to say, heaved himself up and went into the hall. He was not long absent and came back with a face of portentous gloom. Lady Waring laid down her pen in resignation. Her darling husband took such a genuine pleasure in bad news, or rather in imparting it, for his kindness to anyone in trouble was unbounded, that even his wife could not always guess whether their best friend had been killed, or a very old gentleman of no particular distinction, whom Sir Harry had once met at a public dinner had passed peacefully away, regretted by no one, aged ninety-seven.

"Well, Harry, what is it?" said Lady Waring with her unalterable patience.

"That was Ford ringing up," said Sir Harry, determined to enjoy himself in his own way.

There was a respectful silence, but as the oracle vouchsafed no further information Lady Waring inquired what he had to say.

"These things always come as a shock to one," said Sir Harry, settling himself comfortably in his chair again, with the kind of expression King Henry I may have shown on hearing of the loss of the White Ship.

Lady Waring considered. It might have been that some friend of theirs who was a patient of Dr. Ford's was suddenly worse. She could not think of anyone probable, for Dr. Ford did not really practise in their district, but owing to having petrol to visit the convalescent hospital was able to attend a few old friends who liked a doctor they knew. What Sir Harry deserved was for no one to take the faintest notice of him, which would force him, rather sulkily, to disgorge. But as she was busy she decided to forgo this just revenge and asked what had happened. Even Lydia, not oversensitive, admired the way in which she kept the faintest show of long-suffering patience out of her voice, though it would have been impossible not to feel it inside.

"Eh?" said Sir Harry. "Happened? Oh! thought I'd told you. It's old Horniman's sister."

"Do you mean Miss Horniman is dead, Harry?" said Lady Waring.

His defences now being breached, Sir Harry cast aside his pose of indifference and said the old lady had died at two o'clock that afternoon quite peacefully and the funeral was to be the day after to-morrow.

"And none of that nonsense about no mourning," said Sir Harry. "I asked Ford and he says there's a very sensible niece who is arranging everything. What's the use of people dying if they don't want anyone to wear mourning? Might as well stay alive and make nuisances of themselves that way. No patience with them."

"But Uncle Harry, don't you think that they really don't want to be mourned for sometimes?" said Leslie. "I mean if they are frightfully old and ill and really glad to die."

"In my experience," said Sir Harry, "the iller and older they are the more they want to live. Hope I'll die before I get like that."

Leslie said it must be very difficult to know exactly when to die and she supposed that very old, ill people thought they were quite young and well and were annoyed with people who were even older and iller because *they* wouldn't die. She then drifted into remembrance of a talk she had had with Colonel Winter, Philip she meant, and how he had said that the very aged and demented would dance on all their graves. At this she laughed aloud to herself which made her uncle look up at her again and feel glad that the girl was enjoying herself so much.

"After all, we all begin to die the moment we are born," said Lydia, looking round with a gratified expression, for she had only just evolved this highly original thought and was rather pleased with it.

"I certainly should not dream of going to a funeral except in black," said Lady Waring. "It would be extremely discourteous; nor would I wish to dictate to my friends what they should or should not wear at my funeral. Who is taking it, Harry?"

"I think Miller from Pomfret Madrigal," said Sir Harry. "Well, now the Vicarage will be empty, so I'll have to do something about a new Vicar. We can't go on like this."

"Oh, Sir Harry —" Lydia began, violently, and then checked herself.

Sir Harry, who really wanted to read his paper in peace, looked up at the noise, but as it did not continue he gratefully retired behind the attenuated pages of *The Times*.

Lydia was silent. But in this hour a mighty purpose was born in her, which she determined to consult Noel about that very night. Noel, who was used to his Lydia, realized at once that something was brewing in her mind, but as he only got back just in time for dinner he had no opportunity of asking what it was. Lydia managed to get through the evening somehow, though with occasional alarming bursts of what looked like suppressed apoplexy, so that Noel was quite glad when they could be alone together. She then laid before him her plan, which was that Tommy Needham should, while staying with Nannie, so ingratiate himself with the Warings that Sir Harry would appoint him Vicar of Lambton. The Vicarage would then be empty, and if he and Octavia ever did get married everything would be perfect. Noel, while highly approving the idea, said she had better say nothing about it for the present, to which his Lydia very reasonably agreed, though she was slightly disappointed, having had a vision of Tommy being in the Vicarage the very moment old Miss Horniman's corpse was carried out.

"I'm not coming to bed just yet," said Noel. "I've some papers to look at, so I'll work in the sitting-room. There's only Sir Harry there now."

"It *will* be nice when we can have a proper home," said Lydia wistfully. "I mean so that you can have a proper room to write things in. I haven't heard of anything possible round here. What a pity we couldn't take the Vicarage and have Tommy as a lodger."

Noel, a little alarmed lest Lydia should suggest this to Sir Harry, begged her to keep the idea to herself for the moment.

"Besides," he said, "we may not be needing a house. I heard from Robert to-day. He and Edith have bought a house near Nutfield which Edith has always wanted, and he is quite willing to sell Northbridge Manor back to you. If you really want to live there, I don't see why we shouldn't buy it. We could always use the bailiff's cottage while the house is occupied."

"Oh, Noel!" was all Lydia's reply.

"Then I'll write to Robert," said Noel. "I must say you have a very nice, obliging elder brother, Lydia. Nothing from Colin yet, I suppose?"

"It's much too soon," said Lydia cheerfully; which did not deceive Noel in the least. "Oh, Noel," she added, but with a diffidence quite unlike her manner a moment earlier, "you won't mind if I do full-time V.A.D. here, will you? I mean, if the Warings will have us, or we can get another lodging?"

"I don't see how I could mind," said Noel. "At least, I *shall* mind, quite unpatriotically and unreasonably, but as it's obvious that you might be picked up and stuck into a factory in Merthyr Tydvil or what not, this would be more satisfactory."

"Well, first I was ill, and then I got deferment because I had to take care of mother when her heart was so bad, but now I'm as fit as anything and mother is safely at Bournemouth with Aunt Kate, I'd feel a TRAITOR if I didn't," said Lydia with extreme earnestness.

"What did Dr. Ford say?" asked Noel, touched and annoyed.

"He said, 'Proceed, V.A.D. Merton,'" said Lydia.

"That's that, then," said Noel. "I shall tell Ford to speak to Matron about you. Well, farewell to the felicity of unbounded domesticity. I must say I quite agree with Leslie's brother in preferring my womenfolk ornamental. My precious Lydia, you will take care of yourself, won't you?"

"Of course I will," said Lydia. "After all, it's only convalescents here, not woundeds and lifting people. And I'm really frightfully well."

"Yes, I know you are, and that's what frightens me," said Noel. "Now go to bed. Leslie has left me a heap of stuff, beautifully sorted, and I must deal with it now, or heaven knows when I'll get a chance, as I have to be on late duty the rest of this week."

"Noel, I've never asked what you do at the Dower House," said Lydia, "but is it *anything*?"

Noel laughed.

"I sometimes wonder if it is," he said. "We are all so hush-hush, with Army and Air Force and Signals and A.T.S. and W.A.A.F.s all bundled up together pretending no one knows where we are. And what is even more mortifying, no one taking the faintest interest in us. I hear from Corporal Jackson, who gets the information at the Woolpack at Worsted, that the village say we are a lot of lazy blighters and have absolutely no opinion of us at all. And they are usually pretty near the truth. Oh, well."

Lydia clung to him for a moment, as if this were a moment of parting, and then he went downstairs.

CHAPTER
NINE

Selina brought in word next day that her mother had heard from Mr. Needham, who was coming over to-morrow by the morning train from Barchester.

"Mother's been down to the butcher herself about it," said Selina, "and he's letting her have a nice bit of steak for the gentleman's lunch. And he's keeping her a nice bit of best-end neck for the week-end."

"I think Nannie has the whole village terrorized," said Lady Waring, when Selina had gone. "I know she got veal when no one else had any for weeks, and chocolate biscuits when there was a famine, and last time I went to see her she showed me two lemon soles in the larder when we hadn't seen anything for three weeks except frozen cod. Still, it's just as well, because I can always give her vegetables or a rabbit if we have any, but meat and fish I can't, nor can anyone else. We must ask your friend up to lunch soon, Lydia."

"It's Miss Horniman's funeral in the afternoon, so it's lucky he's coming in the morning," said Lydia, who apparently felt this to be a suitable house-warming for a clergyman. "Do you think it would be all right for me to come, Lady Waring? I mean as I didn't know Miss Horniman."

Lady Waring said it would show a neighbourly spirit for anyone at the Priory to go.

"Suppose we drive you down in Crumpet, Aunt Harriet," said Leslie. "We could drop you near the Vicarage and go on to Nannie's and see if Mr. Needham would care to come. He'll hardly want to walk there if he's only got one arm."

"A very kind thought," said Lady Waring approvingly. "Poor young man. Perhaps we could have Miss Crawley over for a night next time you are in town, Leslie." For Dr. Ford had now given Leslie permission to go to London once a week for the night to see friends and pick up the threads of her work, and she appeared to thrive on it.

So directly after lunch Crumpet was harnessed and the three ladies went down to the village. And if anyone thinks that three ladies, one in a neat black coat and skirt, a black felt hat and a fur coat, the other two in tweeds, for they were on a visit and had not brought their blacks with them, crammed into a small pony cart drawn by a cheerful, unclipped pony, attracted any attention, we may at once say that person is mistaken. A few convalescent soldiers who were hanging about the drive cheered; the laundry, who to Lady Waring's great relief was turning in at the lodge gates, for he had not called since last Thursday week, touched his cap and nearly ran into the bank in his attempts to evade Crumpet's downhill charge, and a few quiet people who were living at Lambton for the duration cast wistful eyes at pony and cart. As for the village, it saw no reason to think anything at all about a normal occurrence.

Lady Waring got out of Crumpet near the Vicarage, mysteriously managing to step down backwards out of a small tilting cart with no loss of dignity, and Leslie drove on to Ladysmith Cottages. Marigold's brother, aged ten, was playing in the street with some friends.

"Here, Percy!" said Leslie, who never forgot a tenant's name to the third generation, "come and take Crumpet. You and the others can have a ride up the lane in the cart, but mind, you must lead him all the time."

"They'd have rides anyway," said Leslie as she and Lydia walked up Nannie's path, "but if Percy has Crumpet he'll be all right. Percy's father is Uncle Harry's head carter, if you can call it head when there isn't anyone under you now, and Percy was practically brought up in a stable."

"I half wish I hadn't come," said Lydia, rather to Leslie's surprise, as they stepped into the house. "I mean Tommy's arm. I don't know if I ought to notice that he's lost it or not."

Leslie, rightly judging that the sooner this was over the better knocked at the sitting-room door. A slightly muffled voice, as of someone talking with a very full mouth, said "Come in." Leslie opened the door and stood aside for Lydia, who summoning all her courage went in. At a well-spread table sat Mr. Needham, a heaped plate of grilled steak neatly cut up potatoes and brussels sprouts before him, a glass of beer at his side.

Opposite him sat Nannie with a face of grim satisfaction.

"Oh, Tommy," said Lydia, suddenly half-blinded by her feelings.

"If it isn't Lydia!" said Mr. Needham, getting up and stretching a hand across the table in warm welcome.

"Oh, *Tommy!*" said Lydia again, grabbing Mr. Needham's hand in both hers. Then she looked at it. "Oh, I *am* glad it's the other one," she said, looking at the left sleeve which was pinned across his coat. "It is so *awful* to have to shake people's left hands, because you never know which way round. Oh, Tommy, this *is* nice."

"Nice goings-on," said Nannie indignantly to Leslie, "young ladies coming in while a gentleman's having his dinner. Eat it up now, sir, or it'll all be getting cold, and there's another nice little bit of steak Nannie will cut up for you."

She got up and bustled into the kitchen, with no sign of rheumatics.

"Good lord, Lydia!" said Mr. Needham. "Octavia said you were hereabouts, but I never thought I'd see you so soon. Where are you?"

Lydia explained that she and Noel were at the Priory and that Miss Waring who had brought her was the Warings' niece.

"Do sit down," said Mr. Needham. "I say, excuse my going on with my lunch, but that old lady will probably put me to bed if I don't. I only got here just before lunch and she apparently thinks I'm a mentally defective child of seven. But what a dear old thing she is. When I was in Libya I used to dream about grilled steak and beer and a good fire, with a cold day outside, and by Jove, here it all is. I *am* a lucky fellow. It's a good thing Dr. Crawley isn't here. The Army makes a fellow a bit tough and I wouldn't like to come out with by Jove in front of him. How's everyone?"

Lydia, her face beaming with joy at finding an old friend so well, poured out all the news of family and friends that she thought Mr. Needham would not have got from the Crawleys. Nannie brought in the fresh bit of steak, cut it up into suitable mouthfuls and put it on her lodger's plate, who forked it into his mouth and talked and drank his beer with perfect unself-consciousness, while Nannie went in and out with an air of great importance.

"I've just unpacked your suitcase, sir," she said, as she brought in a fine apple turnover and a jug of custard. "You can eat the custard, sir, it's made with eggs from my own fowls, not those nasty powders. And I can't find a toothbrush nowhere, sir," she added accusingly.

"Not in my bedroom slippers?" said Mr. Needham, entirely unembarrassed.

"No, sir, nor in the sponge-bag," said Nannie.

"Well, then, I left it behind at the Deanery," said Mr. Needham. "I'll write to Octavia and ask. I suppose there's a chemist here."

"Yes, sir," said Nannie, "but it's early closing."

Mr. Needham said that he had always told his scout troop that one could clean one's teeth with a twig and, by Jove, this was the moment to try it.

"Certainly not, sir," said Nannie. "Clean your teeth with a twig! I never heard such nonsense. I'll put a nice new one in your tooth-vase, sir. I always keep some for my young gentlemen and ladies in case they forget."

"I'd like to see her up against our sergeant-major," said Mr. Needham admiringly when Nannie had gone upstairs. "By Jove, I don't think she'd give him a chance."

"I expect she'll want to bath you," said Lydia. "What's the matter?"

For Mr. Needham had suddenly made a curious movement, half-turning his body and then slewing round in the other direction and helping himself to sugar.

"I really *must* cure myself of that," said Mr. Needham seriously. "It's a rum thing, but I often don't believe my left arm's gone. I was trying to reach the sugar with it just then. I wish you'd tell me when I do anything like that. It looks so silly."

Leslie interrupted to say that it was getting on and she would go and fetch Crumpet, and perhaps Mr. Needham would care to come with them.

"It's a funeral," said Lydia as Leslie went away, "so we thought you'd like to come, especially as it's the old Vicar's sister. We've got the pony cart in case you couldn't walk."

"Look here, Lydia, do you think I walk on my hands like an acrobat?" said Mr. Needham. "I was never fitter. And as soon as I get out of these silly habits of thinking I've got an extra arm, I'll be at the top of my form. I'd love to come to the funeral. By Jove, it will be like old

284

times. It will be good to get into harness. That is if I can," he said, suddenly sober, "for one doesn't drop into a living all of a sudden. But I've done a good spot of curating, so I dare say they'll put me somewhere, and Dr. Crawley would recommend me. Or do you think a Dean doesn't count now?"

Lydia said she was sure they counted frightfully.

Much cheered, Mr. Needham folded up his table napkin with his right hand and put it into a ring composed of the largest whorl of a many-coloured shell with "A Present from Frinton" in black upon it.

"My coat's in the passage," said Mr. Needham, "and if you wouldn't mind giving me just one hoick up with it. Thanks awfully. I'll soon get into the way of things, but I don't know what my tailor will say."

"No you don't, sir, not without your muffler," said Nannie, suddenly appearing from the kitchen. "It's in the drawer of the hall stand, and when you come in you can fold it up nicely and put it away."

A very few minutes in Crumpet brought them to the churchyard. Leslie took Crumpet and cart round to the Vicarage backyard and put them in the garage. Lady Waring, who had been in to Bolton Abbey about the weekly working party that took place there, was already in the church, where they joined her. Mr. Miller from Pomfret Madrigal took the little service, the ceremony out of doors was soon over, and the few friends present were invited by the niece-in-charge to come back to the Vicarage and have a cup of tea.

To Lydia's great surprise, who was waiting in the drawingroom among the teacups but Octavia Crawley.

"Miss Horniman was a mistress at the Barchester High School," said Octavia, who appeared to think that her presence needed a little explanation. "So when father said old Miss Horniman was dead and her niece was alone in the Vicarage, I thought I'd see if I could help her. You know, Lydia, she used to do maths, but you never got so high as her form."

"Gosh!" said Lydia, gazing with reverence upon the pleasant, efficient, young-middle-aged niece in whose lineaments she now recognized the ex-maths mistress.

"So I rang her up and said could I help and I'm staying here till the end of the week," Octavia continued, "and then I can see Tommy."

Lydia, lost in admiration of the ruthless methods of the daughter of the Deanery, was struck temporarily dumb.

"How do you think he's looking?" said Octavia. "I haven't seen it yet," she continued without giving Lydia time to answer, "but Tommy says it's pretty well healed now, which is rather a pity, but it can't be helped. He doesn't seem to know if they did it by the Fowkes-Brunter method or the Lanke-Ellerman, but I suppose being under an anæsthetic one wouldn't notice much. Mother thinks we ought to get married soon."

Leaving Lydia to digest this interesting information, Octavia returned to her duties, dealing out tea and small cakes with calm efficiency, speaking a kind word to everyone, occasionally asking Miss Horniman to tell her some guest's name, which it was obvious she would now remember for ever. Miss Horniman introduced her to Lady Waring and rather to Lydia's surprise they fell into earnest talk, while the neglected lover was happily engaged with Mr. Miller, who had been at college with his father.

Lady Waring now felt that the party had lasted long enough, so she began her good-byes, lingering a moment with Mr. Miller to ask news of Mrs. Brandon, who was a great friend of her Vicar and his wife.

"Mrs. Brandon is doing wonders," said Mr. Miller. "What with the way she is looking after the land girls and running the little nursery school in her house, and the way my dear wife is caring for the evacuee children, several of whose parents in London have quite disappeared, we could not be a happier parish. And we hear that Mrs. Grant, her daughter's mother-in-law, is quite safe in Calabria and is allowed to continue her work of collecting folk songs. And how is Sir Harry?"

Lady Waring said he was well and busy and how they hoped to see something of Mr. Needham.

"An excellent young man," said the Vicar. "And though his views on ritual are not quite mine, he is perfectly sound about the Bishop and should go far."

Lady Waring was glad to hear this and asked Mr. Miller to give her kindest regards to his wife. Mr. Miller, gratified, said indeed, indeed he would, and went away.

By this time Lady Waring, standing near the door had, as often happened though without any intention on her part, become the hostess, and good-byes were said to her quite as much as to Miss Horniman, who however took it all in very good part, being a strong-minded woman with no use for what she called social mumbo-jumbo. Lady Waring said she hoped Miss Horniman and Miss Crawley would come up to dinner the following night and Mr. Needham too, if he felt equal to it, and went away.

"I do wish," said Mr. Needham to Lydia, who had lingered to speak to Octavia, "that people wouldn't behave as if they were sorry for me. If they aren't careful I'll get an artificial arm just not to give them a chance."

Octavia said she had seen a man in the Barchester General who had a marvellous artificial arm, but the trouble was one had to wear a glove on the hand and it looked so peculiar as one couldn't always be changing it to match one's real glove. Mr. Needham said he thought a gadget like one of those multiple tools that you can stick a punch, or a gimlet, or a screwdriver, or a tobacco-stopper into would be the thing. So leaving her friends to their lover-like talk Lydia joined her hostess and they all went home to tea.

No one was disappointed when Miss Horniman rang up next morning to say she was starting a cold and thought she had better not come.

"That will make us only one woman too many," said Lady Waring. "Shall I ask that nice Colonel Winter, Harry?"

Sir Harry, who was not going to town that day, seemed pleased by the idea. Philip was rung up and accepted. For though Leslie Waring undoubtedly possessed highly irritating qualities, that was no reason to turn down an invitation to a pleasant house. Besides,

288

one might show her, quite calmly and politely, that one didn't really mind how annoying she was.

Lydia and Leslie spent most of the day in the garden, for the unnaturally mild weather continued and there was much to do. Leslie was now quite up to a couple of hours' work and would have done more but that Lydia, having consulted Dr. Ford, took up an attitude of benevolent bullying and forced her to stop before she was tired. After one morning of defiance, which made her unfit to do much for the next two days, Leslie apologized very handsomely to Lydia and submitted to her authority.

"Stupid things women with brains are," said Leslie, who was helping Lydia to have a bonfire of hedge cuttings in the kitchen garden. "They can't look after themselves and they don't know what they want."

"You would know of course," said Lydia, with entire candour. "But people who haven't got brains are just as silly. I overdid it like anything at that hospital in Yorkshire, and — oh, well."

"It seems to me if one's born silly that's that," said Leslie, "however clever one's mind may be. What one really needs is someone to bully one. You are a splendid bully, Lydia, but when I go back to London I'll probably relapse."

"Everyone ought to be married," said Lydia stoutly, "unless of course they've got a very nice brother like Colin or Cecil to live with."

"I hope I won't have got too horrid to make a nice home for Cecil some day," said Leslie, forking more clippings on to the bonfire, whose high wavering flames crackled agreeably. "I say, you *did* cut a lot off that hedge."

"It needed it," said Lydia. "All gone to height and a lot of dead wood. I'm sure you'll make a very nice home for Cecil. And really, you must, else you'll be settling down in London for ever."

"And sharing a flat with someone called 'My-friend-that-I-live-with,'" added Leslie grimly. "What I'd like to do — but it's no good looking ahead — would be to live in the country and do something useful. I mean if Uncle Harry died and the war were over I'd like to live here and run the estate for Cecil and he might make the house into a sort of hostel for naval officers and their wives. It's only a sort of idea and I suppose I oughtn't to think about it, but I do so want to do something with Cecil. He'll have to live here and if he isn't bothe red with the estate at first he might settle down and really get fond of it. And he could always go away for sailing holidays."

Lydia listened with interest and was glad to hear Leslie making plans, for it showed that she was ready to begin working again, though Dr. Ford had refused to let her go back permanently under the three months, which would not be up for three weeks or so. She too thought of a future in the country, at her old home, perhaps spending the week in town with Noel and coming down for week-ends, perhaps as time went on living more at Northbridge with new ties to the place. But realizing with her excellent common sense that Leslie wished to talk a little about her own plans, not to hear about other people's, she kept her thoughts to

290

herself. They raked earth over the ashes of the bonfire, so that there should be no chance of a light after black-out, and walked back to the house.

In the yard they found Sergeant Hopkins and Selina.

"Oh please, madam," said Selina to Lydia, "Sergeant Hopkins's mother came over to see him to-day and she's having a cup of tea in the kitchen before she goes and Sergeant Hopkins wants to know if you'd like to see her."

"That's right, miss," said Sergeant Hopkins, "seeing as the Captain was so good to me and all."

Rightly interpreting the Sergeant's desire for her to meet his mother as a kind of thankoffering, the best he could bestow, for Colin's care of him, Lydia said she would love it. Leslie said she would go in, and left them.

Lydia Merton was one of those rarely gifted women who can go into other people's kitchens without giving mortal umbrage to the staff, though she never presumed upon this quality. Together with Sergeant Hopkins, she followed Selina into the warm, blacked-out kitchen, where a spare and still goodlooking little elderly woman with a pleasant expression was sitting with Cook and Baker.

"It's the Captain's sister, mum," said Sergeant Hopkins.

Lydia shook hands with Mrs. Hopkins, who conveyed the impression of a curtsy, though not actually dropping one. Sergeant Hopkins stood twisting his cap in his hands, waiting for some clash of intellect between the two powers. Selina's eyes began to brim at the sight of the Sergeant's mother and the Captain's sister in the same room.

"We was just having our tea, madam," said Cook. "I suppose you wouldn't like a cup."

Lydia said, quite truthfully, that she would love it, and hooking a chair with her leg dragged it next to Mrs. Hopkins and sat down. Mrs. Hopkins, at once recognizing Lydia as an equal, and knowing all about her family from her son, was entirely at her ease and favoured Lydia with a long account of her son's good qualities, his deep understanding of the vegetable trade, his happy married life and his grief at his wife's death, to all of which Lydia listened with real interest, telling Mrs. Hopkins in return, with a little exaggeration, how sorry Colin had been.

"You've not heard from the Captain yet, miss, have you?" said Sergeant Hopkins.

Lydia said cheerfully that she hadn't, but one couldn't possibly expect to for some time.

"The sergeant and me we took Mrs. Hopkins down to see mother this afternoon," said Selina. "Mother *was* so pleased. She does like visitors. She showed Mrs. Hopkins Mr. Needham's room, madam, and all his collars," said Selina, her voice impeded by tears.

"Here, Mrs. Crockett, what's the matter?" said Sergeant Hopkins.

"Nothing," said Selina, wiping her eyes. "Only I thought Mother and Mrs. Hopkins were quite a picture together, and when I thought of your poor wife that couldn't see it I *was* so upset."

"Well, it's to be hoped she *did* see it," said Cook, who was a staunch churchwoman. "That's what we're taught, anyhow. Another cup of tea, Mrs. Hopkins."

Mrs. Hopkins thanked Cook, but said she must be going, as she had to catch the train and anyway wouldn't get back to Northbridge till after eight.

"It's a bit dull," she added, "getting back to an empty house. I'll be glad when the war's over and my Ted's at home again. The vegetables could do with a man about the place and I'm not as young as I was. What I tell Ted is he ought to marry again. There's plenty would be pleased to have him. I said so to Mrs. Allen this afternoon."

At this remark all eyes turned on Sergeant Hopkins, who went quite crimson and twisted his cap harder than ever. Selina, still getting over her emotion at the thought of the late Mrs. Ted Hopkins's celestial inability to see her mother-in-law and another old lady having a talk, appeared not to have heard. Lydia said good-bye to Mrs. Hopkins and got up to go. As she turned from the table she saw in the doorway Jasper, leaning against the doorpost.

"Well, come in or stay out as the saying is," said Cook, rather loudly, for she stood no nonsense in her kitchen.

"I heerd someone talk about getting married," said Jasper, looking round the assembly with his slanting gaze, his eyes almost veiled like a bird's against the light.

"They say listeners hear no good of themselves," said Cook sharply, and it seemed to Lydia irrelevantly.

"You must be Jasper Margett," said Mrs. Hopkins, getting up. "I remember your father when I was a girl. Always up to some mischief or other and I dare say you're the same. Come along, Ted, you and Mrs. Crockett can see me down to the station if Jasper Margett doesn't mind making room for us to pass."

Jasper melted from the doorway and the party dispersed.

Octavia Crawley and Mr. Needham were the first to arrive. Sir Harry expressed the hope that the walk in the dark had not been unpleasant. Octavia said there was a moon and she had a torch and Tommy had only stumbled once, but luckily she was holding his arm, so he had not fallen down. Mr. Needham looked as it he were undecided between gratitude or hatred for unnecessary kindness, but controlled himself. Sir Harry, who had been looking forward to a pair of billing and cooing young lovers, was a little disappointed, but his soldier's heart warmed to the young chaplain with an empty sleeve and he determined to pump him after dinner, by which phrase he meant, on the whole, that he hoped to find a sympathetic audience for his stories about the last war.

Philip followed a few minutes later, delighted to meet Mr. Needham whom he remembered at Rose Birkett's wedding, and quite resigned to meeting Octavia Crawley as she was an old acquaintance. Noel was also an old friend of both, so everyone was on very comfortable terms.

Looking across the dinner-table at her friend Octavia, Mrs. Noel Merton, bringing a fresh eye to bear on her, for they had not met in the last two years, thought she saw a faint but decided improvement. It is true that Octavia would always look, as Miss Pettinger had once said, exactly the type she would wish the Barchester High School to turn out, but there was added to her a kind of laborious neatness, just spoilt by a touch of peasant arts, which seemed familiar, though Lydia could not quite place the type. She had acquired a not very good permanent wave in her uninteresting hair; her dress, obviously a standardized utility product, had some faint approach to style, though it might have fitted better across the shoulders; and her talk, though far from sparkling, appeared to be sensible, for Sir Harry was listening to her with attention. As Mr. Needham on her left was talking to Leslie, Lydia listened placidly to Sir Harry and Octavia on her right, and heard her expounding the theory of day nursery-schools with cheap lunches in a lucid and not too overbearing manner. Sir Harry, who was exercised about the growing number of married women in the neighbourhood who either wanted to do part-time war work and were prevented by their young children, or didn't want to do part-time war work because of their young children and were pushed into it by the combined efforts of the Labour Exchange at Winter Overcotes and the lure of easy money, had been considering the possibility of this kind of state foster-motherhood, but had not had time to go properly into it.

"You know I don't like it, Miss Crawley," he said. "It seems all wrong to me, the whole business, and I know the husbands don't like it at all, but one has to face facts."

"I always do," said Octavia. "Of course, as I'm Red Cross I'm all right, but if I had to work in a factory, or wanted to, I think I'd be glad to have my children properly looked after. You know Mrs. Miller has done it at Pomfret Madrigal, at least at Grumper's End, where there are a lot of children, mostly illegitimate, and it's a great success. All the married and unmarried mothers go to the factory over on the other side of the village every day and earn heaps of money and some of them are going to marry properly, the older key-men who come from the Hogglestock rolling mills, which you know are working full time now. Of course a certain number are going to have more illegitimate children," said Octavia in a business-like manner, "but they'd have them anyway."

She then gave a few statistics about the expense of starting and maintaining such schools.

"Well, well," said Sir Harry, a little taken aback by his young guest's knowledge of life, but impressed by what she said, "that's all very interesting. How did you learn it all?"

"I thought I ought to," said Octavia. "You see I'm going to marry Tommy as soon as he gets a living, so I thought I'd better learn something useful. I pretty well know the parish work because I've got two brothers in the Church and two sisters who married clergymen and I've stayed with them a lot. Of course I like nursing better than anything, and the war's a splendid opportunity," said Octavia, her face lighting up in so far as such an uninteresting face could be said to do such a thing, "but I shall give it up as soon as I marry. Besides, it is my duty to have a large family and if I let my own children go to a village nursery school I shall be freer to run the parish front. I don't know what you think about the optional changes in the marriage service, Sir Harry, but I don't approve them at all, nor does my father. The Bishop of course does."

Sir Harry was not quite sure whether the marriage service, authorized or revised, was quite the thing for the dinner-table, but any implied criticism of the Bishop was grateful to him, and he joined his guest in tearing the Palace to ribbons.

At this moment Selina, who had been handing a casserole of rabbit, withdrew to the sideboard.

"Selina has forgotten you," said Leslie to Mr. Needham. "She must be flustered."

But before she could take steps about it, Selina was back with a plate. On it were arranged rabbit, potato, vegetables, all neatly cut up and thoughtfully arranged, even to the cutting of the larger brussels sprouts in two. She then retired to the kitchen to tell Cook how upset she felt at seeing the poor gentleman eating so nicely with only the one arm.

Leslie, feeling that Mr. Needham might be embarrassed by this tender attention, did not say anything, and Mr. Needham now claimed Lydia's notice.

While he talked with great pride of his regiment and its prowess, appearing to consider himself as on the whole higher than the colonel, though not puffed up, Lydia looked at him also with a fresh eye. She thought of the very young Tommy who had been so susceptible to every nice woman or girl that he met; she remembered his incredibly dilatory courtship of Octavia and how, but for her vigorous action, they would never have got engaged at all; she remembered how she had looked upon Tommy with what was almost good-natured contempt, and how Noel had at one time imagined that she might care for the Dean's secretary, a thought that suddenly made her laugh, which she so rarely did.

Mr. Needham stopped talking and looked at her.

"Sorry, Tommy," said Lydia, recovering herself at once. "I was only thinking how different we all were when you think of us before the war. I mean we are a bit different."

"By Jove, yes," said Mr. Needham. "I must say everyone at home seems a bit different. The old ones look a lot older and all my own lot seem to have such a lot of responsibility. Fine fun for me," said Mr. Needham apologetically, "having such a splendid time in Libya with my regiment, but I can tell you, Lydia, I feel a perfect worm to see all your people carrying on here with none of the fun. Look at Octavia. Doesn't she look wonderful to-night?"

Lydia stoutly said she did.

"And yet," continued Mr. Needham, "she's working much harder than I ever worked in my life. It's no good pretending that I'm a good enough chap for her. However," said Mr. Needham with a tone of authority quite new to Lydia's ears, "she's been running round nursing and going to lectures about communal kitchens and State insurance and war damages and land settlement and lord knows what quite long enough. She's got to settle down now and be my left hand," said Mr. Needham, looking anxiously at Lydia to see if she understood the joke.

"Of course, what's the matter with you, Tommy, is that you've grown up," said Lydia, gazing at him with candid, appraising eyes.

Mr. Needham went bright pink.

"By Jove, Lydia," he said, "that's it. I couldn't think what was wrong. And most of us are now. Do you think Octavia is?"

Lydia said she was sure of it.

"Well then, it's high time we did get married," said Mr. Needham seriously. "I'd like to have a living first, but luckily I've got a bit of my own and Mrs. Crawley says the Dean is going to do something, so why wait? It's time Octavia stopped thinking that the Barchester General is the beginning and end of everything. I shall see about it."

"Quite right, Tommy," said Lydia approvingly.

"What a right-hand man to have!" said Mr. Needham looking with real affection at his betrothed's uninteresting face.

"Left-hand woman, you mean," said Lydia, thus showing that she had taken Mr. Needham's point and giving him intense pleasure.

While this conversation was going on, Leslie had hoped to talk to Colonel Winter, but the table had got out of control from the beginning, a state of things that can rarely be put right by peaceful methods. Old Lord Pomfret had stood no nonsense about it. If the couples at his dinner-table were not pairing off properly, he would call loudly down the table to the place where the trouble had begun, eye the unlucky talkers into submission with his fierce little eyes, and not resume his own conversation till every man and woman had turned in the right direction. But at a table of eight in war-time, especially a round table, one could not adopt this lordly control; at least Lady Waring did not feel like it and Sir Harry did not particularly notice, so long as he was happily engaged himself. So Leslie sat and thought her own thoughts, which were partly how she wished Aunt Harriet would stop talking to Colonel Winter so that he could turn to Miss Waring, partly that as Colonel Winter, or Philip, was so rude as to neglect her when it was really her turn to be talked to, she would really prefer not to talk to him at all; with a rider to the effect that he should feel this want of interest and be severely hurt by it.

"I am glad to have met Dr. Crawley's girl," said Lady Waring to Philip. "The Crawleys are old acquaintances but I really haven't kept count of their family and we rarely meet now. You know them well, don't you?"

Philip said he had seen a certain amount of them while he was at Southbridge School. He believed Octavia had done extremely well at the Barchester General and had some intention of taking up nursing professionally, though Mr. Needham's return would probably alter that.

"A much better plan to get married," said Lady Waring. "She is a very intelligent young woman. She has all the latest rulings about the call-up of married women at her finger-tips. We do need someone with that civic kind of mind here. Our nearest Citizens' Advice Bureau is at Winter Overcotes. The village women haven't time to go there and probably be kept waiting in an office. Besides, the very competent woman who was in charge has been bullied into a factory and been replaced by a fool who goes entirely by routine and doesn't understand the villagers."

Philip, who had never looked upon Octavia as anything but so dull that she practically didn't exist, was interested.

"It is much the same with the W.V.S.," said Lady Waring. "Our nearest is at Shearings, just about as far away as Winter Overcotes, only in the opposite direction. We have an excellent head there, but as she has an old invalid mother and the Labour Exchange won't allow her to have help more than three days in the week, she is having to give it up."

Philip sympathized very much with his hostess. If he had known her better, he would have noticed that any complaints she made were never for herself, though her way of living was doomed through enemies abroad and a spirit of change and meddling bureaucracy at home, but for the village, so patient and cheerful under rules and restrictions they could not understand, still looking to the Priory for advice and help.

And then the table suddenly sorted itself and fell into pairs, and Lady Waring and Noel were able to talk about books, while Philip Winter at last found himself free for Leslie.

They were both glad to meet again, but both a little afraid, for each had felt a sense of guilt since their last parting. It had practically been a row, Leslie thought to herself, a common sort of row, and it was perhaps not so much good manners as cowardice which had kept her from being much nastier to Colonel Winter than she was. Philip had inwardly accused himself of being not merely impatient but brutal to a girl who had only just got over a bad illness. Each was anxious to make amends: neither was quite ready to apologize. However, they found neutral ground in discussing Mrs. Spender, whose meteor apparition had profoundly impressed them both.

"I thought people like that only happened in books," said Leslie, "but it all goes to show that authors don't really exaggerate anything."

Philip said he found himself that the older he got the more he realized that everyone in Dickens, without exception, was a real person, and quite a lot of them were among his friends.

"Am I like one, Colonel Winter?" said Leslie. "I would love to be a Dickens person. Perhaps Mrs. Jellyby, only not so sweet-natured."

And why I said Colonel Winter instead of Philip I don't know, she thought. Of course he will think it's a snub because he was so rude, for he was rude, though I really didn't mind.

302

Philip, concluding that the use of Christian names had been going a step too far in Miss Waring's opinion, said kindly that he thought her work must be on the whole more really important than Borrioboola-Gha. And from this their talk meandered very pleasantly on, though no form of address was used by either, for it is a peculiarity of Christian names that if they are used by arrangement they can produce an almost unbearable sense of embarrassment. "Now, you must call me Dolly" is a challenge, to which the only answer is, "Then you must say Gladys"; after which Mrs. Smith and Mrs. Brown are taken extremely self-conscious, use the unwonted names once or twice fervently, haven't the courage to go back to Mrs., and say "you" to each other for the rest of their lives.

It is true that christian-naming is so common as to have almost done away with the use of surnames, especially we regret to say, among men, but among the older generation the formality of title is less easily set aside, as Lydia with unusual perception had noted in the case of Lady Waring. In ordering Philip and Leslie to drop the prefix she had but done what anyone would do with contemporaries, probably thinking, if she did think about it, that she had eased their path. And indeed she would have eased it, or they would quite possibly have dropped into first names of themselves before long, had not each been touched in the heart by the other. To say Philip or Leslie offhand was to each, though they were not consciously aware of it, a faint impropriety, a pulling open of rose-petals which might hurt the rose, a digging up of a plant to see how it was growing. When they thought of each other, which they were apt to do at most odd moments, it was not by name at all. The friendly vision was a personality without a label; which anyone who has been very fond of a member of the opposite sex, without any openly expressed liking, will understand.

After dinner the men had a delightful time. Sir Harry, who had produced one of his last half-dozen of port for his guest, asked Mr. Needham to come up near him, not without a little anxiety as to whether it was too much to ask a one-armed man to move up a place. He watched with pleasure Mr. Needham's enjoyment of a wine of which Sir Harry was glad to see he was almost worthy. He gave Mr. Needham much valuable information about the South African War, India in 1915, the war in 1916–18, and the subsequent decay of everything, and courteously asked his guest to tell him about Libya, a vagueness of phrase which gave the young military chaplain full scope to speak about his men and what a splendid lot they were. By incredible good luck he had been quite near Sir Harry's old regiment and though all the names were new, Sir Harry rejoiced to hear that even in those damned contraptions, by which he meant tanks, the 408th had not abated one whit of its reputation for dash and endurance. And what was more, he found in Mr. Needham a staunch though modest opponent of the Bishop and all his ways.

"We might as well finish the bottle, Needham," said Sir Harry, glancing with a slight prick of conscience at

Colonel Winter and Major Merton, deep in shop of the modern army, and deciding that his need was greater than theirs. "I'm sorry about your arm, my boy. Very sorry."

"It is a bit of bad luck, sir," said Mr. Needham candidly. "I don't suppose I'll be able to play football again, and certainly I can't row. I shall miss that most."

As George Waring had been a keen oarsman in his school days, this led to more sympathetic talk, and when Sir Harry discovered that Tom Oldmeadow, who played Rugger for England, was his guest's uncle, and had been at Southbridge School of which he was a governor, his satisfaction knew no bounds, and if he could have made Mr. Needham a bishop on the spot, he would undoubtedly have done so.

In the drawing-room, by another piece of unprecedented good luck, Leslie and Octavia, though without much in common in normal life, at once conceived a respect for each other as organizers. Leslie admired in Octavia a thoroughness and capacity for taking pains which almost excused her dullness. Octavia, though she took very little interest in Leslie, did realise that she was an excellent business woman and respected her accordingly. Each felt that the other, though not her style, would be an excellent person to work with, painstaking and above all reliable.

Lydia, talking in a desultory way with Lady Waring and knitting socks which she hoped to be able to send to Colin, considered with much interest this blossoming of Octavia. It gradually came over her that Octavia was exactly like a clergyman's wife. Not, it is true, like Mrs. Miller, or Mrs. Crawley, or Mrs. Tompion at Little Misfit, or any other clergy-wife whom she personally knew, but as it were a symbol of all the excellent qualities required in that position, with a larger amount of push and perhaps a smaller amount of charm; certainly dressed for the part. As she considered these things a light suddenly burst upon her. When she had, across the dinner-table, studied Octavia's dress and appearance, she had found it vaguely familiar without being able to place it. It now occurred to her that the person Octavia most resembled, in dress and general atmosphere, was the Bishop's wife, which so interested her, as betokening future eminence for Tommy, that she could hardly wait to tell Noel. Still, wait she did, where Miss Lydia Keith would probably have announced her discovery in a loud voice to anyone handy.

The arrival of the gentlemen was followed by quite dull though agreeable general conversation, during which Sir Harry, as was his wont, suddenly fell fast asleep sitting up. His wife said that he sometimes did it on purpose because he knew how handsome he looked, but it is more probable that it was the result of domestic selfishness in an otherwise very unselfish man.

Selina coming in announced Dr. Ford on a half-sob.

"Anyone ill, eh?" said Sir Harry, waking as suddenly as he had fallen asleep and in full possession of his faculties.

"No, Harry. You know what Dr. Ford is like," said Lady Waring, for as Dr. Ford had petrol to visit various hospitals and convalescent homes in the district, had no home ties, enjoyed society and took no notice at all of the black-out, he was as apt as not to turn up anywhere within twenty miles of High Rising for a friendly chat, thus driving sisters and matrons nearly mad by the irregularity of his hours, though as a bachelor doctor they otherwise adored him.

"Not too late, I hope," said Dr. Ford after a general greeting. "I couldn't get over to the hospital till after dinner. I was at Barchester all day. That man Jenks," said Dr. Ford, whose memory for patients and their names was prodigious, "is making a nice recovery. Sister Macheath said she had never seen Sir Abel operate better. I thought you'd be glad to know. No, Octavia, I am *not* going to tell you all about it. You'll get it from Macheath when you go back."

Leslie said she must tell Selina, as Private Jenks was rather a friend of hers.

"I've told her," said Dr. Ford. "It's a pleasure, profesionally speaking, to tell that woman anything. I never saw anyone who turned on the waterworks with such ease and showed it so little. I'd like to do an article for the *B.M.J.* about her," said Dr. Ford, who was always trying to storm that periodical but had so far never succeeded; this failure being attributed by him to a conspiracy to keep him out, but by Mrs. George Knox, who had very affectionately refused to marry him years ago, to his abominable handwriting and his refusal to let her type his manuscript. "I've got a message for you, Lady Waring, from Mrs. Morland.

Matron said you had asked her about doing a talk for the men."

"I did suggest it," said Lady Waring, "and she was so nice about it, but didn't see how she could get over."

"Well, I can bring her when I come over on Thursday, just as I did with Stoke," said Dr. Ford.

Lady Waring said that would be delightful, but she didn't know if the date was filled or not, and she had an idea that Captain Barclay, the one who married Amabel Marling's girl who had lost her husband at Dunkirk, was coming to talk about dealing with high-explosive bombs.

"That's all right," said Dr. Ford. "He can't come. I got that from Matron last week, or I wouldn't have bothered you and Mrs. Morland. Now, Miss Leslie, I'd like a word with you."

Accordingly he took Leslie away and after a brief absence brought her back, told her aunt she was a most fraudulent affair regarded as a patient, and departed.

Leslie, who was feeling better every day, was in such spirits after Dr. Ford's visit as rejoiced her uncle and aunt. She, Lydia, Philip and Mr. Needham began to talk, rather noisily, about what they would do after the war, while Octavia gave Lady Waring and Noel a short but informative lecture on Social Credit, not one word of which, as they found afterwards on comparing notes, had they understood or wished to understand, though much struck by the lecturer's power of apparently making things clear, while Sir Harry read *The Times*.

Mr. Needham's hopes were definite enough; a living and to settle down with Octavia. And if he did not say that he wanted to help everyone less fortunate than himself, it was only because he took it for granted that everyone felt like that. Philip, when pressed, was at first diffident, but warming in Leslie's good spirits gradually unfolded his old plan of a preparatory school.

"I used to think I'd run a prep. school on as crank and anti-established-order lines as possible," he said, "so that the boys would get it out of the system early and turn into good, dull, law-abiding Tories. But when I thought of the kind of parents I'd have to face with a school like that, I rather selfishly gave up the idea. Fathers with sparse beards and vegetarian shoes, and mothers with bobbed hair and square-necked dresses."

"And peers who are too self-conscious to use their titles," said Lydia.

"And peeresses who bring shame on their husbands by not using theirs," said Leslie.

"And all the daring parents of one peculiar child," Noel, who had stopped listening to, or rather hearing Octavia for a few moments, threw in over his shoulder.

There was then a brief but tense silence, as everyone had thought of some class of parent which ought not to be admitted, but was nervous of showing a decided opinion on any race, religion, or way of political thought, because unexpected passions suddenly rise so high when the world is in what Mrs. Brandon in an inspired moment had called the stockpot.

"And free-thinkers," said Mr. Needham.

This statement from a very loyal son of the Church who, in spite of saying by Jove, most deeply meant what he said, produced complete paralysis conversationally.

Each member of the party was conscious of doing what Captain Hooper would have called a spot of free-thinking, but liked Mr. Needham so much that each would have subscribed to the Thirty-nine Articles on the spot sooner than hurt his feelings. Philip, who was the oldest of them and very much more experienced, went on, almost ignoring the interlude on parents:

"But now I think just a very ordinary school, for very ordinary boys, with very ordinary parents, to keep them ordinary. They will burst out and be peculiar soon enough, without any teaching, and meanwhile my whole effort shall be directed to making the holidays peaceful for their relations and sending them home with a respect for good manners."

Relieved from the slight strain, of which Mr. Needham had not been aware, they all plunged into plans for Philip's future. Before long they had equipped him with a large house, abandoned by its owners yet in excellent repair, in the heart of the country yet extremely accessible, with a home farm that always earned its keep, where the boys would hold communion with cows (Lydia), poultry (Leslie), horses (Philip) and (suddenly contributed with a burst of real enthusiasm by Mr. Needham) pigs and manure heaps.

"You're right, Needham," said Philip. "No education is complete that doesn't include leaning over a pigsty gate on Sunday afternoon scratching the old sow's back with a stick. Also, one could have roast sucking pig occasionally, a piece of old England which is fast disappearing. Has anyone ever had one?"

There was a shamefaced silence.

"Jasper did offer us one before the war when he still kept pigs," said Leslie, "but it was the runt and had a very peculiar back, very long with a great dip in it, so we thought we'd better not."

"Oh, and you *must* have someone like Jasper on the place, to teach the boys about rabbits and ferrets and fishing," said Lydia.

They all plunged into the fray again till Octavia, with a rather married air, summoned Mr. Needham to get ready to walk back. Philip said he would walk with them.

"I think," he said, getting up, "that I'd rather like to specialize in little boys who are going into the Navy. Doubtless being in the Army makes one prefer every other service, but I have a weakness in that direction."

Leslie looked up at him with a smile of such gratitude and friendliness as seriously upset his circulation for a moment. He then, most ungratefully, felt a distinct jealousy of the brother for whose sake she liked little boys who were going into the Navy. Good nights were said.

"I did like your plans about the school, Philip," said Leslie, not noticing that she did not say Colonel Winter. "Let's talk about it again. I'll be out of a job myself after the war, I expect, if you need a secretary. I'll frighten the parents like anything."

Philip said he would love it, if she really meant it. He was going to try to get over to hear Mrs. Morland's talk, he said, because he adored her books with all the lower side of his nature, and perhaps he might come to tea first. Or stay to dinner, said Leslie.

Colonel Winter, Mr. Needham and Octavia walked down the drive. A moon with a bright, hard face, rather swollen on one side, was shining, and their torches were not needed. Octavia appeared to have enjoyed her evening very much and had a good deal to say to her betrothed as she was going back to Barchester on the following day, so Philip was left to his own thoughts, which in their turn we may leave to the reader's imagination as they were of little value to anyone but himself, and consisted largely in an insane desire to say "Oh, Leslie" to the moon, but not wishing to disturb his companions, he refrained.

At the vicarage they stopped to see Octavia safely bestowed. Miss Horniman opened the door, said she wouldn't ask them in as there was nothing to drink, and that she had pretty well finished clearing up and would be going the day after tomorrow. Octavia, bidding an unimpassioned farewell to her escort, went in and shut the front door. The men walked quickly on to Ladysmith Cottages, for the night was cold.

"Mrs. Allen wouldn't let me have a key," said Mr. Needham, "and I'm afraid she's sitting up for me. But if you don't mind risking it I have got a little rum."

Philip thanked him very much. Mr. Needham knocked cautiously at the door. After a brief interval the noise of several bolts, chains and locks being unfastened was heard and the door was half-opened by

Nannie Allen, who in a long pink flannel dressing-gown, a large Shetland shawl and a rather dashing boudoir cap fringed with curling-pins, presented a very impressive appearance in the dimly lighted hall.

"Oh, well, good night, Winter," said Mr. Needham. "I hope I'm not late, Mrs. Allen."

"Straight to bed you go, sir," said Nannie. "I've mended that nasty tear in your pyjamas and they're airing in front of the gas fire. You can take your shoes off down here."

An inner voice told Philip that he was not wanted. Nannie slammed the door, bolted, barred and locked it. Philip pursued his way to the Dower House, thinking as he went of an ideal school, full of delightful little boys, presided over by himself and the perfect secretary, or co-head, or even headmaster's wife, though of course that was simply an idea and one didn't know anyone likely to take on the job.

Gradually he fell into a trance from which he was roused by his own voice remarking, "Leslie, Leslie," to sleeping nature. He then discovered that he was standing still, facing the wrong way, and feeling rather cold. So he pursued his way to the Dower House, where he arrived without any further incident.

CHAPTER
TEN

All Dr. Ford's plans worked, as they usually did. On the Thursday appointed for Mrs. Morland's talk to the convalescents his shabby old car rattled into the yard, where Selina was pegging out a few clorths, the phrase being not hers but Cook's. He got out, as did Mrs. Morland.

"Well, Mrs. Crockett, still breaking all hearts," said Dr. Ford, whose deliberately eighteenth-century manner was much admired by his humbler friends.

"Oh, *sir*," said Selina, dropping a clothes-peg in her confusion.

"That old Silleena's breaking old Jasper's heart," said a slow voice behind them, making Mrs. Morland start. She turned and saw a picturesque figure lounging against the arch that led to the kitchen garden.

"That's Margett, Sir Harry's keeper," said Dr. Ford, thus causing Mrs. Morland to feel an alarmed interest in the family she was about to meet. "Well, Margett, got the old lady yet?"

"No, Jasper hasn't got her yet," said the head keeper, deliberately speaking of himself in the third person to make an impression on Mrs. Morland. "But he's got something as he knows on, and he'll get the old lady yet."

Seeing that his affectation of half-witted rusticity had made its full effect on the strange lady, he lounged away till he was well out of sight, when he fell into his usual purposeful stride and went about his work.

"Old impostor," said Dr. Ford. "But he knows his business. Come on, Tony."

A young officer who had been sitting in the back of the car, watching this scene with inscrutable, age-weary eyes, got slowly out and joined the party. Dr. Ford, ignoring him, as he had always successfully done since Tony Morland was an exhaustingly talkative little boy with a passion for trains, led the way along the kitchen passage into the house, where Lady Waring was waiting to give tea to the speaker, and went off to the hospital. The two ladies had a slight acquaintance and liked each other without intimacy. If the truth must be told, which it mostly mustn't as being apt to cause disagreeableness, Lady Waring almost classed Mrs. Morland in her mind as a very worthy sort of person. Indeed she would have relegated her wholly to this category, had she not, with the pathetic illusion of the well-born who have never tried to write, felt something of the same nervous respect for a female author as the Middle Ages (whatever they were, for certainly no one was ever conscious of belonging to them, but rather to the present enlightened age) felt for the enchanter Vergilius. If she had realized, as she probably did not, that Mrs. Morland earned enough money to keep herself and help her sons, she would have respected her even more and been even more nervous. As for Mrs. Morland, that lady had no illusions at all about herself and never stopped being surprised at her own earning powers, feeling with the calm of despair that each new book would be a failure and the last she would ever write. Much to Tony's annoyance he was secretly impressed by his mother's mild celebrity.

"I hope you won't mind my bringing my youngest boy," said Mrs. Morland to Lady Waring. "He is on leave."

Lady Waring expressed pleasure and Tony inclined his body slightly over her hand, which action made a good impression, as perhaps he had meant it to.

"Hullo, Lydia," said Tony, concealing with Red Indian stoicism his surprise at seeing an old friend.

"Hullo, Tony," said Lydia. "I haven't seen you since we rode on the roundabout at the Pomfret Madrigal flower show and you got the coconut at the shies. I got married to Noel Merton. This is Leslie Waring, she's Lady Waring's niece. I say, you're a gunner, so's my brother, Colin Keith."

This led to a delightful conversation. Tony, it is true, had not seen Colin since he was at Southbridge School, but the fact that they were both attached to the Barsetshires was considered just as good. Tony, with a faint appearance of an early Christian offering incense to Jupiter against his principles, then handed teacups. There was not very much time for talk before the lecture. Leslie thought Tony a quite pleasant young man, like so many other young second lieutenants, but her mind was not in the room. Philip had said something about coming to hear Mrs. Morland speak and possibly coming to tea first. She had said, Or stay to dinner. What a fool she was. She should have said, Yes, do come to tea and then stay to dinner. Why lose any time when time was so short and went so soon. She felt an attack of petulance coming upon her, so was silent, making most commendable efforts to bring herself to a better frame of mind.

Lady Waring asked after Mrs. Morland's sons, rather vaguely, not being quite sure how many there were.

"Thank you very much, all very well indeed, I am glad to say," said Mrs. Morland, pushing her hair off one side of her face the better to get down to her subject and so setting her hat a little askew. "That is, at least, I haven't heard from Gerald for six weeks, but I hardly expected to, and John hasn't written for quite some time, but as I know where he is, though I mustn't say, though of course everyone knows, it's not surprising, for writing-pads are such a nuisance and tanks *not* the best place to write home in, rocking up and down all the time. I do get a cable from Dick from time to time, but whenever I don't hear from them I know they are all right, because if the War Office or the Admiralty *can* annoy you by sending a telegram to say everyone is dead or missing they will most certainly do so. I am trying to arrange a code with Tony and then he can tell me where he is when he goes abroad but it is extremely difficult. Because first," said Mrs. Morland, looking round to see that her audience was attending and dropping a large horn hairpin as she did so, "there are such a lot of places he might go to that there are really hardly enough words; then if we did get a code arranged we couldn't write it down, at least he couldn't, in case he was taken prisoner with it on him, and then the Germans would know where he was; then he might never go abroad at all, and how silly it would be if he were sent to Weston-super-Mare and not allowed to say where he was and hadn't a code word for it. For there are really too many places in England to have a code name for them all. Of course, abroad there aren't so many places, so it isn't so bad. Still, as I said, I have *great* confidence in the War Office telling me anything horrid at *once*, which is such a comfort."

Her hearers, slightly overwhelmed by this lucid exposition, were silent for a moment, sorting out what Mrs. Morland had said, while the gifted authoress picked her hairpin up and pushed it into her head.

"Mother," said Tony, "when I am killed, don't write a little book about me to say the world is the poorer for my loss."

"Of course I won't," said his mother indignantly. "I dare say Adrian will want me to — you know Adrian Coates, my publisher, I expect," she added to Lady Waring, "he married George Knox's girl, Sybil, and never bothers me except to choose jackets for books, and why books go on having jackets when we are *asked* to economize paper, I cannot think. Still, all the jackets are torn off and go into salvage which the Government seems to want, so I dare say it's all right, though you would think it would be simpler just to put the amount of paper you would have used for jackets straight into salvage instead of wasting time and money printing

318

things all over it, or even having pictures — but however much he wants it, I shan't," said Mrs. Morland, triumphantly returning, as she nearly always did, to her original thesis. "And what is more," she added defiantly, "I shall *not* put No letters please in *The Times*, though even if I did I wouldn't put a comma after letters, and anyway it's rather like saying Deliver no circulars, because you can't order people to *not* deliver a thing even if you do split your infinitives. I hope *everyone* would write to me and say how much they liked you, because it's the only time they would take the trouble, though I dare say they do all like you very much only they don't say so. Besides, I should cry so much over the letters and I believe crying is really better for me than anything and then I can tear up all the letters and give them to salvage, which is, I believe, absolutely the *only* thing the Government thinks about sometimes."

Tony appeared to be unmoved by his mother's apologia, merely remarking to Lydia, "Mamma rather fancies her own letters when people are dead," to which Lydia, whose meeting with Tony had sent her back to her schoolgirl days again, said she knew exactly the kind of letter she would like to write when Miss Pettinger died and she hoped the *Barchester Chronicle* would print it, because she knew the *Barcastriana*, the official organ of the Barchester High School, wouldn't.

Lady Waring said, with what in one so well-bred and so self-controlled was almost a sigh, that she and Sir Harry had been very much touched by the expressions of sympathy they had received on their son's death and felt that many friends had given themselves real trouble to write when there was so little to say. But only Mrs. Morland heard what she said, for Leslie, having picked out from Mrs. Morland's disconnected remarks the fact that she had a son in the Navy, was only waiting till that lady had finished to inquire from Tony where his brother was. Dick Morland was in quite another part of the world from Cecil, but the discovery that they had both been in the same ship at the outbreak of war cheered her up very much.

It was now nearly five o'clock, so Lady Waring and her party went through into the big house. Matron had posted a nurse to catch them as they came in, whose colleagues, all deeply interested in seeing Mrs. Morland who wrote those nice books, were clustering round doorways, or industriously straightening the hall furniture. Lady Waring, with her well-trained memory for names and faces, introduced their guide as Nurse Poulter.

"This way, Mrs. Morland," said Nurse Poulter, much gratified. "I hope you don't mind me saying, Mrs. Morland, how I love your books. As I said to Matron this morning, we all feel we are going to have a great treat."

They were then wafted into the Old Bookroom, where Matron was delighted to meet Mrs. Morland, whose nice books she had enjoyed so much.

"But just one weeny criticism if I may, Mrs. Morland," she said, "just a quite professional one. In your last book, or was it the last but one, the one where the wicked Italian count is disguised as the government inspector who goes round the dress shops to see that they are using little enough material, you know the one I mean —"

"That was the last," said Mrs. Morland. "I know it was, because the villain was to have been Brazilian and then they seemed to be becoming allies so I had to change him. I cannot tell you how difficult it is to ring the changes on one's villains. If only Hitler had a few more allies it would be *much* easier."

"Dear, dear," said Matron, "well we all have our trials and that is one which never in my wildest dreams would I have thought of. But as I was saying, when the nurse comes to look after the heroine after the Italian count has drugged her and left her senseless in the stockroom, you mention that she had a smart uniform with slanting pink stripes under her light blue cloak. Now that uniform, Mrs. Morland, simply does not exist. I must say — I was back at the Mid-Central where I trained when I happened to be reading it — that it gave the staff sister and I quite a hearty laugh, for as I said to her, such a uniform simply does not exist. But that is the only little fly on the scutcheon, for I can assure you we were all tearing the copy from each other's hands."

Mrs. Morland, in spite of her large and constant public, was always surprised, interested and pleased to hear that anyone had really read her books, though sometimes a little depressed by the way in which her friends lent their copy, or even the library copy, to one another, and she took very seriously any technical criticism that came her way.

321

"You see," she said earnestly to Matron, "I didn't like to make it a *real* uniform, because the hospital it belonged to mightn't have liked it, for, if you remember, the nurse was really only a half-German woman, who had married an Englishman but only did it to spite England, in disguise, and all she did was to keep the heroine under drugs till the villain could come, but it was really the hero disguised as a doctor and he killed her with a poison that left no trace."

"Of *course*," said Matron. "How you think of your plots I cannot imagine. Only you see, the nurse wearing a light-blue cloak seemed to point to Knight's, and of course we Mid-Central nurses were quite excited, because we just wondered if any of the Knight's nurses had really been spies in disguise. But that quite explains it, and I am most grateful, Mrs. Morland. Now I think the boys are quite ready for what we all know is going to be a thoroughly enjoyable little talk."

After a polite struggle for loss of precedence between Lady Waring and Matron, they went across the hall. Matron led the party along the side of the billiard-room to the further end. Tony, following them, was held up by Lydia as she stopped to speak to Sergeant Hopkins, who wanted to know if there was any news of Captain Keith.

"Not yet," she said cheerfully. "Anyway, I don't expect to hear for ages. Nobody is having letters now, at least no one I know, but I'll let you know at once."

"Sergeant Hopkins," said Tony.

"Sir!" said the sergeant jumping up and saluting.

"We were on a course in Middleshire last year when I was a cadet and the sergeant got run into by a lorry," said Tony to Lydia. "Then my employers sent me somewhere else. What happened to you, sergeant?"

Sergeant Hopkins looked round.

"I *am* supposed to be on duty here, sir," he said, "but the boys will be all right now, leastways till the Sheep's Head opens."

"Six?" said Tony. "Lydia, will you tell my Mamma that I shall report for duty in Lady Waring's drawing-room at 6.15. Come and tell me your troubles, sergeant, and I'll give you the lowdown on Captain Keith. He was a master for one term at the school where I was. And then we'll go down to the Sheep's Head before six, have a quick one together and be back here for me to fetch my mother."

Sergeant Hopkins, delighted to meet an old friend who knew the Captain, glanced quickly round, saw that his flock did not look as if they would be up to any particular mischief, and followed Tony from the room.

"Do they let you smoke here?" Tony asked, handing his cigarette-case to the sergeant, who took one and thanked him. "Hullo, cat. Who are you?"

"He's Winston, sir," said Sergeant Hopkins. "He's a cheeky little beggar. Runs after his own tail like anything."

In proof of this he stirred the kitten up with a finger till out of the corner of its eye it suddenly saw the tip of a highly desirable tail and at once became a living corkscrew. Tony then got an old envelope out of the waste-paper basket, drew from his pocket a piece of string, tied it on to the paper and dangled the paper in the air just above the kitten's head. The kitten leapt into the air with every claw outspread, humped itself like a salmon, fell head over heels, rushed madly away, squashed itself under a chest of drawers, turned round and stuck its face and front paws out, emerged, waved its tail angrily from side to side, rushed at the paper again, skidded on the parquet floor against Tony's foot, and embracing his boot in its fore-paws began to kill it.

"A very good kitten," said Tony, picking it up. The kitten at once went to sleep. "How is your mother, sergeant, and the vegetable shop?"

Under Tony's fatherly influence the sergeant, who was more than twice his age and had been in the last war, told him how his mother was carrying on at the shop and had been over to see the hospital and had tea with Mrs. Allen. Tony asked who Mrs. Allen was. The sergeant said she was an old lady, Mrs. Crockett's mother. Tony gave the sergeant another cigarette and asked who Mrs. Crockett was. At this point the sergeant's replies became a little confused owing to his going red in the face and stuttering.

"I think we'd better go and see this Selina of yours," said Tony. "She sounds all right to me, but I'd better have a look."

The sergeant, who had complete confidence in his young lieutenant, for very little reason except that Tony had sometimes listened to his sad story of his wife's death and the Captain's kindness, said he knew Mrs. Crockett had gone down to the village to see her mother and would be coming back about now.

324

"We might walk down to the Sheep's Head," said Tony, "and see if we can find Mrs. Selina. Then one drink and I must go and rescue my mamma."

Accordingly, the sergeant, who really had no business to be out at all, took Tony by the side door into the garden. The sergeant talking, Tony listening, they sauntered through the garden, admired the view over Golden Valley, and went leisurely down the drive.

"Anyone else looking at your Mrs. Selina?" Tony asked.

The sergeant said he didn't rightly know. Sir Harry's head keeper was about the kitchen a good deal, but he might be after Cook or Baker.

"Is that Margett, the man we saw in the backyard?" Tony inquired. "Dr. Ford told my mamma that he was Sir Harry's keeper and she thought he meant Sir Harry was in a loony-bin."

Sergeant Hopkins, after an interval of thought, guffawed.

"Delayed action, but quite a success," said Tony with scientific interest.

"Yes, sir," said the sergeant doubtfully. "Margett's a good sort, sir. He takes the boys out shooting. But I don't think Mrs. Crockett ought to take up with him, sir. There's something — well, I can't quite explain, sir. There is a word just about fits him, sir, but I don't know as I'd like to say it in front of Mrs. Crockett."

"What is it?" said Tony. "I thought I knew most of them."

"Well, sir, not a word I'd like to use, not in front of an officer," said Sergeant Hopkins.

"Out with it," said Tony. "I'll stand you another one at the Sheep's Head."

"Well, sir," said Sergeant Hopkins, tempted by the dazzling bait, "if I was asked to say what Margett was like, I'd certainly use a certain expression, sir, though it's not one I'd care to use in public. The name I'd have for him," said the sergeant, looking cautiously round as if the Manchester Watch Committee was behind the next tree, "is sinister. I'd call him a sinister man, sir."

Tony, who prided himself on knowing a good deal of really bad language and had hoped to add some Barsetshire word of unprintable obscenity to his vocabulary, was slightly disappointed, but realizing how appalling the implications of the word must be to Sergeant Hopkins, he whistled.

"Yes, sir," said the sergeant, much gratified. "Sinister. That's what I'd say."

"Well then, he mustn't bother Mrs. Selina," said Tony. "What does your mother say?"

"Mother's always at me to marry again," said Sergeant Hopkins, "and seeing Mrs. Crockett's late husband was in the greengrocery, it does seem as if it was meant. I can fancy her handling a nice fresh savoy, or some early rhubarb," said the sergeant rhapsodically, "or picking out the best toms for Mrs. Carter at the school. And we might do a bit of a sideline in flowers, sir, because after all there *is* other things than veg. I'd like to see her with a bunch of daffs, or some nice big chrysanths. My mother and Mrs. Allen, that's Mrs. Crockett's mother, sir, they both say I ought to marry again. I've got another board, sir, and Dr. Ford says he thinks they'll discharge me because of my eyes, so if Mrs. Crockett was agreeable, well you see, sir, that's how it is."

As the sergeant finished his love-plaint, Selina appeared round the bend in the drive. She was looking extremely pretty, her face flushed by the cold air and the walk, and at the sight of the sergeant, or a young officer, or both, her hair appeared to wreathe itself in silvered tendrils more violently than ever.

"Well, Mrs. Crockett, who'd have thought of meeting you?" said Sergeant Hopkins, lying with a fluency that Tony much admired. "Mr. Morland was on a gunnery course with our lot up in Wales and we was just having a talk about old times."

Tony saluted Selina.

"Mrs. Crockett," he said gravely, this statement of a new acquaintance's name being his affectation at the moment.

Selina bridled and dimpled and Sergeant Hopkins looked as silly as a man with an undeclared passion usually looks.

"Did the sergeant tell you about the time we shot the sheep?" said Tony.

"Oh no, sir!" said Selina, her eyes filling with tears, "not a sheep, sir!"

"It was all its own fault for being just where we were aiming at," said Tony. "But the farmer kicked up a frightful row."

"He *must* have been upset, sir," said Selina.

"He was awfully upset," said Tony, "till he got his compensation; and then the sergeants' mess stood him drinks at the Taliesin Arms and he was more upset than ever. Wasn't he, sergeant?"

"Never seen a man so bl — beg your pardon, sir, I mean blind drunk in my life," said the sergeant. Excuse me, sir, but I can't help laughing just to think of it."

"And the sergeant carried him home and put him to bed," said Tony to Selina, "all out of kindness."

"Oh, it *was* kind, sir," said Selina, distracted from the horrors of ovicide to the beauty of the sergeant's kind action. "He must be very strong, sir."

"He is," said Tony. "Wait till you see him lift a sack of potatoes."

Selina said that the late Mr. Crockett had to have a young man to help with the lifting.

"Well, you marry Sergeant Hopkins when he gets his discharge, Mrs. Crockett," said Tony, "and you'll have a young man and the potatoes too."

"Oh, sir!" said Selina, so moved by virtuous indignation and the delightful sense that the officer admired her, that she quite forgot to cry.

Tony saluted; Selina went back as fast as she could to tell Cook that these young gentlemen you never knew what they'd say next, and the men continued their walk.

"Excuse me, sir, have you ever thought of marrying yourself?" said Sergeant Hopkins.

"Not seriously," said Tony. "I mean to catch one young and bring her up to be just what I want. And then I suppose she'll marry someone else like Mr. Day's pupil."

"Was that Mr. Day of the Loyal Barsets, sir?" asked the sergeant.

"Lord, no! A much older man," said Tony. "I like your Mrs. Selina, sergeant. I'd see about it at once if I were you. And here is the Sheep's Head. It's a pity it's not quite six."

"I dare say if we was to go round to the back we'd find Mrs. Pollett somewhere about," said Sergeant Hopkins carelessly.

"I'd like to meet Mrs. Pollett," said Tony.

Meanwhile in the billiard-room Matron had briefly introduced Mrs. Morland to her audience, and then went away, as she had to see Dr. Ford. Mrs. Morland, left alone in front of some forty or fifty convalescent soldiers, nothing but a wooden chair, a card-table and a glass of water to support her, her son vanished, Lady Waring, Lydia and Leslie seated in the front row looking at her, heartily wished she had never been born. She hated any kind of public appearance and had only twice spoken to an audience, in both cases at the request of her publisher with whom she had almost quarrelled afterwards owing to general nervous misery. She had only accepted Lady Waring's invitation because she felt one ought to do anything one was asked to do for convalescent soldiers, though, if her own sons were anything to judge by, the very last thing they would want was to have a middle-aged woman with no allure coming and talking to them about how she wrote books, for such was the subject that Matron had suggested, and Mrs. Morland had accepted it, feeling with dumb despair that she could be just as stupid about that as about anything else, and that certainly none of her audience would have read any. She had typed out again and again a rough synopsis of her lecture, but every time she looked at it she hated it more.

How on earth could one expect convalescent soldiers, or well soldiers, or any sort of soldiers, to read what were really only pot-boilers? Thrillers about Madame Koska, in whose dressmaking establishment her readers demanded to meet a new hero, heroine, female spy and foreign secret agent every year, sandwiched with descriptions of clothes and the difficulties of a fashionable dressmaker, seemed to her the last thing in the world for military circles. After sitting up till one o'clock that morning she had gone to bed with a headache, slept in the company of nightmares and was at the moment on the verge of hysteria with icy feet, trembling knees, shaking hands, bleared eyes, her hat a little askew and the certainty that her hair would come down before long.

A polite clap greeted her.

"It isn't my fault that I'm here," said Mrs. Morland, looking vengefully towards Lady Waring, who was getting her spectacles out of her bag and did not notice it, "and I'm perfectly sure none of you have read any of my books and I really don't see why you should, not to speak of writing them, which is really the last thing I know how to do."

She paused, wondering how long she could drivel on like this, for her typescript was in a hopeless mess and had it been the tidiest in the world she could not have seen the words.

To her eternal surprise a voice near the back of the room said, "I did, miss. I liked them a lot. So did George; didn't you, George?"

George thus appealed to, and told by his neighbours to speak up, said he had read three and his young lady had read them all. Other men, taking example by the courageous action of George, joined their voices, and Mrs. Morland, incredulous, found herself face to face with at least twenty fervent admirers out of her audience.

"I can't *tell* you how pleased I am," said Mrs. Morland, stooping to pick up a hairpin. "I've got a friend in the Air Force who said they were reading some of my Madame Koska stories in the mess, which I thought was extraordinary because one hardly expects airmen to be able to read, I mean to have *time* for reading when they are bombing Germany and Italy, but this is ever so much nicer. None of my sons read my books, because of course one *cannot* think one's mother can do anything, so it is more cheering-up than I can tell you that you like them. Which did you like best?"

George and his friends, having overcome their first shyness, were delighted to have a literary discussion. Names of books flew about the room. Powerful, beefy-looking corporals invoked the names of their young ladies who wished they could be mannequins at Madame Koska's and wear such lovely costumes. Pink-faced privates said they'd like to have been there when that foreign fellow tried to suffocate Rosalba the beautiful receptionist in a thousand-guinea mink coat and they'd have given him something on account for Hitler. A lance-corporal said his sister teased the life out of him to give her one for her birthday. Mrs. Morland could hardly contain her exultation, as the business side of her noticed that nearly fifteen minutes had already gone.

"Thank you all very, very much," she said earnestly. "Lady Waring said Matron said you'd like to know how I write my books. Well, I'm frightfully sorry, but I really haven't the faintest idea."

She paused dramatically.

"Jew mean you go into a trance, sort of?" said George's friend, awestruck.

"Not exactly," said Mrs. Morland, "though I often feel just as stupid as if I had."

"That's the reaction, miss," said George. "I often go that way myself after one of sergeant's talks about the Bren gun."

This allusion raised a loud laugh.

"Well, I'll try to explain," said Mrs. Morland, pushing all her hairpins well into her head by the simple method of banging her hat with both hands. "You see, my publisher *will* make me write books."

She paused dramatically.

George said to his friend it did seem a shame, a lady like her.

"So then," pursued Mrs. Morland, looking earnestly into space, "I get so furious that I simply don't know what to do. So I buy some exercise books, which are a perfectly frightful price now, at least they cost the same but there are hardly any pages so it comes to much the same thing in the end, and some more pencils. And what is perfectly maddening is that nowadays the pencils called B are so soft that you use them up at once, besides the lead breaking every time you sharpen them, and the ones called H don't mark at all. And then I sit down, very angrily, and write a book."

She then realized with horror that though she had come to the end of her subject there were at least thirty minutes of her allotted time to be filled.

"I think it's a shame, miss," said George.

"I don't do it on *purpose*," said Mrs. Morland, pleading her cause as well as she could. "You see, when my husband died I wasn't very well off and I had four boys, so I simply had to do something. I didn't ever *mean* to write books."

George's friend, going very red in the face, brought out an ill-prepared sentence to the effect that the late Mr. Morland's death had been on the whole a gain to humanity.

"Thank you very much," said Mrs. Morland gratefully. "I do so understand what you mean, and it is so kind of you, and I must say that I get on very well as I am and don't feel a bit like a widow."

George said his Dad died before he was born, so he didn't seem to miss him like.

"No," said Mrs. Morland, after considering this statement, "you couldn't. Not unless your mother put it into your head."

"Mum died when I was a month old," said George with some pride, "and auntie she brought me up."

"I *am* sorry," said Mrs. Morland.

Lady Waring now begged for silence so that Mrs. Morland could go on with her most interesting talk, thus earning the lecturer's lively, if temporary, dislike. The convalescents all told each other to shut up and let the lady talk, George and his friend being particularly active in this way.

"Well," said Mrs. Morland, miserably resigned to the inevitable, but without the faintest idea of how she was going to fill up the remaining time, "I hadn't very much money and my third boy was just going into the Navy."

"I got a brother in the Navy, miss," said George.

Not to be outdone, various other members of the audience mentioned the names of brothers, uncles, cousins and brothers-in-law in the Senior Service. George's friend said he wished he was in the Navy because a fellow got treated proper there; rum, they got, not like some people as couldn't even get beer some days.

"You get treated proper, all right, my lad," said George. "What about those drinks I stood you at the Sheep's Head last week?"

This led to a good deal of laughter at the expense of George's friend, who appeared to have a reputation for parsimony.

"I don't know where he is now," said Mrs. Morland, feeling that she could never face her hostess again unless she justified her existence as a lecturer, "but two years ago he was in the *Flatiron*, on the China station."

A voice, unidentified, said his two uncles were out there, adding, "Dirty yellow monkeys." It then apologized, saying it was thinking of the Japs.

Mrs. Morland, having at last realized that Heaven was working directly on her behalf, gave up trying to interfere with it and allowed herself to drift with the tide of popularity. The whole life-stories of her three elder boys were discussed by her sympathetic friends, points of contact were found everywhere, and if Tony was not so analysed it was not from any diffidence on his mother's part, for she was by now in a Delphic frenzy and would have told anybody anything, but that Matron came in and caught Lady Waring's eye. Lady Waring, seizing a moment's comparative calm, got up, thanked Mrs. Morland warmly for her delightful lecture and proposed a vote of thanks, which was carried by acclamation. Mrs. Morland, exhausted but content, had a kind of triumphal progress down the room and at the door was stopped by seven or eight men with sixpenny copies of her books which they wanted her to sign, offering fountain-pens and pencils of all sorts from silver-cased to indelible. In a writing blurred by emotion she wrote Laura Morland in eight different handwritings, thanked Matron for one of the nicest afternoons she had ever spent, shook hands with all the nurses, and went back with Lady Waring and her party to the servants' wing.

Here they found Sir Harry and Dr. Ford talking about fishing in Canada, where neither of them had ever been. Mrs. Morland told Sir Harry that she had had a perfectly delightful time, which pleased him very much, for he wished his guests to enjoy themselves and felt personally responsible for the hospital when his friends spoke there.

"We must be getting along, Mrs. Morland," said Dr. Ford. "Where's Tony?"

Mrs. Morland had received Tony's message, and though she believed him to be fairly truthful, at any rate in intention, she could not help an anxious glance at the clock, for Dr. Ford had always been one of Tony's sharpest critics, and Tony's mother, who adored and disliked her youngest son to distraction, did not wish her old friend to have a righteous cause of displeasure against him. The hands of the clock stood at fourteen and a half minutes past six when these thoughts rushed through her head.

"He will be here at a quarter past to pick us up," she said. "He had to talk to a soldier he knows."

"Seeing a man about a dog, I suppose," said Dr. Ford, a remark which Mrs. Morland decided not to forgive for some time, though she forgot all about it almost at once, for, like the late Count of Monte Cristo, Tony appeared, lingered for a fraction of a second in the doorway to mark his entrance, came in and shut the door.

"I am sorry I couldn't come to my mamma's lecture, Lady Waring," he said with old-fashioned courtesy. "I met an old friend who needed my advice, so I thought I ought to stay with him."

Lady Waring, pleased at the attention, for she had almost given up expecting courtesy from the young, called to her husband.

"Harry," she said, "this is Mrs. Morland's youngest son. He is on leave."

"Sir," said Tony, putting out his hand with a tinge of respectful deference that at once won Sir Harry's heart, who called him "my boy" and made searching inquiries about various local men in the Barsetshires, most of which Tony was able to answer.

Dr. Ford, a little mortified by Tony's punctuality, though really pleased for his old friend Mrs. Morland's sake on the whole, now said they must go at once.

"A splendid lecture, I hear, Mrs. Morland," said Sir Harry, as he conducted his visitor to the door. "I shall hear all about it from my wife. That is a nice boy of yours; he thinks of his men. This mechanized army is all very fine," said Sir Harry, who had all the old cavalryman's proper contempt for modern methods, "but an army still marches on its feet, and if the young officers don't look after the men's feet we'll never get anywhere. Good luck to him."

"Not that way, Sir Harry," said Dr. Ford, breaking into what threatened to be a slightly emotional scene. "My car's in the kitchen yard."

Sir Harry was shocked. Not that he used the front door much himself, as we already know, but to bring an honoured guest, and a lady who wrote books to boot, by the kitchen passage went against his sense of what was fit.

"Well, good-bye, Mrs. Morland," he said, conducting his visitor to the other door. "I expect you'll have us all in a book before long. Good-bye, my boy. You go on looking after your men's feet and you'll do all right for them and for yourself."

Mrs. Morland and Tony followed Dr. Ford down the kitchen passage in silence. Mrs. Morland was trying to forget the remark about putting people in books, a suggestion which always drove her to frenzy and to a strong wish to tell the speaker that no one present was either interesting or funny enough to find their way into a book of hers, and concentrating on Sir Harry's kind and delightful praise of Tony. That young gentleman was meditating on the ease with which one could make a good impression if one wanted to, though it is to be feared that he did not reflect how fatally easy it is to make a bad impression if one does not want to. In the passage, which was dimly lighted, he nearly bumped into Selina who was coming out of the kitchen.

"Sorry," said Tony. "Oh, Mrs. Crockett, I'd back Sergeant Hopkins any day. He really understands vegetables. Goodbye, and I'll come and see you next leave unless I'm killed."

"Oh, *sir*!" said Selina and her lovely eyes misted with tears as she watched the guests depart.

"Tom Jenks is back," said a voice.

"Oh, you *did* upset me, Mr. Margett," said Selina. "I never heard you come up."

"No one does," said Jasper. "Nor the rabbits, nor the pheasants, nor the vermin, nor no one. I saw the ambulance with Tom Jenks. He's doing nicely, he says, and the nurses at the hospital were as pretty as a picture."

338

If Jasper had hoped to provoke Selina to a display of jealousy, he was disappointed. Wiping her eyes she said it was dreadful poor Private Jenks having an operation all over again and she was so glad the nurses were nice.

"Not so pretty as some," said Jasper. "I'll take Tom Jenks out shooting as soon as he's well enough. Give him a shot at a rabbit. That'll do him more good than all the doctor's medicine."

"But don't let him *kill* the poor rabbit, Mr. Margett," Selina pleaded. "It's dreadful to think of killing a poor little rabbit and Private Jenks is such a kindhearted boy. He drowned all the stable cat's kittens for Cook except the one she kept and he said they didn't feel it a bit."

Jasper gave a long whistle, expressive of his opinion of women, and disappeared into the darkness.

Colonel Winter had not forgotten his promise, or at least the wish he expressed to Leslie Waring, that he would come and hear Mrs. Morland's talk; nor had Leslie forgotten it. But though he had every intention of coming to tea, listening to the lecture and staying to dinner, he was a soldier. On the morning of that day he was suddenly summoned to London, which meant getting a car at once to Winter Overcotes and spending at least one night in town. There was not time to telephone to Leslie, so he told Corporal Jackson to ring up the Priory and tell Miss Waring that he had been called away and would ring her up as soon as he got back. Corporal Jackson industriously wrote the message down in his notebook, resumed his occupation of discussing Arsenal's form with Private Moss, and very naturally forgot all about his instructions.

So Leslie, who after telling herself that Philip did not mean what he said, had decided that he would come well before teatime, sit beside her during the talk, and stay to dinner, was hard put to it to behave well. When Philip did not turn up for tea she made up her mind that he had been kept at the camp and would be waiting in the billiard-room. When she looked round the room and could not see him her heart fell into her knees, till imagination coming to the rescue informed her that he was just too late for the lecture, but would be waiting in the hall, or at any rate in the drawing-room when they got back. This position proving untenable, she retreated to the defence that he would ring up before dinner. But these gradations of hope deferred are too familiar to us all. It is enough to say that by dinnertime she was as tired by her own emotions as any sensible young woman can be, and what was more, so feverishly cross that her aunt looked at her once or twice with anxiety and even Noel got bare civility from her. Saying, quite truthfully, that to-morrow was her day in London, she went to bed early, but did not sleep well. After her talk with Philip, the drowsy moments before sleep had been agreeably filled by musings on the perfect school; a building which, without any intention on her part, had a curious resemblance to the Priory. It was rather fun to plan the big rooms as classrooms, to settle the masters' quarters, the dining-hall, the headmaster's private house in the Warings' present quarters, to decide where the playing-fields would be and to hope that the War Office would leave the fixed basins. All this passed through her busy mind with no reference to actual conditions. Not for a moment did she think of the Priory without her uncle and aunt, nor was she really thinking whether Cecil would care for the plan. But to plan a school without a house for it was unreasonable, so she continued her pleasant, competent dreams.

To-night she had no intention of school-planning. Anyone so thoughtless — one did not wish to say untruthful and untrust-worthy — would certainly never be able to concentrate on a school. As for working with or for such a person, the whole idea was fantastic and she was thoroughly ashamed of herself for having entertained it, even in fun. Dismissing Philip Winter from her thoughts, she lay awake till nearly one o'clock, at which hour she fell asleep, disliking him more than ever.

CHAPTER
ELEVEN

Next day Leslie went to town, to work at the office, sleep at her flat, work again next day and come down by the usual afternoon train. Lydia spent a useful morning in the convalescent hospital, helping Nurse Poulter in the wards. Matron had not forgotten Lydia's wish to do full-time work, but what with a scare of chickenpox and Matron going away for a fortnight nothing had been settled. The chickenpox had turned out, as in the case of Master Peppercorn at Southbridge School, to be a rash; Matron had returned from her holiday, but for several days was inaccessible while she dealt with papers and patients and gathered the reins once more into her capable hands. Meanwhile, Lydia had been giving a hand when wanted and otherwise found plenty to do in the garden and in entertaining Mr. Needham, who though grateful to his hostess for her care was glad to escape at times, for the sittingroom, while nominally his room, was used by Nannie as a suitable place in which to pronounce panegyrics on her many ex-charges, always ending with the interesting information that Baby Crawley, for so she called Octavia to the annoyance of that lady's betrothed, never would eat her greens, with various unpleasant details as to Baby Crawley's rejection of the same.

So after lunch Lydia went down to the village. The door of No. 1 Ladysmith Cottages being on the jar she went straight into Mr. Needham's sitting-room and found him smoking a pipe and reading one of Mrs. Morland's books.

"Hullo, Tommy," said Lydia. "Come for a walk."

"I'd love to," said Mr. Needham. "I was going out this morning to do some shopping but Mrs. Allen wouldn't let me because it was raining. I think she has just gone out, so we might escape before she comes back. Anyway it's a lovely afternoon now, so she can't blame me. If she calls Octavia Baby Crawley once more I shall break off my engagement."

The conspirators accordingly tiptoed from the silent house, reached the street and paused. Lydia, with good generalship, would have led a reconnoitring party up the side lane, past the shed, and so fetched a circuit round the village, but Mr. Needham said he must get some tobacco.

"All right," said Lydia. "Don't say you've not been warned."

In the shop they found Nannie, buying beans for early sowing. Mr. Needham began to back, but it was too late, for Nannie had seen him through the little window.

"Oh, go on in, Tommy," said Lydia impatiently.

"Oh," said Mr. Needham nervously, "I didn't know you were here, Mrs. Allen. I only came in to buy some tobacco."

"Just as well, sir," said Nannie. "I meant to ask you where's that other vest of yours, because I want to wash it. You're not wearing it, are you? I told you last night, sir, you'd had it on *quite* long enough."

Mr. Needham, feeling naked and unprotected before Nannie's all-seeing eye and the deep interest of Mrs. Hamp, the tailor's sister-in-law, who sold tobacco, sweets when there were any, small articles of haberdashery, cheap newspapers, seeds and a few home-made buns, said he was most awfully sorry, but he'd dropped it into the bath this morning.

"So I put it flat inside my bath towel to get dry sooner and put the towel on the rail," said Mr. Needham, adding hurriedly "as neatly as I could," in the faint hope of placating his hostess.

"That comes of not telling Nannie at once," said Mrs. Allen. "I saw the towel on the rail, sir, and I thought 'Well, the gentleman has put his towel tidy for once,' so I didn't fold it again. Another time tell me directly, sir."

Mr. Needham, crimson with abasement, paid for his tobacco and left the shop.

"As nice a gentleman as you'd wish to see, Mrs. Hamp," said Nannie. "So quiet, and always in punctual to meals. Not like old Mr. Horniman. Marigold's sister Flo used to work there and she said the old gentleman hadn't been down punctual to a meal all the time she was there. Always reading his books, he was. Now Mr. Needham likes a nice book; I lent him one of Mrs. Morland's that Miss Leslie gave me. But at five minutes to one, or twenty-five past seven, away goes the book,

344

or his letter or whatever he's writing, and the table all ready for me to lay the cloth."

"He's in here most days, Mrs. Allen," said Mrs. Hamp, "for a newspaper, or tobacco, or some little thing and always so cheerful. When you think of his arm, it does seem a shame. It's much to be wished we had someone like him at the Vicarage. Mr. Horniman never came in here, unless it was an odd time, and never a word to say but get what he wanted and out again. Now your gentleman, Mrs. Allen, it's a pleasure to serve him."

Lydia and Mr. Needham continued their progress down the village street. Lydia, in her generous anxiety to forward Mr. Needham's cause, had meant to introduce him to the more important of her village friends, thereby helping him to win the regard of what she hoped might be his future parishioners, but as they went from the post-office to the chemist's, from the chemist's to the china shop, where Mr. Needham insanely hoped to be able to match the tooth-vase which he had knocked off his washing-stand and broken just before lunch, from the china shop to the station to look up the morning trains to Barchester, Lydia found that her old friend was already well known and apparently well liked. Far from feeling disappointed that her work was already done, she was delighted that Mr. Needham was standing so well on his own feet and, being herself, at once wished to share the thought with someone, preferably the nearest person available.

"I say, Tommy," she said, "you're even grown-upper than I thought."

"Not nastily, I hope," said Mr. Needham anxiously.

"Of course not. Very, very nicely," said Lydia. "Only I do feel a bit as if *everyone* was grown up now and I wasn't."

"I always thought you were frightfully grown-up," said Mr. Needham. "You always knew what to do. In fact, if it it hadn't been for you I don't think I'd have been brave enough to propose to Octavia. But I don't suppose anyone feels really grown-up inside."

"What would you call really grown-up?" asked Lydia.

"Knowing about income tax and things, and being a chairman of committees, oh and all that," said Mr. Needham vaguely.

Lydia said like the Dean.

Mr. Needham agreed that the Dean probably felt as grown-up as anyone, but he knew for a matter of fact that the Dean was very frightened of his eldest daughter, though fond of her, and would go miles out of his way to avoid old Lady Norton, because she would tell him what he ought to plant in the Deanery garden and send him cuttings which his gardener, who was an enemy of Lady Norton's gardener, and of whom the Dean was terrified, deliberately allowed to die.

"Well, I suppose no one is really grown-up," said Lydia with a sigh, "not even the King. I did think I'd get grown-up when I was married, but I feel just the same inside. I say, Tommy, when are you and Octavia going to get married?"

346

"After Easter, she says," said her betrothed. "We did think sooner, but the Bishop is broadminded about marriages in Lent, so of course Dr. Crawley wouldn't hear of it, though he doesn't really mind a bit. Dr. Crawley didn't know if he'd marry us or give Octavia away, but Octavia said give her away, so we're going to ask Mr. Miller to marry us. He was at college with my father."

Lydia said she thought there was a law about a Dean having to marry his own daughter if it was in his cathedral, to which Mr. Needham, quickly grappling with the slight want of ordered thinking in Lydia's remark, said he hadn't ever thought about it, but would inquire. Anyway, he said, Dr. Crawley would know, because he knew everything about his job.

Lydia, struck with a new idea and burning to impart it, said she supposed the reason the Bishops of Barchester were always so horrid was that they were really jealous of the Dean.

"I mean, if I were a Bishop of Barchester," she said, "and my cathedral belonged to someone else, I'd feel horrid about him."

Mr. Needham was torn between conflicting loyalties, but the old Adam in him being strongly pro-Deanery, he gracefully yielded to his worse self, and he and Lydia had a delightful talk about the Bishop's wife, who added to the initial fault of having married the Bishop the serious crime of being a friend of Miss Pettinger and often asking her to tea at the Palace. In such heart-warming converse they walked up the village and round the churchyard. While Mr. Needham was reading with great interest the mysterious lists that live in church porches Sir Harry came up.

"I'm just going to the Vicarage, Mrs. Merton," he said. "Would you and Mr. Needham care to look over it?"

The invitation was gratefully accepted. Sir Harry led the way through the little gate into the Vicarage garden and unlocked the Vicarage door.

"Drawing-room this side," said Sir Harry, throwing open the doors, "dining-room opposite. Hatch into kitchen. Bit of glass outside the drawing-room. Like to see the kitchen? There's a gas-cooker and a little coal range and a copper in the scullery. It's heated by gas, but you can use wood if you prefer and if this war goes on we'll be glad to. Hot pipes up and downstairs when we can have the fuel. Nice little cloakroom. Of course it all looks a bit forlorn now, with all the furniture gone, but I'll have it put into proper order. And this room old Horniman used as his study. Shelves all round, you see, and a door into the garden to escape visitors. Like to see upstairs?"

Without waiting for an answer he led the way. Mr. Needham was as near envy as his good and simple nature would let him. If only he and Octavia had a vicarage like that, how easy it would be to help other people a bit. Though the floors were bare, the walls marked where pictures or bookcases had been and the kitchen full of rubbish, the sun shone almost warmly into the living-rooms, birds were singing outside, the garden was in excellent condition, and Mr. Needham, who had never had a real home since his parents died

348

about ten years previously, felt his heart warm longingly to this abiding-place. He followed Sir Harry and Lydia upstairs.

"Bedroom, dressing-room, bathroom," said Sir Harry. "Two other bedrooms with communicating door. Do for guests or children, you know. Other spare bedroom. Linen cupboard here with hot pipes. Housemaid's sink in this cupboard. We needn't go up further. Two bedrooms in the roof for the servants if there ever are any again. Fixed basins everywhere, you see. Power-plugs for all the things the ladies want; Hoovers and electric irons and all that sort of thing. Well, shall we go down?"

But Lydia, always inclined for adventure, had gone up and was examining the attic bedrooms with interest, pleased to find that, although in the roof, there was only one place in each where one couldn't stand upright, and some good cupboards.

Sir Harry and Mr. Needham went down into the garden and took a turn in front of the house in the sun. Mr. Needham tried to express his admiration of all he had seen, but found himself as shy as a child at a party; or, let us rather say, as some children at parties, for heaven knows that the others are self-confident, overbearing and noisy enough, and though psychologists may say that this is merely a form of intense diffidence the results are identical and highly displeasing. He had fallen in love with house, garden, little conservatory, bathrooms. In the study, tucked away in a safe corner with escape provided, he saw the study of his dreams and had already thought how well

349

his college and Leander oars, never to be used again, would look upon the wall, and how well the photographs of himself in a group at school, Oxford, theological training college, and in camp would fit over the mantelpiece, and that at last his father's Arundel prints would find a home.

But he knew that for a young man back from the wars, with only one arm, his way to make and a bride waiting to marry him, such a haven could not be. His thoughts went back to the early days of the war while he was still the Dean's secretary and eating his heart out because he was too safe and comfortable, pining to work in the East End and be stoned, or be a missionary to lepers and come back a human wreck. Now he knew that some forms of usefulness were closed to him and had tried hard to submit. Yet the sight of this little house filled him with such longing that he would have been almost glad if Nannie had appeared and taken him back to Ladysmith Cottages.

All the time while they had been walking up and down, Sir Harry had been talking, but though Mr. Needham tried to listen, he was so unhappy that he had not followed what his companion was saying. Not that this would have been easy, for Sir Harry, as we know from his conversation with Noel about the rent, had the greatest difficulty in bringing himself to the point in any discussion of business between gentlemen. At last Mr. Needham, with a violent effort, concentrated upon the present moment and as if coming out of an anaesthetic heard Sir Harry's voice gradually approaching from a great distance.

"You know, Needham," it was saying, "the Dean is an old friend of mine and Miss Octavia is a very sensible young lady. So if you like to think it over, and if everything is all right and satisfactory on both sides," said Sir Harry, who evidently felt that by this form of words he was insuring himself against interference from the Bishop, the Archbishop of Canterbury, the Court of Arches or any other religious authority, "it would give Lady Waring and myself great pleasure to see you both in the Vicarage. Don't trouble to answer now, my boy," said Sir Harry, seeing his young friend's deep confusion. "Think it over and let me know. Consult Miss Octavia. She's got a head on her shoulders."

Mr. Needham was not sure whether he was standing still and the whole world wheeling and rocking round him, or the world was going on as usual while he stood on his head on the buttend of a spear surrounded with blazing fireworks, but whatever it was he had to get control of it. A wild thought passed through his head that the Bishop, knowing the scarcely veiled hostility of the Deanery party, might refuse to induct him, but he came to the considered opinion, or what in his frenzy he took for such, that the Bishop, though as a cleric practically indistinguishable from Arius or Pope Celestine V, was probably quite reasonable as a man. So he said something incoherent.

"No need to hurry at all, you know," Sir Harry repeated kindly.

But there was every need to hurry. If he did not accept now there was, Mr. Needham felt, every probability that Sir Harry would take offence and at once give the living to one of the Bishop's sons-in-law.

"I'd like it more than anything in the world, sir," he managed to stutter.

"Well then, that's settled," said Sir Harry, much relieved. "That's all right, Needham. We needn't say any more, now. I shall take all the proper steps. You're the third presentation I've made to this living and I hope you'll see me out and get on well with my nephew, Cecil."

Mr. Needham, still quite demented, could only say he hoped he would. He would like to have explained that he meant he hoped he wouldn't ever bury Sir Harry and yet would always be on excellent terms with Commander Waring, R.N., but found himself incapable of formulating this reasonable wish.

"Oh, and one thing, Needham," said Sir Harry, nervously.

Mr. Needham knew the worst had come. Sir Harry probably held views about the Trinity to which Mr. Needham, as a loyal son of the Church, could not subscribe. Farewell vicarage, study, conservatory, wife: welcome a curacy in an industrial town, phthisis and early death.

"You saw the monkey-puzzle down in the far corner of the churchyard," said Sir Harry nervously. "My wife can't bear it, but old Horniman wouldn't hear of its being moved. He said it reminded him of the barren fig-tree. If you wouldn't particularly object to its coming down — ? I'd send Jasper and a man to see about it. No trouble for you at all."

"I LOATHE the thing, sir," said Mr. Needham, relieving his long pent up emotions in one outburst. "I'll cut it down to-day, sir, if you've got an axe. Oh," he added, "I'd forgotten. I can't. Sorry, sir."

"Bad luck, bad luck," said Sir Harry, looking kindly at his empty sleeve. "Now we won't say anything about this till I have got matters in order. Make a surprise for Miss Octavia and my wife and Mrs. Merton. Got to be going. See you again soon, Needham. You must come up to dinner again and tell me about my old regiment."

Mr. Needham wanted to say "God bless you, Sir Harry," but wasn't sure if this would be a proper way to address one's patron, and while he was madly considering, Sir Harry shook him warmly by the hand, clapped him on the shoulder, and strode away, evidently much relieved at having got this piece of business off his mind.

Mrs. Merton, who had taken advantage of being alone in the house to go thoroughly over the kitchen premises, turn on every tap, open every cupboard, see if the windows opened properly, examine the coal and coke sheds and generally inspect everything, now came round the corner of the house and apologized for being so long, giving at the same time a favourable report on all she had seen.

Mr. Needham said he hadn't noticed, he'd been talking to Sir Harry; he meant he had noticed but it didn't matter because Sir Harry was talking to him; he meant it was awfully nice that Sir Harry, he meant Lydia, liked the kitchen and things; he meant —

"You'd better stop talking for a bit, Tommy," said Lydia good-humouredly. "You look as if you'd had a stroke. Can people get strokes from having their arms off? It's a nice Vicarage, isn't it?"

Mr. Needham said yes, but in such a rum and distracted way that Lydia looked piercingly at him and at once knew the truth. Miss Lydia Keith would have hit Mr. Needham on the back and congratulated him in a loud voice. Mrs. Merton only said that it had been a very nice walk and she ought to be getting back to the Priory now. Mr. Needham said, Oh, yes, of course she must, but with such an addled expression that Lydia's suspicions were confirmed.

"Well, see you soon, Tommy," she said. "Give my love to Octavia when you write and say I'm most *terribly* glad."

"What about?" said Mr. Needham, burrowing his head into the sand.

"Well, if you don't know, I don't," said Lydia. "And heaps and heaps of luck, Tommy."

She wrung his hand painfully and went off through the churchyard and away by the wood path to the Priory.

Sir Harry and Lady Waring were enjoying the very rare treat of having tea together, alone, in peace. One of the few advantages of the war had been that Lady Waring could at last put away the massive silver tray, spirit-kettle, long-handled extinguisher for flame under same, teapot, milk-jug (with gilded inside), cream-jug with ditto, sugar-basin, sugar-tongs, muffineer, two special salt-shakers to put salt on muffins, slop-basin and one or two other parts of the service whose use no one had ever discovered. During the whole of her married life she had wished to use one of the really good china tea-services in the Priory, but Sir Harry had a pious feeling that to drink tea with the aid of about a stone of solid mid-Victorian silver was the equivalent of making a daily sacrifice to the memory of his parents and grandparents. Nor, while he had a butler and two footmen, was there any reason why he shouldn't. Now at last Lady Waring's opportunity came, and as soon as they moved into the servants' wing she had all the heavy silver wrapped and put into the strong-room. The results were two. In the first place the butler gave notice, the footmen having already gone, one into the Air Force, the other into the Barsetshire Yeomanry, and went to old Lady Norton who refused to abate one whit of her dowagerial state. In the second place Baker broke the Sèvres, the Dresden and the Crown Derby with punctuality and dispatch. Lady Waring was about to collect and put away the sad remnants when Selina came. Her mother, who had sympathized deeply with her old mistress, gave Selina orders to wash all the china herself. By a miracle of tact Lady Waring kept Baker from taking offence, and it was now Selina's pride to ring the changes on the various tea-sets. Her mistress would willingly have put them away, only keeping one for daily use, but Nannie Allen, coming up on a visit, very loftily forbade any such lowering of the standard, and as Selina loved the delicate objects, things remained as they were.

On the very rare days when Sir Harry was able to have tea in peace with his wife it was his habit to read a chapter or so of *Jorrocks* to himself afterwards. In past times he had tried to educate his wife in his favourite author, but though she had listened kindly, it was obvious that the root of the matter was not in her, as indeed it is not in any woman as far as we know. He had still not lost the habit of reading choice bits aloud to her, swallowing half his words and dropping his voice at the end of every sentence, to which she listened with her affectionate and unalterable patience; and when we say listened, her spirit flew to a Red Cross meeting, or a W.V.S. committee, or whether Mrs. Phipps would come for a fortnight while Cook had her holiday, and if so, exactly how horrid the meals would be.

But on this afternoon Sir Harry appeared to have something on his mind. He read aloud even worse than usual; his wife's comments had not roused him to look over his spectacles and lose the place. Suddenly he put his spectacle-case in the book and closed it, an outrage on books to which Lady Waring could never accustom herself, and said:

"I've been thinking about the Vicarage, my dear. It needs a bit of doing up. Paint and paper and so forth. The drains are all right, so are the fittings, gas-stove and so on. But we want it to look bright again. Old Horniman liked things gloomy, dark curtains and that sort of thing."

Lady Waring quite agreed in principle.

"Wouldn't it be better, though," she said, "to wait till we have a new Vicar? If you get a married man his wife might like to have a say in it."

"Or the young lady he is going to marry, even if she isn't his wife yet," said Sir Harry.

Lady Waring quite agreed.

"It would be so nice," she said, "if we had a really sound Vicar. I mean a man we could comfortably ask to dinner and whose wife would take an interest in the parish without getting across the village. When I think of that dreadful Mr. Moxon who used to be curate at Worsted, and how dear old Dr. Thomas suffered from him, I feel one cannot be too careful."

"Quite right, my dear," said Sir Harry and relapsed into his book. But suddenly, looking round at his wife, half through, half outside his spectacles, he remarked carelessly, "By the way, my dear, what does Nannie think of her present lodger?"

"Mr. Needham? She likes him very much," said Lady Waring, who had not the faintest doubt of what was in her husband's mind. "And of course as Octavia Crawley was one of her babies she thoroughly approves of the marriage. I feel so sorry for Mr. Needham and he makes light of his misfortune in such a courageous and unselfish way. I would very much like to help them if I could."

"Well, my dear," said Sir Harry, again marking his place in *Jorrocks* with his spectacle-case, so that his wife could hardly pay any attention to him in her sympathy for the book, "I have been thinking that too. Now, what would you think of Mr. Needham, and of course Miss

Crawley who would then be able to marry him, for the Vicarage?"

Lady Waring, who had been thinking of this ever since the evening of the dinner party, expressed every suitable grade of surprise, doubt, gradual conviction and complete agreement.

"I thought you'd come round to my way of thinking," said Sir Harry complacently, "and I may as well tell you now that I spoke to Needham about it this afternoon. He took the suggestion very well, in a very nice modest way. But of course not a word to anyone about it at present."

"Of course not, Harry," said his wife. "And I do hope it will be soon, because Canon Tempest gets angrier every week, and last Sunday he really *barked* the service at us." She then went away.

Hardly had she gone when Lydia came in.

"I'm so sorry I'm late, Sir Harry," she said. "I was having a good go over the Vicarage and didn't see how late it was. What *lovely* cupboards there are, and I *do* like the kitchen sink."

"You know a lot about it, young lady," said Sir Harry, amused. "Ring for Selina to bring you some fresh tea."

But Lydia said so long as it was wet she didn't mind what it was.

"I did know quite a lot about sinks and cupboards before I was married," she said, "but I got a bit out of the way living in hotels and rooms and things. It's a pity you haven't got a clergyman living there. Being empty makes it look a bit uninhabited."

"Well, well, we'll have to look round," said Sir Harry. "You are a friend of Dr. Crawley. Perhaps you know of someone."

Lydia, thinking of the vacant living and her friend Tommy had, as we know, laid very deep and diplomatic plans, but now that the moment had come her natural straightforwardness got the better of her and she said, very simply, that she thought it would be most awfully nice if Tommy were there, because he had loved the house and it was all so labour-saving and as he only had one arm that would be such a good thing now one couldn't get servants.

"That's an idea worth considering," said Sir Harry with great subtlety. "But what would Miss Octavia think?"

Lydia gave it as her opinion that Octavia would like it very much indeed, adding that Octavia had always meant to have eight children because she was an eighth, so it was a good thing there was plenty of room for nurseries.

"Eight children, eh?" said Sir Harry, amused. "Well, it's a round number, and we need big families now."

If Lydia felt his friendly gaze fixed on her for a moment we do not know; nor do we know whether he was conscious of it.

"I am going to treat you as if you were Leslie and tell you quite privately that I like your friend Needham very much," said Sir Harry.

Having got so far, and seeing Lydia's look of approval, he could not longer deny himself the pleasure of indiscretion and added, "In fact, while you were looking into the cupboards this afternoon, young lady, I offered him the living."

This was no surprise to Lydia, but the delight of hearing it from Sir Harry himself was so great that she was able to look as surprised and excited as if it had never before occurred to her. While she ate her usual hearty tea they rearranged the whole Vicarage and had even added a downstairs playroom with an extra bedroom and bathroom over it.

"But mind," said Sir Harry, heaving himself up to go out while the last daylight made it possible to saw a log or cut down a piece of dead wood, "not a word to anyone."

Lydia sat by the fire thinking her own thoughts till Selina came in to clear the tea-things away.

"You've been drinking all that cold tea, madam," she said reproachfully. "Why didn't you ring for fresh?"

Lydia said she quite liked it.

"Besides I was so late I really didn't deserve fresh," she said. "I went over the Vicarage with Sir Harry and Mr. Needham. What a nice house it is."

"Yes, indeed, madam," said Selina. "And we're all ever so pleased that Mr. Needham's coming there. Cook had a stranger in her cup at teatime, a funny shape it was, and she says it's the way the leaves tell you if it's a man that isn't all there."

"But Mr. Needham isn't mad!" said Lydia indignantly.

"Oh, no, madam," said Selina. "But he's not all there with his arm goodness knows where. They say the Free French eat frogs and snails and *anything*. Mother *will*

360

be so pleased. I shall run down and tell her before dinner."

"But who told you, Selina?" said Lydia. "I don't know if anything is really settled yet."

"Well, madam, I thought it was quite settled," said Selina, "because I met Sir Harry in the kitchen passage and he said he had a nice surprise for us, so I said that would be very nice and he said, Well, Mr. Needham is going to be the new Vicar, but don't tell anyone. So I only just stopped to tell Cook and Baker and came straight along to clear the tea. I *was* so pleased, madam."

"But ought you to have told Cook and Baker?" asked Lydia.

"Oh dear, yes, madam," said Selina. "Cook knew it because of the Stranger, and Baker said Mrs. Hamp had told her that everyone said it would be Mr. Needham, and they *were* so pleased."

Lydia reflected that Sir Harry must be enjoying himself very much.

Then Lady Waring came back and sat down as usual to her writing-table to deal with her correspondence. Lydia was burning to talk to her about Mr. Needham's new job, but could not feel quite sure whether Sir Harry's recommendation of secrecy applied to his wife or not. So she sat and knitted and made plans in her head for living in the bailiff's delightful little house near Northbridge Manor, working at the Barchester General, and in her spare time doing vegetables in the garden. Lady Waring too would fain have discussed the Vicarage with her guest and the possibility of another bathroom if one built out a little at the side, but as Sir Harry had said it was a secret, a secret it should remain as far as she was concerned.

So quiet was the room that the sound of the door being opened almost made Lydia jump. A rustling, crackling noise told her that it was Matron, so she turned her head and saw Matron in a clean, starched uniform, with Winston walking between her feet, arching his back and trying to rub his head against her shoes.

"Down, Winston, down!" said Matron, "bad pussy. Good evening, Lady Waring; good evening, Mrs. Merton. I must ask to be excused for coming over without ceremony, but I was so interested by the news I felt I really must share the excitement."

Lady Waring begged Matron to sit down and asked what news.

"Why, the great news," said Matron sitting down and taking the kitten on her lap, where it washed its hands, stretched them out to admire them and went to sleep. "I was saying only yesterday, or perhaps the day before, but time does so fly when one is busy, to Nurse Poulter that it really hardly seemed feasible to have a church without a Vicar and all the time Sir Harry had Mr. Needham up his sleeve. Such a nice young man, Lady Waring, and so much liked by the men. He has been up twice to play draughts with them and you will excuse my smiling but it struck me as so humorous, he insisted on the man that was playing with him having his left arm tied to his side, saying it made him feel the game would be more even. Now that I do call a really

362

Christian spirit, so rare nowadays. So Winston and I felt we must come and pay you a little visit. Pussy wanted go walkies with auntie, didn't 'um?"

"But where did you hear this piece of news, Matron?" said Lady Waring. "I hardly know if it is true or not."

"Well, we all like our little mysteries and if I am premature of course I am sorry," said Matron, "but from the way Private Jenks spoke, I understood it was quite a settled thing."

"Private Jenks?" said Lady Waring.

"He had of course no business to be out, Lady Waring," said Matron. "He is supposed to go to bed after his tea for the next few days, but he met your nice maid near the back door and she told him Sir Harry had just told her. All the men were delighted and they are getting up a little subscription for a wedding present."

"But he isn't going to be married yet," cried Lydia, "only to get made the Vicar." Then she looked at Lady Waring and Lady Waring looked at her, and each lady realized that Sir Harry had told the other, but neither dared to laugh, for Matron kept in reserve a very powerful gift for taking umbrage, and would probably have construed their laughter as against herself.

"If Private Jenks says he is to be the Vicar, he probably is," said Lady Waring, so gravely that Matron was quite taken in. "It was very nice of you to come, Matron, and I am pleased to see how well the kitten is."

"He's auntie's own boy," said Matron, "but I must say, Lady Waring, that Private Jenks did not say it in at all a joking way. Indeed he looked quite depressed for him, for he is always quite the life and soul of the ward. Still, the first days of convalescence are always the most difficult and we must make every allowance for him, poor fellow. I suppose you have heard that Sergeant Hopkins is to have his board to-morrow at Winter Overcotes. I much fear he will be discharged altogether. I don't think he'll lose the sight of his eye, but in my opinion he will be better out of the Army than in. Say good night, Winston, there's auntie's good boy."

Winston, proving quite indifferent to this appeal, was presented to Lady Waring and Lydia in turn to be tickled behind the ear and Matron took him away.

Lady Waring looked at Lydia.

"I suppose Sir Harry told you at teatime," said Lady Waring.

"Yes, he did, but he must have told you first," said Lydia, not wishing to appear the earlier recipient of Sir Harry's confidence.

"And apparently Selina third," said Lady Waring, laughing, a thing she so rarely did, in spite of herself. "I must find out about this."

She rang the bell. As a rule Selina was very prompt to answer, but this evening she delayed so long that Lady Waring rang again. Selina then appeared, on the verge of tears.

"Was it for the papers, my lady?" she said in a choked voice. "They haven't come yet."

"What is the matter, Selina?" said her mistress.

"It's Private Jenks, my lady. Oh, I *am* so upset," cried Selina, looking wildly from side to side with mournful eyes.

"I'll hear about that in a moment," said Lady Waring. "Selina, did Sir Harry tell you about Mr. Needham?"

"Oh, yes, my lady, and we were all so pleased," said Selina, her expression of pleasure marred by a fresh outburst of grief. "And he said not to tell anyone, so I only just mentioned it to Cook and Baker, like I told Mrs. Merton, and then Private Jenks came into the yard, my lady, and it didn't seem kind not to ask him in, just out of the hospital again."

"And then I suppose you told him about Mr. Needham," said Lady Waring unsympathetically. "You do talk too much, Selina. Sir Harry will not be pleased."

"No, my lady, of course he won't," said Selina, "and that's what I told Private Jenks, and then Cook passed the remark that Mr. Needham was going to marry Miss Crawley and Private Jenks was *most* impertinent, my lady."

Lady Waring, a little bored by the whole affair, and wishing, though with the greatest fondness, that her darling husband had a little more discretion, was not particularly interested in the impertinence of a convalescent soldier to a woman who was quite old enough to look after herself and was being rather a nuisance. But Lydia, impelled not so much by curiosity as by a wish to help Selina and a feeling that she wanted to unburden herself, asked what he said.

365

"He was *most* impertinent, madam," said Selina, her eyes flashing the mildest fire. "He had the impertinence to say that he would like to give Mr. Needham his first job when he was Vicar, and that would be to marry Mr. Tom Jenks and Mrs. Selina Crockett."

Selina's fiery indignation had now checked her tears and Lydia thought she had never seen her look prettier. Her tears had but made her cheeks the more blooming and caused her hair to curl more wildly. Seeing her audience deprived for the moment of speech, she continued:

"Of course, my lady, I said, Never had I been spoken to like that and I'm old enough to be your mother, Tom Jenks, I said, and joking or no joking I shall ever remain faithful to a very good husband. Cook said I was quite right and so I was, my lady, but poor Private Jenks looked *so* upset and Baker said, No wonder."

"So what happened then?" said Lydia, as Lady Waring appeared to have given up all attempt to control the situation.

"Sergeant Hopkins came along, madam, and said Matron was quite upset because of Private Jenks being out without leave, and he was to go back at once. So one of the boys was going down to the station with the lorry and he said he would give me a lift, my lady. So I went in and told mother, but she said she knew it all the time and she was going to give Mr. Needham the chop for his supper that she was keeping for his lunch to-morrow, just to mark the occasion. So I came back on the lorry, and there was your bell ringing, my lady, and I never heard it till Baker told me and I *am* so sorry, my lady."

Lady Waring, with a detachment that Lydia greatly admired, said that was very sad and now Selina had better forget about it and that was all. But as soon as Selina had left the room Lady Waring looked at Lydia, and Lydia knew that her hostess was longing to discuss the whole story, from Sir Harry's first breaking of the news to her over *Jorrocks*, to Selina's rejection of the ill-advised Private Jenks, who would not, she felt sure, break his heart permanently. Lady Waring then permitted herself, a thing she very rarely did, a little gentle criticism of her husband's methods of keeping a secret, and Lydia liked her more and more, as indeed she had done ever since she and Noel came to the Priory. They also allowed themselves to wonder how soon the news would be broken to Noel. Lady Waring thought Sir Harry would buttonhole him before dinner, Lydia thought Selina would hang about to be near the front door when he came back and so get in first. So busy were they in their talk that Noel, who was rather early that week, came upon them unawares.

"I hope I'm not ruining a conversation about mantuamakers and milliners," he said. "I came in by the back way as my boots were so dirty. What delightful news about Tommy. Is it true, Lydia?"

"Who told you?" said the ladies in chorus.

"It comes of living in a hush-hush camp," said Noel, sitting down. "Sergeant Hopkins at the hospital rang up Corporal Jackson at the Dower House about the football pool. This conversation always goes on for ten minutes or so and I suppose Hopkins didn't know what to say next, so he told Corporal Jackson that Mr. Needham was going to be the new Vicar. And when Jackson brought the last lot of papers in to me, he passed the news on."

So then Lady Waring, feeling that having once betrayed her husband she might as well do so again, told Noel, with Lydia's help, the whole story of the afternoon. They all laughed a good deal, and when Sir Harry came back, bursting with his news, Noel was quite ready to be surprised, and so well did he do it that Sir Harry plumed himself on his secrecy and diplomacy more than ever.

Next day, being Saturday, Sir Harry and Leslie were to come down together on the 6.25. Lady Waring, as on the day when this story began, had a number of Red Cross engagements, winding up at Winter Overcotes, and was going to use her official petrol ration. Having heard from Matron on the previous day that Sergeant Hopkins was having a board at Winter Overcotes, she offered to drive him back if he cared to wait. It was a cold day with driving sleet, so the sergeant was glad to accept the offer. He was to go in by train after lunch and when the board had done with him was to wait at the station where Lady Waring would pick him up together with the passengers from the 6.25.

The day got nastier and nastier. Sometimes it sleeted, sometimes it rained, sometimes it snowed. The wind blew from every point of the compass, weathercocks went nearly mad in their efforts to keep up with the changes, in Boon's Benefit a chimney-pot was blown down from River Woolram and crashed into the garden of River Rising, knocking the other wing off the cherub on Mr. Beedle's rockery.

"I don't like it, Beedle," said Mrs. Beedle. "Last time the rockery was hit was the day Henry got the order to go back to the camp; the day the tile fell off the roof. I hope nothing bad's coming."

"Don't you worry, Mother," said Mr. Beedle. "Our Henry's safe enough where he is."

With which cold comfort Mrs. Beedle had to content herself.

Whether it was the ill-omened chimney-pot's fault or not, nothing seemed to go right at the station that day. The petty thefts from the office lay heavily on Mr. Beedle's mind. Everything pointed to Bill Morple as the culprit, yet there was no proof, and Mr. Beedle was very loath to trouble the police, for he did not wish them to suspect any blemish on the character of the Best Line in England. Bill Morple was over-excited or moody in turns, though that again proved nothing, and Mr. Beedle tried to attribute it to his imminent departure for the Army. But the atmosphere was far from comfortable and even Doris Phipps and Lily-Annie Pollett, as a rule so cheerful and willing, were feeling the bitter cold and wet and inclined to grumble. Passenger traffic had to be altered to make way for some munition and troop trains, people asked more and sillier questions than usual. The telephone to Skeynes Junction was broken by a fall of earth at the other side of the Worsted tunnel, and was not repaired till five in the afternoon. Six boxes of zoned fish arrived long after Cockle the fishmonger had given up any hope of them, in a stinking condition, and as it was early closing he had gone with his wife to Barchester and could not be summoned, so the fish were left at the far end of the platform and stank more than ever, and several people, including Lord Bond, complained, blaming the Government however rather than Mr. Beedle.

By the time the 6.25 was due the whole of the depleted staff was seething with temper, with the exception of Mr. Beedle, who though deeply distressed and sorely worried managed to behave as if the chairman of directors were present. He was a little comforted by Sergeant Hopkins, who got loose from his board by five o'clock and came up to the station to wait for Lady Waring. Mr. Beedle and he were old acquaintances, so the stationmaster invited him into his office to sit before a fire and have a cup of tea. The 5.10 had gone out and there was time for a talk. Sergeant Hopkins inquired after Henry Beedle. Mr. Beedle inquired after Sergeant Hopkins's eye. Sergeant Hopkins said it wasn't any better and wasn't any worse; but the board had turned him down good and proper and he would be back in the greengrocery business before long. And not alone he hoped, said Sergeant Hopkins. Mr. Beedle inquired who the lady was, and hearing that it was Lady Waring's old nurse's daughter, Mrs. Crockett, was much interested, for when courting Mrs. Beedle he had seen Selina and admired her.

"But there's one thing I don't like," said Sergeant Hopkins. "Jasper Margett's after Mrs. Crockett. All that gipsy lot have got a way with them and Mrs. Crockett's like the rest, a slippery tongue goes a long way with her."

Mr. Beedle did his best to comfort the sergeant. His wife, he said, had no opinion of Jasper and he always went by her opinion, besides which, Sergeant Hopkins and the late Mr. Crockett having both been in the greengrocery line, it seemed as if it was to be.

"Well, I've got my work to attend to," he said at length. "You make yourself comfortable till the 6.25 comes in. Pull your chair round the other side of the fire, then you won't get the draught. There's the evening paper in my jacket behind the door if you want to look at the pools. That's where young Morple's money is going I'm afraid. He's in with that lot that came down from London, the ones that took the Cup, though the inspector says I mustn't say so. Seems if a man does a dirty trick on you he's all right, but if you say he's done it you're all wrong. Sometimes I lie awake at night and feel I'll never get over the disgrace to the Line. And Henry was so proud of it too. It's a bad story about Bill Morple, though mind you I've nothing definite to go on. I shall be glad when he's in the Army."

Sergeant Hopkins, who had heard with much sympathy and in great confidence Mr. Beedle's suspicions of Bill Morple, said the pools had done a lot of young fellows a lot of harm, and settled down happily to work out his favourites for the following week.

Presently the 6.25, only a few minutes late, came puffing majestically in. Sir Harry and Leslie got out. The evenings were by now beginning to lengthen and though the cloudy sky gave little light, Mr. Beedle at once saw the arrivals.

"Good evening Sir Harry; good evening, Miss Leslie," he said, touching his gold-laced cap. "Dreadful weather. Have you any luggage, miss?"

Leslie said only a small suitcase.

Mr. Beedle looked round. In the distance Doris Phipps and Lily-Annie were exchanging badinage with Guard Crackman and hauling cases out of the van. His porter was not to be seen.

"Allow me, miss," said Mr. Beedle, willing to demean himself to act as porter for Sir Harry's niece.

"Give me your suitcase, Leslie," said a voice.

Leslie looked round, with a beat of her heart, to see Philip, and even as her heart beat forgot how angry, how justifiably angry, she was with him.

"Are you going by the local, Sir Harry?" said Mr. Beedle.

Sir Harry said Lady Waring was meeting them with the car and picking up Sergeant Hopkins.

"Her ladyship has not yet arrived, Sir Harry," said Mr. Beedle. "Sergeant Hopkins is in my office. The board have turned him down, poor fellow. It's a dreadful state of things, Sir Harry, everywhere. I don't complain for myself, but it is very hard for some. There's only one thing really troubles me, Sir Harry, and that's the engines. Now, there was the Rising Castle, the latest of Our Line's Castle class. She was a picture, all her brass as shining as if a ship's company had been at work, her paint so new and glossy. Tomkins that drove her, and Tom Potter the stoker, a cousin of my wife's he was, were like mothers with a baby, Sir Harry, the way they looked after the Rising Castle, fair petted her you might say. First Tom was taken, and he's been missing since Singapore, Sir Harry. Then they had to cut down on the paint. And now Tomkins has a boy to help, but the youngester's heart isn't in the job, and he'll have to go soon. And as for the Rising Castle, she breaks Tomkins's heart. He'd buy the paint for her out of his own wages if he could. I was looking at her the other day, all so dirty and shabby I really could have cried, Sir Harry, and Tomkins was in the cab, rubbing her down with a handful of waste the way he always does if he has a minute to spare, and he said to me, 'Beedle,' he said, 'I can't look her in the face. It's not my fault and I hope she knows it, but every time we pull out of the station I feel like a murderer.' 'Well, Tomkins,' I said to him, 'there are some that's worse off. Think of old Ted Mitton that used to drive the Gatherum Castle. She's abroad somewhere and Ted can't get any news of her at all.' 'You're right, mate,' said Tomkins to me, 'and I'll never forgive Hitler for that. We all know what those foreign locomotives are and their dirty coal. If Hitler had seen the English railways it might have made all the difference.' But I beg pardon, Sir Harry, keeping you like this. Will you come into the office till her ladyship arrives?"

Sir Harry looked round for his niece, but seeing her occupied with Philip Winter, he followed the station-master.

If Sir Harry had been nearer his niece he would not have thought her occupied, for she and Colonel Winter were walking up and down the platform saying nothing. It is true that their coat sleeves occasionally brushed against each other and a flame leapt between them, but apart from this beautiful and romantic incident, no sign was made on either side.

"You aren't too tired by your night in town?" said Philip in a low passionate tone which conveyed the impression of stifled croup.

"Oh no, thank you," said Leslie, in a curiously high, artificial voice. "I dined with some people and we went to a show."

Philip at once hated and despised the people, but so far constrained himself as to hope the show was good.

Leslie said she hadn't much enjoyed it. It was all very symbolic, about a young man who didn't believe in patriotism and got converted by a street-walker just as they were killed in a blitz. Philip said it sounded pretty mouldy, but not much mouldier than having to play bridge with Captain Hooper, Wagstaffe of Signals, and Major Spender, who would talk about his children all the time.

They then continued their walk, each with a strong impulse to take the other's hand, but thinking it might be considered forward; both very glad that Lady Waring was so late. After a few minutes of this ecstasy Philip, who had already tried six times to speak and found himself quite unequal to it, said:

"Leslie, there's something I want to tell you. I really oughtn't to but I don't care."

He stopped, as if the works had suddenly run down. Leslie felt that something was coming which she had spent her whole life going to meet; something that had been coming towards her from the beginning of the world. But what it was she did not know, or would not let herself think. She only gave him a quick look and turned her head away.

"Have I made you angry?" asked Philip, nervously addressing his love's lost profile.

"Oh, of course not," said Leslie. "I think that's Uncle Harry looking for us."

She began to walk towards her uncle, followed by Philip with hope and despair jostling in him to that extent that there didn't seem to be much room for his breath.

"Come along, Leslie," said Sir Harry. "Your aunt's there. Can we give you a lift, Winter?"

Philip looked at Leslie to see if she wished to be incommoded by his presence, but owing to the darkness could see nothing but a pale oval which was her face.

"Thank you so much, sir," he said with calm despair, "but the local hasn't gone yet and I've got a big suitcase, so I won't trouble you."

He saluted and went away. Leslie, realizing that she had deliberately shattered her life's happiness as well as probably driving Philip to suicide on the first German gun he met, followed her uncle meekly. Lady Waring was in the car with Sergeant Hopkins in the back. Her husband got in beside the sergeant, Leslie sat beside her aunt, and they drove away.

"Most extraordinary thing just happened, my dear," said Sir Harry. "Of course this is entirely between ourselves. You know that porter, Bill Morple, from Melicent Halt. It seems there has been a lot of petty thieving at the station here, and Beedle had his suspicions, just as he did about the cup that was stolen, but he couldn't say anything as he had no proof. But our friend Hopkins here has caught the fellow red-handed."

"Good gracious!" said Lady Waring, quite moved from her accustomed calm. "What happened, sergeant?"

Sergeant Hopkins, who found consecutive speech very difficult unless his hands were occupied, looked wildly round, for discipline forbade him to take off his cap and roll it. His hand found something soft, he picked it up and began to twist it.

"It was this way, my lady," he said. "I was alone in Mr. Beedle's office by the fire till your ladyship and the car came, and I was doing the football pool, not that you would be interested in that though it's surprising the way the Barchester Roamers are doing in spite of the war, and I felt a draught, though I was on the other side of the fire, so I looked, my lady, and there was a hand came round the door."

"You see, my dear," said Sir Harry, acting as chorus, "the office is always empty just then, when the 6.25 is in the station, so if the door isn't locked anyone can get in."

"What *did* you do?" asked Leslie. "I would have screamed."

"I watched that hand," said the sergeant, who was enjoying himself deeply, "and it crope round the corner of the door, miss, and began feeling in the pocket of Mr. Beedle's jacket that was hanging behind the door."

The exclamations that burst from his female hearers were of a gratifying nature.

"Whoever it was thought the room was empty, you see, my dear," said Sir Harry.

"I watched that hand," said the sergeant, "and just as it came out of the pocket I made a jump and grabbed it and pulled the fellow in and put my back against the door."

"And it was Morple," said Sir Harry, who could not bear to keep silence any longer, "with three and twopence worth of loose change in his hand and an envelope."

"That's right, my lady," said Sergeant Hopkins, who had a generous nature and did not resent Sir Harry's poaching on his story. "So I said, 'Everything you say will be taken down against you, my lad,' and I waited till Mr. Beedle come back and I told him what had occurred, and then Sir Harry was calling me, so I came along."

"You don't think Morple will hurt Mr. Beedle, do you?" said Lady Waring anxiously.

"He was as white as a jelly and his knees shaking, my lady," said Sergeant Hopkins. "But I passed the word to

Doris Phipps to stand by. She and that Lily-Annie are as good as a couple of men any day."

The story was discussed with pleasurable horror all the way back by the Warings and Sergeant Hopkins. Leslie sat in her corner thinking how she had driven the one love of her life out into the snow to perish miserably. If there had been a telephone in the car she would have rung him up at once. She would have given the world to have the last half-hour again, but she could not, and none of us can. When they got to the Priory, Sergeant Hopkins took the car into the garage and went away to report to Matron, not without a caution from Sir Harry to say nothing of what had happened, a caution which he scrupulously respected.

"What an extraordinary state my muffler is in," said Sir Harry. "I laid it on the seat in the car and it looks as if it had been twisted into a rope."

No one could account for this, though Lady Waring offered some very improbable explanations.

"Nothing from Cecil," said Leslie, who had been looking through her accumulation of letters in the hall.

"I expect his letters will all come in a rush now," said Lydia, who had stood sympathetically by. "I haven't heard from Colin yet, but I'm sure they'll all come in a bunch."

The Warings also spoke words of comfort, but Leslie, her face suddenly small and peaked, said she was so sorry but she was tired; it had been a tiring day in London; the party the night before had been rather tiring; would no one mind if she went upstairs.

Lydia picked up Leslie's suitcase and followed her. She overtook Leslie at the door of her bedroom, put the suitcase on the floor, lighted the gas-fire for her and helped her off with her coat, for Leslie looked incapable of doing anything for herself.

"Cheer up," said Lydia very kindly, thinking that conventional words of comfort would be as good as any other. "I'm perfectly sure you'll get heaps of letters from Cecil soon. Probably he and Colin have met each other among the oranges if Colin has gone where I think he has."

"I know something has happened," said Leslie. "I can't bear it. I know something has happened to Cecil. And I was beastly to Philip. I wish I were dead."

She began to cry in a desolate way.

"Look here," said Lydia, half-guessing what might have happened between Leslie and Philip. "If you are going to have a breakdown I'll tell Selina to bring you up some dinner and tell your aunt you were overtired. But if you could possibly not have a breakdown it would really be better. I don't know what Philip's done, and I can't ring up the camp because a lorry skidded into a telegraph-post and the Dower House is cut off, but I swear I'll get at him to-morrow if it's important. Try to have a bath quickly and come down to dinner."

"All right," said Leslie, with real heroism choking back the hysteria that she longed to indulge in. "I expect I'll be all right to-morrow. I was really a bit tired, not much — but not getting Cecil's letter — I'd been waiting so long. I wish I knew what had happened. Thanks awfully, Lydia."

Lydia went away and Leslie drank a greal deal of cold water, had a bath and told herself not to be a fool. Luckily the affair of Bill Morple overshadowed all other conversation and she was able to go to bed early without disturbing her uncle and aunt.

When Sergeant Hopkins had left the office, Mr. Beedle sat down and looked at Bill Morple.

"You've not got anything on me, Mr. Beedle," said Bill Morple suddenly.

"There's the three-and-twopence I had in my pocket," said Mr. Beedle, pointing sadly to his desk.

"There's no one can say it's yours," said Bill Morple sullenly. "I s'pose you go marking all your money."

"And there's that envelope," said Mr. Beedle, still looking at his porter. "It's Henry's last letter from Germany. I wouldn't have liked to lose it."

Bill Morple looked at the floor, the ceiling, the desk, anywhere but at Mr. Beedle.

"I ought rightly to ring up the police," said Mr. Beedle. "You're giving the Line a bad name, Bill Morple. It's bad enough to see the station the way it is now, without having a thief on the station staff."

Bill Morple was heard to mumble that he was going to put it back.

"What Mrs. Beedle would say if she knew, I hardly like to think," said Mr. Beedle. "Nor Doris and Lily-Annie. A nice example you're setting them. On your last night here, too."

Bill, now sniffing as well as mumbling, said he owed some chaps eleven shillings and was afraid they'd write to the Army and get him into trouble.

"Well," said Mr. Beedle, unlocking his desk, "there's eleven shillings. Hold your tongue and no one will be the wiser. I'm not going to touch that three-and-twopence. Put it into the box for Prisoners of War in the general waiting-room. Good-bye, Bill, and good luck."

Bill Morple, his face a disagreeable compound of fear, defiance, mortification, dirt and a tear or two, ignored Mr. Beedle's hand, turned and slouched out of the office. Mr. Beedle's face showed no emotion. He carefully smoothed the letter that Bill had crumpled, put it in his pocket-book, and applied himself to his papers.

Outside the office Bill found Doris Phipps and Lily-Annie Pollett sitting on a truck smoking.

"So long," said Bill, affecting a devil-may-care air. "It's the Army for me to-morrow. Glad to get there."

"You've been long enough thinking about it," said Doris.

"Waiting to grow the moustache I expect," said Lily-Annie.

"All right, you girls," shouted Bill Morple, "I s'pose you think I'm a thief. Old Beetle's been talking to you."

Doris said she didn't *think* anything.

"Well, let me tell you old Beetle called me in to say good-bye and wish me good luck," said Bill angrily. "And if you think I'm a thief, I'll show you something. Just you wait till Monday. If he was in Russia —"

"There wouldn't be no football pools," said Lily-Annie, finishing his sentence for him.

"That's enough, Lily-Annie," said Doris Phipps, putting out her hand to the porter. "Good-bye, Bill. Mind your step and don't trouble to write."

Cowed by his fair and muscular friends who each stretched out a slightly threatening hand, Bill Morple sulkily shook them both, looked sheepish and turned away.

"You just wait till Monday morning," he repeated. "If you think I'm a thief, I'll just show you I *am* a thief. You look out the day after to-morrow and you'll see something."

"See the last of you," shrieked Lily-Annie.

Hoots of laughter followed the ex-porter as he went away to take off his official jacket for the last time. Seeing no further call for their services the girls applied themselves to their usual duties with a great deal of talk about what Bill Morple had meant, but getting no nearer any explanation. When the platform was clear Bill Morple came out of the porters' room and went into the general waiting-room. He came out again almost at once and disappeared from Winter Overcotes station into the darkness.

CHAPTER
TWELVE

The second post, which had not brought Cecil's letter to Leslie on the Saturday, had brought to the Mertons letters containing the delightful news, first that everything was in train for them to buy back Lydia's old home of North-bridge Manor, and secondly that the bailiff was staying in the Army and would be very glad if they would live in his little house for an indefinite period. An old housemaid had been kept on as caretaker at the Manor and the Keiths' old nurse Mrs. Twitcher was only a short distance away, so Lydia saw no great difficulties about housekeeping and said she could go back to the Barchester General Hospital. Her only regret, she added, was that she would have to give the Warings notice and would feel like a murderess. She was however cheered by Noel, who reminded her that the Carters would now be within easy reach by bicycle and her mother would be able to stay with them after or before her annual visit to Kate. Fortified by these reflections, Lydia was able to go down to breakfast on Sunday morning without feeling too murderous, having arranged with Noel that she would break the news to Lady Waring when the fit moment arrived.

The Warings and the Mertons walked across the park to church as they had done when the Mertons arrived, nearly three months ago. The days in February are not so very much longer than the days in early November, but the new year has begun and the light is winning, the darkness losing. Primroses or catkins no longer seemed unseasonable and the world was turning to the sun. Leslie, who had made heroic efforts to conquer her depression, did her very best to appear normal and certainly succeeded in making her uncle and aunt feel less anxious about her. After taking their seats in the Waring pew and indulging in the usual moment of silent thought whose vagaries it is so difficult to control, the Priory party looked discreetly about them and were rewarded by seeing Nannie Allen, in her best Sunday grey coat and skirt and her uncompromising black hat trimmed with white roses, escorted by Mr. Needham. Nannie was looking out the hymns and psalms for the day and inserting bookmarkers, made very badly in cross-stitch on perforated cardboard by various ex-charges, in the right places. Mr. Needham, who knew all the hymns for the day by heart and the one psalm which is the most a degenerate age can stomach, was bearing it all very well.

Canon Tempest then entered in an angry way, hurled a sentence about the wicked man at his congregation and launched into Dearly beloved brethren, giving it the effect of an anathema, but not, we are glad to inform our readers, curtailing it as is the present reprehensible and lazy practice. As he reached the words "saying after me," there was a slight noise from the direction of the church porch and an officer came in. Nannie, recognizing him as the gentleman that came to tea the day the new curtain-rod was put up, beckoned to him to come into her pew, and Philip would no more have dared to refuse than he would have brawled in church. The party in the Warings' pew were by now kneeling and did not turn to look, so it was not till Canon Tempest had blessed and dismissed them with ill-suppressed rage that Leslie saw Colonel Winter in Nannie's pew.

Although she had thought of him till she fell asleep, although she had woken to a thought of him, it had never occurred to her that she would see him again so soon and her heart bounded violently. She saw Philip leaving the church with Nannie Allen and Mr. Needham, but it was impossible to hurry down the aisle, for she was on the inside of the pew near the wall. Gradually her uncle and aunt moved towards the door and at last they were out in the faint sunshine. She saw Philip at the churchyard gate, but Canon Tempest came out to speak to the Warings and courtesy bade Leslie stay and greet him, while Noel and Lydia, not wishing to intrude, walked slowly on. She saw them join Nannie and her party, she saw Philip say something to Lydia and then she had to drag her attention back to Canon Tempest who, having been informed by Sir Harry under the seal of secrecy that he hoped to have an excellent new Vicar as soon as possible in a young Mr. Needham, an Army chaplain engaged to Dr. Crawley's youngest daughter, took the wind completely out of his sails by turning out to be Octavia's godfather and knowing all about Mr. Needham, whom he thoroughly approved; for the Canon had been a great oarsman in his time. Then Sir Harry called to Mr. Needham to come and be introduced to Dr. Tempest, Noel came with him, one or two other important parishioners joined them, and Leslie, quite hopeless now, saw Philip and Lydia disappear by the lane into the Priory woods. By the time the little group had dispersed they were lost to sight, so Leslie walked back by the road with her uncle and aunt, being very pleasant, and wondering how much longer she could bear her anxiety about Cecil and her need of Philip.

Meanwhile Philip and Lydia walked up the lane through the woods where the young trees, though no green appeared, seemed to vibrate with life, as if with a motion of their branches they might shake out their spring leafage.

"Anything wrong?" said Lydia, using the same direct methods with Colonel Winter as Miss Lydia Keith would have used with the assistant master at Southbridge School.

"Everything," said Philip.

"Well then, you'd better tell me," said Lydia. "Is it about Leslie?"

Philip, looking straight in front of him, said he supposed it was.

"She said she was beastly to you yesterday," said Lydia, by way of a delicate hint.

"So she was," said Philip furiously. "She wouldn't listen to a thing I said. I told her I wanted to tell her something important and she simply walked off to Sir Harry and left me feeling like a fool."

"Was it that you want to marry her?" said Lydia, interested.

"Good God, no!" said Philip, standing still and prodding violently in a bank with his stick. "I mean I'd marry her to-morrow, or to-day for that matter, but I know it's no good trying. I only wanted to tell her I'm off to-morrow. It's all secret and I mayn't say where, not even to you, but I expect I'll see Colin soon."

"Oh, Philip!" said Lydia, her whole face lighting at the thought.

"Bless you, my girl," said Philip, laughing in spite of his depression. "If Colin and Noel are all right I believe you don't care for anything else. Look here, will you do something for me?"

"Of course I will," said Lydia. "When do you go?"

"To-morrow morning," said Philip. "Black Monday. The Dower House is sending me to Winter Overcotes in a car to get the London train. Why this waste of petrol when I could just as well get the through train at Worsted or Lambton I don't know, but the Dower House is like that. You remember our compact, Lydia?"

"Do you mean about the ring?" said Lydia.

"I do. Here it is," said Philip, taking it out of a pocket. "And in accordance with my vow I give it to you in token that I love Leslie quite distractedly and if she isn't married when I come back I shall ask her at once. Perhaps she won't hate me so much when I come back with one arm and one leg and one eye."

"Why don't you ask her now?" said Lydia, slipping the ring on to her finger.

"Because she doesn't want me to. She as good as turned me down at the station yesterday and I'm not going to make a nuisance of myself. Also I'd look like a fortune-hunter. If anything happens to her brother, which God forbid, she will be an heiress, for what that's worth nowadays. Oh, how could I ever have thought I loved Rose?"

"You didn't think, you did love her," said Lydia. "People get different when they get older. I've often noticed it and we're all growing up. We can't help it."

"Well, thank God, you've got Noel," said Philip. "I must fly, for I've a deuce of a lot of work to do before I leave the Dower House. Our telephone's still out of order, blast it. Good-bye, my precious Lydia. I'll write to you and tell you all about Colin, and if you can ever tell me anything about Leslie that you think would cheer me up, please do. If we are growing up, you are one of the nicest grown-ups I know."

They embraced heartily. Lydia stood watching Philip till he was round a turn in the lane and then walked homewards, meditating upon the sad story of her friend's passion. The more she thought of it all the sillier it seemed that Philip should not rush over to the Priory, batter Leslie into submission and, though this Lydia admitted was not very probable, get Mr. Needham to marry them at midnight with a curtain ring. These thoughts made her slightly pensive at lunch. Noel looked at her once or twice, wondering what had

388

made her so quiet, but seeing that her excellent appetite was unimpaired he did not worry.

After lunch Leslie and Lydia took Crumpet out to collect wood for the house. Lydia remembered their first drive, the day after she and Noel had come to the Priory, and thought how different Leslie looked. The nervous, exhausted young woman was now obviously fit to command any number of subordinates, take responsibilities, and probably emerge from the war with at least a D.B.E. if she wanted to take it. That she had suddenly looked so peaky in the last few days was a pity, but the peakiness appeared to be in her looks, not in her general health, for she collected and piled wood, filled the little cart and walked beside Crumpet with no sign of fatigue. Of course to be worrying about a brother was enough to make anyone look haggard, thought Lydia, and then blamed herself severely for not looking haggard about Colin. She thought of him a great deal, she looked eagerly for the post twice a day and rather disliked Sundays, but she ate and slept with her usual equanimity. Examining these facts in her mind she came to the very obvious conclusion that having a husband whom she loved very much made it easier to bear anxiety. If Noel went abroad, when Noel went abroad if one was to face things squarely, it would all be more difficult, but Lydia knew in her heart, as she had known after Dunkirk, that alive or dead Noel would keep her sane and in her own way happy. She didn't think anyone but herself would really understand this, except perhaps Philip. And now Philip was unhappy and so was Leslie, who so needed someone to steady her in her too feminine career; and Lydia was for once completely at a loss as to how she could help them. So she very wisely decided to wait upon events and give them a shove in the right direction if occasion offered.

As the cart was now heaped with firewood they walked, at Crumpet's pace, for any other would have been impossible, by much the same way they had followed on their first outing. Golden Valley was waking to life. A delusion of green mistiness hung above the bare trees, there were early wild flowers everywhere. The purling brook swollen by the rains had overflowed its banks and in places the road was so deep in water that they had to lead Crumpet round over last year's fern and the newly springing brambles to get to dry land.

From the chimney of Jasper's cottage the thin blue smoke rose straight towards the tree-tops, but the front door was shut.

"Of course the garden is flooded as usual," said Leslie, "and I expect it is all over the kitchen floor. I can't tell you what a mess it is. I went in last year about this time and everything was swimming about the kitchen and the smell quite dreadful. I can't think how he doesn't die of rheumatism. No place for Selina. I hope all that nonsense is over."

Lydia said she didn't know, but as Private Jenks seemed to have made Selina an unsuccessful offer, she probably wasn't thinking of matrimony at all.

"Go on, Crumpet," said Leslie, giving the pony a hearty whack with a bit of stick, for he had taken advantage of their conversation to stop and assuage the pangs of hunger with a few young shoots. Crumpet shook his head and ambled forward, so that his companions had to run to keep up with him till the rise of the road checked his course. At the top of the hill they turned and looked back at the little valley, so safe, so untouched, among the wooded hills. The sound of a gun broke the silence, echoed from the hanger and was lost.

"Jasper mending Private Jenks's broken heart, I expect," said Leslie. "I believe he has ordered Uncle Harry to tell Lord Pomfret that Tom Jenks is to succeed his father as head keeper after the war. Come on, Crumpet."

"Noel and I shall simply hate leaving here," said Lydia, thinking this as good a moment as any other to tell Leslie their plans. "But we can get my old home back, and then we'll be near my sister at Southbridge School and I can go to the Barchester General."

Leslie said she would be very sorry when they went, but of course she understood how much Lydia wanted to be in her old home.

"I think I would die if I couldn't live here," she said. "My job is all very well, but this is more and more the real thing. And if Cecil agrees, we can turn the Priory into something really useful some day."

"Like a school for boys going into the Navy, I mean what Philip was talking about," said Lydia.

She said this with no deeper meaning, merely considering the possibilities of the Priory, but Leslie suddenly stopped and looked at Lydia as if appealing for help. Crumpet stopped too, jerked his head away from Leslie and made another attempt to sustain languid nature by cropping the roadside grass.

"It's no good," she said. "Philip hates me. He said he wanted to tell me something yesterday at the station and I wouldn't listen."

"Did you know what it was?" asked Lydia.

"I suppose I did," said Leslie, looking away. "But it's no use now, so it doesn't matter."

"He told me what it was," said Lydia.

For a woman who is in love to hear from another woman that the adored object has confided his passion to her is enough to wreck most friendships, but so much did Leslie like and respect Lydia, and so great was her need of help, that she was in no way offended. She looked at Lydia, mutely questioning.

"It's rather horrid," said Lydia compassionately, "but he is going to-morrow and that's all he may say. He wanted to tell you because of saying good-bye."

On hearing this, the competent and self-possessed head of an important organization put her arms round Crumpet's neck and began to cry into his mane.

"I say, don't," said Lydia, alarmed.

"I'm not crying about Philip. I'm crying about Cecil. I'm crying because I *want* to cry," said Leslie; in proof of which she put her face into Crumpet's mane once more.

"Look here, Leslie, you can't. Jasper or anyone might come," said Lydia.

A choked voice remarked that it didn't care.

392

"Oh, well then," said Lydia, "if you won't be sensible I'll have to tell you, even if it's dishonourable. Look!"

Leslie obediently stood up straight and looked at the gloveless hand that Lydia stretched towards her.

"That's the ring he got engaged to Rose Birkett with," said Lydia, "and he said he would send it to me whenever he really fell in love again. He gave it me this morning after church when he told me he was ordered abroad. It's yours if you want it."

She took it off and laid it on the palm of her hand.

Any young woman of spirit, if offered by a third person the ring which had celebrated the engagement of the beloved object to another young woman, would dash it to the ground. But so unhappy was Leslie that she picked it up and held it as if she had found a lost treasure.

"You see," said Lydia, determined now to make a job of it, "he thought you being rather well off and the Priory and everything, he might seem as if he wanted to marry you for money, and anyway he thought you'd turned him down on the platform, so he said he'd ask you to marry him when he comes back. All this is very private," she added, "so that's why I'm telling you."

"I must see him," was all Leslie said.

"I don't see how you can," said Lydia compassionately. "The telephone's still down at the Dower House and he is going to London to-morrow morning. Unless of course you like to go to Winter Overcotes and take your chance. Like when I went to see Colin off."

"Do you think I can wear the ring?" said Leslie.

"Of course you can," said Lydia a little impatiently, "unless it doesn't fit you. That's why I gave it you."

Still showing no resentment at this peculiar form of proxy for an absent wooer, Leslie put the ring on her third finger, noted with a certain satisfaction that her finger was slimmer than that of Miss Birkett, and jerked Crumpet's head up again. They soon reached home and took Crumpet round to the stable where they stacked the wood.

In the yard they found Nannie Allen, who had walked up from the village to have tea with the kitchen and was enjoying the afternoon sun in a sheltered corner. On her hands she held a skein of wool which Selina was winding.

"Hullo, Nannie," said Leslie. "Is that for the troops?"

"Of course not, Miss Leslie," said Nannie. "It's for poor Mr. Needham. His socks are in a shocking state and it's a shame to give coupons for them, so I'm knitting him some. I had a nice lot of wool put away. Where's Mr. Cecil now?"

Leslie said she didn't know, but Lydia noted with approval that though she spoke sadly, her face did not suddenly become as small as a kitten's, from which she augured the best.

Sergeant Hopkins, who had been loitering about the yard gate, now came in with Winston at his heels. Nannie received him with great condescension and inquired after his mother. Selina picked up the kitten, who arranged himself comfortably in her arms and began to purr. Lydia and Leslie spoke to the kitten and were just going in when Jasper appeared. Nannie gave a loud disapproving sniff which had no effect upon him at all.

"Good afternoon, ladies all," said Jasper, at the same time sketching a salute to Sergeant Hopkins. "I've got old granny at last."

They all looked at him. Lydia and Leslie thought of the gunshot, Lydia remembered her silver button. A horrid pang assailed her and she wished she had never been hypnotized by the visit to Jasper's cottage into being so silly and school-girlish.

"Some say you need a silver button to shoot a witch," said Jasper, "but I hadn't no time for old silver buttons. There was old granny cleaning her whiskers on Copshot Bank, and I got her first shot. That'll learn her to lay quiet in her grave."

"Do you mean you killed the black hare?" said Selina in a trembling voice.

"Hare or old granny, it's all one," said Jasper.

"Don't talk like that," said Nannie sharply. "It's not Christian. Before the young ladies, too. I never did!"

"You didn't kill the poor hare!" said Selina, crystal drops falling on to Winston's fur. "Oh dear, I was *never* so upset."

"What you need's a bit of comforting, my lass," said Jasper.

Leslie, representing her uncle, felt that things had gone quite far enough, but so unusual were the circumstances that she hardly knew how to begin. She had no wish to offend her uncle's excellent keeper, but she saw that she would have to intervene. Heartily wishing she and Lydia had gone indoors before Jasper's arrival, she opened her mouth to speak, when to her intense relief Sergeant Hopkins stepped forward.

"If there's any comforting to be done, I'm the man," he said. "Mrs. Crockett and me's engaged to be married. Aren't we, Mrs. Allen?" he demanded, as his affianced appeared to be dissolving in grief and Winston had twice angrily shaken his head as her tears fell on it.

"Of course she is," said Nannie, taking up her cue with incredible dexterity. "And going to be married as soon as the Sergeant is out of the Army. So I'll thank you to leave her alone, Jasper Margett."

Jasper looked slowly round the circle. Although he was entirely in the wrong, having killed his grandmother and offered wedlock, or at any rate comfort, to a respectable widow about to make a second marriage, everyone felt a distinct disinclination to meet his eye, or his mysterious smile.

"But thank you kindly all the same, mum," he said, advancing to Lydia, who really felt alarmed for a moment. "I'm much obliged, but I don't need no old silver button now."

He gave the button to Lydia, disconcerted the whole party by another of his sidelong looks, and went off on his own business.

"Well, of all the impudence," said Nannie. "Put that cat down, Selina, and finish winding my wool."

Sergeant Hopkins with great gallantry said Winston was much too happy where he was to be disturbed, and offered to wind the wool himself. The skein was nearly wound, and as Lydia and Leslie turned to go into the kitchen passage, they saw the sergeant hand the ball to his future mother-in-law and kiss her. Glancing through the open kitchen door as they passed, Leslie saw Cook and Baker looking out of the window and felt that the sooner she and Lydia were on the other side of the green baize door the better.

When they got to the drawing-room they were laughing so much that they could not properly tell the Warings and Noel what had happened, but as the story was unfolded even Lady Waring had to join in the laughter, and said she was extremely glad it was settled, as Selina was becoming almost a menace.

"But I'm afraid, my dear, it means you'll lose her," said Sir Harry, at once thinking of his wife. "Hopkins lives at Northbridge."

"Then she can come and do things for Lydia in her spare time," said Leslie.

"But not if she is at Northbridge," said Lady Waring, puzzled.

Leslie, realizing now that her aunt had not heard of the Mertons' new plans, managed to change the subject to Mr. Needham, which put Sir Harry in high good humour. Presently he went out to see Jasper and if possible get his account of the afternoon's event. Noel and Leslie withdrew to the dining-room to do some work and Lydia was left alone with her hostess.

She then told Lady Waring that owing to her brother Robert's willingness to sell her old home, and the bailiff's house being empty at present, it would be possible for her and Noel to go and live there, as she had always wanted to do. She thanked Lady Waring again and again for all her kindness and said they would hate leaving the Priory and hoped they hadn't been a bother. Lady Waring was genuinely sorry to hear that her guests would be leaving her, but loving her own home as she did she could understand Lydia's longing to go back to Northbridge Manor.

"In any case," she said, "I hope it will not be at once, for Harry and I have grown very fond of you, my dear. And we have liked your husband so much too. I don't want to interfere, but you must stay here just as long or as short a time as suits you. You and Major Merton have been such delightful guests and friends that we shall not want to have anyone else, even if Captain Hooper recommends them."

This approach to a joke made Lydia feel that there was no shadow between Lady Waring and herself, so in the gratitude of her heart she got up and kissed her. Lady Waring looked surprised, then pleased, and kissed Lydia very kindly in return.

"So that is why Selina will be able to help you in her spare time," said Lady Waring, smiling. And then they had a very pleasant conversation about plans and how the old housemaid could be got and how Mrs. Twitcher would come in and cook and how Lydia would be free to nurse at the Barchester General. Lydia thought Lady Waring seemed slightly dashed by the mention of the hospital, but gave the matter no further thought.

Dinner passed without incident except that Selina dropped and broke two of the good plates and Sir Harry said he supposed she was thinking of Sergeant Hopkins, which drove her in a wild mixture of tears and giggles from the room, with a most becoming colour and wildly wreathing hair.

Everyone was sleepy after dinner. Sir Harry wrote a few letters to old country friends to boast about the excellent Vicar he had secured, and then said he was going to bed.

"Are you going to town to-morrow, Uncle Harry?" said Leslie.

"Only to Winter Overcotes," said Sir Harry. "Do you want anything? I'm going by the 8.25."

"Nothing you could do, thank you, Uncle Harry," said Leslie, "but I'll come in with you if you don't mind."

"All right, young woman. Breakfast quarter to eight sharp," said Sir Harry. "I can't wait for you."

Then they all went to bed. Lydia for once did not tell her Noel all that had happened to her during the day, but he did not notice. After reading some Gibbon, she turned off her light and lay awake thinking of Leslie and Philip. It suddenly occurred to her that Leslie, whom she had always looked upon as someone really grown-up, who had committees and ordered people about and probably even knew about income tax, was only an ordinary person who could be very unhappy and need help, apparently regarding herself, Lydia Merton, as a real grown-up person who understood the world and could give advice. The idea struck her as so peculiar, though fascinating, that she was impelled to share it.

"Noel," she said in the dark, "would you say I was grown-up?"

"What?" said Noel, who was nearly asleep.

Lydia repeated her question.

"The answer to that is yes *and* no," said Noel. "And for goodness' sake go to sleep, my precious love."

With this further food for philosophical consideration, Lydia was soon asleep.

As for Leslie, she was a prey to so many feelings that she almost felt her bed reeling. A longing to see Philip, a fear of seeing him, anxiety for Cecil, then a fear of not seeing Philip, then a certainty that Cecil was well and letters only delayed, then a remembrance of her unkindness to Philip, her awkward stupidity, then Lydia's words about the ring, then a sickening anxiety for Cecil again; all these so tossed and turned in her head that sleep did not come, and when it did she woke often, sure that she had overslept herself and would never get to Winter Overcotes in time, or that if she did she would find that Philip had gone the previous evening, or by car. Her last waking was at half-past six, so she got up and dressed and worked at Noel's papers till it was time for breakfast.

If Lady Waring had been there Leslie would have forced herself to eat, but her uncle was buried in his paper and did not appear to take any notice of her beyond a greeting, so she was able to drink some coffee and eye with disgust the scrambled eggs which many households had not seen for months. As they went down the drive they met the postman, who obligingly sorted their letters from his pile and handed them over. The short delay so irritated Leslie's feverish impatience that she walked hurriedly on and her uncle, who had

400

pushed all the letters into his overcoat pocket, only caught her up as they neared the station. When they were in the train he took the letters out and handed Leslie her share. Much to her annoyance her hands were shaking and her fingers very clumsy at unripping the envelopes. Her mind was racing ahead to her meeting with Philip, to the chance of his not being at the station, to what she should say if he were, again to the certainty of Cecil being dead or missing, so that she opened and began to read her first letter without understanding a word. When she did, she became so pale that even her uncle would have noticed; but he was going through his own post.

"It's Cecil!" Leslie gasped.

Sir Harry looked up.

"Cecil? Eh, where?" he said, looking over his spectacles.

"He's quite well, Uncle Harry, he's at Washington. He says he couldn't tell me till he was there and he hopes I got his letters but he knows a lot were lost."

When this news had sunk into Sir Harry's mind he was almost as pleased as Leslie.

"Well, young woman, now you can stop worrying and eat some breakfast," said Sir Harry, eyeing his niece.

"Oh, Uncle Harry, I *am* so sorry," said Leslie. "I didn't think you noticed. I was so unhappy I simply couldn't. Not even scrambled eggs."

"You women are all alike," said Sir Harry. "Except your aunt. And Mrs. Merton. She wouldn't go without her breakfast because she hadn't heard from her brother. Nice fellow he was. I hope she'll get news soon."

On hearing these words Leslie fell into an abyss of self-blame and remorse for having been such a general nuisance, but decided not to say she was sorry, because she knew Uncle Harry hated scenes. As far as Winter Underclose she sat in a golden haze of relief and joy, her letters unregarded on her lap. Then, as the train started again, the familiar feeling of sick anxiety came over her with redoubled force; would Philip be there, what could she say? So that by the time they drew into the low level station at Winter Overcotes, she could not see or hear and was almost incapable of walking.

On the platform Mr. Beedle was anxiously scanning the windows of the train as it moved past. Seeing Sir Harry he came to the door and opened it.

"Good morning, Sir Harry; good morning, Miss Waring," he said with a subdued excitement very unlike his usual calm and stately manner. "Could you be kind enough to come up to my office for a moment? There's something I want to show you."

"Certainly, Beedle," said Sir Harry. "Come along, Leslie. We've just had news of Commander Waring, Beedle. He's in America."

Mr. Beedle expressed pleasure, though not with the deep interest that he usually showed in the Waring family. Leslie was nearly sick with misery. She had just seen Philip come onto the platform and Uncle Harry and Mr. Beedle wouldn't stop talking.

"Just one minute, Uncle Harry," she said. "You and Mr. Beedle go up and I'll come in a moment."

Sir Harry nodded, and he and Mr. Beedle went up the stairs to the high level.

Leslie saw Philip get into a carriage and shut the door. She ran down the platform and knocked at the window. Philip saw her, jumped up and opened it.

"Leslie! Anything wrong?" he asked.

"Oh no," said Leslie, seeing with heartfelt gratitude that the guard was still talking to Doris and Lily-Annie just beside her. "I've heard from Cecil. He's in America."

"How kind of you to come and tell me," said Philip, afraid of somehow again offending her. "I can't tell you how glad I am."

Leslie tore off her glove and laid her hand on Philip's.

"Lydia gave it to me. May I wear it?" she said.

Philip looked at Rose Birkett's engagement ring, once spurned and thrown into the pool at Northbridge Manor, now on the hand of the only woman he loved.

"Do I understand?" he said, holding her hand as if he would never let it go.

"Well, will you marry me?" said Leslie, desperate as the moments passed and Mr. Crackman began to unfurl his green flag.

"The very minute I come back," said Philip. "Oh, Leslie!"

"Oh, Philip!" said his love.

Neither looked at the other, but their hands clung.

The guard blew his whistle and waved the flag. The London train began to pull out on the loop to the main line. Leslie laid her cheek on Philip's hand, let it go and stood back. Philip remained at the window, but made no sign, frozen by his incredulous joy and the heavy weight of parting. In a few seconds she could see him no longer, so she went up the stairs to find her uncle, followed by Lily-Annie and Doris whose duties now called them to the high level.

"Seeing the colonel off to the front, she was," said Doris Phipps to Lily-Annie Pollett.

"Are they engaged?" asked Lily-Annie.

"Of course they are," said Doris Phipps. "He's been after her ever since he came to the Dower House. Mum says Cook told her Selina said he couldn't take his eyes off her at dinner. Didn't you see her showing him the ring? It's time Bert got *me* a ring. I fancy forget-me-nots myself, in terkwoises."

"Bit old-fashioned," said Lily-Annie. "Now I'd like a diamond cluster."

"Better ask Bill Morple for one," said Doris Phipps, which made both the girls laugh so much that the new under-porter, who was a Lambton girl, was terrified.

"All right, young Rene," said Lily-Annie kindly. "We're a bit bats, you know. Come on and we'll show you where the brooms and things are."

Meanwhile, Leslie had gone into Mr. Beedle's office, where she found Sir Harry. On Mr. Beedle's desk was a large untidy parcel loosely wrapped in dirty newspaper.

"Most extraordinary thing, Leslie," said Sir Harry. "I don't know that I was ever more surprised, or pleased, in my life. But you tell her, Beedle."

404

Without a word Mr. Beedle pulled aside the torn paper. Under it was a large silver cup, iridescent with tarnish.

"THE CUP, miss," said Mr. Beedle.

There was a silence so full of awe and general overcomeness that Mr. Beedle could almost be heard swelling with joy.

"But how?" said Leslie.

"That's just the question," said Sir Harry. "But Beedle will tell you."

"It was on my desk this morning, miss," said Mr. Beedle. "And what's more the key of the office door was lying beside it and the window was unlatched. Whoever brought it must have had another key, for I have only the two, one on me and the other at home, and then gone out by the window."

"But who?" said Leslie.

"That's exactly what we are not going to ask," said Sir Harry. "The inspector was in a moment ago. He has known where the cup was ever since those London people stole it, but he hadn't any evidence. One of them, or someone who was in with them, must have stolen it back and brought it here."

Mr. Beedle gave Sir Harry a grateful look.

"Yes; that's all we shall ever know, miss," he said, "unless you know this writing."

On a dirty piece of paper inside the cup were printed the words, "From a friend."

Leslie shook her head and laughed.

"What are you going to do with it now?" she said.

"Give it a good polish, miss, and lock it in the safe," said Mr. Beedle. "It'll be a nice surprise for any of our directors that come here."

Sir Harry and Leslie again congratulated Mr. Beedle and shook his hand warmly.

"Oh! Mr. Beedle," said Leslie, "have I time to get the train back to Lambton?"

Mr. Beedle looked at his watch and went to the door.

"Doris!" he called.

Doris Phipps appeared.

"Run down, Doris, and see if the local's in, and tell Sid Pollett I said to hold her. Miss Waring's going back on her."

"O.K., Mr. Beedle," said Doris.

"Thank you very much, Mr. Beedle," said Leslie, shaking his hand again. "Please remember me to Mrs. Beedle. And have you good news of Henry?"

"Thank you very much, miss," said Mr. Beedle, "he's fine. He's got a harmonica now the Red Cross sent him and one of his mates tried to pinch it, so the officer's writing for another so they can play duets."

Then Leslie hurried away while Sir Harry lingered to tell Mr. Beedle about Cecil and rejoice with him again over the cup. On the low-level she found Doris Phipps engaged in badinage with the engine-driver.

"Get in, miss," said Doris, opening a carriage door. "And me and Lily-Annie'd like to wish you all the best, miss, you and the colonel. Mum says Mrs. Hamp's sister that cleans up at the Dower House says he's a lovely man. All right, Sid!"

She slammed the door and Leslie sank back on the hard dirty seat to reflect upon the publicity attaching to her position. And then she thought of Philip, and so absorbed in these thoughts did she become that she only got out of the train at Lambton just as it was moving and walked towards the Priory in a waking dream.

Leslie's joy was so great that she could not bear to part with it at first, resolving to wait till she could get her uncle and aunt together before dinner. But meeting Selina in the drive she stopped to ask her if Mrs. Allen had enjoyed the teaparty.

"Oh, yes, Miss Leslie, mother *did* enjoy it," said Selina. "And Sergeant Hopkins said would you be so very kind as to tell the officer he took his advice and he's very glad he did."

"What officer?" asked Leslie, to whom there was only one in the world at the moment and he a colonel.

"The young gentleman that came with Mrs. Morland, Miss Leslie," said Selina.

"Oh, Mr. Morland," said Leslie. "Yes, I'll ring his mother up and tell her. When are you going to be married?"

"Mother says after Easter," said Selina. "But of course I shan't leave her ladyship unless she wishes. Sergeant Hopkins wanted to give me a ring, but Mother said it wasn't proper as I'm a widow, so he's going to give me some silk stockings off his own coupons as soon as he's out of the Army."

Leslie could bear it no longer.

"Would you like to see my ring, Selina?" she said, and took off her glove.

"It *is* pretty," said Selina. "Is it Colonel Winter, Miss Leslie?"

"Yes," said Leslie. "But we can't get married till he comes back. He's going abroad."

"Oh, Miss Leslie, how dreadful. Oh, I *am* upset," said Selina, wiping her lovely eyes. "Can I tell mother?"

"Yes, do," said Leslie, realizing that her joy was now exceedingly public property. "And tell her I'll come down and tell her all about it myself soon."

"She *will* be pleased, Miss Leslie," said Selina, "and so will Mr. Needham."

Leslie had forgotten Mr. Needham. She went into the backyard and stood thinking. As the whole countryside appeared to know already, it would be better to tell her aunt at once, for it would be very wrong to let her hear it from an outsider. Mrs. Phipps came out with a bucket of dirty water which she emptied down the outside drain.

"Good morning, miss," she said. "You might tell her ladyship I shan't be staying with my Monday, Wednesday and Thursday lady after Easter. She's got a foreign girl and I don't hold with them. So I can oblige if her ladyship likes and I might come the Saturday morning too. Phipps can manage for himself."

"All right, Mrs. Phipps," said Leslie. "Oh, I expect Doris will have some news for you when she gets back, so I might as well tell you now. I'm engaged to Colonel Winter."

"That's what I thought," said Mrs. Phipps. "Well, I'm sure I wish you joy, Miss Leslie. I little thought when I married Phipps that I'd have a daughter in the railways, but you never know."

Feeling certain that Cook and Baker would take offence if they heard from Mrs. Phipps, Leslie looked into the kitchen and announced her news. Cook said she saw a marriage in her cup last night, but she had thought it was Selina's.

"So it was, Cook," said Baker, "but you remember there was those tea-leaves on the other side. I told you it meant a double marriage."

Filled with terror lest Selina, Mrs. Phipps, Cook, Baker, or even Doris should somehow bring the news to her aunt before she got there, Leslie hurried through the green baize door and found Lady Waring in the sitting-room.

"What *has* your uncle been telephoning about?" said Lady Waring to her niece. "He rang up from the station and it was a bad connection. Something about Cecil and Doris Phipps and an engagement. Have you any idea?"

"Yes, Aunt Harriet," said Leslie sitting down. "I had a letter from Cecil this morning and he is at Washington, and I got engaged to Philip Winter at Winter Overcotes and Doris Phipps saw us getting engaged. I didn't have time to tell Uncle Harry."

Lady Waring bore the news very well. Her relief at hearing of her nephew's safety was great, so great that it overshadowed her pleasure in her niece's engagement at first, but as things settled themselves she showed as much quiet satisfaction as even Leslie could have wished.

"Oh, and Mrs. Phipps asked me to tell you that she will be free for the whole week after Easter if you want her, Aunt Harriet," said Leslie.

Lady Waring said if Selina married and went to North-bridge, it might be very convenient, and was Leslie going to put her engagement in *The Times*.

"Yes, I suppose so, Aunt Harriet," said Leslie. "But I'll have to do it on my own because I don't even know where Philip is till he writes to me. I didn't even have time to kiss him, because the train went," she added, looking out of the window.

Lydia came in to lunch after a morning's gardening and was overjoyed by Leslie's news. The talk, unchecked by Selina who took the liveliest interest in it, was all of Philip and Cecil, Cecil and Philip, to which Lydia listened with the greatest interest and sympathy. Not till they were having their coffee did Leslie think of Lydia's anxiety.

"I wish you had heard from Colin," she said, "then everything would be perfect."

"I did," said Lydia. "This morning. He says he has had a bath and the water was very dirty and he has found lots of friends and the oranges are heavenly and the red wine. I'm so glad."

"But why didn't you tell me before?" said Lady Waring and Leslie, almost in one breath.

"I thought it might be rather dull for you," said Lydia with perfect simplicity.

The day passed peacefully. Leslie slept all afternoon, making up for her bad night and her past anxiety; refusing to think for the moment of the anxiety to come. Lydia gardened till dusk, not coming in for tea as Lady Waring was out and would not need her company. Then she came in, had her bath and sat before the looking-glass steadily brushing her thick, shining, dark hair. Noel, returning from the Dower House, came into the room and found her so engaged.

"Any news?" he said, taking off his belt and sitting down by the fire.

"Leslie is engaged to Philip, which is very nice and not a bit surprising," said Lydia. "And I had a letter from Colin. I'll show it you."

"I'm glad, glad, glad," said Noel with unusual vehemence. "I mean about Colin. But I'm very glad about Leslie and Philip too. I wonder if they'll keep a school or what. Perhaps there won't be any little boys for them to teach by then. It's a rum world."

"Noel," said Lydia, brushing her hair till it crackled. "Do you think people who have babies are traitors?"

"Good lord, no," said Noel. "Whatever put that into your head, my love?"

"I mean," said Lydia, brushing away all the time, "the Government does want a high birth-rate, but if people are having babies they can't very well go on the land or into hospitals or anything."

"I should think the babies came first," said Noel. "Oh, decidedly first."

"Because I couldn't *bear* to be a traitor," said Lydia and went on brushing her shining dark hair in pensive contentment.